# THE FLIGHT OF THE SWAN

Also by Elizabeth Webster:

*Johnnie Alone*
*To Fly a Kite*
*Bracken*

# THE FLIGHT OF THE SWAN

## ELIZABETH WEBSTER, *1918 -*

St. Martin's Press
New York

All of the characters in this book are fictitious, and
any resemblance to actual persons, living or dead, is
purely coincidental

Library of Congress Cataloging-in-Publication Data

Webster, Elizabeth.
    The flight of the swan / Elizabeth Webster.
        p.      cm.
    ISBN 0-312-04991-9
    I. Title.
PR6073.E2312F5    1990
823'.914—dc20                                                                90-37261
                                                                            CIP

First published in Great Britain by Souvenir Press Limited

First U.S. Edition: November 1990
10 9 8 7 6 5 4 3 2 1

# CONTENTS

PART I
*THE HIDE*
7

\* \* \*

PART II
*TAKE-OFF*
77

\* \* \*

PART III
*FREE FLIGHT*
161

\* \* \*

PART IV
*LANDFALL*
293

# PART I

# THE HIDE

The thrumming sound came across the sky, high and sweet and strange. Laurie looked up, hugging her arms round herself to stop the trembling. The ache of shock and fear did not go away—and the bruises on her body and on her marked face did not stop hurting—but the far, rhythmic thrum like distant music was coming nearer, and for some reason it seemed to bring with it a kind of peace . . . or maybe reassurance. Out there, it said, high in the sky, is a world of blue air and sunlight, a world of clear, open spaces and no pressures beyond the lift and fall of the wind—no fears, not even of your own strength and endurance. A world of freedom.

She craned her neck to look higher, above the sooty trees of the cramped back gardens, and there—sailing in majestic, steady flight—were three white swans. Their necks were stretched out in a perfect straight line, pointing towards the glowing west, and their wing-beats were slow and strong and filled with music.

'Free . . . free . . . free . . .' sang the pulsing wings. 'Fly . . . fly . . . fly . . . ,' they sang as they passed over, gilded by the sun, high above her head.

She watched them out of sight, her throat aching with the tears she could not shed. Yes! she thought: Fly, fly, fly! It's all very well for you, you beautiful things, with all the wide, empty sky to sail in. And she stood there, shivering in the shabby backyard with its scuffed, brown grass and grimy stones and the overful dustbins spilling out along the blackened creosote boards of the broken fence.

'Mum,' called Jason's voice from the kitchen door. 'Mum, . . . I've made some tea.'

She drew a long, shaky breath and looked up once more at the pale London sky. She thought she could still hear the faint thrum of wings on the wind, far and still sweet, 'Coming,' she said, and went back inside to the untidy kitchen.

Really, she thought, pushing her hair back from her bruised forehead, I ought not to let it get as bad as this . . . But I'm so tired—and so confused. And the more he shouts and hits out, the more muddled I get.

'Come on, Mum.' Jason's arms were round her, leading her to a chair. Jason's kind young voice was trying to soothe her. 'He's gone out. We've got the place to ourselves.' He set the cup of tea before her and awkwardly tried to smooth the long, fair hair into place. 'Shall I fetch the sponge for your eye?'

She shook her head. 'It's all right.' But it wasn't all right. Not at all. Especially the matter-of-fact, unsurprised voice of her young son, speaking with the casual acceptance born of many such occasions: Shall I fetch the sponge for your eye? Shall I sweep up the broken plates? Shall I find the sticking plaster? Shall I phone the doctor?

She reached out an unsteady hand for the cup.

'I put three sugars in,' said Jason, and grinned. He did not add 'for shock', but he knew what it was for. Yes, he knew. The boy's concerned young face was pale with the effort to be some support and comfort. The blue eyes were anxious and too big in his pinched face, and the freckles on his nose seemed to stand out extra strong.

She put an arm round him and hugged him close. 'Don't worry, Jay. I'm fine . . . Where's Midge?'

He gave her an odd, stern look—adult and aware— far beyond his eight years. 'She crawled into the broomcupboard and went to sleep. So I left her there—where it was safe.' He bent his head and looked down at his own cup of tea, stirring furiously. Then he glanced up again and added, 'She's OK. I did check. She's still asleep.'

Laurie sighed. A sudden wave of grey desolation seemed to wash over her, sapping her energy and will. What was the use? She was trapped here in this cramped, squalid little council house with a violent man who did nothing but shout and flail at the unjust world with his fists . . . who could not find the work he was used to and

10

could not bear to accept the fact that he was an unwanted failure . . . and who spent most of his time and his money drinking himself into oblivion down at his seedy local—a man who took out his own anger and frustration on his exhausted wife. And her small daughter, Midge, crept into the broom-cupboard out of sight and cried herself to sleep while her young brother, Jason, stood by, his eyes wide with too much knowledge, and tried to comfort his frightened mother.

It was too much. It was all too much, and she didn't know what to do about it or where it would end. While out there, high in the blue empty air, those pure white wings pulsed on . . . and on.

There was a sudden knock on the door, and Laurie reached for her handbag, remembering vaguely that it was the day for paying the milk bill. When she opened the door, the kind, observant gaze of Dave, the neighbourhood milkman, looked compassionately into hers. Dave knew what was going on at No. 14. Dave knew what went on in most of the households round about. He couldn't say much, of course, or do anything—unless things got really bad. More than his job's worth— though he had reported a thing or two from time to time. He rather liked young Laurie Collins. A brave, uncomplaining sort of girl, she was—and her kids were OK, too. A shame she had to take so much stick from that cocky bastard of a husband. Sometimes—like today—she looked almost at the end of her tether. And her face . . . must have given her a right old pasting this time, the creep.

'Everything all right, Missus?' he asked, his blue eyes so full of kindness and concern that Laurie suddenly wanted to weep.

'Yes, thanks.' She took the milk bottle from him and handed over the week's money with a shaking hand. 'Everything's all right.'

But it wasn't, of course. It wasn't all right at all. She watched Dave turn away, and felt as if her last lifeline of support was gone. But out there, beyond the milk-float and Dave's broad shoulders, was a smiling, sunny street—a whole world of trees and grass, and a sky where swans' wings pulsed in radiant flight.

'Jay,' she said suddenly, 'get your coat. I'll wake Midge.'

She got to her feet swiftly, before she could change her mind, and opened the broom-cupboard door. The child lay curled up on an old ironing-blanket and a pile of dusters. One flushed cheek was resting on the head of an old string mop, and her hair—honey-gold like her mother's—was spread out round her head in limp, tangled tongues. One hand was clutching the woolly mane of her favourite toy—an ancient yellow lion whose velvet coat had worn very thin. Like me, thought Laurie, with a desperate flick of humour. I've worn very thin . . . In fact, almost through . . . I think I'm almost through.

She scooped Midge up in her arms, found her coat and pushed her unresisting, sleepy arms into it. Then she picked up her own coat and handbag and turned to follow Jason into the narrow hall.

'Where are we going?' he asked, as they went down the dark little corridor.

'I don't know. To the park . . . for some fresh air.'

But as they reached the front door, someone stood in their way.

'Where the hell d'you think you're going?' said Jeff.

Laurie's heart seemed to leap and clench in terror. She could see at a glance that he was drunk again—drunk and seethingly angry with the heedless, uncaring world in general, and his young wife in particular.

'I was . . . taking them for a walk.'

'Oh, you were, were you? Well, you can just walk back in again.' His hand shot out and spun her round, shoving her back towards the kitchen door. 'D'you know what the time is? Or are you too far gone to notice?' The voice was heavy with sarcasm. It seemed to ring and jangle in her head like actual pain. 'I suppose it's too much to ask to have a meal ready when I come home.'

'But you're early . . .'

'*Early*? When I've been down at the Job Centre scouring the ads all day!'

She looked at him. It was clear where he had been most of the day. But it wasn't worth protesting. He had been violent enough at lunch-time—and already fairly drunk then. Now he was violent and very drunk . . . She shivered.

'Don't put on that martyred look, you cow!' he shouted, suddenly furious. Even her silence was a reproach, and he knew it. 'For God's sake, get back in there and cook something, or I'll . . .' His hand went up.

She backed away, feeling Midge's soft, sleep-warm limbs go tense in her arms. 'All right,' she said. 'All right . . .'

Beside her, Jason's taut young hand slipped into hers. She looked down and saw the warning look in his eyes. Not now, he seemed to be saying. *Not now!* Don't let him start another fight now.

Defeated, she turned away and went back to the kitchen. There she carefully put Midge down to play, as far from the door and Jeff as possible, and wearily began to sling some food together.

But Jeff's anger was not spent yet. When she put the plate of food in front of him, he stared at it in disgust. 'What's this?'

'Bean and lentil stew.'

He prodded it. 'Where's the meat?'

'There's some mince in it.'

'Where?' He pushed it round with his fork.

'I can't afford meat every day. You don't give me enough money.'

He slammed a hand down on the table, so that all the crockery jumped. So did the children, who were trying to keep out of sight, playing on the floor.

'Look, Midge!' said Jason, desperately trying to divert her attention. 'Look! Leo's riding in your car . . . He's going very fast . . . Look!'

'I give you plenty,' growled Jeff. 'You're just a bloody bad manager.'

'If you didn't spend so much in the pub,' she said, suddenly brave and as angry as he was, 'you could have meat all day—every day!'

13

He picked up the plate of stew and threw it at her. The hot, sticky mess hit the wall and splashed back on to her face, scalding it so that she gasped and stepped back. The plate smashed, and a piece of jagged china flew up and cut her cheek. Blood and gravy mingled, trickling down her face.

Jeff got up and came towards her, toweringly angry. 'I drink', he said, 'to forget I'm married to a snivelling slut like you.' He slammed her hard against the sink, bruising her backbone against the sharp rim. 'Look at you! You bleeding slag-heap! Wash that muck off your face!'

Blindly, she turned to reach for a wet cloth in the sink, and as she turned he hit her again. Her head contacted the wall, hard, and for a moment she could not see. A strange, high singing began in her ears, almost like the flight of the swans.

'And I drink—,' he shouted, looming over her with sickening emphasis, 'because I can't get a job and no one cares a damn what happens to me. D'you know what they offered me today? Tar-spreading on the roads—and I'm a *salesman*!'

She was holding the wet cloth against her face, staring at him out of dilated eyes. The wings were still beating in her head, trying to get out. Everything seemed to be tilting slightly out of focus: Jeff's distorted face seemed to grow tall and thin one moment, and then to shrink and grow sideways like a monstrous balloon. It was a strange sensation, like being very high on drugs, and it terrified her.

'Dear God, a *salesman*!' he cried, and began to shake her wildly. 'Dragged down to this!' He swept an arm round at the littered kitchen and the frightened children on the floor, and then brought it back smartly across her face. 'No decent suit,' he yelled, 'No decent shoes. Not a clean shirt in the place. And this!' Once more he swept an arm round, and once more he hit her. 'How can I bring a prospective client home to this? Let alone a prospective boss!'

His words were slurring now, and she had an insane desire to laugh. Prospective? Since when had he had any

14

prospective clients? Or bosses? Who would look at him like this?

He must have caught the desperate flick of laughter in her face, for he hit her again—even harder—slamming her head back against the wall again and bruising her back even more against the rim of the sink.

'I suppose you think I should go and spread tar, don't you?

She did not answer. His head looked even taller and stranger, weaving before her in a most peculiar manner. But her thoughts went on: It would be more money than the dole—even a labourer's job—and tar-spreading didn't seem a particularly degrading occupation. Certainly not worse than drinking yourself silly in the pub, and knocking your wife silly as well . . . It was as if her thoughts were vocal: he understood them all too clearly.

'Don't you?' he said, and shook her even harder.

She knew, dimly, that she must make an effort to reach him. For the children's sake, at least, she must try to stop this somehow.

'Jeff,' she began, still holding the wet cloth to her cut face, 'please . . . I know it's frustrating . . .'

'Frustrating!' he screamed. 'You can say that again! With you and the kids hanging round my neck like bloody millstones!'

She looked down at little Midge cowering on the floor— Soft, gentle little Midge with her wide grey eyes and honey-gold hair. A millstone?

'Then why don't you leave?' she heard herself say—a spurious kind of courage in her despairing voice.

'Leave?' He sounded totally uncomprehending. Then he seemed to take it in, and he began to laugh. It was an ugly sound, and it made the hair rise on Laurie's scalp and her overworked heart thump even faster with alarm.

'I might at that!' he said, still laughing. 'Except that you'd like that, wouldn't you?'

And when once more she did not answer, he hit her again.

She understood then, in a curious, crystal-clear flash of comprehension, that he would never leave her. He liked

15

having someone to hit—and he liked having a reason for his anger and his grudges. She and the children were his excuse for violence—his escape from his own failures and shortcomings. While they were there, he could blame them for everything that happened or failed to happen in the descending spiral of his down-at-heel existence. It was their fault that he had come to this. He did not have to blame himself for anything. He only had to punish them.

*Them?* At this point in her thoughts, she realised all at once what this implied. Her children were in danger. How could she let this go on? How could she not have realised what was happening to them? Midge was already terrified and cowering—afraid even to play or laugh in front of her father. And Jason—dear, brave Jay—was far too adult and far too carefully good for a boy of his age.

As she gained this brief glimpse of reality, Jeff took a lurching step away from her and tripped over the yellow lion, which Midge had dropped in terror on the floor before crawling under the table. Now, he advanced on the child with a bunched, uplifted fist and a look of glazed fury in his eye. 'You bloody brat!' he began.

'No!' said Laurie, and moved swiftly in front of the table. 'No, Jeff! Not Midge!'

He had never hit the children—till now. It had always been Laurie he wanted to hurt—Laurie he wanted to humiliate and defeat. He seemed to need the release of violence in some twisted way—to vent all his own rage and frustration on her. And in a way she had been thankful that he had never seen the children as a threat to his pride and independence, as he saw her. Never—till now.

But now the look on his face was past reason, and Laurie was afraid. She stooped down and gathered the little girl into her arms—moving very swiftly, though the floor and the table seemed to be weaving about even more than Jeff. 'Jay!' she said sharply. 'Come on. It's past your bedtime. I'll put you both to bed.'

'You won't!' shouted Jeff. 'Leave them there!'

'No!' answered Laurie, and backed quickly away, keeping Jason behind her.

Jeff overturned the table with a crash of crockery, and

16

came after her. But one of the upturned table legs caught him as he lurched drunkenly forward and sent him sprawling in a shower of broken glass and curses.

The wings were very strong in Laurie's head now. 'Fly, fly, fly!' they said, pulsing and singing, and the sound of their swift, sure flight was louder than Jeff's voice. The white flash of their wings got in front of Jeff's face and dazzled her eyes.

Somehow, without quite knowing how she got there, she was out in the street with Midge in her arms and Jason by her side, and she was running—running through the blue dusk of the September evening; running along the darkening road and leaving the tiny, shouting figure of Jeff and the cramped imprisoning little house far behind. And with her, as she ran, the wings pulsed on.

\* \* \*

When the stitch in her side got too bad, she paused to get her breath. They were in a part of London she did not know, but the streets seemed well lit, and there was an all-night coffee stall on the corner.

She looked down at the children, suddenly seeing them clearly—their faces turned to her in mute enquiry. 'What do we do now?' they were saying. She was glad they still had their coats on from that abortive earlier attempt to escape. She also had her coat on, she noticed vaguely, and her hand was clutching the leather strap of her handbag. Thank God for that, at least. There was a little more money left in it, Jason's school bus fare for tomorrow. . . . Tomorrow? . . . She couldn't think that far ahead. Right now, they needed a hot drink and something to eat.

She approached the coffee stall warily. She did not know how she looked, of course, with her marked face and the cut below her eye still oozing a thin trail of blood, her hair dishevelled and hanging in long straggling wisps, and her eyes seeming huge and almost black—dilated with shock—in the blazing pallor of her face.

The coffee stall owner took one look at her and poured out a steaming mug of tea, sliding it along the wooden counter towards her.

17

'What'd the kids like?' he asked.

'Tea,' said Jason promptly, 'please.'

'And the little girl? Milk-and-a-dash? Warm her up a bit?'

Laurie nodded.

'Here,' said the man kindly. 'Sit her on top . . . Give your arms a rest. Come on, luv—oops-a-daisy.' He set Midge down on the counter so that her four-year-old legs dangled down and her face was level with her mother's. She reached out a small quiet hand and patted Laurie's bruised cheek. 'Poor Mummy,' she said. 'All fall down.'

Laurie gulped down some hot tea hastily. Midge's absurd tenderness was almost the last straw. 'Could they have a hot dog?' she asked, trying to smile at the weather-beaten face before her.

'Sure.' He slapped two sausages into two bread rolls and spooned on some onions. 'Sauce?'

'Yes, please!' nodded Jason.

'Sauce!' agreed Midge, smiling seraphically from the counter.

'What about you, lady?' The alert brown eyes were watching her, unsurprised but not unsympathetic—arrested by that tired, dim smile.

'No, thanks. Not hungry.'

It was true, too. She was too tired to be hungry. Too tired to think what to do, where to go . . . Too tired to think at all.

'Had it rough tonight?' he asked gently, rubbing at his counter with a careless hand.

'You could say that.' The smile came again, almost with a glint of mischief in it.

'That cut wants seeing to,' he said. 'Needs a stitch, I'd say.'

She was warming her hands on the mug of tea, but she couldn't stop trembling. 'It doesn't matter,' she murmured.

He seemed to be assessing the situation, with his head cocked to one side in a considering manner. 'Going home, are you?' he asked, and waited with seeming inattention for her answer.

'No,' she said, and shivered again. 'Never.'

He nodded to himself, as if he understood the situation all too well. The seamy old-young face was set in lines of weary compassion. He had seen it all before. 'Where will you be going, then?' he asked, still carelessly polishing his counter, still not looking at her too keenly.

'I don't know,' she sighed. Then she leant forward and said to him with great earnestness, 'It's the wings, you see. They won't let me think.' And before he could say any more to her, the sigh in her voice became longer and she slid into a heap on the pavement, while Jason and Midge looked down at her in wonder.

\* \* \*

She woke to a strange room in a house full of strange sounds. She was lying on a camp-bed, covered in a grey army blanket. There was another camp-bed by one wall, and against another were two bunk beds. But there was no sign of her children.

She started up in terror; but the sudden movement caused a violent, searing pain in her head, and she leant back, clutching her throbbing temples and rocking to and fro in distress.

'It's all right,' said a voice close by. 'Take it easy. I've brought you some tea.'

'My children . . .'

'They're fine. They're with the others. Penny's looking after them.'

Laurie opened her eyes. The pain subsided a little, and she could see. She found herself looking into the face of a strong, gaunt woman with short grey hair, a straight, determined mouth and unexpectedly beautiful eyes of a curious golden colour that seemed to generate warmth and reassurance.

'Where . . . ? What is this place?'

'This is Hyde House—a refuge for women.'

'A . . . a refuge?'

'That's right.' A fleeting grin touched the stern mouth. 'They call it "The Hide". And I'm its founder—Jane Everett.' She smiled at Laurie more openly. 'There are a lot of women here in your predicament. We do our best to give them temporary shelter—and some kind of help and comfort, if we can.'

Laurie still looked confused. 'How did I . . . how did we get here?'

'Joe brought you in. D'you remember Joe? The coffee stall owner? He often brings people in. He's seen a lot of this, our Joe. And he's a kind little man.'

Laurie sighed. 'Yes . . . I remember . . . He was very kind.'

Jane Everett nodded. Then she sat down on the end of Laurie's bed and said quietly, 'Your sensible boy, Jason, told me your name—and Midge's. But there are one or two things I want to know. Do you feel up to it?'

'Yes.' She remembered just in time not to nod her head. 'But I don't know any answers.'

Jane smiled again. 'No, I don't suppose you do at the moment. But, you see, I want you to go to hospital and get that head injury checked, and they will ask questions.'

'I don't need . . .'

'Oh yes you do.' She was silent for a moment, and then went on. 'And if, as I suspect, you have no intention of returning for another battering—at least for the moment— you may need the hospital's evidence of your injuries. Do you understand?'

Laurie looked at her. All at once, the whole frightening process of the law, and the consequences of Jeff's actions and her flight, seemed to stretch before her like some nightmare road.

'Or do you want to go back?' asked Jane, still speaking gently.

'No,' said Laurie. 'No, I can't go back.' She looked anxiously into the other woman's face, as if trying to justify her decision. 'It's the children, you see,' she explained, and was horrified to hear her own voice shake on the edge of tears. 'They're not safe any more. They're not . . . safe.' And she put her hands over her face and began to weep.

Jane Everett put an arm round her shoulders. 'Don't worry now. They're quite safe here. No one can get at

20

them here. I'll send them in with Penny, and you can see for yourself. But then I think I'd better take you down to the hospital myself. You needn't explain anything—I'll do all the talking, if you like.'

Laurie nodded, forgetting the pain in her head, and then gave a small gasp of agony. 'Sorry,' she murmured helplessly. 'Sorry . . . to be such a nuisance.' But the tears still fell out of her eyes and she could not stop them.

Presently Jason came in, carefully balancing a tray with some bread and jam and another cup of tea, and Midge brought a bright-red geranium and put it in Laurie's hand. Then she climbed up on to the bed and curled up to watch Laurie eat. With them was a cheerful red-haired girl, pregnant and ringless but seemingly undismayed by Laurie's tears or the children's anxious attempts at comfort.

'I'm Penny,' she said, and grinned. 'Your two have taken to me OK, so it's all right to leave them while you go and get checked at the hospital.' She winked at Jason out of a blue, merry eye. 'Him and me's good friends, see? We'll take care of Midge, won't we, Jay?' She turned back to Laurie, half-serious now. 'There's a lot of kids here. Not much to play with, but we get by. And there's some swings out the back. They won't fret.'

Laurie was trying to eat bread and jam and stop crying, both at once. She choked, and took another gulp of tea to cover herself.

'Don't cry,' said Jason, and put his arm round her shoulders and held the cup of tea for her. 'Don't cry, Mum. It's OK. We like it here.'

The room spun in front of her eyes, and Laurie lay back exhausted. Penny took a look at her and quietly beckoned to Jason to come away. Then she picked up Midge and went out of the room.

In a little while Jane Everett returned. She got Laurie to her feet, wrapped a blanket round her shoulders, and steered her out of the room. They went down a long corridor with scuffed brown paint at the edges, and out through the front door to an ancient Ford van waiting at the kerb.

'I'll explain things,' repeated Jane to that bewildered, cloudy gaze. 'Don't worry.'

'No,' said Laurie, with her teeth clenched to stop them chattering. 'I'm past worrying now.'

The hospital was brisk and efficient—and unexpectedly kind. Jane gave a brief explanation of the situation, and Laurie fancied they were quite used to this. She then announced that she would be returning with a social worker and possibly a policewoman to hear the results of their examination.

The young houseman on duty took one look at Laurie and decided to postpone any questions till later. She was taken away for X-rays, and when they undressed her and stood looking at her bruised body even she was mildly surprised at the extent of her injuries. She seemed to be black-and-blue all over, her ribs hurt like fire when she breathed in, and her backbone where Jeff had rammed her against the rim of the sink was painfully stiff and sore and had developed a deep, crippling ache.

They stitched up the cut on her cheek and X-rayed her head, ribs and spine. Then they took her back to the ward and put her to bed. She was shaking badly by this time, and deathly cold, but they piled blankets on her and even brought her a lukewarm hot-water bottle (unheard-of cosseting in a busy hospital ward). The little nurse in charge leant over, smiling, and said, 'Don't worry. It's only shock.'

Laurie went on shivering, even when they brought her some hot, sweet tea.

Eventually, the young doctor reappeared and sat down beside her. 'How are you feeling now?'

'All right. Just c-cold.' She drew a shaky breath. 'Can I go soon? I've left my children . . .'

'They are being well looked after. Jane Everett promised me.' He smiled at her reassuringly. 'She is very experienced. We see quite a lot of her here.'

'Do you?' Her head still felt strange. The wings were still fluttering about inside it, trying to get out. It made it difficult to concentrate.

'We want to keep you in for the night.'

'But I can't! My children . . .'

'Yes you can.' He laid a hand on her wrist, feeling the erratic, jumping pulse with cool, competent fingers. 'After a bang on the head, we like to keep patients under observation for a little while. Just in case.' His smile was still friendly. 'I can assure you we won't keep you longer than necessary—we are too short of beds!'

She tried to answer his smile. 'Then . . . what's the damage?'

He looked at her, gravely now, but without any particular anxiety. 'You have a mild concussion, and a possible hairline fracture. You also have three cracked ribs, but they will heal in time. And a severely bruised spine, which will be very painful for a while but will also get better on its own.' He gave her arm a cheerful little pat and got to his feet. 'It sounds bad, but in fact they are all things that only require rest. You were lucky.'

Her smile was tired but relieved. At least she would be able to cope with the children . . . and finding somewhere to live . . . and all the rest of the difficult rearrangements she would have to make. 'Yes,' she murmured. 'Very lucky.'

At that point, a voice behind the doctor said busily, 'Can we get her particulars now? Who is the next of kin? Shouldn't we send for her husband?'

'No!' exclaimed Laurie, and tried to leap out of bed then and there. 'No! You *can't*!'

'Don't be so stupid!' snapped Jane Everett's voice beside her. 'It's her husband that's put her here in this condition.'

'But,' persisted the voice, uncomprehending, 'next of kin must always be informed.'

'Very well,' said Jane. 'Inform him. I have a policewoman here, and a social worker. They want to hear the doctor's report. When that has been done, you can inform her husband that if he attempts to come here to see her, or to make any disturbance, he will be arrested for common assault and causing grievous bodily harm.' She looked at the hapless official from the records office with grim dislike. 'You people,' she said, 'with your built-in forms and set procedures! Can't you use a little discretion?'

23

'But'—the woman sounded exceedingly affronted—'we have to abide by the rules.'

'Why?' said Jane belligerently. 'Haven't you any humanity? Or at least common sense?'

'Well, what about her mother?' insisted the bossy voice.

'My mother is in Sunderland,' said Laurie, very distinctly. 'She is arthritic. She couldn't possibly come. Besides, she couldn't care less.'

There was a rather shocked silence at this. But young Dr Lang, who had stood by during this exchange, now said firmly, 'I don't think this helps my patient. Leave the forms for now and come to my office.'

Laurie was still trying to get out of bed, and the little nurse was still trying to restrain her.

'I can't stay here!' she said wildly. 'He'll come! Let me go!'

'Now look what you've done!' snarled Jane.

The doctor signalled with his eyes to the ward sister, who had come up during the argument. She turned away to prepare an injection, and Dr Lang took Laurie's wrist in his hand again and said firmly, 'No one will come. I won't allow it. We're going to give you a shot to make you sleep. Forget everything—you are quite safe.'

Somehow the calm voice and steady pressure of his long, cool fingers got through to her. She relaxed and fell back on the bed, exhausted.

The sister returned with the injection, and presently pain and shock retreated into a warm haze.

They waited till she was drowsy before they looked at her injuries and heard the doctor's report. Then they went away, grim-faced and silent. Jane Everett returned to her houseful of shattered refugees from violence and set about her endless tasks of reassurance, practical advice and plain honest comfort. She also set in motion the social service procedures that would help Laurie and her children to survive.

When Laurie woke next, it was late at night and the ward lights were low. There was a dim glow over the sister's desk, and Laurie could see her head bent over the report sheets in front of her. Laurie turned her head restlessly and saw a note propped up on her locker. It said, 'Your children are fine. Everything is taken care of. The doctor says NO VISITORS. See you tomorrow. Jane E.'

Sighing, Laurie turned on her side, trying to ease her aching spine. There was a small rustle of starch beside her, and a young nurse's voice said softly, 'I've brought you a cup of tea, since you're awake. It'll help you to sleep.'

Obediently, Laurie sat up and leant back against the pillows, sipping the hot tea. She had a sudden vision of her young son, Jason, trying to comfort her and saying, 'I put three sugars in' and not adding the words 'for shock', though she could see them in his eyes.

'What time is it?' she asked suddenly.

'About two in the morning. Why?'

'Am I still in shock?'

The young nurse smiled at her and leant over to plump up her pillows. 'You're over the worst.' She gave her a reassuring pat. 'A good night's rest will help.'

Wearily, Laurie agreed, and lay back with her eyes closed. But her thoughts went round and round in her head and would not let her rest. What was she going to do? . . . Where would she go? . . . How could she support the children? . . . Would the social security people give her any money? . . . Would they find her somewhere to live? Or would they tell her to go back to Jeff?

She shuddered, and found herself unable to stop shivering—caught in the throes of an attack of uncontrollable rigors. When she opened her eyes, she found the night sister there, observing her with a quiet, perceptive gaze.

'I'm s-sorry,' she muttered, her teeth chattering. 'C-can't stop it.'

'It's all right.' The sister's voice was calm. 'We'll give you another injection. You may sleep on rather long in the morning, though!'

Laurie tried to smile, but her face felt stiff and it came out like a grimace. 'I want a bath,' she said, in a voice like a lost child's.

'In the morning,' said the sister kindly. 'It will all seem better then. Now, try to sleep.'

Presently, Laurie slept.

* * *

In the morning they let her have a bath, watched over by a cheery young probationer to see that she didn't pass out. But even the soothing touch of the hot water on her bruised flesh could not wash off the feel of Jeff's hard hands—the endless, punishing flail of his fists and his angry voice which seemed to go on and on shouting in her aching head.

When she came back into the ward, wearing a hospital dressing-gown, Penny was there with an armful of clean clothes.

'Thought you could do with 'em,' she grinned. 'Can't get into 'em now, meself. Not very posh, but we can wash yours when we get back.'

Laurie looked round for permission to get dressed, and found the little probationer beside her. 'Better wait for the doctor's rounds,' she said. 'He'll be here in a minute.'

Penny sat down on the end of Laurie's bed. 'OK if I wait here? Come to take her home, see?'

Home? thought Laurie. Where is home? Aloud she asked swiftly, 'The children? Are they all right?'

'Course they are. Right as rain. I'd've brought them, but Jane said better not—hospital might frighten them.' She smiled encouragingly at Laurie. 'You'll see them soon.'

'Penny, . . .' began Laurie unsteadily. 'It is Penny, isn't it?'

'That's me.'

'I don't understand what's happened.' She looked up at Penny anxiously, struggling to bring her bewildered mind into focus.

'Don't suppose you do.' Penny's grin was still cheerful. 'With a bashing like that, you're bound to be a bit fazed. But Jane'll sort things out for you. She usually does.'

'Does she?' Laurie sounded vague and uncertain still.

Her head hurt when she tried to think. And those wings were still there . . .

At that moment, Dr Lang arrived by her bed. He looked at her eyes, studied her chart for a moment, and once more took her wrist in his firm, cool hand.

'You'll do,' he said, smiling. 'But I want you to take it easy for at least a week. And I want to see you again a week from now. But if your headache gets much worse, or you start seeing double, come back at once.'

Laurie stared at him. How could she promise to return when she didn't even know where she would be in a week's time?

'Jane Everett has arranged for you and the children to stay at the refuge for a fortnight', he said, seeing the doubt and confusion in her eyes. 'I made sure of that with the authorities. After that, we shall see.'

'She said *at least* a fortnight,' interrupted Penny sturdily. 'And I can look after the kids. You'll be able to do just what the doc says.'

Laurie put her hands up to her face and said in a stifled voice, 'I wish . . . everyone wasn't so bloody kind!'

Dr Lang laughed. 'I daresay you'll get used to it. Though I can see you haven't met too much kindness just lately.'

Just lately? thought Laurie bleakly, a new wave of defeat overwhelming her. How long had all this been going on? How long since Jeff had shown any kindness—either to her or to the children? How long since she had been afraid every time he walked in the door?

But it had not always been like that. She could remember a far-off time when Jeff had been considerate and friendly—even loving, sometimes . . . And he had brought them home small presents and taken them all out for a meal . . . And his eyes had been warm—not accusing.

'Come on,' said Penny. 'Climb in!' She was holding out a clean pair of jeans. 'Doc says you can go.'

Laurie did as she was told. It seemed simpler.

When she was ready to go, the ward sister came over to her and handed her a packet of tablets and an appointment card. 'These are for your headache', she said. 'The instructions are on the packet. Don't take more that it says.'

'No.' agreed Laurie. Vaguely, she wondered whether other women in her kind of plight had been driven to suicide—and if that was the meaning of the sister's careful warning. Suicide? How could she? There were the children. In a way, they were her salvation, as well as her responsibility. Then, nervously, she asked the vital question: 'What . . . do you know what they did about . . . notifying anyone?'

The sister smiled. 'Yes,' she said. 'Dr Lang instructed the records office to notify your husband—but the letter was not to be posted until today.' A suspicion of a wink seemed to touch her eye for a moment, but she kept a perfectly straight face.

'Oh!' Laurie suddenly answered her smile with a brief flood of radiance. 'Oh . . . *thank* you!' And she turned and moved away down the ward to the door, with Penny's guiding arm round her shoulders.

Outside the hospital Penny went confidently up to the old green van parked on the corner and rapped on the window. It was the same van that Jane had used to bring her to hospital, she thought vaguely, but this time a man was driving it.

'This is Joe,' said Penny. 'Remember him? He runs a stall in the market. Get in.'

Still dazed and obedient, Laurie climbed in, and Penny got in the back with a load of cauliflowers and cabbages. Joe, Laurie discovered, was a squarish, brownish man with a sardonic twist to his mouth and very bright, very observant brown eyes—and she recognised him in a sudden flash of memory.

'I thought you ran an all-night coffee stall?'

'I do,' agreed Joe, smiling at her sideways. 'Veges, mornings. Coffee, nights.'

'You were the one who got me into Jane's refuge.'

'I was.' He was still smiling at her, knowing and kind.

'Well . . . thanks,' breathed Laurie. 'You probably saved my life—and the kids' as well!'

His grin got wider. 'Think nothing of it, luv,' he said, and slammed in the gears and shot out into the traffic.

'Often does us a good turn, Joe does,' remarked Penny, from the back. 'Even brings us 'is left-overs for The Hide.'

'You be quiet,' growled Joe, dodging between a bus and a taxi, 'or I'll crown you with one of me turnips!'

He turned into a road of tall, shabby houses in a long, curving terrace, with stucco falling off the old-fashioned pillars of the Victorian porticos, and rusty iron railings flanking the steep area steps. At the end of the row was one slightly larger semi-detached house with a straggly back garden running along the edge of a side-road. Here, Joe stopped and opened the back of the van to let Penny out. Then they both came round to help Laurie up the steps.

'I can manage,' she said. But her legs felt very wobbly and strange, and she was ashamed of her own weakness. Also, the steps seemed to weave up and down in front of her eyes, and distances and heights seemed to change as she looked at them.

'Hold up!' said Penny cheerfully. 'Nearly there.'

Inside, the house was filled with the sound of children—babies crying, with mothers soothing, toddlers running about and shrieking with alternate joy and rage, and small boys zooming up and down the corridors as planes and space-rockets. It was also filled with the sound of women's voices talking—some loudly, and some in desperate, grief-stricken monotones. The weight of their despair seemed to fill the dim corridors like an almost tangible force. It made Laurie shiver.

There was a long narrow hall reaching from the front to the back of the house, stuffed with push-chairs, prams, bundles of clothes, coats and shabby suitcases. On one side was a large, crowded day-room with ancient arm-chairs set round in groups and a faded cord carpet on the floor. Various little knots of women and children were gathered here. Some were talking among themselves, some were trying vaguely to keep order among the tumbling children, and some were just sitting there in helpless silence, staring into space. Most of their faces showed some signs of shock or exhaustion, and though some of them had clearly made an effort to look tidy and presentable, and had also cleaned up their children, there were others who still looked unkempt, unwashed and uncaring.

'Not in there,' said Penny, and steered her past the door. 'Jane says rest for you today—and what Jane says goes!'

Laurie did not answer. She was occupied in trying to still the wings which were beating in her head again, beating and beating, trying to get out. They made her eyes see things strangely, too. The walls seemed to tilt inwards and grow enormously high and tall, forming a dark tunnel down which she was walking. And there was a white, clear light at the end of the tunnel—very bright and pure—if only she could reach it.

She stumbled a little, and Penny's strong young arms came round her and held her steady. 'In here,' she said. 'Where you were before. You can have the kids with you—and me as well, I'm afraid, but Jane thought you wouldn't mind. We're terribly short of beds.'

Laurie smiled vaguely. 'I'm glad . . .' she managed to say, 'glad . . . you'll be here.' She fell on to the bed and seemed to float off at once towards that brilliant, pulsing light at the end of the tunnel.

'You lay there and relax,' commanded Penny. 'I'll fetch the kids.'

'Mm . . .' sighed Laurie. But then her eyes flew open, filled with anxiety. 'Penny . . . does . . . does anyone know we're here?'

'No.' Penny's voice was calm and flat. 'No one. Except the doctor—and he won't tell. Come on, Laurie, you're *safe* here. Relax!'

Once again Laurie gave up the struggle to control her own life. She was too tired, and her head wouldn't think. All she could feel was a thousand aches from her bruised and battered body, and a heavy sense of dread and uncertainty—as if she hung over an abyss and did not know whether she was going to fall in or not.

But while she was silently wrestling with this swimming

darkness, there was a rush of small feet at the door, and Midge and Jason burst into the room. 'Mummy!' cried Midge, and hurled herself on to the bed and flung her arms round Laurie's neck.

Jason was quieter, but his eyes were full of relief and welcome. 'Are you better?'

'Much better,' lied Laurie. 'Quite all right, in fact.'

'*Quite*?' Jason put his head on one side and looked at her consideringly.

'Well . . . almost!' She smiled, and disentangled one arm from Midge's convulsive embrace and drew him close.

'Jane says we can bring you your dinner in here,' Jason explained, "cos you've got to be quiet.' He looked at Penny for confirmation, and she nodded, smiling.

'That's right, Jay, keep her quiet!'

'And Jane's coming to see you after dinner,' he went on, trying to take the cloudy bewilderment out of his mother's eyes. 'She said to tell you—and you weren't to worry—not about anything yet.' He sounded absurdly adult and serious, and Laurie wanted to cry again because her young son was far too responsible and far too aware of trouble for his eight years.

'Come on,' said Penny. 'Let's go and see about that dinner. Give your Mum a chance to rest a bit, see?' And she took them off to investigate the meals being got together in the kitchen, leaving Laurie alone.

But even when they brought her a plate of stew, she could not eat it. Her throat closed tight, and her hands shook so much she could not hold a spoon. She was still sitting there, staring at it, when Jane came in to see her.

'How are you feeling?' she asked, noting the plate of untouched food.

'I'm sorry,' began Laurie. 'I know food must be . . . must be precious here . . .'

'Never mind.' Jane's voice was calm and unemphatic, but there was a hidden strength about her that Laurie felt could be steel-hard if pushed. Somehow this reassured her more than her initial kindness.

'I . . . I haven't touched it,' Laurie went on anxiously. 'Maybe . . . you could put it back.'

Jane knew then that Laurie understood poverty—and how every scrap of food had to be saved and used with infinite care.

'I've no money,' Laurie's voice was wavering again, though she was trying gamely to keep it under control, 'except £2 for Jason's school bus fares. You could have that. He won't be needing it now.'

Jane smiled and patted Laurie's hand. 'You keep it. In any case, I've arranged something with social security for the moment—till you're fit to cope.' She was silent for a little while, as if considering what course of action would upset Laurie least.

'Now,' she said at last, 'I'm only going to tell you enough to reassure you about the present. We can talk about the rest later. All right?'

'Yes,' agreed Laurie. But then she added awkwardly, 'Only, I oughtn't to expect . . . I mean, why should you . . . ?'

'Just let go and accept things as they are!' said Jane, smiling. 'I have a grant for running this place now. I get a subsistence allowance for you and your children while you're in my care. I've told the hospital you can stay at least a fortnight—and you can! I suggest you make use of that time to get well. And don't try to think too far ahead or make any plans—not yet. The time to make decisions is when you are rested and feeling strong.' She leant forward and laid a friendly hand on Laurie's arm. 'Some of the women here are basically very weak, you know . . . and a bit, er, limited. But I don't think you are either! Just give yourself time—time to heal and time to consider. We can talk again later. Now I think you should sleep.'

'Yes,' agreed Laurie dutifully—and admitted to herself that her head was flying off in circles and she was longing for sleep again. 'I . . . I can't begin to . . .' she started to say.

But Jane cut her off short. 'Don't try. Just thank God Joe had the sense to bring you here.' She got up and gave Laurie's arm another friendly pat. 'Sleep well!'

\* \* \*
32

Jeff was confused. When Laurie ran out of the house with the children, he supposed she would come back soon, contrite and placatory, as usual. But she didn't come back. He surveyed the wreckage of the kitchen, and the stew spread all over the wall behind the sink, and was a little ashamed of his own violence. It made him shudder. Had he really done all that? What had made him so angry? He couldn't remember now, but the thought of that scene appalled him. He wanted to blot it out—so he decided to go back to his mates in the pub. He could get a pie or something, and they would be sympathetic.

'My wife's run off,' he said, gulping down his drink.

'Don't blame 'er,' muttered someone in the corner who knew him a bit too well.

'What's that?' He turned belligerently towards the speaker.

'Nothing.' The voice was neutral, without malice. 'Same again?'

Jeff agreed with alacrity, and sat down rather heavily at the nearest table.

'She'll come back,' said someone else, and laughed. 'They always do.'

Everyone round Jeff laughed as well then, so he did too—though he had a sneaking feeling of shame about it. But when he got home, late and even more belligerent with drink than usual, there was no one to take it out on—no one at all.

He fell into bed in a haze of alcohol and self-pity, and dreamt that he was on a merry-go-round which was spinning faster and faster so that he got dizzier and sicker with every whirl. And Laurie and the kids were standing hand-in-hand at the side, watching gravely while he spun and spun and could not get off. They weren't laughing, though—just watching. And he couldn't get off.

He woke feeling very sick and curiously frightened about something, and rushed to the bathroom. There was no one in the house, and its silence and emptiness seemed to mock him. Cursing, he looked at his pallid face and stubbly chin in the bathroom mirror—and winced. Was that him—that sagging, flaccid, grey face with the bitter

33

mouth and hot, angry eyes? Where was the handsome lively lad that had charmed all the girls from here to Bethnal Green? Or was it Gretna Green? He should never have run off with Laurie—never have married her, an inexperienced child who couldn't cope with a man of the world like him, who only whined when things got difficult and made him want to hit her. What he needed was someone stronger and more mature who could manage his life for him properly—like his mother had once. He shed a maudlin tear or two into the wash-basin as he shaved. What he needed was a mother. . . . No, what he needed was a drink.

He went downstairs, and once more stared at the kitchen in disgust. It did not occur to him—yet—that he would have to clear it up, since there was no one else to do it for him. Instead, he went out—slamming the door—and staggered down to the workmen's café on the corner. There he ordered himself a plate of bacon and eggs, but when it came his stomach heaved and he could not eat it.

'Take it away,' he snarled at the café owner's solid wife, who had slapped it down in front of him. 'Can't eat that stuff! Why don't you feed it to the pigs?'

She looked at him, hands on hips. 'I thought we had,' she said.

Jeff stared—almost too befuddled to be insulted. Then he lurched to his feet and stormed out of the café without paying.

'Hey!' shouted the woman.

'Let 'im go,' advised her husband from behind the coffee machine. 'Trouble, that one is.'

The rest of the day passed in a haze of pubs and drinks and uneatable pies that stuck in his throat—and a sense of loss that he could not quite understand. When he got back to the house there was still no one there.

He began to wonder in a muddled sort of way whether anything could have happened to Laurie. No, he thought. She's just paying me out—or trying to. She's probably staying with one of the neighbours—or even gone back to her mother's, like last time. But no, she wouldn't have the fares for that. He kept her pretty short—needed it all himself these days to keep his end up—and she didn't ever seem to save anything. (Nor did he, come to that, niggled a little voice in his mind.)

He cursed again, and kicked angrily at the overturned table on the kitchen floor. He only succeeded in stubbing his toe. Better clear up this mess, he thought. Can't live like this. But he did not. He left it where it was, and stumbled up to bed.

In the morning, he found the letter from the hospital. It was a printed form with bits filled in by hand. 'Mrs Laura Collins, wife of Jeffrey Collins of 14 Wetherby Terrace . . . has been admitted to Ward 10 of this hospital, suffering from: fractured ribs, hairline fracture of the skull, concussion, severe spinal bruising and multiple contusions.' Nothing else was said. No word about how long she would be there, or how bad she was. Or how the injuries were acquired.

His stomach gave a heave of fear. Did they know it was him? What had she told them? Surely all those injuries couldn't have been his fault? True, there had been two rows in one day, but she couldn't have . . . he couldn't have . . . could he? No, she must have been knocked down by a car, or mugged or something.

He'd better got round there and see how she was, hadn't he? But supposing they accused him of—what was it they accused people of?—assault? Or grievous bodily harm? Maybe he ought to stay away and wait for them to get in touch again. Or send her home. After all, they didn't say she was very ill, or in danger or anything. Yes, better wait and see. Meanwhile, he needed a drink—bit of a shock, news like that.

But after a morning at the pub he felt more courageous, and he began to think. Suppose he didn't go to see her— wouldn't they think he didn't care what happened to her? Wouldn't that make it look as if he really might've beaten her up? Maybe it would be better to go round after all, and seem concerned. *Seem*? Well, he *was* concerned. They wouldn't believe it could have been him then, would they? And he could take her home. Things would get back to normal then.

He wondered vaguely what had happened to the kids. She couldn't have them in the hospital with her, could she? Someone else must be looking after them. Well, good luck to them! He'd find out soon enough where they were. Maybe they'd keep them a day or two longer—give him a breather. He could do with it.

It occurred to him then that if he was going to bring Laurie home, like a good husband, he'd better clear the place up a bit first—just in case someone wanted to come and see for themselves or something. Clean himself up, too. He gulped down another drink, and as an after-thought bought a half-bottle of whisky with his last fiver. He might need it—things might get pretty hairy at the hospital. You never knew how people would take things.

Then he went back to the house to clear up. He swept up the broken glass and crockery and threw it in the dustbin outside the back door. He cleaned the sink and washed up all the plates that were left whole. Then he washed the stew off the walls. He was a bit shaken to find blood on the walls as well, so he washed that off too.

He looked round. It wasn't very good, but it was better than nothing—though the floor was a mess. Maybe he'd better mop it over. There was even a bit of blood on the floor as well. It was all over that confounded yellow lion of Midge's! He picked it up and threw it in the dustbin with the broken glass. Then he looked round for a mop.

By this time his courage was evaporating again, so he stopped to pour out a stiff whisky. He needed it. He didn't like hospitals at the best of times, and this interview might be tricky. Still, he was good at tricky interviews—part of his job, tricky interviews were. He'd always been a smooth operator, a clever manipulator, a good talker.

After another drink he felt quite jaunty. He changed into his one and only suit (a bit shiny at the edges, but still quite respectable), picked up his salesman's briefcase to add to the professional image, and went off to get the tube. The hospital was in another part of London—a part he didn't know very well. Still, he'd find it—he was good at finding his way around.

* * *

36

'I've come to see my wife, Mrs Laura Collins,' he said. 'Ward 10, I believe.'

The woman at the reception desk said automatically, without looking up, 'Second floor. Take the lift at the end of the corridor.'

Jeff took the lift. He also, surreptitiously, took another swig from the bottle of whisky concealed in his pocket.

At the entrance to Ward 10 he met a pretty nurse. Smiling, he put on all his charm and said, 'Are you going my way?'

'I shouldn't think so,' she replied tartly. 'Who did you want to see?'

'My wife—Laura Collins. This is Ward 10, isn't it?'

The pretty nurse stopped and looked at him. 'Did you say Mrs *Collins*?' She turned back towards the ward door, and made for the sister's office just inside. 'Wait there,' she said crisply. 'I'll make enquiries.'

Inside the sister's office there was a brief colloquy. 'What's he like?' asked the sister, looking at the young nurse with grim attention.

'Drunk,' said the nurse. 'Or at least the worse for wear. I think he could get nasty.'

The sister reached for the phone. 'Bleep Dr Lang, will you? He's needed on Ward 10.'

Outside, Jeff's courage was beginning to wane again. But he did not dare take out the bottle and have another swig—there were too many people passing to and fro. Presently the pretty nurse returned, with the sister beside her for reinforcement, and said politely, 'If you would wait in here, Mr Collins, Dr Lang will be down to see you.'

The doctor? thought Jeff, with another slight lurch of alarm. Was she bad, then? Why couldn't he go into the ward like the other visitors?

'Is she . . . ? Can't I go in?' he said, and tried to push past the two women in his way.

'In here, if you please,' said the sister, adroitly stepping in front of him and steering him through a door into a small waiting-room. 'The doctor won't be long.'

Defeated, Jeff sat down on a chair, next to someone

else who was also waiting. There was a copy of *Autocar* on the table, and he reached out for it with an unsteady hand. The glossy pages mocked him. It was a long time since he had a shiny company car: a long time since life had been easy and comfortable—and full of promise.

Presently the other waiting man was shepherded away. It gave Jeff just time to take another quick swig before a stern-faced young doctor stood in the doorway. 'Mr Collins?'

'Yes. That's me.' The jaunty tone rang false, and he stood up, not knowing quite what line he should take.

'What can I do for you?' The tone was clipped, uncompromising.

'I . . . came to see my wife.'

'I'm afraid you're too late.' He seemed to pause deliberately, watching the flick of terror in Jeff's eyes.

'*What*?'

'We discharged her this morning.'

Jeff was suddenly furious. Frightening him like that. He had thought for a moment . . . and there was nothing wrong with her at all!

'Discharged her? Where to?'

Dr Lang shrugged his shoulders. 'I've no idea. She said she had somewhere to go—where she would be looked after—so we let her go.'

'But . . . I want to know where she is! She's my wife!' He glared at the young doctor with mounting anger. 'Didn't she leave an address?'

'Only *your* address, Mr Collins—and that reluctantly.'

'What? Did she . . . did she say anything?'

'About what, Mr Collins? About how she got her injuries, perhaps?'

Jeff felt a new flick of fear. 'Well, did she?' His voice came out too loud, too truculent.

'She didn't say much at all, Mr Collins. She was concussed. And in shock.'

'She must've fallen,' he muttered. 'Been knocked down by a car or something. Or mugged. Didn't she ask for me?'

'*Ask* for you?' The doctor sounded extraordinarily cold

38

and contemptuous. 'No, Mr Collins. She did not. In fact, the only time you were mentioned she got so frightened that she tried to get up and leave the hospital there and then.'

There was a pause while Jeff took this in. He seemed unable to decide what to do next. Finally he allowed fear and anger to get the better of him. 'It's ridiculous!' he raged. 'Refusing to tell me where she is! Making all these accusations!'

'No one has made any accusations, Mr Collins,' said Dr Lang in a cool, clear voice.

'I demand to know where she is! She's my wife! And where are my children? She has no right to go off without leaving an address! And you've no right to let her!' He advanced on Dr Lang, pointing an accusing finger. 'You must know where she is! And I shan't leave here until you tell me!'

The young doctor stood there, with his hands in the pockets of his white coat. 'I'm afraid I can't help you.'

Jeff lunged at him blindly, but a hard, swift hand caught him by the wrist and forced his arm down.

'I wouldn't advise you to get rough, Mr Collins,' said Dr Lang pleasantly. 'I think we've already had enough of that. I suggest you leave now, before I call a couple of porters to escort you.'

'I'm not leaving!' shouted Jeff. 'My wife's run off some-where and you tell me a cock-and-bull story about injuries and . . . and shock or something! That's all bullshit! She's my wife and I want her back!' His eyes focused in a hot, angry glare on Dr Lang's quiet, set face. 'And you can stop looking so bloody disapproving, too! What goes on between me and my wife is *my* bloody business—no one else's!'

'Indeed,' murmured Dr Lang. 'And a bloody business is what it appears to be.'

Once again Jeff tried to hit him. But this time the sister came in, followed by two burly porters who each took Jeff by an arm.

'I should go quietly if I were you,' said the doctor mildly. 'Or do you want me to call the police?'

'The *police*?' Jeff was startled. He remembered that bit of paper from the hospital with the list of injuries—and he remembered the blood-stained kitchen wall. Good thing he'd cleaned it up a bit.

'I'm sure your wife will contact you in due course,' said Dr Lang, still sounding cool and quite pleasant. 'When she has recovered. Good afternoon, Mr Collins.'

But Jeff was an obstinate man, and the hard hands of the two porters gripping his arms made him mad. He flung them off, saying between his teeth, 'Let go of me! I've told you—I'm not leaving till I know where she is!'

The two porters grabbed him again, and a running fight ensued. The sister went back into her office and called the police.

At the police station they were used to calls from this hospital—especially from Casualty, where the drunks came in on Saturday night. They sent a man round right away. By the time he had got there, Jeff was beside himself with frustration and fright. He hit out at the porters, he hit out at Dr Lang, and he hit out at the police constable.

'Let me go!' he shouted. 'I want my wife! I want to know where she is! How dare you keep her from me!'

They led him away, still struggling and shouting. It was a nice clear case of assault, drunk and disorderly behaviour, and public affray. They put him in a cell and wrote out a report.

'Well,' said Dr Lang, looking at the sister somewhat grimly. 'There's not much doubt about where those injuries came from.'

'No,' she agreed. 'It seems fairly clear!'

* * *

In the bare cell, when the drunken rage wore off, Jeff sat and cried. He wanted to go home. He wanted his wife. He even wanted his children. He was appalled at what had happened to Laurie—and to him. He couldn't understand how life had suddenly gone so horribly wrong.

'Come on,' said the constable in charge, pulling him to

his feet. 'No need for that. You can go home when you've made a statement. Desk-sergeant's waiting.'

When that confusing ordeal was over, and he had been charged, the desk-sergeant said—quite kindly—'Court on Monday. Released on bail. Mind you're there! And you'd better stay sober till then—and keep out of trouble!'

'Oh, I will,' said Jeff piously. 'I will.'

* * *

The next day, Laurie got up determined to be some use and do something to help with the running of the refuge. But she found that her legs would scarcely hold her up, and she still shook badly whenever she tried to hold anything—even a cup.

She went in search of the children, and found them playing with a noisy group round the swings and the grubby sand-pit in the back garden. They ran up to her at once, smiling, and she hugged them both to her briefly and then let them return to their game. They seemed happy enough—though Jay's eyes were still too anxious.

Since they were cheerfully occupied, she went indoors again, on cottonwool legs, and went to look for Jane . . . or Penny . . . or anyone who could tell her what to do next. She seemed incapable of making up her mind about anything—even the simplest of decisions was too much for her.

She found Jane with a paintbrush and a pot of bright blue paint, patiently explaining to one of the women residents how to paint a door.

'Can't I do that?' asked Laurie.

Jane looked at her pale, shadowed face. 'Not today you can't,' she said, smiling. 'Perhaps tomorrow. We're trying to brighten up the place. It makes everyone feel more cheerful.' She looked round rather ruefully at the greyish-beige walls and dark-brown paint of the long, dark hall. 'Everywhere needs doing,' she sighed, 'but we'll get round to it in time.'

Laurie said in a choked sort of voice, 'I must do *something!*'

Jane glanced at her again, and handed her paintbrush

41

over to the waiting woman. 'There you are, then, Molly—see what you can do.' She turned back to Laurie and led her away into the kitchen. 'I know it's dull,' she said, smiling, 'but you can help me with the vegetables—while we talk. I don't think you should tackle anything too strenuous at first—especially with three bust ribs. Painting's not a good idea!'

Laurie saw the sense of that—and it was true that her ribs hurt like fire when she moved too suddenly, especially if she lifted her arms. Even holding Midge in her arms seemed to send knife-blades through her.

'All right,' she said, and returned Jane's smile with a tentative one of her own. She looked like a small child not sure of her welcome, with her long, fair hair and anxious blue eyes, and Jane felt moved to ask suddenly, 'How old are you, Laurie?'

'Twenty-seven.'

'And Jason is . . . ?'

'Eight. I married Jeff when I was eighteen.'

Jane picked up a bag of sprouts and a bowl and handed them to Laurie, and rummaged in a drawer for a knife. 'You can do those. I'll do the potatoes.' She was wondering whether it would upset Laurie to talk, or if that was what she needed to do. In any case, it was time Jane found out a thing or two if she was ever going to help her to put her life in order again. What questions would distress her least? she wondered. But in the end she decided to be straightforward. After all, Laurie could always tell her to mind her own business. It had happened to her before!

'How long has all this been going on, Laurie?' she asked in a gentle voice. She watched the desolation in the girl's eyes, and almost wished she had kept silent. 'I mean—this latest bust-up isn't the only occasion, is it?'

Laurie looked at her. 'No,' she said sadly. 'Oh no . . .' How to describe how it had been? How Jeff had changed from the jaunty, affectionate, laughter-loving man he used to be? How she had changed too, she supposed, from the green girl who had loved him so much—who had been so bedazzled by his charm?

42

'When did it begin?' asked Jane softly, seeing the regret, the rueful, unwilling tenderness in the pain-filled eyes.

Laurie took a deep, shaken breath. 'Begin? Yes, I suppose . . . I'd better start at the beginning.' She tried to focus her flying thoughts. 'Well . . . I ran away with Jeff when I was eighteen. I'd just started a job in the bank—after my A-levels—but I threw it all up when Jeff asked me to go with him. That made my parents angry—or my mother, anyway. She—my mother—didn't like Jeff. He was a salesman for a software company—a good bit older than me, and very . . . very good-looking and full of charm.' She glanced at Jane, half-sorrowfully but with a hint of humour against herself. 'I was so young—so easily impressed! My mother said he wasn't to be trusted—and all salesmen had extra women on the side and were unreliable. She was right, of course.' The sadness and resignation were back in her voice.

Jane, being an ardent champion of women, wanted to shake some sense into Laurie and get rid of that forgiving sadness. Instead, she merely said, 'You found this out for yourself, I imagine, in time?'

'Oh yes. Quite soon.' Again the faint glimmer of a smile touched her, though it wasn't really funny—not for her. 'He was all right till . . . till I was heavily pregnant with Jason. Up till then he was quite loving and . . . and attentive—though he had moods, even then.' The gleam of tenderness came back into that faint reminiscent smile. 'But then . . . he seemed to go right off me. Men do, I suppose, when their wives begin to look big and ugly.' She sounded almost detached now—even indifferent.

'Pregnancy isn't ugly, Laurie,' protested Jane.

'Isn't it?' Laurie looked at her, almost contemptuously. 'Well, Jeff thought so, anyway. So he found a slim, pretty girl somewhere else.'

'Weren't you angry?'

She gave a small, careless shrug. 'What was the use? I didn't make a fuss about it. He was still quite kind to me, most of the time—even quite loving, really—when he came home!' She sighed a little. 'But when the baby came, he didn't want to know. He didn't even like it being a boy. I don't think he's a natural father.' She looked away from Jane, seeing the distaste in Jeff's eyes, his reluctance to help, his resentment of all those broken nights and dirty nappies. 'He didn't like the mess, and he didn't like having to stay in at night. He was used to having a good time, and he couldn't really understand why things had to change.' Once again she sighed. She understood Jeff's fun-loving nature, really. He was like a small boy who couldn't believe that life wasn't all treats—all ice-cream and funfairs and endless pocket-money, and going out with the gang. 'So . . . he took to going out on his own, more and more . . . and found . . . other distractions.' Her voice was dry.

'Leaving you literally holding the baby?'

'Oh yes.' Her smile was bleak. 'It's a familiar pattern, isn't it? But I was very young—and silly enough to protest. 'She shut her eyes and swallowed. 'That was . . . when it all started.'

Jane could see it. The small, cramped rooms; the crying baby; the endless washing; and the tired, inexperienced young mother who had once been a pretty, adoring wife and a lively good-time girl to take out and show off to his friends. And the smart-alec young salesman who liked life to be bright and full of parties—and plenty of feminine admiration—who wondered—bitterly, no doubt—where all the sparkle had gone from his young wife, and why his life had become so drab.

'What about your parents?' This was one of the crucial questions Jane had to ask. 'Weren't they any help?'

Laurie sighed. 'They lived up north, remember. And my father died of a heart attack not long after . . . after I ran away. My mother said it was my fault—and I believed her. She blamed me for everything—my father's death, the shortage of money, having to sell the house, the lot. She wouldn't come to our wedding. She wouldn't have anything to do with us—not even when Jason was born.' She looked at Jane's stern expression, and added awkwardly, 'It wasn't her fault. It's just the way she is—a bit rigid and old-fashioned.' Then she went on, more slowly. 'But I did go home once . . . when things got very bad.'

'When was that?'

'I . . . when Jason was about two. I had a miscarriage.'

'Was that Jeff's fault?' Jane's voice was grim.

Laurie opened her eyes wide. It suddenly occurred to her that she had been covering up this thought—even in her own mind—for years. Pretending to herself that it was a normal accident—the kind of thing that could happen to anyone. How blind and stupid could you be?

'Yes,' she admitted—seeming to admit years and years of self-deception and wishful thinking as she did so. 'At least . . . partly. We had a row, and in the excitement he pushed me downstairs.'

'I wondered about the gap between Jason and Midge,' murmured Jane.

Laurie pushed the hair out of her eyes, as if trying to free her mind from webs of camouflage. 'I've never admitted it before,' she said wonderingly, 'even to myself. But it wasn't *all* his fault. I must've provoked him. 'She paused, and then continued in a flat voice. 'The doctors at the hospital said I'd twisted the womb or something, and I oughtn't to have another child.' 'She looked at Jane again, almost apologetically (though how could you apologise for Midge—loving, gentle little Midge?). 'I *was* careful . . . But Jeff . . . he was so unpredictable. He would go off me for weeks—especially when he'd got another woman somewhere—and then, suddenly, he'd get all contrite and affectionate. Or . . .' But there she stalled, and shut her eyes and shuddered. Not even to Jane, with her cool, neutral assessment, could she talk of the degradation that she had endured at his hands: of the violence that was almost rape, that left her bruised and shamed and unable to face her neighbours or her friends, who had none of them known what was going on—who had all been puzzled by her withdrawal and seeming unfriendliness.

Sometimes she had wondered which was worse—the violence or the abject remorse that came afterwards: the tears and apologies, the need for reassurance. 'You do still love me, don't you?' like a naughty child that has to

45

be forgiven for his mindless tantrums. Once again she shuddered.

'So, you did go home that time? What happened?'

'Oh, it was hopeless. My mother had moved into a flat when my father died. It's rather small, and my mother is obsessively neat and tidy—and her arthritis makes her extra crotchety. She kept on and on at Jason, and at me. And she kept on and on about my marriage being a failure. "I told you so!"—and my selfish actions killing my father.'

Jane gave a short, explosive sound. 'What rubbish! More likely it was her nagging that killed him, by the sound of it.'

'Oh yes.' Laurie smiled a tired smile. 'Probably. But I . . . then I believed her. I suppose I was a bit weak after the miscarriage. I remember I cried a lot—which didn't help. I couldn't stand up to her. And Jason was just at the age when he was into everything, and everything he did was wrong. She kept scolding and fussing, and in between telling me that Jeff was no good and it was only what she expected.'

'Didn't she tell you to leave him?'

'Oh no. She told me to go back.'

'You've made your bed and you must lie on it?'

Laurie gave a helpless little laugh. 'It sounds absurd, doesn't it? Today! But . . . but she's old-fashioned, like I said. She believes a wife is morally bound to put up with whatever treatment her husband chooses to mete out—however bad!'

There was another small silence while Jane tried to imagine a woman who could send her daughter back to the kind of violence that she had clearly endured for so long.

'What did your father do?' she asked, trying to take Laurie's mind away from pain for the moment.

'He was assistant manager at the local bank. It was only a small branch, but he was good at his job. People liked him, and he was very . . . very respected in the town.' Her voice shook for a moment. She had loved her father. He had always been good to her—always fair-minded and kind. It was through him that she had got her own job in the bank. And she had rewarded him by throwing it all up and running away with Jeff. And the shock—had it been the shock?—the shock had killed him. She still felt guilty.

'A respectable, quiet profession,' commented Jane, waiting to see the grief recede a little in Laurie's expressive face.

Laurie gave her a rueful glance. 'Oh yes. Very respectable. That was part of the trouble, really. My mother thought Jeff wasn't good enough for me. I don't know who she thought I ought to marry—a banker, perhaps? But the idea of a . . . a wife-beater in the family, and the scandal, that was too much'

'So she sent you back—to that?'

'I went back,' said Laurie, her small chin setting as firmly and squarely as Jane's much older one. 'I made up my mind to try . . .' She turned her head and looked at Jane very earnestly. 'It wasn't all bad, you know—at least at first. Sometimes things went all right, and Jeff was . . . like he used to be—kind, I mean, and friendly—even generous. He would suddenly buy me things—to make up. And I . . .' Once more she glanced at Jane, almost pleadingly. 'I *did* try . . .'

'I'm sure you did.'

'But . . .' Again she pushed the long, limp hair out of her eyes, as if trying to clear her head of cobwebs and fantasies—'the trouble is, when all that's going on—rows and fights, and then reconciliations and attempts at patching things up, and then more rows—you get to a point when you can't think straight any more. You don't know what's happening. You can't see it clearly.' She hesitated, thinking it out, while Jane nodded, agreeing with that pattern of confusion and distress of mind. She had seen it all before—many times.

'And then Jeff lost his job. He couldn't get another— it's a bad time for unemployment, especially salesmen, and it was bad for him. I understood how he felt. He lost status. It somehow . . . took away his image.'

'What?'

47

'I mean . . . he saw himself as a clever-talking, smart salesman—well-dressed and successful. Taking clients out to dinner at expensive restaurants, chatting up the birds, having a high old time, and being one hell of a fellow.' Her voice was dry again, but there was a sadness about her smile that said she really did feel sorry for Jeff and his crumbling image. 'And then, you see, all at once he wasn't one hell of a fellow any more. And he thought it was all my fault.'

'Why?'

'Well, he was convinced I had trapped him into marriage.'

'And had you?'

'Oh no!' Laurie's eyes were wide again. 'Of course not. He persuaded *me* to run away with *him*! And I wasn't pregnant or anything—not till later. But he believed—he convinced himself—if it wasn't for me and the children he could have got another job: gone off anywhere, been smart and single and unattached—and wanted. You know the kind of things men tell themselves, when things go wrong.'

'I do, indeed.' Jane's voice was also dry.

'And so . . .'—Laurie looked at her painfully—'he began to drink a bit more here and a bit more there—to boost his courage for interviews and so on. He'd always been a bit on the heavy side about spirits. Part of his job, he used to say—oiling the works with clients. Only it began to get out of hand.' Laurie shivered, remembering the drunken rows, the constant threat of violence erupting over trifles, the increasing shortage of money at home as he drank more outside, the slow slide into poverty and debt and down-at-heel shabbiness (his only good suit getting shinier and shinier no matter how carefully she pressed it), and Jeff's own deepening despair as the new job never came along. The cramped, untidy council house she could never quite keep up with; the children needing clothes they could not have, shoes for their growing feet, and food she couldn't afford to buy.

'What finally made you go?' asked Jane, curious to know what had eventually pushed her beyond recall.

48

'He started to go for Midge,' she said, staring out beyond Jane's fierce, compassionate gaze. 'And I suddenly realised that the children weren't safe any more. Jeff was . . . was over the edge at times. He didn't know what he was doing. I ought to have seen it sooner. I ought to have realised. My little Midge was reduced to crawling into the broom-cupboard for safety, and Jay . . . Jason was already aware of the danger. He tried to get between Midge and his father—even between me and Jeff. He's absurdly brave for his age. And it wasn't fair on them. It was totally wrong. I can't think why I didn't see it! . . . And I don't know what harm it may have done them already.'

'Had he ever hit them before, do you know?'

She looked at Jane with growing horror. 'I don't know. Never while I was there. But I . . . I used to leave them with him sometimes when I went to the shops. I don't know what happened then.' Her voice was filled with self-reproach. 'I didn't think . . . I always made excuses for him, I suppose . . . But . . . but sometimes they did have bruises I couldn't account for. I thought they were just childish tumbles . . . But now I'm not so sure.'

'Did they ever complain?'

'No. Never. But sometimes . . . Jay's eyes looked . . .' Almost black with the thoughts he was trying to hide, she thought. That was how it was. My poor, brave young son, Jason, hiding fear and hurt from his mother—until she understood what she was doing to him—to him and little Midge—and could not let it go on any longer.

'But it was the swans, really,' she murmured, in a strange voice of dream.

'The swans?'

'Yes.' She kept her eyes shut. Far behind them she could see those dazzling white wings beating against the sun—beating and beating in perfect unison—the music of their passing clear in the listening air.

'So *beautiful*,' she whispered. 'Flying very high. They flew right over the house. I watched them go. The sound they made was like . . . like nothing on earth I'd ever heard. Like music—only wider. So strong and free. I

49

listened a long time—a long, long time—until they were gone.' She opened her eyes and stared at Jane with a dark, dilated gaze. 'I knew then that I must go,' she said. 'It all came clear to me then. Somewhere . . .' she lifted her head to look out of the window, above the sooty house-tops to the clear sky beyond. 'Somewhere out there . . . is a world. I'd forgotten how beautiful it is. But I can't ignore it any longer—or let my children grow up without knowing it. I've got to get out . . . and find it.'

'Yes!' agreed Jane. 'Yes! Of course you have.'

\* \* \*

It was late that afternoon that the hospital telephoned Jane with news of Jeff's arrest. She immediately rang the police and suggested that they should talk to the policewoman who saw Laurie—and read the doctor's report. It seemed to her that there was enough evidence to bring a more serious charge of assault and grievous bodily harm, and also get an injunction restraining the husband from molesting his wife further. What did the police think?

She knew from past experience that the police were reluctant to get involved in what they called 'domestic' disputes. It had always made her very angry that men in authority—both police and magistrates—seemed to consider beating up your wife till she was reduced to pulp a lesser offence than taking a swipe at a man in the street. She hadn't asked Laurie yet if she had ever been to the police for help, but many of her women had—and had got precious little response. Now, though, since they already had a clear case of common assault that would bring a conviction, and responsible witnesses to Laurie's condition, the police would probably agree to co-operate. It made her smile, though somewhat grimly, to realise that they would prosecute Jeff for merely attempting to hit the hospital staff and the arresting officer, but would be reluctant to do anything about Laurie's much more serious injuries. However, for Laurie's sake she felt she had to try. And presently the young policewoman who had first seen Laurie in hospital came round to discuss the matter.

50

Jane thought she'd better prepare Laurie for yet more shocks, but to her surprise Laurie was quite calm about it.

'Yes, I'll see her. You'll be there, though, won't you?'

'Of course—if you want.'

Laurie thought for a moment. 'If . . . they just convict Jeff on the first charge . . . what will happen?'

'He'll probably get a fine and be bound over.'

'To keep the peace?' Her smile was brittle.

'That's the official term!'

'He won't, you know.' Laurie began to laugh.

'No. I know.' She looked at Laurie with a glint of humour in her strange, golden eyes.

'But if'—Laurie was pursuing her own line of reasoning—'the second charge sticks?'

'He'll get a month or two in jail—according to how lenient or how tough the magistrate is. Usually, in your kind of case, they're much too lenient!'

Laurie nodded wearily. 'So I've gathered. Not that I'm trying to make things worse for Jeff. I just want a bit of peace and safety . . . for me and the children.'

Jane agreed. 'An injunction will help. Also,' she went on carefully, 'a cooling-off period in jail might bring him to his senses a bit. At least he'd be off the drink.'

Laurie said painfully, 'I think he may need help over that—it's got beyond his control.'

Jane was almost impatient with her then. These women! They always believed their men would reform and become paragons of virtue—and they scarcely ever did! And when they went back after a touching reconciliation, the wives usually ended up with a worse battering than before.

'Are you saying you'd go back to him if he was permanently off the drink? You think he's an alcoholic?'

'No,' said Laurie flatly. 'He was violent before . . . before the pub took over. I could never trust him again. But I . . . I just thought it might help him.'

Jane looked at her in astonishment. After all she had been through—and was still going through—this girl could still think with real compassion about her husband's future.

51

'Well, all right,' she said at last. 'There'll be social welfare contacts we can make—on his behalf. But meantime I'd better fetch the policewoman in, and you can tell her what you know.'

Laurie agreed.

The policewoman was sympathetic—and patient. She had seen Laurie in the hospital, and she could see that she was still very shocked and by no means over her recent battering. She took careful notes and asked only relevant questions.

'Have you ever been to the police before?'

'Yes,' sighed Laurie. 'Twice. Once, I got frightened and locked him out, and he broke the door down. So I panicked and took the children round to the police station.'

'What did they do?'

'Nothing. They gave me a cup of tea and sent me home.'

The policewoman made no comment, but wrote it all down. 'And the second time?'

'He threw me through the window into the backyard. I was . . . I was afraid the children might get hurt by all the glass. So I went back to the police and asked them to come and . . . and speak to Jeff.'

'Did they?'

'Oh yes. A constable came back with me. But by this time Jeff had calmed down. He was very reasonable. He said it was an accident—and I was young and easily frightened. He more or less suggested I was hysterical and making it all up—or at least exaggerating. He can be very persuasive and charming when he likes, and I think the constable believed him.'

'Yes,' murmured the policewoman, busily scribbling, 'I see.' She glanced at Jane, and a look of grim understanding flashed between them. They were both aware of the uphill task they had undertaken to get these desperate women taken seriously. 'Well,' she said kindly, 'that'll be all, thanks, Mrs Collins. You've been most helpful. I hope we can get something sorted out.'

'One thing . . .' said Laurie, trying not to sound too nervous. 'Will I . . . would I have to give evidence in court? Because I . . . I don't think I could face seeing him—though I'll try, if you think I should.'

The policewoman and Jane looked at one another.

'I would suggest,' said Jane crisply, 'that the doctor's report might be sufficient. You're clearly not fit to attend the court at present. Concussion and a hairline fracture are quite serious injuries. They have to be watched. And you have been told to keep very quiet.'

The policewoman agreed. 'I'll put that to them.'

'And the . . . the injunction?' Laurie still sounded tense and anxious.

'That will go through, I'm sure,' said the policewoman. 'But if there was any doubt, you could take out a civil injunction yourself.' She turned to Jane. 'I'm sure Mrs Everett would arrange it for you.'

'Yes,' nodded Jane. 'I would.'

They left Laurie then and went off, discussing one or two other cases that had come up. But as soon as they had gone, Laurie began to shake. A cold sweat broke out on her forehead, drenching her hair, and she could not stop her teeth from chattering. The wings, which had been quiet for most of the day, suddenly began their urgent beating in her head. They seemed to swirl and grow until the mighty pinions filled the air and blotted out the light. Before their powerful onslaught, Laurie went down without a cry.

*　*　*

It was Penny who picked her up and put her back to bed; Penny who brought her a hot-water bottle for the shakes, and a cup of tea to warm her hands on, and Penny who perched on the bed and said with cheerful good sense, 'You oughtn't to let them get at you. I don't. Bugger the lot, I say!'

Laurie tried to laugh. 'You're such a comfort, Penny.' She looked at the friendly, easy-going face of the girl before her and said suddenly, 'You've never told me what you're doing here—among all us tired old battered women! You're much too young to be mixed up in all this, aren't you?'

53

Penny swung her foot to and fro as she sat on the edge of the bed and looked down consideringly. 'It depends what you mean by "too young" ' she said.

Laurie was horrified. 'You? Battered?'

'Beaten-up,' she agreed, nodding at Laurie quite briskly. 'Oh yes. But I wasn't exactly a *wife*.'

Laurie was puzzled. 'What, then?'

'A *daughter*,' she said—and now there was real bitterness in her voice.

'You mean . . . your father beat you up?'

'Oh no. Well, not exactly.' She stared at Laurie almost pityingly. 'You don't understand a thing, do you?'

'No,' agreed Laurie, half-smiling. 'Not a thing!'

'Well, I'll tell you.' The hard, flippant note was back in her voice. 'My Ma married a man younger than her, see? A bit randy. Fancied little girls.' Once more she glanced at Laurie's uncomprehending face. 'So he . . .' She looked down at her bulging stomach.

'Oh, my God,' said Laurie. But . . . how old were you?'

'About eight or nine when it began. I couldn't tell my Ma—or anyone, come to that. He threatened to beat me if I did. He said he'd deny it anyway, and no one would believe me—They'd think I was just . . . a tart.' There was a small, rueful smile tugging at the corners of her mouth. 'And in the end that's just what they did think—my Ma included.'

'*What*? When you . . . when he got you pregnant?'

'Why should they believe me? I told my Ma what he was like. I told her all of it. But she wouldn't believe me. She didn't *want* to believe me. She liked her life the way it was, and my . . . her husband . . . the way he was—or she thought he was.' The blue-green eyes just met Laurie's appalled gaze. 'So, my Ma gave me the most God-awful hiding I'd ever had—for being a liar and a trouble-maker and having a sick mind, she said. And when my . . . when *he* came in, he gave me a beating, too—for telling my Ma. I told them I was desperate—I was pregnant, and what was he going to do about it? And he said—"Nothing". How did he know the child was his?

54

It was most unlikely, he said. And then my Ma came home, and threw me out.'

'Just like that?'

'Just like that. She came on me trying to talk to him—after the beating. I was crying a bit, and he was . . . trying to calm me down. She took one look and went upstairs and fetched my clothes and put them out in the street—and shoved me out after them and slammed the door in my face.'

'But, *Penny*! What on earth did you do?'

Penny sighed. 'Nearly lost the baby, didn't I?' Might've been better if I had. Joe found me in the street—like he found you. And then Jane took over.' She grinned at Laurie—the old, perky cheerfulness coming to the surface again. 'Thank God for Jane, eh?' Her smile dimmed suddenly and she added in a changed voice, 'Mind you, she was very, very angry when I told her. Never seen her so angry. I reckon she'd have gone round and beaten *him* up, if I'd let her. But I didn't.'

'Why not?'

'I dunno. First of all, I couldn't prove it was him, could I? Not without blood tests and things after the baby's born. And then I thought: What the hell, I don't want him—and my Ma does. So let her have him. I don't want nothing more to do with either of 'em!'

'Yes, but Penny, how old are you now? What will you do?'

'I'm nearly sixteen. And I shall *manage*! Jane says I can stay here till it's born, if I like. And if I kind of give her a hand with the kids, she can say I'm a helper and then I can stay longer than the others.'

'Do you want the baby? Could you have . . . ?'

'An abortion? They'd probably have given me one—seeing how young I was and all that. But I left it too late, see? When things started to go wrong after the beating, Jane got me a doctor. I nearly lost it then, and he said he would have . . . but he couldn't take it away now—not unless I was dying. And I wasn't!'

Laurie was silent for a moment—still horrified at

55

Penny's story and the bleak prospect for her future. 'So . . . will you have it adopted?'

Penny hesitated. Her clear young eyes were shadowed now with uncertainty and doubt. 'I dunno. Jane thinks I should. She says I'm too young to cope with being a single parent, and I oughtn't to have my life ruined before I start, and all that. But I'm not sure.' She looked at Laurie, almost shyly now. 'Thing is, I like kids. I'm good with 'em. I like *your* kids, Laurie. And I . . . I think I'd like looking after a baby. Not sure I'd want to part with it. Poor little bugger didn't ask to be born, after all—or to be foisted on someone else.' She looked round at the walls of the bedroom and out through the window to the scruffy garden beyond, and added half to herself, 'And I'm not sure I'd want to keep it here, either. Not permanently, whatever Jane says.'

Laurie was also staring out of the window. 'Don't you like it here?'

'It's all right.' Penny was swinging her foot again, and frowning a little. 'It's safe. No one gets at you—and we all get enough to eat. And Jane's done wonders with the place—and with everyone who comes here. I'm not saying I'm not bloody grateful. She's been wonderful to me.' She glanced up at Laurie again, smiling a little. 'But . . . Oh, I dunno . . . I think a baby needs . . . a more settled sort of place—not with all these women and their problems . . . not for ever!'

Laurie sighed. It was what she was already feeling about Jay and Midge, though she knew she couldn't change things for them yet—she simply wasn't strong enough. But, like Penny, she felt oppressed by the crowded rooms full of scared and bitter women. It was not the right atmosphere for children to grow up in, however hard Jane tried to make them welcome.

'Anyways,' said Penny, suddenly brisk and cheerful again, 'this isn't doing you no good. I'm going to fetch us both some more tea. And then I'll bring the kids in to see you. They've been asking for you.'

'Have they?' Laurie instantly felt guilty and tried to get out of bed.

'Trouble with you is,' said Penny, pushing her back, 'you're too responsible! Lie down, or I'll crown you!'

Smiling, Laurie lay back against her pillows. She would have to pull herself together somehow. She couldn't go on like this—it was ridiculous. The wings had subsided now a little, and her head felt strangely empty. But she thought with longing of that far, clear blue sky, with the white swans flying.

* * *

Jason and Midge had devised a way of avoiding trouble with the other kids. After all, they were very skilled by now at avoiding trouble. So when squabbles broke out, or one tougher than the rest took to imitating his Dad and hitting the nearest and softest face, Jason and Midge retreated from the edge of the crowd of yelling children and went round the other side of the shed. There was an old rubbish tip there, cluttered with bits of rusty pram and a sagging mattress or two, and there was a little hollow where there had once been a tree. It didn't take long to pile a few cardboard boxes together and make a kind of shelter—a small, safe house of their own.

It was here that Penny found them next day, when Jane had sent her to fetch them to see the social worker. But Penny was much too used to trouble herself—and too near childhood, perhaps—to blunder in upon their private sanctuary without asking.

'Jay?' she whispered loudly, knowing he wouldn't want the other kids to find them. 'It's me—Penny. You coming out?'

After a moment, Jason crawled out backwards, looking a bit anxious.

'I won't tell,' said Penny quickly, and watched the anxiety fade from the boy's eyes. They were like his mother's, Penny thought—blue and far-seeing. In fact he was very like his mother altogether, with that honey-gold, straight, thick hair, and that pointed, determined-looking chin. Midge was like her, too—only she was younger and softer, still with the rounded curves of babyhood about her. And Penny—much to her own surprise—felt a sudden surge of affection for these two children caught up in the awful battleground of their parents' marriage.

'There's a lady wants to see you,' she explained. 'Two of 'em, actually.' She looked down at Jason and grinned. 'But you don't have to.'

'Don't I?' Jason grinned back. 'What do they want?'

'Only to help, Jay—really. But they might ask a few questions.'

Jason's face closed. 'Like what?'

'Like . . .' Penny paused, and then decided to be frank. It was always best with kids to be honest—they saw through you too fast. 'Like . . . what happened at home . . . And did your Dad hit you or Midge, as well as your Mum?'

Jason was silent.

After a moment, Penny said conversationally, 'My Dad often hit me.'

'Did he?' Jason's eyes were fixed on her face now, looking almost black with his secret thoughts. He seemed to consider a long time before he spoke again. 'What do you want me to say?'

'The truth, of course.' Penny sounded quite definite. 'What really happened.' (Poor little sod, she thought. Ought they to make him remember?)

He thought even more deeply. 'Would it help my Mum?'

'It might. Give you all a bit of peace for a bit longer.'

He nodded, as if he understood that all too well. But his glance fell on the makeshift cardboard shelter and he said doubtfully, 'Not Midge?'

'No,' said Penny firmly. 'They'd like to see Midge—just to know she's OK—but they won't ask her anything. She's too small.'

'Good.' Jason got to his feet and dusted himself down. Then he bent down and called softly, 'Midge—it's all right. You can come out. We're going with Penny.'

\* \* \*

Laurie was feeling more at bay than ever. They were in Jane's office, and the atmosphere was charged with

58

unsaid things. There was the social worker, Lois Brown, who was kind but persistent. And there was a calm-looking woman solicitor called Madeleine Williamson, who seemed to be a friend of Jane's and very well acquainted with the problems at the refuge. And there was Jane—watchful and neutral.

'If you have no objections . . .' Lois Brown was saying politely. But Laurie plainly had.

'You see,' explained Jane patiently, 'Madeleine is used to dealing with these situations. She helps a lot of the women here. And if she is to help you—even over the injunction—the question of custody and access may come up. So she needs to know how the children feel about it—and whether it's safe or not to let your husband come near them. So does Lois—for social security purposes as well as the children's welfare.' She paused to see how much Laurie was taking in. 'In ordinary circumstances,' she went on gently, 'you'd go to see Madeleine in her office, and she might ask to talk to the children there. And Lois would want to see them separately, too. This way, at least it will only happen once. And anyway, you're clearly not well enough to go traipsing across London. That's why Madeleine and Lois came here to see you.'

'Aren't they . . . isn't Jason a bit young for questions?'

'It might help,' said Lois carefully, 'for us to get the whole picture.'

The whole picture? thought Laurie in despair. How can they possibly know? How can I possibly tell them? Or how can Jason, either?

But aloud she just said, 'So long as they're not bullied—or frightened. They've had enough of that.'

Lois Brown looked shocked. 'Of course not! We'll be very careful.'

Laurie looked helplessly at Jane, who said as gently as before, 'We're very experienced here, Laurie. We would never browbeat a child. In fact, that's the whole idea of The Hide—no browbeating, not of *any* kind!'

'Lois can ask all the questions,' said Madeleine pleasantly. 'I'll just listen. He won't be badgered, I promise you.'

Laurie gave a pale smile and pushed the hair out of her eyes. 'I'm sorry. I know I'm over-anxious . . . but, you see . . .'

'We do see, Laurie, believe me,' said Jane. 'You can trust us.'

But Laurie could not trust anyone. Not yet.

At this point, Penny came in with the children. Midge ran straight to Laurie and climbed into her arms. But Jason stood still, looking from his mother to the others in mute enquiry.

'Jay . . .' Laurie drew him close into the protection of her arm. 'You can tell them what they want to know, I'm sure. Just answer them truthfully, won't you?'

'Yes,' agreed Jason, still looking at his mother. 'If *you* want me to.'

Laurie smiled. 'I do, Jay. And Jane does, too. And so does Penny. All right?'

'All right,' answered Jason, and kept his head high.

Jane got up purposefully. 'Then we'll go and make everyone some tea,' she said. 'Midge, are you going to stay with Jason?'

But Midge—for the first time since they came to The Hide—made a scene. She clung to Laurie, her arms tight round her neck, and screamed.

'Never mind,' Lois Brown spoke quickly. 'We'll just talk to Jason.' She gave Laurie a reassuring smile.

'In any case,' remarked the solicitor in a cool, clear voice, 'I think Midge has told us what we want to know.'

Laurie, confused and not very happy about it, turned rather desperately to Jane. 'Couldn't you stay?' After all, Jane was neutral. She wouldn't try to influence them either way—but she would make Jason feel safer.

Jane looked over Laurie's head at the other two, enquiringly. They both nodded. 'Very well,' she said quietly. 'I'll stay.'

Penny, after a swift glance round, took Laurie and Midge away to make tea in the kitchen.

So now it was Jason's turn to stand at bay.

'First of all,' began Lois Brown, quite gently, 'do you want to go home?'

'No!' flashed Jason. And then, flatly, 'Not if *he's* there.'

The two women exchanged glances. Jane sat mutely in her corner—grey and neutral, as requested—and did not say a word.

'Then,' Lois Brown still sounded casual and not too insistent, 'do you like being here?'

Jason considered. 'It's all right.' He looked at them, almost with contempt. They asked such obvious questions. 'It's safe,' he explained.

'Safe from what, Jason?' asked Lois, even more gently.

'From harm,' he said. And then, seeing them waiting for him to go on, he spelt it out for them. 'From my Dad.'

They nodded to one another quietly. Madeleine Williamson made a note.

'Did he . . . often hit your mother, Jason?' A careful note had crept into Lois's voice.

'Oh yes.' The contempt had come back. 'All the time.'

'And . . . did he ever hit you—or Midge?'

His face seemed to close like a frosted flower. He did not answer.

'Did he, Jason?' persisted the social worker. 'It's all right. You can tell us.'

'Yes,' he admitted. 'Sometimes.'

'When?'

'When Mum was out.'

'And Midge, too?'

A kind of darkness seemed to come into his eyes then. 'Only when she cried . . . I tried to stop him . . .' He looked at them helplessly. 'But he was too strong.'

They were silent—shaken by the grief and self-reproach in the young voice.

'I did tell her not to cry,' he went on, with painful honesty. 'And she managed not to, mostly.'

Once again there was a stunned silence. Then Lois Brown followed it up in a deceptively casual tone. 'I suppose . . . your mother never hit you?'

He suddenly flared into anger then. His eyes seemed

to spark with incredulity. 'My *Mum*? She wouldn't hurt anyone!'

'Not even your Dad?'

'No.' He spoke decisively. He saw their watchful, unconvinced faces and tried to think of a way to make it clear to them. 'She told us . . . after a row, she used to tell us he was tired and it wasn't his fault.' His voice was flat again with scorn. 'She used to say . . . people get cross when they're tired—and we mustn't hate him.' He looked at them again, and his face was suddenly as bleak as his cold young voice. 'But I *do* hate him. I hate him for hurting my Mum—and Midge!'

He stood there, taut and defensive, defying them all. But before they could ask any more—even if they had wanted to—Laurie came back into the room, with Midge running after her. She crossed swiftly to Jason and laid an arm round his shoulders, and turned to face his inquisitors.

'That's enough!' she said. 'Can't you see he's had enough?'

And Penny, behind her, added cheerfully, 'Look, Jay, we've brought *you* a cup of tea first—and a chocolate biscuit.'

Jason did not say any more. But he leant tiredly against his mother's arm and gave up trying to stand up straight and tall, like an adult.

Everyone relaxed then, and Madeleine Williamson said to Laurie, under cover of the general conversation, 'He's a brave boy, your son. You must be proud of him.'

'I am,' agreed Laurie. Then, somewhat hesitantly, she asked, 'Did you . . . did you find out what you wanted to know?'

'Oh yes.' The solicitor nodded briefly. 'We did.' She looked round at the others, and seemed to get a faint nod from Jane, so she spoke for all of them. 'I'll be representing you in court—though it probably won't be necessary. You'll get legal aid, of course. And we'll take out an injunction against your husband to prevent him from approaching or molesting or harassing you in any way—just in case the magistrate doesn't do it automatically.'

Laurie pushed the hair out of her eyes again, in the familiar gesture of stress and confusion. 'Ought I . . . ? Do you think I ought to be in court, too?'

The solicitor looked at Laurie appraisingly, and shook her head. 'No. It would be distressing for you, and I don't think you're well enough.' She paused for thought. 'In my experience, the magistrates are apt to consider wives in your position unreliable witnesses! I think your doctor's report, and the statement that you are still too ill to attend, will impress them more.'

'She *is* too ill,' interrupted Penny stoutly. 'Look at her! Last time there were questions, she passed out on the floor.' She glared at Jane.

Jane nodded and said levelly, 'I agree.'

The solicitor glanced from her to Laurie, and added quietly, 'For the rest—if you want to take other legal steps concerning your marriage or your maintenance and so on, I can come back here to discuss it with you. Or you can come to me at my office when you are feeling stronger.' She smiled at her encouragingly, at last allowing her friendliness to show. 'These sort of decisions need a clear head. I gather yours is still, er . . . ?'

'Woolly,' said Laurie, smiling a little, too. 'Distinctly woolly. But . . . but thank you for coming here specially— and for your help.' She turned to the social worker, Lois Brown, and added politely, 'Thank you as well. I'm sorry if I seemed a bit prickly.' Her smile was perilously fragile now. 'We've all . . . all been through a bit too much just lately.'

Then, without waiting for anyone to reply, she took Jason and Midge with her and went out into the sooty garden to breathe. It was true—her head felt very woolly indeed. And the swans' wings were back inside it, beating and beating to get free.

'Is she all right?' asked Lois Brown anxiously.

'No,' said Jane. 'But she will be—given time. They usually recover.'

'Just leave her be!' exploded Penny, full of righteous indignation. 'All this argy-bargy! What she needs is a bit of peace!' And she flounced out of the room and stood on guard by the door into the garden.

The other three women looked at each other and sighed.

'Don't we all?' murmured Jane.

*　*　*

That night, Laurie could not sleep. She lay in her narrow camp-bed, tossing and turning, while her thoughts went round and round in her head and every bruised bone and muscle seemed to ache more than ever.

The two children were asleep in their bunk beds. Laurie could hear their quiet breathing, and Penny also lay fast asleep in her corner. The house wasn't quiet, though. Somewhere a child was crying, and someone was calling out 'No! No! Don't!' in her sleep.

No. No. Don't! thought Laurie. All these desperate, unhappy women under this roof . . . Don't hit me . . . Don't hit the children . . . Don't rape me . . . Don't drive me to run away and leave you . . . Don't destroy my will and my confidence—my mind as well as my body . . . Don't make me glad you're going to be punished—instead of sorry . . .

She shuddered, and got restlessly out of bed. There was a light on in the passage. There was always a light on somewhere in the house, and always someone wide awake and needing comfort or counsel. And Jane was usually there, giving what was needed. Laurie wondered when she ever slept herself.

She hadn't got a dressing-gown, so she pulled on her jeans and a jersey and wandered out into the passage. The child had stopped wailing, but there were voices coming from the kitchen, and Laurie followed them there.

At the kitchen table sat Jane and another woman, while a third was at the cooker, pouring boiling water onto teabags in three mugs. When she saw Laurie coming, she smiled and reached for another mug without comment.

'You got the heebies, too?' said the woman at the table, looking up and giving Laurie a faint grin.

'Come and join us,' invited Jane, pulling out a chair.

64

Laurie hesitated, wondering if she was interrupting a private counselling session, but Jane calmly laid a hand on her arm and drew her down beside her.

Up till now, Laurie had been too ill and too confused even to notice the other women in The Hide. She had been vaguely aware of the hordes of children and the overcrowded rooms—the yards of washing festooning the yard outside and the only bathroom, the endless comings and goings of feet, and the many voices. Once or twice she had heard shouts and an angry man's voice outside, and had supposed an irate husband had turned up. Her heart had jumped in terror then, in case it was Jeff. But it hadn't been Jeff, and in the end the shouting had stopped and the angry voice had gone away. Someone had dealt with it, and the women and children in the house had crept out of hiding and gone on moving about and talking—still safe from harm.

But now, Laurie suddenly began to see these three women as real people—not just shadows outside her own grief and despair. There was Jane, iron-grey and compassionate, but strong—strong enough to control a frightened, hysterical woman or a disturbed, aggressive child; even strong enough to fend off an angry husband? (Or did she have help there?) And, in spite of all that toughness and strength, those beautiful, expressive golden eyes.

Then there was the one making tea—thin, almost to the point of emaciation; wispy hair; brown eyes quick with observation and a faint touch of humour but still scared; and a face that was neither old nor young but carried a heavy mark on one cheekbone and a tell-tale nervous tic at the edge of her mouth.

'Viv, that's me,' she said, handing Laurie her tea. 'And you're Laurie. Sugar's on the table.'

'Thanks,' Laurie smiled up at her, and the quick brown eyes seemed almost to flinch at the sudden radiance.

Laurie turned to look at the third woman sitting at the table. She was heavier and bigger-boned, and probably older, though you couldn't tell—violence did such awful things to a woman's looks. Her hair was almost grey a'

the edges and hung in long, sad straggles round her face. Her eyes were a pale, sparkless blue—somehow flat and without hope—and the downward curve of her mouth was bitter. Someone—Laurie could guess who—had broken two of her front teeth, so that her welcoming grin was distinctly piratical.

'Molly,' she said briefly to Laurie's enquiring look. 'Join the club.'

Laurie sipped her tea and said nothing.

'Taking him to court, are you?' Molly flipped a spoon and the sugar-bowl across to her. 'And now, I suppose, you're having second thoughts and guilt complexes! Well, my advice to you is—*don't*.'

Laurie looked at her, startled.

'Listen,' said Molly, and glanced at Jane for a moment, almost as if for approval. 'None of my business, of course, but I've had more than fifteen years of it. I've left him three times—and each time I went back. I thought, at first, maybe it's my fault—maybe if I manage better, do this or do that, he'll be different.' Her glance was contemptuous now, but seemingly turned against herself. 'Different? Flipping hell!' She gave a short, mirthless little laugh. 'Each time was worse than before.'

'Why did you go back?' asked Laurie, wondering if she ought to ask.

'The kids, mostly. Nowhere else to go. No money of my own.' She took a gulp of tea and looked at Laurie over the top of her cup. 'See, Welfare wouldn't house us—not unless I was taking legal action for divorce. They said I'd got a home and I'd better go back and live in it! So I went.' Her voice was flat—as flat as the lightless blue eyes, opaque with anger.

'What happened?'

'The first time, a dislocated shoulder and a smashed big toe. He took the coal-hammer to it—so's I couldn't go out, he said.'

Laurie shuddered.

'The next time, broken collar-bone and three cracked ribs.' She was reciting it all without any apparent emotion. It was something that had happened. That was all.

66

'And the third time?' Laurie didn't quite know why she was asking so many questions. Maybe the other women's plight would help to put hers in perspective.

'I came here, didn't I?' Molly said, and grinned wolfishly at Jane. 'That is, after hospital. Threw boiling water over me this time, he did.' She rolled up her sleeve and showed a red and terribly scarred arm and hand. 'That was enough,' she said. 'And it wasn't right for the kids to see it, either. I don't know why I didn't see it before. They're all affected—all over the place, they are. Jeanie, my eldest, can't speak without a stammer. Mark, the next one, goes round hitting everyone in sight.'She glanced at Jane again, apologetically. 'Proper handful, he is—But Jane has got him more or less sorted out by now. And the little one, Sarey-Ann, cries every time anyone shouts or a door bangs.' She leant over the table and tapped Laurie's arm. 'He said he was sorry—every time. He said he'd never do it again. He said he'd never touch the kids, but he did. I don't know why I stuck it so long.' She looked down thoughtfully into her tea and added in a strange, difficult tone, 'You always think they'll change . . . and I s'pose . . . I must've thought I loved him once.'

She took another gulp of tea and went on, now looking hard at Laurie. 'Reconciliations! They don't work. Men are like kids themselves—bad, mindless kids. A few tears and a weak promise—the sods! And back they go again to the same old tricks.' She shut her eyes and shook her head. 'Don't you believe 'em, kid. Don't you believe a single word! They don't mean it. They'll never change. Once a hitter, always a hitter—that's my experience.'

'And mine!' said thin Viv, in a voice as sharp as the point of her nose.

Laurie sighed. She supposed it was true. It was certainly true of Jeff up to now. There had been many reconciliations—too many—and Jeff's maudlin tears had revolted her almost more than his violence. Yes, she too had learnt not to believe him. It had happened too often. He would never change.

She looked at Molly and asked in a curiously dead

67

voice, 'Did anyone ever tell you that you must *like* violence if you went back?'

Molly swore. 'Did they hell! The police did, once. And so did the social worker. "Why do you go back, then?" she asked.' Molly mimicked her bland, uncomprehending voice. 'And she'd just told me I couldn't expect to get anywhere else to live—or any money either!' She glared at Laurie. 'What else could I do but go back, with three kids to look after and no roof over our heads? Beg in the streets?' Her expression softened a little at Laurie's bleak look of acknowledgement. 'Did someone say that to you?'

'Yes,' said Laurie shortly. 'My mother.'

'Christ!' exploded Molly, genuinely shocked. 'Some mother!' She patted Laurie again, with a sudden spurt of comradely understanding. 'I never met a woman yet who liked getting her ribs bust or her nose broken.' She turned to Jane abruptly. 'Did you?'

'No,' agreed Jane. 'Never.' She paused for consideration. 'I daresay there are a few who like it rough. But for the most part I think that's a clever myth put out by men. Husbands, magistrates, police—the lot! They all believe that lie. Why not? It saves them from feeling guilty.'

'Too bloody right,' confirmed Molly, nodding her head.

And Viv waved her mug of tea in salute and added vaguely, 'Cheers! Couldn't have put it better meself!'

Jane laughed. Then she grew serious. There was another side to all this which she had to make them see, if all these tragic, embittered women were ever to find happiness again.

'There are some good men about, you know.'

Viv and Molly made scornful noises. 'Oh yeah? Show me some.'

'Well—Joe, for one.'

They sobered up at that. They all knew Joe, and what he had done for them.

'Yeah, Joe's all right,' admitted Molly. 'I'll give you that.'

'And my father,' said Laurie suddenly. 'He was all right. There must be lots of fathers who . . .' But then she remembered Penny, and the words died in her throat.

But Jane was of sterner stuff. 'Of course there are. And husbands. And lovers.' She smiled at the women with more than a hint of mischief. They needed to let off steam, she knew. They had years and years of abuse and stress and bitterness to overcome. But they needed hope, too. Of course they did. Everyone needs hope. Everyone needs to believe that the world is not a totally brutal, totally unjust and evil place.

'When you get over all this,' she told them, 'you'll find that there really are some decent, kind men around. You'd be surprised.'

'I would be surprised,' agreed Molly.

'That'll be the day,' said Viv, her voice dry with disbelief.

'Believe me,' said Jane steadily. 'I know.' And there was all at once a radiance of memory in her face, transforming it into something much less bleak and much less stern.

Laurie sighed. 'I believe you.'

The others looked at her with tolerant amusement— clearly thinking she was too young and too soft to see the truth.

Jane glanced at them all shrewdly. It was a bit corny, she knew, but she thought she had said enough to start their thoughts off on a different track that was not wholly dark—not wholly coloured with present bitterness. A glimpse of hope—however naïve they thought it was— wouldn't do them any harm.

'You know,' she said mildly, 'it's nearly four in the morning. Couldn't any of you sleep now?'

Molly lurched to her feet and took her cup over to the sink and rinsed it out. 'Selfish sods, we are. You've been coping with us all day.' She turned to glance over her shoulder at Laurie, and added with sudden bluff kindness, 'Don't weaken, girl! You owe it to your kids, if not yourself!'

'Yes,' agreed Laurie sadly. 'I know.'

'Can't take it lying down, can we? growled Molly, like a rallying battle-cry. And then suddenly began to giggle.

'Can't take it standing up, either!' retorted Viv sharply, and also began to giggle helplessly.

For a moment they all fell about laughing. It seemed inordinately funny—but then laughter was very near to tears.

Even Jane was laughing.

Viv put a spiky arm round Laurie's shoulders. 'Come on. Back to bed with you. White as a bleedin' mothball, you are!'

Briefly, dimly, Laurie smiled at them all. 'Thanks for your advice,' she said, and they all giggled again, though more feebly. then she drifted away back towards her room.

But when Penny and the children got up in the morning, they found Laurie in a high fever, tossing and muttering, and crying out—like the other women in the house—'No! No! Don't!'

* * *

Meanwhile, life was not being very kind to Jeff. He got home to a cold, cluttered house, an echoing emptiness all round him, and nothing in the kitchen fit to eat.

He was angry about the mess, angry with the hospital and the police, angry with himself, and—obscurely—even more angry with Laurie who had caused all this uproar by running off.

He kicked a few things in frustration, but it didn't make him feel any better. He needed to hit something—or someone—but there was no one to hit.

Cursing, he went out again and slammed the door behind him. His mates in the pub would be better than this—and to hell with the police sergeant and all his dire warnings.

But the next day he got dragged down to the police station again, where he was told there was a second charge against him, And, on top of that, someone came round to the door and served him with an injunction. He was astonished. Had Laurie done all this? That creeping mouse? He wouldn't have thought she had it in her.

She must've found a pushy lawyer somewhere. And that reminded him—he'd better find one, too.

Down at the Dog and Bear, he asked his mates about lawyers, and someone recommended a bloke he knew who wasn't very expensive. That he probably wasn't very good either did not occur to Jeff—or that he might have applied for legal aid. Instead, he swallowed a couple of drinks to give him courage and went and hired his mate's seedy friend on the spot.

After this, he felt better. Things would be looked after for him now. He'd probably get off with a caution anyway—so the lawyer said.

He went back to the Dog and Bear and leant on the bar to talk to Brenda, the barmaid. She was large and plump, and usually jolly—but she was also as strong as a horse and very good at chucking people out. Everyone liked her, but they also minded their language and kept a wary eye on her muscular right arm—it had been known to shoot out and propel an unwanted reveller right out into the street.

'Have one on me,' invited Jeff, waving a note in a reckless hand.

'Don't mind if I do,' agreed Brenda. 'Port and lemon, thanks. What's yours?'

'Whisky,' he ordered. 'Drowning my sorrows.'

'Oh yes? Why's that?'

'Lonely,' he sighed, and looked at her like a little boy lost. 'Wife's gone off.'

'Sorry to hear that.'

'Got a court case coming up, too.'

'Bad luck.' She raised her glass. 'Cheers! Don't let it get you down.'

'No.' Jeff stared at his glass. Then he looked up at Brenda appraisingly. She wasn't bad-looking, really— Good skin, and a nice smile when she bothered. Too much frizz in the hair, and it was too blonde, but those brown eyes were all right: they weren't cold—not cold at all—and he rather liked them plump, especially after that skinny, whining cow, Laurie.

Once again he wondered briefly at Laurie's temerity.

How could she go off? And how could she land this on him? Must be more in her than he'd supposed. But his thoughts returned to the problem in hand. He was lonely. The house was empty. He needed company. Well, he needed more than company—let's face it, he needed sex. And Brenda wasn't half bad, when you came to think of it.

'What're you doing when you come off duty?' he asked, taking a gulp of Dutch courage.

'Nothing you'd be interested in,' replied Brenda, and smiled a fat, jolly smile.

'Are you sure?' asked Jeff, putting on all the appeal and all the charm he knew.

'Well . . .' Brenda considered him, 'we'll see . . .'

\* \* \*

By the time the court case came up, Jeff was feeling quite perky.

Brenda wouldn't come to the house—she said she didn't want to get involved in any trouble—but she let him come to her flat over the greengrocer's shop on the corner. She bestowed her favours cheerfully, but Jeff suspected she would throw him out quite forcibly if she got bored. It didn't occur to him to try taking out his frustrations on her, like he had on Laurie. In any case, she was a big girl—and tough with it: not soft and frail and just asking to be hit. No, this one could probably knock *him* about if she tried. And in the meantime, she was solid and comforting to be with—and pretty good in bed. It made him feel ten feet tall again, and brought back the swagger into his step.

All the same, he needed a bit of boosting before the court. By the time he met his lawyer, he was jaunty and aggressive outside and very frightened underneath. Things seemed to happen in a haze.

He did not understand what was going on. When they asked him questions, he answered sullenly, with flashes of rebellion—and then tried to remember to be smooth and charming.

'I wanted to see my wife,' he said reasonably.

'When I understand you had put her in hospital with your brutality?'

That was the woman solicitor. She was a clever one.

'Mistake . . .' he muttered. 'A one-off thing . . . Lost my temper . . . Sorry . . .'

'When this state of affairs had been going on for years? I have here a statement that your wife had asked for police protection at least twice before—and had left home already once.'

There was a bit more talk, but the magistrate seemed indisposed to prolong things. 'Three months on the first count,' he rasped, 'and a further one month on the second. And you will be bound over to keep the peace—and not to approach or molest or harass your wife in any way—for one year.'

Madeleine Williamson thought bitterly to herself: Yes. Three months for not quite knocking down a policeman, and one month for half-killing your wife. So it goes! But at least he'll be out of the way while that poor girl gets on her feet.

Jeff could not believe it. Prison? Him? *Three months?* No, *four!* What had he done to deserve it? A man had a right to do what he liked to his own wife in his own home, hadn't he? It wasn't fair.

He suddenly stood up and shouted all this out loud. But it did not do any good. They hustled him away, still shouting and trying to explain. He went to prison feeling aggrieved and hard done by, and it was all Laurie's fault.

* * *

Laurie was ill for nearly a week. She missed her hospital check-up, and she missed Jeff's court case. When the fever was high, she raved; and when it went down, she shook uncontrollably. Jane fetched her long-suffering local doctor, and he pronounced a case of accumulated stress and anxiety, together with some unexplained virus. It would all die down and resolve itself with rest and no worries, he was sure.

No worries? thought Jane. You must be joking. But she did not say so. Instead, she appointed Penny to watch over Laurie until she was fit to get out of bed, with strict instructions to send for Jane if she started asking questions.

In the end, though, a white and weaving Laurie appeared in Jane's office and demanded to know what was going on.

Jane told her quietly.

'Four months?' said Laurie, wonderingly. 'Then . . .'

'That gives you a chance to get your life sorted out,' Jane intervened. 'By the time he comes out, you can be well out of reach, with everything settled.'

'Can I?' She still sounded confused and uncertain. Jeff, she thought. Poor Jeff. What will he do?

'And I shouldn't waste any sympathy on your husband,' added Jane drily. 'He made a scene in court and more or less told them he could do what he liked with his own wife in his own home.'

'Did he?'

'And I gather from Madeleine Williamson, who had been checking up on him, that he was having it off with the local barmaid by way of consolation—just to cheer himself up before the court case.'

Laurie sighed.

Jane looked at her quite sternly. 'Laurie—you've made the break. You've got to build your life again. You are a free and independent woman. And—as Molly said—you owe it to your children, if not to yourself. Or are you having second thoughts?'

'No.' Laurie was quite definite about that. 'No. It isn't possible to go back, I know that. I know I've got to start again.' She stared out of the window, over Jane's stern, fighting head. 'You're quite right—and I'm grateful for all you've done—but . . . but that doesn't stop me feeling sorry.'

Jane's expression softened. 'No, of course not. Human relationships are a sad and sorry business. But now you have to think of the future. You're still young, Laurie. You have a whole life before you.'

'Yes,' agreed Laurie, still staring out of the window. 'A whole life . . .' She turned back to smile rather shyly at

Jane, seeing the warmth and understanding in those beautiful golden eyes. 'I'll . . . I'll go and see Madeleine Williamson tomorrow.'

'No need,' said Jane. 'She's here now, seeing someone else. I'll fetch her for you. In any case, you don't look fit yet to go anywhere. Sit down and rest. I won't be long.'

Sighing, Laurie agreed, and almost fell into the nearest chair. It was true—she wasn't ready to go anywhere yet. Her legs felt like jelly, and her head still swam if she moved too quickly. Better to acquiesce and let things take their natural course. Jane was right. She had to start somewhere. It was time to plan for the future. If only she didn't feel so tired and so confused! She ought not to leave it all to other people. She had to take charge of her own life now. She took a deep breath, and tried to think ahead.

PART II

# TAKE-OFF

The morning after Madeleine Williamson's consultation, while Laurie was still trying to sort things out in her mind, Penny came into the bedroom, smiling.

'You've got a visitor.'

Laurie's heart jumped. Not Jeff, surely? He couldn't have found her here. And anyway, he was in prison. It couldn't be Jeff.

'Who?'

Behind Penny, a square, brownish figure came forward. 'It's me. Joe. Remember me? How are you now, then?'

'Better.' Laurie smiled her relief. 'Much better, thanks.'

'We was wondering—Penny and me—if you'd like a trip to the country. You and the kids, I mean.' He was looking at her shrewdly. 'Gotta go get some veges, see? Thought maybe—cooped up here, like—you could do with a breather?'

Radiance flooded into her face. 'Oh, Joe! What a lovely idea. I certainly could—and so could the children.' She glowed at him. 'Real country?'

'Real country.' He grinned. 'Green fields an' all!'

'Come on,' urged Penny. 'Don't waste time! I'll fetch the kids.' She turned to Joe. 'Shall I make some sandwiches?'

'No,' growled Joe. 'Fish and chips on me. Make a day of it.'

They all laughed. It was like a Sunday School treat already.

\* \* \*

The ancient van rattled down the Old Kent Road and out into the sprawling suburbs. Before long, the green fields that Joe had promised were creeping up on either side,

79

and they turned off the Maidstone road into the rich Kentish countryside. Orchards and market gardens and hop-fields spread out before them, and the old green van lurched down the lanes until it came to a farm gate leading into a long, sandy track with a farmhouse at the end.

On one side of the track were flat fields of sprouts and cabbages, carrots and onions, and even rows of late strawberries, with the pickers still moving among them. And on the other side were neat green orchards, their apple trees laden with rosy fruit, while beyond them were the tall aisles of the hop-gardens like a solid, leafy wall. There was a man with a tractor and trailer moving through the orchards, loading bushel baskets of fruit as his companion filled them from the trees. And in the hop-garden there were knots of people clustered round the hop-bins, picking the green, spicy bobbles of the hops, while another tractor and trailer collected the filled sacks and took them off to the drying kilns.

At one end of the farmhouse buildings, as they drew up in the yard, Laurie saw a strange-looking barn with a beautiful circular roof of ancient reddish tiles with a tall cowl on top.

'What's that?' asked Jason, pointing to it.

'Oast house . . . ,' Joe explained. 'Where they dries the hops.' He jerked a thumb at the moving tractor between the high walls of cascading hop-bines. 'They're picking the hops now, see? Right time of year. Most farms use the machines nowadays, but this one likes the old ways — Stan's old-fashioned.' He grinned sideways at Jason and Laurie. 'Used to use a lot of Londoners in the old days — they all come out to "see the breeze and taste the sun" — men, women, kids, the lot. Three weeks picking, camping out in the hoppers' huts, fresh air and sing-songs round the camp fire every night — had the time of their lives!'

'Don't they do it any more?' Laurie sounded quite disappointed.

'Not so much. Machines took over the picking, see? But a few of 'em still come down for casual labour — apples, sprout-picking, strawberries. The only holiday they ever get, some of 'em.'

He pulled up the van in the yard and went round to open the back doors. 'Everybody out!' he said cheerfully. While Joe went off to load up his van with produce, Penny and the children scampered off down one of the long green lanes of hops to join a tumbling knot of kids playing in and out of a heap of bushel baskets lying between the end of the hop-garden and the beginning of the apple orchards. Laurie followed them more slowly. It still hurt to walk fast, and her aching ribs still made breathing a bit difficult. But it was wonderful to be out in the air, with these huge washed skies and sailing argosies of bright cloud above her. The strange, pungent smell of the hops seemed all around her, mingled with the sweeter scent of the apples from the orchards beyond. Her head began to feel extraordinarily cool and clear—clearer than it had been for many bewildering days. The wings didn't seem to be beating inside at all—in fact, she had a curious sense of freedom, as if they had got out already.

One of the nearest group of women pickers looked up and smiled. She was busy stripping the hops from the trailing green bines that the men had pulled down from their trellises of hop-poles and wires above their heads, with the rest of her family working as a team round her. She was wearing a hessian apron wrapped round her cotton skirt, and her hands were stained green and gold with the hops as she dropped them in aromatic heaps into the open hessian sack stretched on withies that made up each hop-bin. All around them was the clean, spicy scent of the hops, and the laughter and chatter of the pickers and the children.

'Joining us?' the woman asked, dropping a spent bine on to the ground and pulling at another.

Laurie hesitated, watching how neatly the woman's fingers stripped the hops from the bine and separated them from the leaves before dropping them into the bin.

'Used to be more on us,' said the woman wistfully. 'But machines is quicker. They don't want us nowadays—most places.'

Laurie nodded. 'But here they do?'

'Sure. Stan's a good boss.'

'That means you've been coming down here a long time?'

The woman laughed. 'Longer than I wants to remember!' She squinted up the hop-garden, shading her eyes against the sun slanting through the dark-green columns of the bines. 'Tallyman's coming!' She jerked her head towards the far end of the orchard where the hop-garden began. 'Competition today to see who's the fastest picker—prizes an' all!' She pointed a stained green finger at another group of pickers farther down. 'Them's casuals from Rochester way—come in by bus every day.' She winked at Laurie. 'But they don't know the job like we do!'

Laurie grinned. 'What's the prize?'

'Dunno. Bottle of flamin' beer, I expect! Or cider!' She laughed again—a deep, throaty chuckle—and then glanced sideways at Laurie and added, 'You down for long?'

'No,' sighed Laurie. 'Wish I was . . .' She suddenly thought: And that's true. I wish I was. I like it here with the tangy scent of hops and apples, and the hop-fields all round us, and these cheerful women.

'Look as if you could do with it,' commented the woman shrewdly. She looked down the tall green aisles at the scatter of children dodging about and said in an oddly softened tone, 'Does the kids a power of good an' all.'

Laurie agreed. She could see Jason and Midge dodging about among the dark, shadowy tunnels, following a shrieking mob of children intent on some game of cops and robbers. It occurred to her that she hadn't seen them look so carefree and unafraid for a long, long time. And when had she ever managed to take them out to the country like this before? Even Penny seemed to have shed some of her own increasing heaviness and slowness and was running with the kids in the dappled shade. She was swerving and laughing, kicking up her heels like a young colt, and Laurie was somehow absurdly touched by the sight of her childish abandon. After all, she reminded herself, Penny was still only a child herself in many ways, and her childhood had been dreadfully shadowed with stress for far too long.

'Can't catch me!' She heard Penny's voice floating back to them down the green aisles of hops. 'Look at me running! Can't catch me!'

'Why don't you stay?' said the woman softly. 'There's room in the huts. Some of 'em went home this week—and there's still a lot of hops to get in while the weather holds. Dessay the boss could do with you.'

Laurie stared at her. All kinds of possibilities were milling around in her head. But she did not speak.

Just then, a small moving knot of people headed by 'Spider'—the tall, rangy tallyman—came down the hop-ride towards them. He looked round with a practised eye at the green mounds in the bins, and dipped his long tally-stick into them to measure the volume of picked hops. But this was only a token measurement—stemming from long years of ancient tradition. After a shrewd guess at the volume, he began to shovel the hops out into his bushel basket, counting as he went and tipping them into the big sacks which would be loaded on to the tractor and taken away for drying. '. . . three . . . four . . . five . . .'—his voice droned on. Then he totted them all up and wrote them down in his little black notebook.

'Most bushels so far, Dorrie!' he said to the woman, grinning. 'You're winning!'

'What about them other lot?' asked Dorrie, still stripping hops into her empty bin as she talked.

'Nowhere near!' he said, and laughed.

Dorrie's fat chuckle answered him. Then she leant over to the pile of newly pulled bines that lay on the ground near her and started on another one.

Spider, the tallyman, tipped his cap back on his red hair and squinted at Laurie through the leafy sunlight. 'You're new, aren't you?'

'Just visiting,' said Laurie shyly. 'Joe brought us down.'

'Oh, you're with *Joe*,' he said, as if that gave her instant status. He smiled at her, noting how her long, fair hair glinted in the sun, and how those blue eyes—so heavily

83

shadowed with fatigue—were looking back at him out of some deep and hidden fortress of resolve.

'Well, . . .' he said lamely, 'enjoy yourself!' and he passed on to the next group of hop-pickers down the hop-garden.

Somewhere down at the far end, near the road, a bell like an ice-cream van's carillon chimed across the hop-spiced air.

'Grub's up,' said fat Dorrie, and started waddling off towards the sound of the bell. From all over the hop-field, and from the orchards and fields beyond, pickers and children streamed out in a cheerful, chattering crowd.

'Fish and chips,' said Joe's voice close behind Laurie. 'Promised you. Come on.'

They sat on a dusty, foot-scuffed bank near the end of the hop-garden and ate fish and chips out of greasy newspaper, licking the salt off their fingers. It was the first time Laurie had felt hungry since . . . since goodness knows when . . . and she saw that Jason and Midge were demolishing their share very swiftly and even looking round for more. And Penny was laughingly handing out her own chips to keep them quiet.

Joe was watching them all with a shrewd and knowing eye. But he didn't say anything just then—he simply went off to buy everyone an ice-cream as an extra treat.

'Mum,' said Jason, with his mouth full, 'I like it here. Couldn't we stay?'

'Stay!' agreed Midge, and stuffed in another chip.

Laurie looked from them to Penny and sighed.

'Well, why not?' said Penny sturdily. 'Do us good.'

'Us?' murmured Laurie, a deeper question in her mind.

'Yeah, us!' stated Penny. 'Where you goes, I goes—or words to that effect!' And then she blushed with sudden shyness and tossed her red hair in the sun. 'That is—if you don't blurry well mind?'

Joe came back with the ice-creams then, and Laurie tried vainly to pay for them. 'I've got some money, Joe. The Welfare people gave me an emergency grant, to tide me over. Jane fixed it for me.'

'I know,' growled Joe. 'She told me. But this is a present, see?'

Laurie looked at his implacable face, and saw. She thanked him gravely. 'You're right, of course. I mustn't squander it. God knows where the next lot's coming from. But I was wondering—couldn't I earn some down here?'

'*Here?*' asked Joe, surprised. 'You mean . . . hop-picking?'

'Why not?' She glanced at the children's faces turned towards her in mute entreaty. 'They love it here, Joe—the space and the . . . the greenness. After London, it's so . . . *clean.*'

If Joe heard the note of pain in her voice, he chose to ignore it. 'You fit to work, then?' he asked. 'Only just out of bed an' all?' He looked at her severely. 'Wouldn't want you falling in heaps again.'

Laurie caught the glint in his eye and laughed.

'Another thing,' he said seriously. 'Jane's very pushed for space, you know. If you stayed on down here, she mightn't have room when you got back—not that she wouldn't try, mind.'

Laurie nodded. 'I know. But, in any case, I can't stay there for ever, Joe. I've got to move on somewhere.'

Joe thought for a bit. 'I s'pose . . . the Welfare'll house you? They're obliged to, if you're homeless.'

Laurie nodded. 'Yes—a couple of rooms, or bed and breakfast, they said.' She pushed the hair out of her eyes in the familiar, anxious gesture. 'That's no good for the children, Joe. Not permanently, I mean.'

Joe agreed. 'What would you like, then?'

Laurie took a deep breath and looked up at the blue, clear skies and the dazzling towers of cloud moving majestically across them. 'I'd like . . . to go right away,' she murmured, in a strange, far-off voice. 'Right away from London . . .' (and from Jeff and his resentment and rage which I know will follow me) 'to somewhere small and quiet—maybe by the sea or something—where it was empty and . . . and *clean* . . . and I could work.'

Joe was silent for a moment. Then he said, half-smiling, 'What can you do then—besides picking hops?'

Laurie sighed. 'Not much! I can cook a bit, and clean a house, I suppose. And dig a garden. I like gardens.' She sighed again. 'I used to help my father with the garden—when we got home from the bank.'

'The bank?' Joe's voice was sharper.

'Oh yes, I forgot.' Laurie grinned at him apologetically. 'I can add up—a cash balance.'

Joe laughed. 'Worth your weight in gold, girl!' He looked round at the sunny orchards and hop-gardens. 'You really want to stay down here?'

'If there's any work.'

'I'll see,' said Joe, looking at her doubtfully.

'What about me?' Penny demanded. 'I can pick. So could the kids, come to that.'

'Not too much pulling down of bines!' protested Joe. 'Not in your condition, gel! Stan wouldn't like it!' He thought for a moment. 'There's sprouts,' he said slowly, 'and late strawberries still. But that's a lot of stooping.'

'So what?' Penny snorted. 'I'm not made of glass!'

He shook his head at her, laughing. 'Bloody hell, kid—what've I let Stan in for?'

But they were still looking at him, urgent appeal in their eyes.

Joe sighed. 'OK, OK—I'll ask him.' He looked at Laurie's expressive face and had an urgent desire to dispel that look of stress and anxiety. 'You've got your green fields,' he said, smiling. 'Anything else you'd like?'

'Swans,' said Laurie suddenly, looking beyond Joe into the wide, clear sky.

Joe looked startled. But he remembered how she had babbled about wings that night at his coffee stall, before she collapsed on the hard London pavement. 'Swans?' he said. 'Well, there's the river just down the bottom—the muddy old Medway. Why not go and see, while I talk to Stan?'

Together, he and Laurie—with Penny and the two dancing children ahead of them—walked down through the busy hop-gardens and orchards until they came to the green water-meadows and the slow-moving river beyond them. There he left them and turned back towards the farm buildings, with a vague, appreciative gesture of his hand and the cheerful words, 'Help yourself!'

The banks were rusty with late September grasses, but still flowery with balsam and loosestrife and meadow-sweet—and tall, spiky reeds grew in long islets of green swords among the tangled arms of the willows. The brown, sluggish stream flowed gently by, with cloud-shadow and trees reflected in its unbroken surface. A few moorhens and coots chugged busily about among the reed-beds, and a pair of mallards sailed jauntily down-stream on the twirling eddies.

'There!' breathed Jason, pointing an excited finger. 'There they are! That what you wanted?'

And there, drifting peacefully on the river's smooth-flowing surface, were two calm and graceful swans.

'Oh!' whispered Laurie. 'Aren't they *beautiful!*' And she sank down on the rough grass of the river bank to watch them, her eyes suddenly abrim with unexpected tears.

Penny looked at her sideways, and then turned away and began to talk to Jason very earnestly about mallard ducks, and swans, and boats on the river. Still talking, they wandered away along the river bank, with Midge held firmly by the hand in case she toppled into the water—she was so eager to see everything growing and green and new, and even more enchanted by the fleet of perky young ducklings who swam out of the reeds to join their parents. The gaudy drake flaunted his bright plumage in the sun, but all the same he kept a careful eye on his adventurous offspring and his neat brown wife.

'Ooh . . . look!' said Midge, pointing a small finger at the orderly little flotilla sailing past. And she laughed in the sun and tried to run after them down the river bank. Laughing, Penny and Jason ran too.

Laurie sat on in the sun, watching the quiet swans who sailed so proudly before the wind like trim, deep-breasted clippers. She, too, seemed to be drifting into a world that was all green and gold and white wings reflected in brown water—all stillness and peace, with no shadow of fear behind it.

Presently the two swans seemed to wake from their

slumbrous drifting, almost as if they had been called, and began to swim together towards a small, jutting finger of land reaching out from the river bank. As they reached the reedy shallows, Laurie saw the figure of a man outlined against the sun. He too seemed all green and gold and brown—and as still and quiet as the river—as calm as the swans. He seemed almost to merge with the landscape and to belong to it, he stood so still—squarely planted on the river bank like a growing tree.

'Men as trees walking,' thought Laurie vaguely, and pushed the hair out of her eyes to look again. He lifted a hand to the swans—as if greeting old friends—and they came quite close so that he could lean out and stroke the beautiful curve of their heads and long white necks. He reached into a pocket and brought out some food for them, and they both took it from his hand with unhurried dignity. Then he gave them a final, loving stroke, and she caught the faint murmur of his voice as he turned away from them and came on towards her. 'Grow strong,' she thought he said.

She did not move, but sat watching him as he came nearer with slow, long strides. She seemed almost as mesmerised by his presence as the swans. He was so calm and quiet, and seemed to walk in an aura of steady, purposeful intent, but without haste or anxiety.

An extraordinary sense of release and gladness seemed to well up inside Laurie as she watched him come—a feeling almost of recognition. Here was someone unafraid—someone untouched by the seeds of anger or spite—who reached out to the swans with gentle, compassionate hands that had never known violence . . . and who walked through the dappled world of the watermeadows not as if he owned it but was part of it.

As he came close, she found herself looking into a brown, lean face with finely etched lines round the far-seeing eyes which were a deep cloud-shadow grey and were regarding her with friendly enquiry. There were two small wings of grey in his hair, which was brown and faintly curly and sprang away from a broad, lifting brow.

88

And his mouth was curly, like his hair, and very kind—
though Laurie suspected it could be stern on occasions.

He for his part saw a small, pale girl with long, fair hair
that glinted in the sun, and eyes that were too big and
too dark with shadows but should have been a clear,
unclouded gentian blue. And a mouth that was resolute,
but trembled on the edge of tears—he could not tell why.

'Are they yours?' she asked.

'What?'

'The swans.'

'Oh. Oh, no. They're wild swans—entirely wild and
free. They belong to no one but themselves.' He smiled
at her, and sunlight seemed to brim and dance in his face.

'But—they knew you!'

'That's because they were injured, and I took them in.
But they are well again now—and free to come and go as
they please.' The smile still lingered as he stood looking
down at her.

'Free?' murmured Laurie, as if it was a strange word
she did not know.

'They only come back because they know I'm friendly—
and it's safe,' he said, and there was tenderness in that
faint, still lingering smile.

*Because they know I'm friendly—and it's safe.* Laurie shut
her eyes for a moment, blinking back absurd tears. When
she opened them again, he was sitting on the bank beside
her.

'Do you . . . are there a lot of swans on the river?'

'Quite a few still. Not nearly so many as there used to
be.'

'Why?'

'They get hurt . . . and they die.'

'Many of them?'

'Far too many.' His expression changed and grew grim.
'Well—even *one* injured swan is one too many.'

'What happens to them?'

'Everything.' His voice was as grim as that stern,
uncompromising mouth. 'They get tangled up in fishing-
line. They get shot. They get fish-hooks embedded in

their throats. They get attacked by people on the banks—
by people in boats . . .'

'*Attacked*? Swans?'

'Oh yes. Beaten with paddles. Tied to a tree and used
as a dartboard. Dragged behind an outboard motor and
chopped up by the propeller. Thrown on a bonfire and
burnt. Their beaks cut off; their wings torn off. You name
it, people have done it.'

Laurie's eyes were huge and almost black with anger.
'*Why*? What is it about us human beings? *Why* are we so
violent?'

She shuddered, and the quiet man watching her knew
she was talking of more than the swans.

'It's a kind of despair,' he murmured. 'I think . . .'

'Despair?'

'Yes. Despair—that life can be so ugly and disappointing.'

Laurie nodded. 'So they hit out?' She knew that pattern.

'At the nearest thing—yes.' He looked at her. 'Nothing
has any right to be so beautiful and so pure. They hate
it.' Once more he glanced fleetingly at Laurie. 'Innocence—they *have* to destroy it. It's like walking on new
snow. It seems to mock them with its purity.' There was
a strange edge to his tone. 'And it's the same with the
swans.'

Laurie sighed. So beautiful and so pure, she thought,
watching the two wild swans sailing on the river.

'It isn't, of course,' he added, his eyes also on the
swans.

'What isn't what?'

'Life isn't—disappointing and ugly.'

'Isn't it?'

'No,' he said, not missing the wistful note in her voice.
'Not all the time.' He lifted a quiet hand and gestured at
the river and the gently drifting snowy birds beyond
them. 'Look at it! Looks peaceful enough, doesn't it? But
the worst thing for the swans is right here in front of our
eyes—buried in the mud.'

'What's that?'

'Lead weights. Fishermen's lead weights. You wouldn't

think of fishermen as particularly cruel, would you? Except to the fish, of course!' There was a sardonic gleam in his eye now. 'But to the swans they are lethal. The lead pellets get lodged in their gizzards, and they can't swallow. It's a terrible slow death, lingering and agonising. They are slowly poisoned, and they die of starvation in the end.'

His face was dark with sorrow. Not with anger, thought Laurie, surprised. Sorrow.

'But . . . you save them?'

'Some of them.' He shook his head sadly. 'Not all of them. We find some of them in time. But for a lot of them it's too late.' He spoke, thought Laurie, as if they were friends of his that he loved—and as if 'people' were the enemy.

'Is it . . . a kind of sanctuary that you run?'

'Sort of.' His eyes were crinkling again with laughter, but it seemed to be directed against himself. 'I had a caravan first—on the river bank. But now it's a small, rather derelict cottage on a backwater. It's just right for the birds—enclosed and quiet, with a stretch of safe water. But even so, I've had to dredge it for lead at the bottom. The injured ones stay in the house when they're really sick, and then they move out by stages. That pair over there—' he nodded at the swans affectionately, 'they're two of my successes.'

Laurie nodded. 'I'm glad. But I suppose there are always more to deal with?'

'Always more,' he sighed, and his voice was still flecked with sorrow.

'Not much room for you, by the sound of it!'

He laughed. 'I don't mind. I came to an arrangement with the wildlife people. I've got a roof over my head—and a bed to lie on!'

A roof over my head and a bed to lie on, thought Laurie. And I haven't. The children haven't, either—except the awful, crowded chaos of Jane's hostel. *'You've made your bed and you must lie on it!* But I won't! she said. I must pull myself together and find somewhere to live. I wonder if Joe will have persuaded the farmer to let us stay.

Behind her, in the distant orchards, what sounded like a shot rang out, and then some shouts and a whole series of sharp whip-crack detonations.

Laurie jumped and began to tremble.

'It's all right,' said the Swan-Man, smiling. 'Bird-scarers. They usually start them up in the orchards when the pickers go home. Saves a lot of fruit.'

'Oh.' Laurie was vainly trying to stop herself shaking. 'Silly to be scared . . .' she muttered, through chattering teeth.

He looked at her gravely. 'It takes time,' he said obscurely. 'Sometimes my swans take a long time.'

'D-do they?' She seemed to be asking more than a simple question.

'They can't bear to be touched at first.' He was not looking at her now, but gazing quietly out at the slow-moving river. 'They start at every sound—even a spoon doling out food on to a tin plate makes them go rigid with fear. They hate men.' He still did not look at her. 'You can't blame them, can you? Violence goes very deep.'

'Yes,' breathed Laurie.

'But in the end they learn to trust me,' he said gently, his voice alive with compassion. 'In the end, they eat out of my hand—as you saw!'

Laurie smiled a pain-washed smile. 'Yes. I did.'

'They even let me stroke them,' he said, and now he was smiling too—even half-teasing—as he turned his strange cloud-grey gaze on her.

Far down the bank, Laurie heard the sound of Penny and the children returning—their clear young voices carrying across the quiet air.

'It will get better,' he murmured, to no one in particular, and watched the small figures of the children coming towards them.

Midge ran up to her mother, babbling happily of ducks and babies and water-lilies. But Jason came up to her slowly, his eyes anxiously on her face, and held out a long, white swan's feather which he had found on the river bank.

'Mum?' he said, and laid the feather in her lap.

He did not say any more, but Laurie looked up and smiled at him through tear-dazzled eyes. In the strangely adult gaze of her young son she saw reassurance and clear understanding. I know, he was saying. I know there's never been time to sit on a river bank and look at swans—not for ages and ages. I know when a thing is beautiful it makes you cry. But I'm here. And Midge is here. And Penny. And we're safe. There's nothing here to frighten us. Everything is all right.

Laurie put out a hand and picked up the smooth, white flight feather. A sudden terrible longing assailed her to plunge into the river beside the snowy swans and dive down and down until all her old self and her old life had been stripped from her and washed away, so that she could come to the surface all new and clean—like the sparkling mallards; like the pure, unblemished swans sailing so proudly, entirely healed and free.

But aloud she only said, 'One small piece of freedom, Jay!' and held up the gleaming feather in the late September sunlight.

The man at her side touched the feather with a gentle finger. He smiled at her, and there was the same awareness and reassurance in his compassionate gaze as she had seen in young Jason's eyes.

'There will be others,' he said softly, and got up and walked away from them into the sun.

\* \* \*

At the end of the golden afternoon, they wandered back towards the farm and met Joe returning. With him came the farmer—a stocky, sandy-haired man with big, freckled hands and a steady, summing-up stare.

'This is Stan,' said Joe. 'Might take you on for a week—if you think you're up to it.'

Stan looked at Laurie hard, and then at Penny and the children, who were all returning his stare with appealing looks of their own.

'*All* of you?' he enquired.

'All of us!' said Penny firmly. 'All or nothing, that's me.'

93

Stan looked from them to Joe and began to laugh. 'Accommodation's rough.'

Laurie smiled. 'We're not fussy.' How could they be—with nowhere else to live, except the overcrowded squalor of The Hide?

She looked at Joe suddenly and said doubtfully, 'Jane . . . ?'

'You'd better talk to her,' Joe answered. 'Stan'll let you phone—if you're sure?'

'I'm sure,' murmured Laurie, with her eye on the children.

'We're sure,' confirmed Penny.

'Sure!' echoed the children.

'Wages . . . ,' Stan was saying: 'Piece-rates . . . tally-man will tot it up for you. . . . Up to you . . .' He looked at Laurie again and added kindly, 'Don't set yourself too fast a pace. Work as a team. It's a race against time anyway, what with the weather and the blight.'

'Blight?' asked Joe, with swift sympathy. 'You got it here?'

'No. Not yet.' Stan's face creaked into a smile. 'But it's not far down the valley.' His smile grew solider and rested on Laurie. 'Glad to have some extra pairs of hands this week. There's an empty hut, and the kitchen's at the end. The others'll show you. Fix yourself up with food and such tomorrow.'

'Tomorrow?' said Laurie, confused.

'Mobile shop. Comes up here most days. Keeps his prices down—I see that he does!' His mouth took on a grim but humorous quirk. 'Bring her up to the house, Joe. She can phone from there.'

He turned on his heel and stumped off. Laurie looked from Joe to Penny and the kids—still not quite sure what was happening. She supposed they were hired, but she must talk to Jane first.

Jane, when she heard the proposal, said at once, 'Yes, Laurie. Stay. Fresh air and sun will do you good. But don't stoop too much—with that head injury. And don't let Penny do too much reaching up!'

'That's going to be difficult!' said Laurie, laughing.

94

She heard Jane laugh too, and then add cheerfully, 'A week, you say?'

'That's all. The picking's nearly over.'

'I may have to use your room.'

'Never mind. You've been wonderful to let us have it so long, anyway.'

'You'll have to start thinking about the future.'

'Yes,' agreed Laurie. 'I am.' She paused and added shyly, 'I'm hoping . . . the air and the work . . . will help me to get things clear.'

Jane agreed with that. 'The social security people will want to see you about housing.'

'Yes.' Laurie sighed. 'When I come back . . .' She hesitated, and then went on awkwardly, 'And I . . . I suppose I'll have to go round to the house and collect some clothes for the children. I've been putting it off.' And another school for Jason, she thought—when we know where we're going to live. And, meanwhile, a week in the country won't hurt him.

'. . . stronger when you come back,' Jane was saying. 'Make the most of it!'

Laurie went back to Penny and the children, and found Joe with them—looking almost as anxious as they were.

'Well?' they all cried.

'Jane says—make the most of it!' She stood there smiling, while Penny and Jason did a kind of jig, with Midge jumping up and down in the middle.

Then Laurie did a surprising thing. She turned to Joe and put her arms round his neck and hugged him. 'You're a crafty devil, Joe! I believe you planned this all along!'

'What, me?' Joe was all injured innocence. 'As if I would!'

*   *   *

For Laurie—and for Penny and the children—there began a time of quite unexpected peace and freedom.

Accommodation was certainly 'rough'—but the long line of old hoppers' huts was clean and newly whitewashed inside, and divided into separate rooms rather like loose-boxes, with bunk beds along the sides. Each

95

family was allocated one of these rooms, and a variety of blankets and rough coverlets was laid out for them—though most of them brought sleeping-bags as well. There was a communal kitchen at the end of the huts but, even so, some families preferred to make their own cooking arrangements, with camping-gas or more elaborate contraptions, and some with open fires on the flat, trampled field outside the huts. This led to convivial gatherings, with the aromatic scent of bonfire smoke curling round them in the cool September evenings.

Everyone was friendly, and someone lent Laurie a tin of baked beans and an old, blackened cooking-pot until she could stock up at the mobile shop next day. Penny had also managed to get some eggs and milk from the farmer's wife, and someone else gave her a screw of tea and half a stale loaf of bread—'to be going on with'—so that first night seemed like a feast.

They got up early, when the others did, and after some smoky tea and a hunk of bread they all trooped out to the hop-gardens for the day's work.

Jason and Midge scampered about, their faces unshadowed and eager, exploring everything in sight—and sometimes out of sight. Laurie didn't call them back—there was no danger here, and it was so good to see them running and laughing in the sun. But, even so, Jason remembered that Penny had said, 'I can pick—so can the kids,' and Laurie would be paid for the amount in her bin when the tallyman came round, so he came galloping back, out of breath and happy, with Midge by the hand, and began to strip off the pale green bobbles from the bines like the rest of them.

All day they were out in the wind and sun, and in the evening they sat by the camp-fires and drowsed over more baked beans and sausages on sticks, and baked potatoes in the embers.

The tallyman, Spider, had taken a fancy to Laurie. He often stopped by her bin for a chat, and in the evening he strolled up to her cooking-fire and stood looking down at her in the fading light.

'Mind if I join you?'

'Suit yourself,' said Laurie, ladling tinned Irish stew on to plastic plates for the children and Penny.

He glanced at her shrewdly before he sat down on the scuffed grass. Her long hair looked even fairer after the sun and wind, and her face had lost some of its pinched, weary look. But there were still shadows under those very blue eyes. Shadows—or were they really bruises just beginning to fade?

'On your own, are you?' he said, with a mixture of friendliness and enquiry in his voice.

Laurie looked at him squarely. 'Yes,' she said. And then heard her own voice continue—almost without conscious volition—'And I intend to keep it that way.'

Spider laughed and stretched his long legs along the grass. 'Don't be like that! I was only asking.'

Laurie sighed. She poured some tea out of the old boiling kettle someone had given her into a tin mug, and tipped some milk into it. 'Here,' she said. 'No sugar, I'm afraid.' She watched him for a moment in silence as he sipped his tea and clearly wondered how to approach her next.

'Listen, Spider,' she said suddenly. 'Just because I've got long hair and baby-blue eyes doesn't mean I'm fair game for any man that comes along.'

'Hey—hold on, I didn't mean . . .'

'No?' she said, disbelieving. 'Well, anyway, I'm not!' She looked at him again, almost despairingly. 'I'm a *person*, Spider. Not a dolly-bird. Not a sex symbol. Not *anything*. I'm just *me*.' Her expression was hardening even as she spoke. 'And to tell you the truth, Spider, I've had my fill of men.'

He glanced at her then, half-smiling. 'Really?'

'Yes, really. Unless, that is, you could treat me like any other worker—male or female. A mate, I mean.' She was looking at him again, searchingly—almost as if she hoped to see something in his face that was not there. 'I could do with an ordinary, common-or-garden friend or two,' she murmured, half to herself.

Spider grinned, and emptied his mug of tea. 'Message

97

received and understood,' he said, and stood up, ready to go.

Laurie felt a faint stirring of disappointment. Given the brush-off, he didn't want to know. Was ordinary friendship with a man impossible?

She was just reaching out a hand to take his empty mug when a fight broke out farther down the line of fires. She had not really noticed till now that there were three distinct factions in the work-force. There were the cockneys from London—cheerful and cheeky and self-reliant. There were the itinerant workers from East Kent, who followed the fruit-picking harvest round from farm to farm and resented the influx of cockneys from the Smoke. They came in bus loads and went home for the night—most of them. But some stayed on, drinking in the pubs—getting steadily more belligerent. And then there were the gipsies, who came and went as they pleased in smart new trailers and turned up wherever the best work was—and the piece-rates were highest. And they were touchy about their status, and belligerent, too.

Now a largish, dark gipsy lad had picked a fight with a Londoner, and before long blows were flying as fast as oaths, and the various factions closed ranks behind them and rallied to the assistance of their friends.

Friends! thought Laurie, watching them, half-fascinated and half-horrified at their violence. Did I say *friends*? With friends like that, who needs enemies?

'Don't mind them,' said Dorrie, the woman who had been kind to Laurie when she first arrived and who now considered herself Laurie's protector. 'It don't mean nothing. They're always at it!' She snorted, and turned back to poke at the glowing embers of her fire with a long stick. 'Men!' she said, poking viciously into the heart of the fire. 'A few drinks in the boozer and they're spoiling for a fight . . . Nothing better to do!'

Laurie said, still a bit horrified, 'Don't they . . . hurt each other?'

The woman laughed. 'A few sore heads in the morning! Serve 'em right.' She straightened her back and brushed down the ancient musquash fur coat she was wearing over the shapeless print dress that covered her ample form, and stood staring down the field, trying to distinguish which was which among the group of heaving, struggling men. 'Gets bad, though, if they start using broken bottles.'

She turned sharply to Spider, who had not gone away but was also staring down the field. 'That's Slattery's boy. He's a mean one—likes glass. Better get down there quick, Spider!'

He nodded and went off down the field, stopping to enlist a few burly bystanders on the way.

It was then that Laurie noticed the children had gone. 'Penny!' she said sharply. 'Where are the kids?'

Penny had been tending the fire with a few chips of wood and had not taken much notice of the fight. Now she looked up in dismay. 'Jay? Midge?' She gazed round the circle of fires and then back at Laurie in growing horror. 'I thought they were eating their stew . . .'

Laurie sprang to her feet. 'It's the fight,' she said. 'They're scared of violence.' And so am I, come to that, she thought—aware that her stomach was churning in a hard knot of fear, especially at the mention of broken bottles.

'We'd better search,' said Penny, and went first to the long row of huts where they slept. The children weren't there.

They toured round all the camp-fires, except near where the fight was now being quelled by a determined group of tough men headed by Spider. There was no sign of Jason and Midge, though. Not anywhere.

'Would they run off into the hop-garden?' asked Laurie doubtfully. 'Or the orchards?'

'They might. They could hide there and feel safe,' answered Penny, trying to put herself in their place.

Laurie turned rather desperately to Dorrie. 'Where can I borrow a torch?'

'Storm-lantern,' said Dorrie, and waddled over to her sleeping-quarters, returning with a paraffin lantern which she lit from the fire with a long spill of paper. 'Kids gone off, have they?' She looked into Laurie's face for a moment, seeing the fear and dread in her eyes, and added softly, 'Seen too much of it, I dessay.'

'Yes,' agreed Laurie; and added bitterly, 'Far too much!'

Dorrie grunted. 'No good me coming—too slow. But I'll get a few folk together. You go on.'

Laurie swung the lantern in front of her and almost ran into the dark lanes of the hop-bines. The ground was dusty and beaten hard by the feet of the pickers and the constant movement of tractors and trailers, but even so it did not echo to footsteps—and there was no sound of children's voices up ahead.

Penny followed her, calling anxiously, and stumbling a little over the stony track.

'Be careful,' warned Laurie. 'Don't want you falling, on top of everything else!'

'If I fell on top of everything else,' said Penny tartly, 'it'd be flattened!'

They laughed shakily, and went on along the tall lanes of the hops, calling and searching—the lantern held high. But though they stopped and listened at intervals, they heard nothing except the owls calling in the tall trees at the end of the field and the distant shouts and laughter and occasional thumps and curses from the pickers' encampment.

'We'd better split up,' suggested Penny, when they came to a kind of crossroads in the lines of hops.

Laurie was doubtful. 'Are you sure? It's getting dark. You might get lost.' She stood irresolute in the dusty clearing, looking down each deep-shadowed ride in turn.

Behind her she heard voices, and another lantern swung into view, followed by several men and a woman with two lanky teenage boys waving torches.

'You two go on,' instructed the lantern-swinger cheerfully. 'We can take the other lanes between us. And someone's checking the orchards. They can't have got far.'

Laurie and Penny plodded on, stopping to call again and listen intently every few yards. Presently, Penny stopped and said, 'That little hut at the end—where they keep the baskets. It's like the back of the shed at Jane's where Jay and Midge used to hide.'

Laurie turned to look at Penny in the glimmering light of the lantern. 'Do you think . . . ?'

'That's where they'll be. They could make a kind of shelter with the baskets—like they did with the cardboard boxes. It's the way they'd think, if they were looking for somewhere safe.'

Somewhere safe? thought Laurie, filled with a sudden ache of grief and guilt. What had she done to her children—allowing them to see so much violence and suffering in their young lives that they were afraid of any raised voice and any lifted hand, however remote from them? So afraid that they would run off into the dark night and hide in a shed full of empty baskets?

'Where is it?' she asked Penny sharply. 'Can you remember?'

'Right at the end of the hop-garden—where the tractors turn round. I think it's this way.'

They hurried on—more surely now that they had some idea where they were making for—and soon came to the end of the row of hops and a long stretch of trodden ground and discarded hop-bines, with the lowered hop-poles lying between them where the picking was already finished. The reddish-brown dust was covered in wheel-tracks and footprints, but there was no sign of the children—or of the hut they were looking for.

'Bloody hell,' said Penny, who always swore more when she was upset. 'It must be at the other flaming corner. This way!' And she set off confidently enough down the flattened rows of wilting leaves.

All at once there was a wild screech and a sudden clatter as a cock pheasant started up right under their feet and flapped clumsily away into the darkness. Laurie felt her heart almost stop, she was so absurdly scared. And if she was scared in this sounding country darkness, what must Jason and Midge be feeling?

'Here!' someone was shouting, from the other end of the hop-row. 'Over here!'

Laurie began to run, with Penny pounding after her. She reached the other clearing and found the small knot of people waiting for her, the lantern swinging to show her the way. They were standing—as Penny had pre-dicted—by a heap of old bushel baskets stacked against the wall of a small ramshackle shed with a broken roof of corrugated iron. And there, curled up in a tight ball of misery and fear, was little Midge—with Jason standing protectively beside her, defying anyone to come near.

Laurie took in at a glance what was happening, and simply knelt down and put her arms round Midge, saying, 'It's all right. It's all right, Midge . . . No one's going to hurt you.'

And when Midge buried her head against her mother's shoulder and burst into tears, Laurie just gathered her close and looked down at Jason over the top of Midge's golden head.

'Jay . . . ?'

'I'm sorry,' he said. 'It was the fight.' He looked at his mother anxiously. 'Midge ran off, and I couldn't make her come back. So I thought I'd better stay with her.' He took a deep breath and added in a small, bleak voice, 'She's too little to be left alone in the dark.'

Too little—and too frightened—to be left alone in the dark. And her brave young son, Jason, stood guard . . .

'Never mind,' she said gently. 'You're both safe now. And you were quite right to stay with her. Only, you see, we didn't know where to look for you.'

'I did,' said Penny sturdily, smiling at them with relief. 'I guessed where you'd be—but I went the wrong way!'

Everyone laughed then—as filled with relief as Penny. A child—two children—had been lost, and they had all been anxious. Now they were found, and it was an occasion for rejoicing.

'Come on,' said one of the men, 'let's sing you home!' And he started up 'Roll out the Barrel'—that most tra-ditional of old cockney songs—in a cheerful, musical tenor. Soon they were all singing, and one of them hoisted Jason on to his shoulders and let him ride high among the green hops all the way home. But Midge clung tight to Laurie, with her arms fast round her neck, and would not let anyone else attempt to carry her.

When they got back to the encampment, Dorrie had

made a huge pot of soup, and everyone sat round her fire and went on singing. Some of the other groups were singing, too, and there were rival pop songs and dancing and clapping going on all round the cooking fires.

Laurie saw then, with surprise, that Spider the tallyman had come back to join them, having quelled the fight, and was smiling down at her.

'Glad you found 'em,' he said, and turned to put a piece of sticky chocolate in Midge's small clenched hand. 'You see, Little Miss Muffet, not *all* men are ogres,' he said softly.

But, though Laurie smiled an astonished smile at his understanding, Midge was not impressed.

* * *

Late that night, Laurie said to Penny as they lay side by side in the hop-scented darkness, 'Could you cut my hair?'

Penny was a half-asleep, but she leant up on one elbow to peer at her in amazement. 'Cut your hair?' What—off, you mean?'

'Yes. Off. Quite short.' Her voice was crisp.

'I suppose so—given a pair of scissors.'

'Dorrie will probably have some.' She appeared to be going to get up and ask her there and then, but Penny said in a calm, cheerful voice, 'Tomorrow morning—when it's light. Can't do it now—might hack your head off!'

They giggled feebly in the dark.

'Why?' asked Penny—but on second thoughts she knew really. 'Not because of Spider?' She laughed a little. 'That'd be cutting off your hair to spite your face!'

Laurie laughed, too—somewhat breathlessly. 'No, but . . .' She hesitated. 'I've decided I've got to be different from now on.'

Penny nodded, though it was almost too dark to see her face. 'Yeah. You're the kind men can't keep their frigging hands off—one way and another!'

Laurie agreed, somewhat bitterly.

'Right!' Penny's voice was dry. 'No more innocent victim stuff. Not from you—or me, neither!'

'Exactly.' Laurie sounded equally matter-of-fact. 'So—scissors. Tomorrow.'

Sleepily, Penny assented. The air and sun and the long day's picking were getting to her—and to Laurie, too. Soon they both slept—dreamlessly and deep.

\* \* \*

When they had borrowed Dorrie's scissors and the long gold streamers of hair lay in swathes at Laurie's feet, Midge looked as if she might cry.

But Jason said stoutly, 'She looks smashing. Like a boy—only smarter!'

Laurie laughed. She did indeed look rather like a slender, fragile boy, with the jagged urchin-cut Penny had given her and the small sprinkling of freckles that the autumn sun was already dusting on her nose. But her eyes were still too big in her heart-shaped face—in fact they looked bigger than ever, and still very clear and blue despite the darkness they had seen. Penny's vivid red hair, on the other hand, was already short—but it flamed in the September sunlight and would not be tamed, and her strange grey-green eyes were full of mischief.

'You can sell hair,' she said. 'I'll ask Dorrie. Might as well make something out of it!'

She picked up the golden heap and turned to look for the cheerful cockney woman who was boiling tea on her fire. But, as an afterthought, she pulled out a small honey-gold strand and laid it in Midge's hand. 'What we need,' she said, 'is a locket. I'll see what the shop can do. Though it won't be gold, mind!' She smiled at Midge encouragingly. 'Then you'll have a bit to keep for ever.'

Midge looked at her doubtfully. 'Ever?' she said. It was clearly a word she didn't believe in much.

Laurie was trying to see her own reflection in the saucepan of water heating on the fire. A pale, glimmering image of a new, crisp stranger looked out at her. New, she thought. All new. I must start anew. But aloud she only said, 'I like it. Makes me feel quite tough!'

They went out to the hop-fields cheerfully that day, like old hands. The sun shone out of a cloudless sky—though there had been a sharpness in the early morning air and a heavy silver dew on all the cobwebs.

'Frosts aren't far away,' muttered one grizzled man, snuffing at the small, light breeze that ruffled the leaves of the hop-bines. He glanced at Penny and added, 'Pickin's cruel when the frosts come—specially sprouts!'

But Penny didn't care. The frosts hadn't come yet. She was standing in the sun, looking up into the clusters of dangling hops. The world was all green and gold, and she was with Laurie and the kids. It was a lovely day.

\* \* \*

After picking that day, Laurie went up to the farm for some more eggs and milk. She passed the oast-house with its scented load of drying hops (oil-fired drying, now, they told her— not slow-burning coke and sulphur fumes) and came to the farm office next to the dairy. Stan was sitting at his desk, painstakingly going over the tallyman's figures and trying to assess the day's harvest. Spider was standing beside him, pointing to something with a blunt finger.

He glanced up as Laurie came by, and his jaw seemed to drop a little at her appearance. He whistled appreciatively. 'Good grief!' he said. 'What have you done to yourself?'

Laurie grinned and tossed her fair cropped head in the fading twilight. 'New me!' she said. 'Needed a change.' She started to walk on towards the open door of the dairy.

'Wait a minute,' called Stan, getting to his feet. 'Joe said something about you doing accounts. Is that true?'

Laurie hesitated. 'I could add up money—and get a balance!'

The two men looked at one another and laughed. 'More than we can do!' said Spider, still laughing.

Stan beckoned her over and showed her his lists and the crabbed, crossed-out entries in his books. 'Make any sense to you?' he asked.

Laurie looked at them cautiously. After a few moments, she nodded and said: 'Could be . . .'

Stan sighed with relief. 'Would you take them on? It'd be less like hard labour than picking.'

Laurie shook her head. 'No. Not by day. I have to be with the children—they'd fret otherwise.' She looked at him apologetically. 'They . . . need me with them at present. It's important for them to feel safe, just now.'

Stan and Spider were looking at her attentively, but they were clearly disappointed.

'And then there's Penny,' she added. 'She needs someone to keep an eye on her!' Her smile was mischievous now. 'Or she might have her baby right there in the hopgarden.'

'God forbid!' said Stan.

She laughed, and then went on more slowly, 'Maybe I could come up for an hour in the evenings?' She glanced round the little farm office appraisingly. 'You've got electric light out here. I could manage after dark.'

Stan's face split into a cheerful grin. 'Could you? Take a real weight off my mind!' He looked from her to Spider somewhat ruefully. 'Not much head for figures, I haven't!'

'That makes two of us,' said Spider.

Laurie smiled. 'OK. Tomorrow.'

'Not tonight?'

'No. Sorry. I promised the kids eggs for tea. Got to get back.'

She went out of the little office quite calmly, and left the two men standing. I do believe cutting off my hair *has* made me tougher! she thought. And she went on to the dairy, where Stan's wife handed over some eggs and a jug of milk.

On the way back, she called through the office door, 'By the way, I s'pose you'll pay me a bit extra?'

'Of course,' agreed Stan, still grinning his relief. 'Stands to reason.'

'Shall I see you back to the huts?' asked Spider, who never gave up when there was a pretty woman in the offing.

'No,' said Laurie. 'No thanks. I can manage on my own.' And she turned and left them again, her bright head held high.

'Wow!' breathed Spider. 'Independent, that one!'

'She's been through it,' said Stan sagely. 'Joe told me. Bloody husband half-killed her.'

'Oh,' said Spider. 'No wonder . . .'

They both stood looking after her as she walked away in the gathering dusk.

\* \* \*

What with the hop-picking and then cooking supper over a slow fire, and, on top of that, working on Stan's accounts in the late evening, it was some days before Laurie could get down to the river again to see the swans. Or was it the Swan-Man she wanted to see? She did not know—but something pulled like a new ache in her mind and drew her towards that slow brown river.

And one afternoon it rained, so they were laid off early—unable to pick the hops when they were wet. Penny and the children volunteered to cook the evening meal, if they could get the fire to go—if not, they would use the over-crowded kitchen at the end of the huts. So Laurie went off on her own to walk in the rain.

There were still times when thoughts of Jeff and the awful turmoil of her life with him besieged her. Times when she felt racked with guilt because the poor sod was in prison, without a drink, without a friend in the world, and certainly needing help. But then those recurrent scenes of violence would come back into her mind, and she would shudder—her stomach would lurch with remembered terror, and she would give herself a mental shake and say: No. I will *not* be sorry for him. Not any more. I *can't*. I've got to think of the kids and the future now. I've got to build a new life of my own and stop having regrets or second thoughts. Looking back is *fatal*!

She was walking along the river bank, pursued by these thoughts, when she almost cannoned into the Swan-Man, who was crouched on the edge with a swan in his arms.

'Sorry,' she whispered, anxious not to frighten the injured bird. 'Can I help?' And she sank down on to the wet grass beside him.

'Fish-hook in her throat,' he said. 'No time to get her back to my place—she's suffocating.' He looked up at

Laurie assessingly. 'Yes. See if you can hold her still while I swaddle her wings.'

He brought out a long strip of cloth and swiftly bound it round the powerful wings, holding them close to the swan's body so that she could not struggle. 'One blow from those', he said, 'can smash an arm or a leg just like that!'

Laurie held the limp bird still in her hands, feeling the warmth of its silken breast under her fingers and the wild, frantic beating of its heart as it fought for breath. That's how I felt, she thought. Frantic and desperate—almost dying of fright. Poor bird—I know just how you feel.

As soon as the swan was safely held, the man's long, brown fingers reached for a pair of thin forceps in the medical bag which was spread out on the grass beside him. Gently, delicately, he forced open the swan's beak and began probing. 'It's a long way down,' he muttered. 'I may not be able to reach it.' But he went on trying. And Laurie went on holding the bird steady between her hands, and instinctively began to croon to it and to stroke its smooth, white feathers to keep it calm.

'That's good,' nodded the Swan-Man approvingly. 'If you can keep her quiet . . . Sometimes they just die of fright.'

Yes, thought Laurie, unsurprised that he had echoed her own thoughts. Sometimes they just die of fright. I know about fright and how it makes your heart thump . . . and all your limbs go rigid with shock. But it's not going to happen again—not ever again. Not to me. Not to Midge or Jason. Not to Penny, either—or her unborn baby. Not ever again. 'Keep still, swan,' she crooned. 'He won't hurt you . . . Soon be better, swan . . . soon . . .'

'Ah!' said the Swan-Man, and seemed to twist his forceps a little and give them a small, sharp tug. 'There!' he exclaimed in triumph, and withdrew his hand from the swan's arching throat. Between the narrow blades of the forceps was a vicious steel fish-hook with a trail of nylon line attached to it, and after it came a mess of blood and clogging grit. The swan gave a convulsive heave and seemed to gasp for air—and then began to breathe more normally.

'It's all right, my friend,' he said, smiling a little now and stroking its long neck with a comforting hand. 'All over. You'll be fine after a little rest.'

Gently he let his hand run down the smooth, pliant neck, feeling for more obstructions. The bird did not try to struggle. It lay passive in Laurie's hands and leant its head tiredly against the Swan-Man's shoulder, as if he was an old and trusted friend.

'She's a bit shocked,' he said. 'Usually I get them home first—but this was too urgent to wait.' He stood up and looked down at the exhausted bird with a quiet, considering gaze. 'Maybe she'll let me take her home now,' he murmured. 'She'll need a week or two under my eye—and feeding up a bit.'

Laurie still had her hands round the swan. She sat in the long wet grass, looking up at him in mute enquiry.

Now that the swan was out of immediate danger, the man seemed to see Laurie more clearly. She looked like a slim, shy boy sitting there, with her cropped golden head and her big anxious eyes. It occurred to him, though, in a lurch of surprise, that she was looking at him like the swan—with acceptance, almost with trust. The wariness of the other day was gone.

He reached out a tentative finger and lightly touched a frond of the closecut blonde hair. 'Another small piece of freedom?'

She smiled at him, and kept her hands round the swan till he stooped and tucked the drooping bird under his arm.

'Coming?' He stood looking down at her, while she hesitated. 'You can help me put her to bed!'

'All right,' said Laurie. And she fancied that those penetrating grey eyes were aware that it was a small victory.

Together they walked along the bank, not hurrying, for fear of disturbing the swan even more.

'What do they call you?' asked Laurie, feeling all at once that it was absurd to be walking peacefuly beside this man—to be aware that he was like an old friend already, almost like someone she had known all her life — and not to know his name.

He turned his head and smiled at her. 'Mostly they call me that batty swan-man. But my friends call me Clem.'

She nodded. It seemed entirely right to her. Clement means merciful, she thought, with her eyes on the swan's limp head lying against his arm. 'Clement?'

He laughed. 'A bit pretentious, that! Clem's short for "always starving!" ' He cocked an eyebrow in her direction. 'What about you?'

'Me? I'm Laurie.'

He seemed to consider for a moment. 'Laura,' he said slowly. 'Are you a fighter?'

It was her turn to consider. 'I am now,' she said.

He looked again at the bright tongues of hair curving round her head. 'Yes,' he agreed. 'That figures. Battle array!' He lengthened his stride a little, so that she had to stretch her own legs to keep up with him. 'Come on,' he said. 'I'm starving — true to tradition! Rescues always make me hungry!'

They came presently to a bend in the river and a small backwater with a rickety wooden bridge over it that led across to the river bank on the other side of the narrow strip of water. Here, on the edge of the next water-meadow, stood an ancient caravan, propped up on stilts of brick; and beyond it, half-hidden in a tangle of green willows, was a small cottage with a reddish-tiled roof and a jumble of sheds and outbuildings at its side. There was a sizeable pond carved out of the backwater close to the cottage, and here Laurie saw a number of swans and other waterfowl swimming about in peaceful seclusion.

She turned to Clem, her face glowing. 'It's so *quiet*.'

'Mm. Lovely. Nothing to disturb my lodgers.'

The cottage was unlocked, and he shouldered his way in through the kitchen door and set his burden down in a wide, shallow basket filled with dried reeds and grasses, which stood near the old-fashioned kitchen range.

'Just a minute, my friend,' he said gently, and stroked the swan's languid head. 'A nice drink and you'll feel better.'

110

He had a long work-bench, neatly arrayed with a variety of medical supplies and instruments, and he busied himself mixing Complan, glucose and vitamins to counteract the swan's exhaustion and shock.

'Just hold her head up,' he instructed, and when Laurie held the small, gallant head still, he pushed open the swan's beak again and tipped the fluid down. 'Now you can rest,' he said. 'No one'll bother you any more. Just sit still and get strong.' And he gave the swan one last gentle pat and left her alone.

'Bread and cheese?' he asked.'And tea?'

'Wonderful!' breathed Laurie. 'But not a lot. Penny and the kids are cooking supper.' She suddenly felt guilty about being away so long, and glanced round wildly for a clock.

He looked up from cutting slices of bread at the kitchen table and said calmly, 'No need to worry. You were going for a walk anyway.' He slapped some cheese and a knob of butter on to a plate, added a slice of bread and handed it to her. Then he went over to the Aga—which Laurie now realised was alight and keeping the kitchen warm enough for Clem's injured birds—and tipped boiling water from the big, black kettle into a brown teapot.

'Let's sit outside and watch the swans,' he said. 'The rain's stopped.'

They sat together on the kitchen step and ate hunks of bread and cheese and drank scalding tea. They did not talk much, but a sense of companionship and curious unspoken unity was growing between them. They neither of them understood it—neither questioned it. They sat enclosed in a green and watery world—serene and tranquil.

Laurie felt years and years of tension and fear falling away from her—scales of armour, high walls and battlements and last-ditch barricades dissolving like the autumn mists across the river.

At last she stirred and said quietly, 'I must go now.'

He did not try to keep her. He turned on her his slow, gentle smile and nodded agreement. 'I'll come with you to the bridge. Will you be all right from there?'

111

'Of course. It isn't far.'

They stood side by side and gazed at the quiet water. 'I'll see you again,' he said. He was stating a fact, not asking a question.

Laurie looked into his face and answered: 'Yes. You will.'

* * *

But by the end of the week she had not seen Clem again, and Joe was due to come down for another load of vegetables and take Laurie's little party home.

She found that she was dreading it. She did not want to go back to the crowded rooms and dark tensions of The Hide—or to her own pressing problems of housing and maintenance, and lawyers and divorce papers, and social workers and prison officers. (Prison officers? Did she really mean to go and see Jeff? Her mind shuddered at the thought.) She wanted to stay here in the green-gold orchards and hop-gardens of Kent, with the slow old Medway flowing by, and the swans . . . and Clem? Clem *because they know I'm friendly, and it's safe.'*

It wouldn't be difficult just to let things slide and stay down here near Clem and the swans and the peaceful brown river for ever. But she knew she could not. There were things to do. There was a life to be rebuilt—three lives, because Jay and Midge were as damaged as she was by all the violence and stress. They, too, needed security, calmness, a roof over their heads and money coming in; a friendly school to go to, and a real, warm, loving place of their own to come home to—not a battleground. But how she was to achieve all this, she had no idea.

And then there was Penny. Penny of the bright flame-red hair and sturdy common sense and ready laughter. Penny who had attached herself firmly to their lives and had already become a part of it that Laurie would find hard to do without. Penny, who was due to have her own father's bastard child within the next three months, and who also had nowhere to go and nothing to live on except social security. What was she to do with her? Could she really send her back to Jane's hostel—among all those

112

frightened, bitter women with their histories of violence and despair? What kind of a life would it be for her, struggling to bring up her own child and manage everyone else's disturbed children in that dark, overcrowded house?

'That's enough brooding for one day,' said Penny, standing over her with a mug of of tea in her hand. 'Look, the sun's shining. And it's Sunday. No picking—just lazing around.'

Laurie laughed and took the tea from her hand. 'No sign of Joe?'

'There is. And he's got a passenger.'

'Who?'

'They're coming towards you,' said Penny grinning. 'Look!'

Laurie looked up into the warm September sunlight and saw Joe strolling towards her, with Jane beside him. *Jane*? How could she be here? How could she leave the hostel?

She got to her feet and went towards them, leaving Penny to collect the children, who were running about the scuffed field of the camp. 'How lovely!' she said, smiling. 'How did you manage to get away?'

'Joe said I needed a break.' Jane was smiling, too—and looking younger and less harassed out in the mild autumn air.

'So she did!' confirmed Joe, in his bluff growl. 'High time!'

'So here I am.'

'Things to discuss,' went on Joe, and looked from Jane to Laurie with his button-bright knowing eyes.

'Come and have some tea,' invited Laurie, and led them over to their smoky morning fire.

'Tea coming up,' sang out Penny cheerfully, 'And then I'll go and round up the kids.'

It occurred to Laurie that this was all carefully orchestrated, and Penny knew quite well what she was doing. 'Tell me what's going on,' she demanded, and watched Penny walk away across the camp-site to look for Jay and Midge.

'First of all,' said Joe, still with half an eye on Jane's watchful face, 'Stan wants you to stay on another week. Picking isn't finished—and he says your book-keeping is spot-on.'

'Really?' Laurie felt an absurd leap of pride. There was actually something she could do quite well—and get paid for! And they could stay on—another week! Could they? She realised then that it was not only pride she felt but joy—real, simple, bubbling joy. She could stay on—in the green hopfields; near the river; near the swans. Near Clem?

She saw that Jane was watching her gravely. There seemed to be knowledge in those tired, beautiful eyes— knowledge and understanding.

'It would be lovely,' she sighed. 'But . . . there are so many things I should do.' She looked at Jane again, almost with appeal. But then she thought swiftly: No. I mustn't ask Jane to order my life—not any more. I must do it myself. 'There's so much to decide,' she added half to herself.

'Such as?' demanded Joe.

'Well, . . . somewhere to live . . . a job . . . money coming in . . . a school for Jay . . . and . . .' She paused. There was Jeff. Something had to be done about Jeff. She couldn't face it really, but she knew she ought to. Somehow, sometime, she had got to face it. She *must*.

'It's too soon,' murmured Jane, as if reading her thoughts.

'Is it?' She looked at Jane again, almost piteously. 'I'm stronger now. I ought to see him.'

'In prison?'

'He's got no one else.' She spoke without bitterness.

'What do you hope to achieve?' asked Jane.

'Nothing.' Laurie's glance was steady now. 'I know it won't change anything. And I'm not going back on any- thing, either.'

'You want the divorce to go through?'

'Oh yes. I can't go back. I have to manage alone now.' Her voice was calm and full of new resolution. 'But . . .

but he *was* my husband for nine years. And he's in much worse trouble than I am.'

'He asked for it!' growled Joe.

'Yes. But that doesn't make it any better,' said Laurie, and her smile was sad. 'I just feel . . . I ought to see him— once more.'

Jane nodded. 'All right. It will be an ordeal, but it can be arranged.'

'As to the rest, . . .' Joe cleared his throat, and looked— a little anxiously—from one to the other again. 'Gotta proposition.'

Laurie's mind snapped to attention. 'Yes?'

'My Dad,' said Joe, as if it solved everything.

'Your Dad?' Laurie was mystified.

'Gotta small-holding, see? In Cornwall. Grows veges— and daffs in spring. By the sea.' His sharp brown eyes seemed to have a sudden warmth. 'You said you'd like to be by the sea.'

'Oh!' Laurie smiled at him. 'You remembered!'

'Course I remembered.' His own engaging smile flickered briefly out. 'Rang him up, didn't I?' He sounded quite pleased with himself. And then he stopped, suddenly unsure.

'So?' Laurie prompted him.

'Gotta cottage,' he explained. 'Empty in winter. Lets it for the holiday season.' His lively intelligent eyes were dancing with humour now. 'If you can do his books— and, mind, he's worse than Stan at figures—and help with packing veges and daffs, you can have it rent free and get paid a wage on the side.'

Laurie gazed at him, open-mouthed. '*And* get paid? He must be bonkers.'

'No, he's not. Weight-in-gold, book-keeping—I told you. It's kinda like a *tied* cottage.'

Laurie shook her head in disbelief. 'By the sea? Are you sure?'

'Course I'm bloody well sure. Hundred yards down the cliff.'

'No, I mean . . .' she was laughing now—'are you sure he means it?'

'He's my Dad,' said Joe, his mouth one straight, firm line. 'What he says, he means. Getting on a bit. Could do with some help. Sends his stuff up to me for the market by lorry, or by train—especially the daffs. Or some of it goes to the Penzance market and a couple of shops. Gets in a rare old mess with his books, see? All them different orders and prices. You'd be a godsend.' He looked at her sternly. 'Can't have my old Dad done in by his own books, can I?'

Laurie laid a hand on his arm. 'Joe—I think you're the kindest man I've ever known.' Bar one, she thought sadly. But that's another story.

'Rubbish!' said Joe crossly. 'Gotta think of me own, too! My Dad's special, see?'

Laurie and Jane looked at each other and laughed.

'What do you think, Jane?' asked Laurie.

'I think Joe's right—it's a godsend,' said Jane. 'Though maybe not quite the way he meant!' She glanced at Joe affectionately, and then turned back to Laurie. 'You know what the housing people suggested?'

'No?'

'That you go back to Jeff's house and squat in it.'

'*What?*'

'And they'd pay the rent for you—and get another injunction to keep him out.'

Laurie was appalled. 'But . . . it wouldn't keep him out!'

'I know.'

'He'd know where we were . . . I'd never have a moment's peace of mind.'

'Exactly.' Jane's mouth was as straight and hard as Joe's.

'Is that really all they could suggest?'

'Yes. Or a bed-sitter. One room. But there's a waiting list even for those.'

'It's crazy,' said Laurie. 'With Jeff the way he is, . . . there'd be murder done.'

'I quite agree,' snapped Jane.

'So . . .' Laurie was thinking furiously. 'You suggest . . . ?'

'I suggest you accept Joe's offer—with alacrity!'

Laurie looked from one to the other of them and laughed again. Then she grew serious. 'Jane, there's another thing. What about Penny?'

'What about her?'

'Well . . . she's kind of attached herself to us. The kids love her—and she loves them, I think.'

'And you,' remarked Joe surprisingly.

Laurie gave him a fleeting grin. 'Yes. Well. Her baby's due in less than three months. What ought I to do about it?'

'What do you want to do about it?' asked Jane, watching her quietly.

'I . . . I could take her with me. It would be a sort of home, at least. She could keep an eye on the kids while I worked, at first. And later on, maybe we could take it in turns or something. And the baby would fit in with my kids. Once it was born, no one would really question it—Penny would be free to do what she liked.'

'You mean—you'd take the baby on?'

'Why not?' said Laurie, tossing her bright cap of hair in a faintly defiant gesture. 'What's one more? We'd manage somehow—if we could manage at all!' She glanced at Jane. 'It would be . . . a kind of solution.'

'Better than most!' murmured Jane.

'I'll say!' agreed Joe in an approving growl.

'Yes, but . . . after the winter—when we have to move on—what then?'

'I should cross that bridge when you come to it.' Jane was smiling.

Laurie nodded soberly. 'But she'd be more secure with you.'

'No. Not really.' Now Jane was regarding her with a straight, level gaze. 'Love makes security—not a place.'

Yes, thought Laurie. Love, not a place. And a sudden vision of Clem's face bent lovingly over the swan's limp head and his long, gentle fingers stroking its neck came into her mind. She would have to leave Clem and his swans—Clem who seemed to understand everything without being told; whom she was just beginning to trust.

117

But Joe's offer was too good to refuse. The children's safety and happiness depended on it—and Penny's too.

'Then . . .', she said slowly, 'you think Penny ought to come with me?'

'I should ask her,' said Jane.

\* \* \*

Penny, when asked, went very pale—so pale that the freckles stood out on her face like a screen-printed pattern. She looked at Laurie with a kind of desperate candour and said, 'Do you really want me?'

Laurie did not hesitate. She realised suddenly that no one had ever told Penny she was wanted or loved in the whole of her young life—except perhaps her father, in a way that he had no right to use.

'Yes,' she said. 'And so do Jay and Midge.'

Penny's smile was like the sun coming out. 'Then I'll come!' she said.

Jane and Joe looked at one another and nodded their approval.

'What do you think, Jay,' said Laurie, smiling, 'we're going to live in a cottage by the sea!'

'Our *own* cottage?' asked Jay, serious eyes fixed on his mother's face.

'Not our own exactly. It belongs to Joe's Dad. But we can live in it on our own.'

'No Dads,' said Midge suddenly. 'I don't want no Dads.'

Laurie and Jane both sighed and gave Joe a rueful glance. But Penny said sturdily, 'Don't be daft, Midge. Joe's Dad is kind, like Joe. He's letting us have his cottage, isn't he?'

Midge looked doubtful.

'Not all Dads are bad,' said Penny—Penny who had been wronged more than all of them—'are they, Joe?'

'Course not!' growled Joe. 'Mine isn't anyways. The best, my old Dad is. You'll see!' He leant forward and gave Midge a friendly pat. 'You don't mind me, do you, little 'un?'

118

'No,' said Midge. And, as an afterthought, 'You're nice.'

'Glad to hear it.' Joe looked inordinately pleased.

'You bought us an ice-cream,' went on Midge, pursuing a thought.

'Did I, now?' Joe grinned, and got to his feet. 'Gotta load up my veges now. Mind, if anyone was to help me, I might buy them another . . .'

Midge smiled seraphically and took his hand. 'I fought you might,' she said.

* * *

Penny and Jason went with them—protesting laughingly that it wasn't just for the ice-cream—and left Jane and Laurie sitting by the fire. It was still quite warm in the sun, though the late September air was beginning to have a spicy chill to it at night and early morning, and there was a heavy dew on the orchard grass which took a long time to disperse. Laurie had been obliged to buy some second-hand wellingtons for the children from a family who were going home. It was the only way to keep their feet dry—and even so they had long since given up any idea of wearing dry socks. She would have to go back to the little house in London soon, to collect all the clothes she could find. It cost too much to buy new ones, though she was loath to take anything out of the squalid, doom-laden house.

'I like your hair,' commented Jane, smiling. 'More positive!'

Laurie laughed. 'I know. I feel more positive, too.' Then she looked at Jane soberly and added, 'Though I still find it difficult to make decisions.'

'It'll take time.' Jane's voice was full of knowledge. 'It always does.'

That's what Clem said, thought Laurie. It takes time . . . Aloud, she asked suddenly,

'Jane—what is it with Joe? Or with you either, come to that? Why do you bother?'

Jane was still half-smiling, but now a curious expression—almost of anger—flitted across her face. 'Joe,' she said thoughtfully. 'Yes, Joe. Well . . . his wife died of cancer, some five years ago. And his only daughter married a wife-beater. Joe tried to stop her, but she wouldn't listen.'

'Rather like me.'

'Very like you. Only, she died of it.'

'Oh God,' said Laurie. 'How?'

'She got pregnant. And he beat her up. The usual pattern.'

'A miscarriage?'

'Yes.' Jane's voice was hard and bleak. 'They couldn't stop the bleeding. She haemorrhaged all night long—and that was that.'

'Was he . . . ? Did they manage to hold him responsible—the husband, I mean?'

'What do you think? It was an accident . . . She slipped . . . The bruises were inflicted when she fell . . .'

Laurie swore softly. It was a familiar sequence.

'Verdict: accidental death, when it should have been murder. The coroner expressed his sympathy with the bereaved husband. Joe never forgave him.'

'I should think not!'

'But . . .' Jane turned to smile at Laurie—'the result was, when I set up The Hide, Joe volunteered to do all he could to help. He's been a tower of strength ever since.'

'I'll say,' agreed Laurie. 'But I still don't understand why he's so specially kind to me.'

'I think you remind him of Lois—his daughter.'

'Do I?'

'He's never said so. But the way he looks at you sometimes—sort of nostalgic and regretful—I'm sure that's what it must be.'

Laurie was silent—more touched than she knew how to express. At last she said tentatively, 'That leaves you . . . ?'

Jane looked away across the scuffed field with its smoky fires, to the orchards and hop-gardens beyond. Her face was remote and sad—even stern.

'It's a long story, Laurie—and a fairly typical one. Are you sure you want to hear it?'

'Yes,' said Laurie. Please. I do.'

Jane sighed. 'Very well. I watched my mother being abused and reduced to pulp for sixteen awful years. My father was a so-called respectable business man—outwardly charming, and well-liked by his colleagues and friends. But at home he was a tyrant—a sadist and a bully. He frightened my mother to death in the end. She died of a heart attack brought on by a savage beating. By that time my brother had run away to London and disappeared without trace—and I had married the first man that would get me away from my father's house and his appalling violence.'

She was still looking away from Laurie—still far away in thought; still remote and stern.

'What happened?' asked Laurie, somehow convinced that Jane wanted to talk.

Jane turned her head, and a grim smile played round that straight mouth for a moment. 'What you'd expect. The man I married wasn't violent—at least, not until I found out how continuously unfaithful he was. He was away on business a lot, and of course he had women on the side. It was inevitable. But I was fool enough to object—and then he hit out.' Her eyes closed for a moment. 'I put up with it for about a year, but then, my mother died and I came to my senses. I realised I was all set for a repetition of the same pattern. So I upped and ran.'

'Where to?'

'Australia.'

'*Australia*?' Laurie was startled. 'That was far enough!'

Jane laughed. 'You'd have thought so. I was young then, remember. I took a sort of au-pair job with a family going out to settle in Melbourne. I hadn't been there more than a month when the man began making passes, and I realised the job had other unexpected duties! When I threatened to tell his wife, he sacked me on the spot.'

Laurie uttered an explosive sound. 'So you were stranded in a completely strange country.'

'Too right, as they say.' She grinned again. 'By this time, as you can imagine, I had had enough of men. I

121

was totally disillusioned, and aggressive with it. I wanted to hit out at every man I came across. I considered them vain, stupid, violent, possessive and utterly selfish. I vowed to myself that I would never, *never* let one of the ghastly creatures come near me—not ever again!' Her smile was gentler now, full of wry self-knowledge and a kind of unwilling pity for that young, angry girl she used to be.

'How did you survive?' asked Laurie, for this seemed to be the crux of the matter.

'Oh, I worked at all manner of jobs. Chamber-maid in a big hotel—more men trouble there!. Barmaid, ditto. Petrol-pump attendant—waitress—you name it, I've done it!' Her face became bleak again for a moment as she remembered that time. 'Then I got ill. I was picked up in the street with pneumonia and taken to a nearby hospital for the destitute, run by nuns.' Once more her smile glimmered out. 'I think they took me for a local prostitute—and I guess I might have been, except that I hated men so much! Anyway, they were very kind to me. In the end I recovered, and stayed to work in their hospital as a sort of ward orderly.'

She paused, as if almost unwilling to say any more, but Laurie was caught by her story and wanted to know the rest. 'And?' she said.

Jane sighed, and glanced at Laurie half-humorously. 'Well, there I saw the same damn problem all over again. The ward was full of 'em. Broken women of one kind or another. Battered, confused, terrified. Nervous wrecks, alcoholics, drug addicts (anything that gave them a kind of oblivion!)—I saw the lot!' Her voice was dry. 'And I came to realise that my own problem was not unique— there were thousands of us.' She sighed again. 'But then the nuns took me across the road and showed me the other side of the question—the men's ward.'

Laurie looked astonished. 'Men—battered?'

'Oh yes.' Her tone deepened a little. 'It's not all one-sided! A few weedy types who had large aggressive wives! They were just sort of broken and defeated—their pride and masculinity gone. (At the time, I was glad!) But there were others who just couldn't take the nagging—the mental pressure and torment. They had mostly gone over to drink or drugs, too—like the women. One or two had suffered breakdowns—a few had been acutely violent— even served prison sentences—and were suffering from remorse. I hated them most!'

'Yes!' breathed Laurie, remembering Jeff's drunken tears.

'They told me not to waste my sympathy on those— they would only go straight back and beat their wives again—and I believed them. But all the same, I did begin to see both sides of the sorry picture—the wreckage people made of their own lives as well as each others'.'

Laurie sighed. 'How long did you stay there?'

'Over a year. But then the nuns told me to get out while the going was good. They said I was too young to spend the rest of my life dealing with all that human flotsam. They advised me to go and train as a nurse, since I was good with the patients. So I did.'

'Just like that? A whole nurse's training?' Laurie looked surprised.

'Yes. Five years in a Melbourne hospital. When I qualified, I took a job in the outback with the flying-doctor service. We flew all over the place, dealing with emergencies on sheep-stations and ranches and remote farmsteads—and with the Abo settlements. I met a lot of tough, enduring people—and brought a lot more tough, enduring babies into the world, too!'

Laurie laughed. 'How long did all that last?'

'Over ten years.' She hesitated then, and again seemed reluctant to go on. Then she decided she must. 'All that time I still had a profound contempt for men. They were such cowards compared to the women. You should've seen them moaning about a boil on their bottoms from a saddle-sore while their wives struggled with childbirth and sometimes quite horrific complications, and running the farmstead as well!' She glanced once more at Laurie and then went on. 'But then I met someone who changed my whole outlook.' A curiously tender smile seemed to touch her for a moment. 'He was a patient, actually—an ex-farmer—and he'd got cancer. I don't know quite why I fell for him, but I did—and he . . . felt the same. At first I only visited him as a nurse, to give him medication. But in the end I moved in to nurse him.' Her face seemed to soften then, washed by a radiance of memory. 'He was very sick, but he was always optimistic—always gentle and uncomplaining. He seemed to open up a whole new universe for me. I learnt that a man could actually be kind and unselfish—and full of quiet courage.' She sighed a little. 'In fact, he changed a bitter, self-opinionated young woman into a human being!'

Laurie nodded. There was someone she knew herself who could do that for her—who was already beginning to show her a different world of compassion and gentleness. She glanced up at Jane's vulnerable face, not wanting to prompt her any further.

But Jane saw her shy glance and went on steadily enough. 'In the end, of course, he died. Cancer doesn't make any concessions. For a time I was too heart-broken to think. But at last I decided to resign from the flying-doctor service and come home. I got a job as a nurse on a cruise-ship going to Europe, and I came back to London.'

'How long ago was that?'

'About . . . ten years.'

Laurie looked surprised. 'Is that all? I thought . . . how long have you been running the hostel, then?'

'Eight years—nearly nine!' She was smiling now—the shadow of past grief firmly put in its place. 'I made up my mind what I wanted to do while I was coming home on that damned bloated cruise-ship with all its spoiled brats of passengers! I remembered all those women in the hospital—and my mother. I still felt guilty, even after all those years, about walking out and leaving her to face all that alone. And then . . . somehow, Mark had taught me so much about . . .'

'Compassion?' murmured Laurie, remembering how Jane had sat by her bed during those first awful days when she had had the shakes.

'You could call it that,' said Jane awkwardly.

'I could,' smiled Laurie.

There was a pause while each of them sorted out private thoughts. Then Jane said slowly, 'Women have a lot of courage, you know. They are incredibly brave and enduring, really. And loyal. The trouble is, they go on too long with a situation that is impossible.'

Laurie agreed.

'They always believe things will get better—and they don't!'

'I know.'

'And by that time they're nervous wrecks, and they're too exhausted to think straight—or to take any decisions.'

'You . . . don't despise us all for being so weak?'

Jane looked shocked. '*Despise* you? Of course not! And it isn't necessarily weakness that makes you go on enduring something till you break.'

'But it's weakness not being able to pull yourself together and start again!'

Jane laughed, and patted her arm kindly. 'You'll do, Laurie! Give yourself a chance!'

Laurie sighed. 'And you don't . . . hate men?'

Jane's face grew stern again. 'Oh yes, I do. I hate them for what they do to the women—and the children. Particularly the children.' She paused. 'But I also . . . pity them for being so inadequate—so unable to cope with family life.'

Laurie nodded. 'Yes. I hated Jeff. I still shudder when I think of him. But, now that it's all over, I believe I shall end up just being sorry for him.'

Jane patted her again, smiling. 'That's my girl! Women have a lot of dignity, too, you know—and compassion. I just want to see them get all that back, and their independence—their own freedom of spirit.'

'You don't want much!'

'Oh yes, I do!' said Jane, laughing. 'I want the lot!'

They saw Joe returning then, with Penny and the children beside him.

Jane said gently, 'Take this extra week, Laurie. You need it. You're not well yet. And there will be plenty to face when you come back.'

'Yes,' agreed Laurie. 'I know.'

'Besides—' Jane's smile was somehow more aware of things than Laurie had expected—'I think this place is changing your outlook a bit.'

'Do you?' Laurie was giving nothing away.

But Jane was still watching her, still with that faint, approving smile. 'Well, something seems to have given you back a few small springs of hope—hasn't it?'

Laurie nodded, keeping her face hidden.

'Or someone?' Jane's voice was soft.

Laurie looked up, startled—and found herself blushing. 'Could be,' she admitted. Then she added, with swift and surprising warmth, 'Not someone. Several. And you and Joe most of all.'

Before Jane could answer, the children had arrived, carrying dripping ice-cream cones for everyone, and the conversation ended in laughter.

Jane would not stay longer—even though Penny offered to cook them all a meal. She said she must get back. After Saturday nights, Sundays were the busiest and most crucial times at The Hide. That was when most of the emergencies happened—when the terrified victims knocked on her door—and sometimes the angry men came and tried to batter it down. She had left someone in charge, she said, but she'd better get back, just the same. She might be needed.

So she gave little Midge a friendly tweak and ruffled Jason's hair in passing. 'Have a nice week, kids. I'll see you all next Sunday—providing Joe's van is still on its wheels!'

Joe grinned. 'Not on our last legs yet,' he said, and winked at Laurie. 'Grow strong, kid,' he added, unconsciously echoing Clem's words to his swans. Then he turned away and followed Jane across the dusty grass to his old, rusty van.

Behind him, Penny said in a voice that seemed lost between awe and laughter, 'Well—talk about flippin' angels in disguise!'

*   *   *

126

So there was another golden week to spend in the hop-gardens—if the weather held. Laurie could scarcely believe her own luck. And the next six months of winter solved, too. It was almost too good to be true. She was a bit superstitious about luck. For too long, things had always gone wrong for her. It seemed improbable that they could ever go right again—not entirely. Not without something dire happening to spoil it all.

She had felt almost guilty watching Jane and Joe walk away from the green orchards and spicy hopfields to return to the hard grind of their life in London, while she was safe from all that anguish and squalor for another week. She could stay and work in the clean-scented air and watch her children running about in the sun, growing ever browner and more confident. And Penny cheerfully lumbering after them, undismayed by any hardship. And she could sleep at night—an ordinary, tired sleep: dreamless and deep—in the uninterrupted safety of the old hoppers' huts, and wake in the mornings without fear or dread.

And she could wander down to the river to see the swans.

She knew she must talk to Clem sometime, and tell him she was going away. But something deep inside her was loath to say anything, to do anything—to admit even to herself that there was anything more than the most fleeting acquaintance between them. She wasn't ready for relationships—not of any kind. Her mind was more bruised than her body, and it still recoiled from any demand, any emotional tie, any feeling at all beyond a thankful acceptance of exhausted peace.

Clem, with his deep, cloud-shadow grey eyes and slow smile of welcome, and his instant, unspoken understanding, was somehow more than she could bear. She wanted to run from him—run from the beginnings of closeness stirring between them. It was not the time—she could not cope with it. Not yet . . . perhaps never. Everything seemed too fragile: herself, the children and Penny, the golden September sunshine—even Clem and his swans. She felt they might all shatter like thin, transparent glass

127

at the merest touch, the merest breath. The whole bright new world she was beginning to see around her might disintegrate like an exploding bubble if the slightest pressure was put on it.

And yet, even so, something drew her to those dazzling swans on the tranquil river—and to the gentle, quiet man who watched over them.

It was, therefore, in a somewhat confused and contradictory mood that she set out with Penny and the children, after Jane had gone, to walk by the river.

Penny had gone on ahead, with Jason and Midge running in front, when Laurie heard her shout. Jason's voice, too, was raised, and Laurie thought she heard the shrill words, 'Let go!'

Panic-stricken, she began to run. She came tearing round the curve of the river bank and almost ran full tilt into a couple of leering louts who had Jason by both arms and were saying to each other, 'Shall we throw 'im in, then?'

Penny was hitting at them wildly with a stick she had picked up from the grass, but a third, overgrown, gangling youth was grabbing at her from behind. Little Midge, transfixed with horror at yet more violence, was slowly backing away towards a clump of reeds right at the edge of the water.

'Stop that!' shouted Laurie, suddenly far too angry to be frightened. She also seized a stick from a broken piece of fencing and began to lay about her on either side. 'Leave them alone!' she yelled. 'You stupid thugs!' (Whack!) 'Why don't you try someone your own size!' (Thwack!)

'Bleedin' cowards!' joined in Penny, and whacked and thumped with a will.

The three louts let out a few surprised oaths and one or two minor screams, while the tallest one hit out wildly at their supposed victims, catching Laurie a sharp blow on the side of her head. Then they turned and ran. They hadn't expected such painful opposition.

But they had to pass Midge, and she saw them coming.

She took one terrified step backwards, trod on nothing but floating reeds, and fell headlong into the river.

Their attackers gave one scared glance and went on running, making no attempt to rescue Midge. Jason, on the other hand, took a deep breath and plunged straight into the water after her.

'No, Penny!' snapped Laurie—seeing her also go towards the edge of the bank. 'You're too heavy. Stay there to pull us out!' And she too jumped into the oozy reed-bed and reached out for Jason and Midge.

The water was deeper and colder than she expected, and the little girl had already gone under twice, but Jason had got hold of her hair and was gamely holding her head up. But he, too, was almost out of his depth, and his feet were sinking deeper into the river mud with every second. Laurie realised, with a flick of sudden terror, that what had started out as a mere tiresome incident was fast turning into a real tragedy. She floundered out towards the children, kicking her legs to free them from the clinging mud and water-weed.

Penny, meanwhile, had wrenched another, longer piece of paling from the fence and was reaching out with it, hanging dangerously over the water from the crumbling bank. But the stick was too short, and the children were being steadily pulled out into the slow current in midstream.

'Hang on!' called a voice from the river beyond them. 'I'm coming!'

Laurie found herself swimming frantically after the drifting children. She reached Jason just as Clem's ancient punt came across the river with a powerful thrust from his paddle.

'Hold on a minute,' he said calmly. 'I've got the little girl.' And he reached out a strong brown hand and heaved Midge into the punt.

'Now you,' he said to Jason, who had swallowed too much river and was gasping and spluttering. 'Take my hand.'

Then it was Laurie's turn, and she too landed in a sodden heap on the silvery planks of the old punt.

'Is the little girl all right?' asked Clem, manoeuvring the punt into the shallows.

Laurie had already picked Midge up and was instinctively holding her upside down and shaking her. A whole lot of river water suddenly came out of her mouth and she began to splutter like Jason.

'Oh—thank God!' muttered Laurie, and turned her right-side-up and cradled her in her arms. 'It's all right . . .' she murmured to the wet gold head against her shoulder. 'It's all right, Midge—you're safe now.' And she reached out her other hand to grasp Jason. 'Are you OK?'

He nodded, still too choked up to speak. But Laurie saw that his colour was good and he did not look too frightened.

Clem, meanwhile, was looking up at Penny on the river bank and saying kindly, 'No harm done—everyone safe.'

'Oh my God,' said Penny, and promptly sat down on the bank and burst into tears. 'I thought they were goners!'

Clem laughed. 'Look at them! Nothing gone about them!' He turned to glance at his sodden cargo and added, half to himself, 'Quicker by boat, I think.' Then he waved a hand at Penny and said, 'Follow us down river. My house is round the next bend,' and he turned the punt back into the stream with a skilful twist of his paddle.

Before long, they were safe inside Clem's house and he was filling his bath with hot water for them.

'Take everything off', he commanded, 'and get into that bath before you all get a chill. Good thing I lit the stove. I'll lend you some blankets to wrap round you when you come out. Hot tea all round, I think.' And he shut them all in his little bathroom and went off the brew the tea.

Meanwhile, Penny had arrived—breathless and anxious. But Clem just said, 'They're fine. Go and see for yourself. And bring out their clothes. We'll have to dry them over the stove.'

Penny found them immersed in hot water and clouds of steam, washing river mud out of their hair. 'Here,' she said, 'let me help.' And she rinsed off little Midge and picked her out of the bath and wrapped her in a towel. Jason got out next. He decided he was too old to be helped, but he submitted to a hug of relief from Penny when she wrapped the towel round him. Laurie was looking at her own body in the water dispassionately, noting that the heavy bruising over her ribs had not faded yet— though the other marks were getting fainter. When she stood up, Penny saw that there was still a heavily discoloured patch across her back where she had been rammed against the kitchen sink, and it was obviously still stiff and painful when she straightened her spine. 'You poor thing!' said Penny, instinctively wrapping her arms round her, towel and all. 'You must've been frightened to death!'

'We all were,' agreed Laurie, smiling. 'You as well! But it's all right now—thanks to Clem.'

Presently they were all sitting round Clem's stove, draped in blankets, drinking tea. Jason seemed none the worse, though he was rather silent. But Midge was still tearful and clung to Laurie rather too hard. Laurie herself was still pale with fright, and her head was feeling strange again where the glancing blow from the departing thug had hit it, but she looked from the children to Penny and then to Clem with thankfulness. Everyone was safe and warm, and Clem's calm good sense reduced the feeling of crisis to one of companionable adventure.

'You seem to make a habit of rescuing things,' she said, smiling.

Clem laughed. 'Makes a change from swans!'

'How's the one with the fish-hook? Did she recover?'

'Oh yes.' He waved a vague hand towards the kitchen door. 'She's out there with the others.'

'What others?' asked Jason, interested.

'Finish your tea and I'll show you,' said Clem. He eyed Jason's blanket-covered form doubtfully and then added, 'I could fix you up with a T-shirt and some shorts. They'll be miles too big—but I daresay a belt would hold 'em up!'

He went off to look for them upstairs, and returned with an armload of clothes for them to try. 'You'll look absurd,' he said to Laurie, grinning, 'but at least they'll

131

be dry!' He glanced at Penny and added with a gleam of mischief, 'Good thing I haven't got to fix you up, too!'

'It'd be like the Battle of the Bulge,' agreed Penny, laughing.

'I'm going to feed my birds,' he announced, withdrawing with tact. 'See what you can do.' And he left Penny in charge of the pile of garments.

When they were all more or less clothed, they looked at each other and fell about laughing. An old blue T-shirt reached nearly to Jason's knees, and the sleeves hung down like dangling scarves. He had tied Clem's khaki shorts on with a piece of string, but, as they were almost invisible under the T-shirt, it didn't matter how baggy they looked. Midge was wearing another towelling T-shirt, also down to her ankles, like a nightdress tied in the middle with a piece of orange twine; and Laurie had climbed into a faded pair of jeans, far too big but not so bad with the ends turned up and a belt holding the waistband in, and another elongated T-shirt over the top.

'Well, he said we'd look absurd,' she said, giggling helplessly.

Clem, hearing the laughter, put his head round the door. 'That's better!' he said—though it was not clear whether he meant the clothes or the laughter. 'Who wants to come and help me feed the birds?'

Jason was the first to follow him. But in the end they all trooped outside to have a look.

There were half a dozen swans swimming quietly on the little pond that Clem had made for them, and several pairs of mallards. There were also coots and moorhens that Clem said had no right to be there but he hadn't the heart to disturb them. There was also a tall, grey heron with a damaged bill, and a couple of seagulls who had been brought in with their feathers oiled. And there was one wet, sleek head that came swimming towards him as the birds all sailed up for their expected food.

'What's that?' asked Jason, pointing.

'That? Oh, that's Jaunty. He's an otter I found in an eel-trap farther down river, near the estuary.'

'An *otter*? . . . I've never seen a real live otter before.'

'Not many people have, these days,' replied Clem. 'They're getting rarer and rarer.' His voice was sad.

'Why?'

'Oh, various reasons. People hunt them and kill them.'

'What for?' The boy's question was entirely innocent, but Clem looked down at him and sighed.

'Search me. They can't eat 'em. They don't use their fur. And the poor creatures don't do much harm to anyone — except take a few fish. And I reckon they're as much entitled to the fish in the river as men are. More so, really — because men can eat something else!'

Jason's eyes were on the beautiful, intelligent head thrusting out of the water to look at them. 'I don't know how they can hurt them!' he muttered.

'It's not only the hunters — the rivers get polluted, the reeds get cut down and the dredgers move in. All the wild, secret places where otters like to live are gradually disappearing. That's why Jaunty stays around — it's quiet here, and no one can cut down his reeds and willows.'

'Do you own it?'

Clem hesitated. 'Well, . . . sort of. It's rather complicated. When I stopped being a town vet, my partner bought me out, so I had some money to spare. And then the wildlife people and I got together, and between us we bought this cottage and as much land round it as we could afford. No one can cut anything down now. It's registered as a nature reserve and a bird sanctuary.'

'I'm glad,' said Jason simply.

He watched, fascinated, as Clem threw out some carefully balanced food for his convalescent swans, and delved into another blue plastic bucket to find a small fish, which he tossed in the air for Jaunty.

'The thing is,' he said seriously to Jason, 'you mustn't feed them too much, or they'll never go away and forage for themselves. But some of these swans are still a bit weak, and they need a little extra help, and some vitamins and things.'

'What about Jaunty?'

'He had an injured leg. It made swimming very difficult, and he was too slow to catch a fish. But now he's much better. He goes farther afield each time. Sometimes he stays away for several days, but he usually comes back for an extra tit-bit.' He smiled at Jason's round eyes. 'Would you like to throw him a fish?' He handed the boy a small, silvery minnow. 'The trouble is,' he went on, watching that alert, clever head in the water, 'otters get too friendly.'

'*Too* friendly?' Jason sounded amazed.

'Yes. I mean, too tame—too dependent on human beings. They like company. They like feeling safe and secure . . . and then they find it hard to go away.'

His eyes were still on the bewhiskered face in the water, but Laurie felt sure he was not only talking about the friendly otter.

'Do they have to go away?' asked Jason wistfully.

The big, quiet man at his side glanced at him sympathetically. He understood the sadness in the boy's voice—the longing to be safe and secure, like Jaunty . . . to have someone big and safe to turn to—like Clem himself.

'Yes,' he said firmly. 'They do. They have to learn to be independent—and free. That's what they were born to be.' His eyes strayed for a moment to Laurie's face, rapt and vulnerable beside him, and he saw a curious, brilliant look of recognition and resolve flash into it.

'But of course,' he went on softly, 'if they return now and then for a spot of comfort and reassurance, I'm only too pleased to see them. Only, it has to be up to them!'

Jason nodded wisely. 'I see,' he said.

Laurie said nothing at all.

Eventually the dignified swans decided they had exhausted Clem's bucket of food and sailed gracefully away to preen themselves in the shallows. The moorhens and coots chugged busily in and out among the lily-pads, and the brown mallards finished off the crumbs on the surface, wagged their tails and swam off into the green shade of the willows. Only Jaunty remained, and he dived and swam and displayed his lissom agility in the water for a few minutes, stood on his head and then on his hindlegs, and smiled at them from the middle of the pond as if to say, 'See? I'm better now. Aren't I clever? Aren't

I handsome? Don't you think I'm worth knowing?' And then he dived deep and swam away from them towards the main flow of the river.

'There he goes!' said Clem, smiling affection clear in his voice. 'But he'll be back.'

'Will he?' There was regret in Jason's voice, and in his expressive face.

'Of course. Sometime or another.' His smile rested on Jason. 'Maybe tomorrow—or the next day. He won't forget me now.'

Jason sighed. He could not express the curious ache that was in his mind.

'You know,' said Clem, looking up at the sun judiciously, 'unless you want to go back looking like Worzel Gummidge, you'll have to stay for lunch—or is it tea?'

'Oh, but . . .' Laurie began to protest.

'No buts,' he said calmly. 'I've got some tins in my larder. I'm not a bad cook.'

'Nor am I,' volunteered Penny, smiling. 'Just show me where.'

Laurie was watching Penny's face, noting her paleness under the freckles, and the shadows under her eyes. Clearly she had been as frightened as Laurie—and probably more shaken, for she had been struggling with one of the louts as well.

'Penny, . . . are you sure you're all right?' she asked suddenly, out of some deep anxiety.

The girl's ready, cheerful smile broke out again. 'Course I am. Now that you're all safe and sound! Takes more than a bit of a fight with some thugs to throw me!'

Clem was looking from her to Laurie, and shaking his head. 'I only came round the bend of the river in time to catch a glimpse of them running away. But they looked fairly tough to me.'

'What did they want?' asked Laurie, mystified. 'Why pick on Penny and a couple of small kids?'

'They probably thought it was just a lark,' said Clem. 'These mindless hooligans do!' He paused, his face set into grim lines again. 'As a matter of fact, I think I know

135

them. They're the same lot I caught tormenting a swan the other day.'

'What were they doing to it?' asked Jason.

'I'd rather not tell you.' Clem's face was stern. 'But they'd tied it to a willow branch, near their camp-fire.' He pointed across the water. 'There he is. His feathers are beginning to grow again, but the singed parts are still a bit brown.'

'It's diabolical!' Laurie exclaimed.

'Oh yes,' agreed Clem. 'It is. And there was one this week that I couldn't save. Her neck was broken.' For a moment there was such anger and grief in his voice that Laurie was startled. But then he seemed to recollect that he had four shocked and distressed human beings on his hands—besides the swans. 'Come on,' he said. 'A hot lunch is what we all need. Yes, I think I know those nasty sadistic louts. I'll have a word with the village bobby. He's on my side already!' He glanced at little Midge, who was still clinging to Laurie's hand. She could so easily have drowned. 'What a good thing you have such a brave and resourceful brother!' he said gently, and saw a flush of pleasure rise in Jason's face at the unexpected praise.

It was at this point that Laurie suddenly passed out. Without warning, the river bank began to spin, the sky wheeled and went black, and she fell like a stone at Clem's feet.

Midge screamed. Jason came running. Penny stooped over her and tried to raise her head. But Clem simply picked her up in his arms, carried her indoors and laid her down on his lumpy old sofa in the corner near the stove.

'It's her head,' explained Penny, looking down at her anxiously. 'She's got a hairline fracture anyway, and I think one of them louts managed to hit her.'

Clem nodded quietly. 'She'll come round in a minute.' He turned to the children, his voice calm. 'There's an old sponge and a bowl in my sink. Bring a drop of water.' He knew that action of some kind would reduce panic. Already Midge had stopped crying and was following Jason. They returned, carefully carrying a bowlful of water, and he showed them how to bathe Laurie's forehead, which did indeed have a new angry red lump on it, and how to hold the cold sponge against her pale and throbbing temples. 'But don't entirely swamp her,' he added, smiling. 'She's already been half-drowned once today!'

In a few moment, Laurie's eyelids began to flutter and the desperate pallor began to recede from her face. She opened her eyes to find a ring of anxious faces looking down at her. 'Sorry,' she muttered, struggling to sit up. 'What hit me?'

Clem smiled. 'A thug's fist, I should think.' He glanced from her to Penny, and laid a quiet hand on her shoulder, pushing her gently back. 'You rest there a while. Penny and I will see about some lunch, and Jason and Midge can lay the table—can't you?' He turned his slow, reassuring smile on the children.

'Yes,' agreed Jason, and reached out to touch Laurie's face with a strangely adult gesture. 'You stay there, Mum. We can manage.'

'Manage!' agreed Midge, and followed the others away on tiptoe.

Thankfully, Laurie lay back and waited for the world to right itself. Her head still felt strange and throbbed with a dull kind of ache, but this was lessening steadily. She would be all right in a minute . . .

Penny was good at whipping up scratch meals out of tins—even with only a kitchen range to cook on. But she discovered that Clem also had a small electric boiling-ring which he mostly used to sterilize instruments, and between the two she soon had a savoury concoction of corned beef, baked beans, tinned tomatoes, spinach out of Clem's vegetable patch, and fresh mushrooms from the fields. She set it down in triumph on the kitchen table. By this time Laurie had recovered sufficiently to sit down beside them all and to comment on the delicious smell—mostly from Clem's herb patch outside the back door. It even made her feel quite hungry.

Before the meal was over, Midge's head began to droop

against Laurie's arm. The excitement of the day had been too much for her.

'Put her down on the sofa,' said Clem softly. 'It's a bit lumpy, but she probably won't notice!'

Carefully, Laurie laid the sleepy child down and covered her with a blanket. Midge stirred a little, and clutched at Laurie's hand, but she soon sank into sleep again.

Penny, with her eyes on Laurie's pale face, said easily, 'I think Jay and I'll go and have a look round, while you have a rest.' She turned enquiringly to Clem. 'If that's all right by you?'

'Of course,' agreed Clem. 'Just go quietly—so that you don't disturb the birds.'

Laurie watched them go and thought in panic: I don't know what to say to this man. How can I explain what has been happening to me—or how I feel?

But Clem surprised her. 'When are you going away?' he said.

Laurie gazed at him in wonder. 'Not till . . . the end of the week.'

'And then?'

Haltingly, she explained about Joe and the cottage that went with the job in Cornwall. 'I've got to take it,' she explained. 'It's a godsend, really—and just what they all need just now.'

Clem nodded thoughtfully.

'And I . . . I wanted to be near the sea.' Her voice was strange and dreaming. 'It seemed to be the only way . . . to feel clean.'

He did not comment on this. But he said suddenly, 'Can they swim?'

'What?'

'The children—can they swim?'

Laurie's face seemed to go even paler. 'N-no. As you saw today, Jay can just keep afloat. But Midge . . .'

'Bring them here,' he said.

She stared at him. 'What?'

'Bring them here. Every day—after work. The bit of

138

backwater I've cleared is quite clean—and not too deep or muddy.'

'But . . .'

'*Every day!*' he said decisively. 'I can teach them in a week. At least I can make them safe in the water. I used to be a lifeguard once.'

'Did you?' she sounded totally confused.

He smiled at her stunned expression. 'Listen,' he said. 'You know as well as I do that you nearly lost little Midge today. If it hadn't been for your young son, you probably would have. And he was none too safe, either!'

Laurie took a shaky breath. 'I know.'

'Well, then—it makes sense. We'll make them as safe as we can in the time. Penny, too—even in her condition she can learn to float!' He laughed, and added cheerfully, 'The water's fairly warm at this time of year—after the summer—and swimming is quite good for pregnant ladies, I believe.'

'How do you know?' asked Laurie, laughing.

He laughed, too. 'Stands to reason. They're buoyant in the water—takes a weight off their feet!'

They were still laughing when Penny and Jason came back. Nothing serious had been said—nothing sad or perilous or important—but Laurie felt strangely comforted. Clem knew how she felt. He accepted her going. He even understood about the sea, and her unquenchable longing to be scoured clean by the blowing sands and sharp, fierce winds and deep sea-swell of the Atlantic shore. Maybe, one day, she would feel clean again, and new again, and ready for other people to come near. Maybe, one day, she would return to this quiet backwater, like the swans—like Jaunty the otter, who knew where he would be welcome.

But in the meantime there was this last golden week—and a swimming lesson every day! And Jason and Midge already accepting Clem as a safe and friendly companion, not an enemy. Particularly Jay. There was a natural bond growing between them, for Jason loved wild creatures too—that was already clear. And Clem's eyes, resting on the boy, were full of warmth. He loves Jason, she thought. He already loves Jay—where is this quiet man leading *me*?

'What's the joke?' asked Penny, smiling.

'You are,' grinned Laurie. 'You don't know it, but Clem's going to teach you to swim!'

'Me?' said Penny, with a hand on her swollen stomach. 'Are you sure?'

'All of you!' stated Clem. 'Starting tomorrow!'

'Smashing!' breathed Jason, his face aglow.

'No,' said Clem gravely, unable to suppress a twinkle. 'Not smashing, Jay. *Swimming!*'

\* \* \*

Clem was a quiet man. Quiet, and slow to anger. But, when he thought about it, he realised that he was very angry indeed—so angry that he couldn't keep still, So he set out to walk it off along the river bank.

It was peaceful by the river. Long evening shadows lay across the water-meadows from the tall old elms, and the westering sun cast a veil of gold over the slow-moving water. A coot called in the stillness, and somewhere down among the tangle of willows a warbler was trilling a late song. Clem knew every inch of that river bank. He recognised each tree, each clump of reeds, each stooping willow trailing green fingers at its own reflection; and he knew most of the water birds and wild creatures that it sheltered—even the water-rats. It was a calm world, enclosed and green—and infinitely soothing. But Clem wasn't soothed.

He knew, when he considered it, that his anger was out of all proportion. Those mindless louts who tortured his swans, and bullied young Jason and frightened little Midge into the river, were not really monsters. They were ignorant and crass, yes—probably a bit sadistic, too, like a lot of boys—but not monsters. And yet he wanted to kill them. They had hit Laurie and scared her children, when violence still cast far too real a shadow over them— when they were all just beginning to come out into the sun and smile. And he couldn't bear to see that new bright radiance quenched.

140

That told him something about himself that he did not know, or had not quite admitted. Was it possible that in so short a space of time another human being could come to mean so much to him? Yes, of course it was. He had seen the unwilling recognition in her eyes, too. Maybe she did not want to acknowledge it, either—and, knowing a little of her history, he could understand why. But it was there—that unspoken, unlooked-for bond growing between them—and he was as afraid of it as she was.

For a long time now, Clem had walked alone. By choice. He found the company of his wild creatures easier to deal with—and far more rewarding. He had sworn, when the final show-down had come with Sylvia, that he would never again allow a human being to come close enough to shatter his life and destroy him. And here he was, caught inextricably like one of his own swans in a tangle of fishing twine—by a small, slender girl with bruised, shock-dilated eyes and a smile as fragile as glass.

Sylvia had not been fragile. She had been very sure of herself. Glossy and secure. And while he was out night after night on call, as a busy vet always was, she had her fun. He hadn't known about it at first, but he got to know. One always did get to know about betrayal. But when it turned out to be his own partner—his friend and colleague—it had been the last straw. It was also the last (almost the only) time he had allowed himself to get really angry. When Sylvia laughed, he had found himself trying to throttle her. And when his friend and partner had intervened, he had knocked him down. Then he had fled—appalled at the rage within him.

Rage, he knew, was a killer. And he wanted no part of it—not any more. Not ever again. he had resigned from his practice—let his partner take over his share, and his wife as well. He had walked out on the tame pussy-cats and overfed poodles and their well-heeled owners, just as he had walked out on Sylvia and her glitzy suburban bedroom and her mocking laughter. He had left the lot and fled to this green and golden sanctuary behind the tangled willows, and devoted his life to the simple needs of wild creatures in distress. It was a long time ago now, and he had built a good, quiet life for himself here. He loved his work and the trust and affection that he managed to build up between his frightened patients and himself. And his weekly lectures in the evening institute kept him on his toes. He quite liked imparting knowledge, and he supposed any interest that the public had in wild life ought to be fostered. It might eventually stop even louts like those river-bank thugs from being quite so mindlessly cruel.

It was a calm, steady enough existence. It filled his days and nights with unceasing activity. There were always new crises, new challenges to be met, new battles to be won or lost. He felt reasonably useful and content. And when he saw a newly mended wing take flight, or a broken leg move comfortably in the water, he knew he was well rewarded. So why this sudden, searing anger? He knew why. And he knew what anger did to him. And he was afraid.

It was at this point in his thoughts that he rounded a bend on the river bank and came upon the three young louts in question. They were stooping over something on the ground and, judging by its squeals of fright and pain, they were up to their usual tricks.

Clem strode forward. This time it was a kitten, and they seemed to be intent on burning its fur off with a cigarette-lighter. The tiny, bedraggled creature mewed its terror in a diminishing wail, and looked at Clem out of desperate, dilated eyes.

'What the hell d'you think you're doing?' he thundered, towering over them like an avenging angel.

They did not at first recognise Clem's strength, or his anger. One of them looked up, grinning, and said, 'Got oiled, see? We're burning it off.'

'Oh not you're not!' shouted Clem, a red rage getting into his eyes.

Two of the scruffy boys got up then, and one of them drew out a flick-knife whose wicked blade flashed in the sun.

'Who says?' he sneered.

Clem was just about to tackle all three of them at once—

knife and all—when another spurt of bright flame farther off caught his eye. Close to them, in the field that flanked the edge of the hop-garden, Stan, the farmer, was using a flame-gun to burn off the long grass in a last-ditch attempt to ward off the dreaded plague of red spider that was creeping down the valley. He was quite close to the tow-path, and now he came over to see what the trouble was.

Clem, still hugely angry, took one long stride towards him. 'Here, Stan,' he said, 'lend me that. There's a few weeds over here I want to get rid of.'

Straight-faced, Stan handed over the flame-gun, taking in at a glance the belligerent trio and the terrified kitten at their feet.

Casually, Clem advanced on the disbelieving louts. He held the gun to the side of him so that its flame and searing heat shot out and withered the dying September grasses in one hot blast. It was close to the boys, but not too close.

'Put that kitten down,' he said.

The third boy, now thoroughly scared, dropped the kitten on the ground and backed away. Clem pointed the flame to the other side of him, and another yellowing swathe of grasses crackled and died.

'Now you know,' he said pleasantly, 'how it feels to have your fur scorched off. Move back.'

The three seemed paralysed by the flame-gun, though at no time did Clem actually point it at them. Instead, he steadily and remorselessly diminished the little space they stood on, and drove them back towards the edge of the river. Careful, he said to himself. Don't get too angry. Don't let it get out of hand. When one of them tried to break and run, he innocently turned the gun on another clump of thistles just beyond them, and they stopped, dismayed. Clem smiled. But even in the rage that consumed him, he kept the bright tongue of fire just far enough away.

The boy with the flick-knife, who seemed both cockier and more vicious than the others, suddenly lunged wildly at Clem's arm. But he was afraid of that darting flame and he missed his aim, only tearing the sleeve of Clem's old tweed jacket.

'Keep away,' said Clem. 'You don't want to get hurt.' He let the flame-gun attack yet another tall tussock of grass.

The boy took one step backwards too many and fell with a splash into the muddy reed-bed.

'Very wise,' said Clem. 'Much cooler in there.'

The space where the boys stood was still untouched, but the second lout lost his nerve and stepped unwarily on to the oozy reeds and sank up to his knees.

Clem looked at his friend Stan, and saw that he was grinning from ear to ear. He turned the flame-gun away from the bank, meaning to hand it back to the cheerful farmer, but the third boy mistook his intention and jumped into the river after his companions without being asked. Clem turned the gun off and handed it to Stan. 'Thanks,' he said. 'Very useful.' Then he stooped down and gathered up the terrified kitten and gently thrust it inside his coat.

He stood for a moment watching the boys flounder among the broken reeds and lily-pads. It wasn't very deep just there, and they weren't in any danger, but it was certainly muddy. 'Oh, come on, Stan,' he said at last. 'Let's give them a hand.'

Together, they leant out across the mud-caked bank and pulled the dripping boys on to dry land. They were a sorry sight. Weed clung to their hair and dangled in wet, green strands round their sodden jeans. They looked thoroughly shaken, but Clem wasn't a bit sure they had got the message. In fact, he was a bit afraid he might have made things worse for his patients in the sanctuary. There was still a spark of venom in the eyes of the knife-carrier — though the knife itself seemed to have sunk in the watery ooze of the river bed.

He looked at them and spoke crisply. His anger was cooling now, and he was a bit ashamed of it, but he thought he'd better make things doubly clear.

'I could, of course, go to see my friend Sergeant Moss and tell him you assaulted a woman with a stick, knocked down a pregnant girl, twisted a small boy's arm, and frightened a four-year-old girl into the river and then ran away and left her to drown.' His glance was cold. 'Not to mention burning the wing feathers off a swan and the fur off a kitten. Quite a catalogue, isn't it? You, on the other hand, could also go to Sergeant Moss and tell him I waved a flame-gun and forced you into the river yourselves. Shall we call it quits?'

They looked at him wetly and sulkily, but they did not answer. They had been in trouble with Sergeant Moss before. There was always trouble at hop-picking time, and he was used to it. They would cut no ice with him, and they knew it.

Then Stan took a hand. He fixed the flick-knife owner with a beady eye and said, 'Jim Slattery's boy, aren't you? I know you. Better cut along before I tell your Dad. Tan the hide off you, he will—especially if I was to mention attacking Mr Harper with a knife.'

The boy got to his feet, muttering something about 'I didn't touch 'im.'

'Just as well,' snapped Stan. 'Criminal offence, that is. And I'm a witness, mind. Now get along.'

The three of them looked from him to Clem. It seemed to them that they didn't have much choice. They got along. In fact, they took to their heels and ran.

Clem looked after them and sighed. 'Will it do any good?'

'Dunno,' shrugged Stan. 'Always in trouble, that one.'

'I lost my temper, Stan.'

The farmer grinned and clapped him on the shoulder. 'I'll say—and a right old mess you made of your river bank!'

Clem began to laugh. But he was still a bit shaken by his own towering anger. If Stan was surprised, he did not show it. Like the rest of the village, he knew Clem as a mild and gentle man. But it did not seem to him unreasonable to get angry about senseless cruelty like that. Do them a power of good.

'I'm off to the Bull,' he said. 'Dessay you could do with a pint after that.'

145

Clem looked down at the singed little bundle under his coat. 'Yes—when I've fixed up this little fellow. I'll follow you down.'

But when he got to the Bull, intending to get very drunk, he somehow found that he could not. He sat staring into his drink and seeing, behind the smoky haze of the pub, Laurie's cropped golden head and pale, resolute face as she told him how she wanted to go to the sea and swim till she felt clean.

Damn it all, he thought, if I ever caught up with that husband of hers I'd get him with more than a flame-gun! No one should be allowed to make a girl look like that. He was surprised at his own anger which was still burning inside him, and had nothing whatever to do with the boys on the river bank. No. It went much deeper than that. And anger as deep and fierce as that was somehow very close to love.

'Same again?' said Stan, seeing his absent stare, and wondering a little about it. But he was much too wise to ask.

'Why not?' agreed Clem, and held out his glass for more.

\* \* \*

Jason was a bit worried by that encounter with the thugs on the river bank. Not that he'd been frightened, of course—a boy his age ought not to be scared by three weedy louts who tried to twist his arm. He had met bullies at school, and in the street. He knew how to take care of himself. But they had frightened Midge, so that she nearly drowned, and made Penny so wild she fell over, and they had actually hit his Mum and made her head bad again, and that would not do. Since he was the man of the family now, he knew he ought to protect his Mum and Midge. It was his job. He ought to make sure they were looked after, and he had made a private promise to himself that no one was ever going to hit his Mum again. And now they had, and he was troubled. Was it going to be like that all over again, wherever they went? And would he be strong enough to prevent it? He hadn't been this time—

146

though he had managed to go after Midge and hold her up till Clem got there. But what kind of a help was he going to be to his Mum if he couldn't even manage those boys on the river bank?

He was not really surprised by the new violence. There had always been violence in his young life. It wasn't only at home, he knew. It was all round him—even in the hopfields when fights broke out. But, even so, he was worried about how to protect his family. So he went to ask the only person he knew who was strong enough and kind enough to look after them all—his new friend, Clem.

He arrived, breathless from running down the tow-path, and found Clem feeding his birds. He watched him for a moment in silence, trying to get his breath, and wondering how to explain his problem.

But Clem forestalled him. 'Well, Jason? What's on your mind?'

The boy hesitated, and then said obliquely, 'Does swimming make you strong?'

Clem smiled. 'It does. Strong, and independent.'

'How soon?'

Clem looked in surprise at the anxious little face beside him. 'Well—not all at once. It takes time.' And then, seeing the boy's disappointment, 'Why?'

Once again Jason hesitated, as if he could not find the right words. But at last he said shyly, 'It's Mum. And Midge.' He paused, and then added as an afterthought, 'And Penny, too, really.'

'What about them?'

The boy looked up trustfully, sure that Clem would know the answer. 'How can I keep them safe?'

Something seemed to change in Clem's eyes then. They grew so dark and so filled with sudden grief that Jason almost faltered. He thought he saw the glitter of tears behind them—but of course that couldn't be true.

Dear God, thought Clem. *How can I keep them safe?* He's only eight years old, and he asks me that?

'Jay,' he said at last, and laid a warm, comforting arm round his shoulders. 'You *have* kept them safe—all of them. But it shouldn't be nearly so bad from now on.'

Jason looked at him straight. 'It was bad by the river.'

'Yes, I know. But that was a one-off thing. It won't happen again.' He smiled at the boy's doubtful face and added quietly, 'I've dealt with those lads. They won't come back.'

Jason nodded sagely. 'I thought you would. But . . . there'll be other times.' There was a world of flat knowledge in the young voice, and it cut Clem to the quick.

'Yes, Jay, there will,' he said gently. 'But they won't be important.'

The boy looked puzzled. 'Not important?'

Clem pointed a brown finger across the pond to where Jaunty, the little otter, was playing in the shallows.

'Remember him? Young Jaunty? When I first got him, life had been very bad for him. He was frightened of everything. He even bit me when I tried to help him. If a bird-scarer went off in the orchard, he nearly died of fright. But now—' he glanced at Jason, wondering how much more he needed to say— 'he's strong again. He can cope with anything that comes his way. I don't have to protect him any more.'

There was a silence while Jason thought about this. Then he said slowly, not looking at Clem, 'Mum's nearly well.'

'Yes, Jay, she is.'

'But Midge is still little.'

Clem laughed. 'Give her time, Jay. She'll grow.' He gave his shoulders an affectionate squeeze. 'Of course you'll need to look after them—I know that. But not nearly so much as before.'

He wondered if he had taken any of the absurdly heavy burden of care from those young shoulders, or if he had only made matters worse.

Jason looked out over the little brown pond to where Jaunty the otter was chasing his tail. 'I wish . . .' he began, and then knew somehow that he must not say it. Instead, he turned it into another thought which was equally true. 'I wish I was bigger.'

Clem's smile was wide and loving. 'Do you? You seem pretty big for your age, one way and another.' He stooped

148

down to his feeding-buckets and found a fish for the otter. 'Here. Give Jaunty a treat. He might turn a somersault.'

Jason threw the fish high in the air so that it glinted in the sun, and Jaunty leapt to catch it and did indeed turn a somersault. Then he came up in a swirl of brown water and laughed at them both in the sun.

'There!' said Clem. 'That's how life's going to be, Jay, from now on. All sunshine and somersaults.'

Jason looked at him seriously. 'I don't think Penny could turn a somersault right now.'

Clem began to laugh again. 'Not now, perhaps,' he said, still chuckling. 'But she will, Jay—she will!'

And there was such certainty in his voice that Jason almost believed it.

\* \* \*

When it came to it, Clem was very clever with Midge. He had already worked out for himself that she would be scared of the water, after falling in so dramatically the day before. So he took her to see one of his patients—a mallard duck whose wing had been shattered by shot, but who was just about ready to go back on the water.

'She'll be scared at first,' he said, stroking the bird's iridescent head. 'But you're littler than me, so she won't mind you so much.'

Midge looked pleased.

'Do you think you could hold her like this? With your hands round her wings so that she can't struggle? . . . Very gently, mind. . . .' Talking all the way, he led Midge down to the shallow reaches of the backwater. 'Now,' he said, 'take her out as far as you can into the water so that she's got plenty of room to move her legs. . . . That's it. . . . Walk on a bit. . . .'

Gently, bit by bit, he coaxed Midge on until she was standing waist-deep in the water, with her small, brown feet placed firmly on the sandy bottom that he had dredged out with so much care for his birds.

'Now!' he said. 'Let her go . . . And watch what she does with her feet. She's a brave little bird—she'll soon get her balance.'

149

Midge took another step forward and opened her hands and let go. For a moment the bewildered mallard did not know where she was, but almost at once she felt the familiar, comforting buoyancy of the water under her, and she thrust out happily with her strong webbed feet and swam away.

'Oh!' cried Midge. 'Look at her go!'

Clem smiled. 'D'you see how she paddles with her feet? One-two, one-two—like a little steam engine. If you lean forward on my hands, you can do it, too.'

'Can I?' Midge was doubtful.

'Then you could follow her. Look—she's going to join her friends over there.'

'Won't we frighten her if we splash?' asked Jason, close beside them.

'No.' Clem shook his head. 'Good swimmers don't splash!' His smile was full of mischief. 'Besides, none of my birds are frightened here. They know it's safe.' His glance met Jason's. Messages were given and received.

Midge looked at the swans sailing peacefully up and down, and the cheerful mallards quacking among themselves in the shade of the willows, and the cheeky moorhens darting in and out among the reeds. 'I'm not frightened, too,' she announced. And she leant forward on Clem's outstretched arms and kicked her legs out behind her, trying to swim like a duck.

Clem's eyes met Laurie's this time—over the top of Midge's head. He did not speak. But the first battle had been won.

\* \* \*

Clem was well aware that Laurie had won a battle too. Several, in fact. She trusted him now, and was even beginning to allow that unspoken bond between them to grow unchecked. But he knew, all the same, that he must go carefully. Very carefully and slowly. Like he did with Midge. It would take a long time—a long, slow time of growth and discovery—before she, too, learnt to be unafraid, to believe in happiness again—to turn somersaults? A smile twitched his mouth as he remembered Jason's

150

serious young face. He had been quick to understand—with Jaunty and the otter as a living example. But what Clem had not told him—perhaps had not even told himself—was how long it took.

His swans, now—they had to fly free and strong before they made their own choice to go or return. He never held them back. But it took time—time for things to heal; time for the moment of choice. Time.

Normally, Clem was patient. He had learnt to be in a hard, exacting school. You couldn't hurry things. You couldn't banish fear and built up trust overnight. But, he had to admit, with Laurie it was different. He didn't want to be patient at all. He was a naturally loving man—loving and protective. All his instincts made him want to put his arms around her and comfort her—like Jay . . . like Midge. To hold her tight against all comers and protect her from every hurt. *Smother her?*

Of course, he could not. Like Jaunty, like his swans, she had to find her own way, her own strength and independence, her own courage—not rely on his. What he had said to Jason, he must put into practice himself. But it was hard. He hadn't realised how hard it would be—to let her go and say nothing. Nothing that would put that wary, cautious look back in those anxious eyes. Only just enough warmth to let her know that he was there—would always be there—when she needed him.

But it seemed a bit tame and craven-hearted somehow, and he badly wanted to do something wild and incautious. But he knew, all too well, how his injured wild creatures shrank away if he made a sudden movement—how they froze into immobile terror and looked at him out of dark, dilated eyes. No—he couldn't do that to Laurie. He couldn't—however much his arms ached to hold her. Not now.

But, in the meantime, there was this last golden week, and the swimming lessons. Time to let her confidence grow a little more. Time to let their closeness flower like the water-lilies in the sun. So long as he said no word.

\* \* \*

151

So, each warm evening, after a day in the hop-fields, they all swam together in the little backwater—keeping to the open, sunny side so as not to disturb Clem's shyer birds among the reed-beds. But for the most part the swans and mallards took little notice of them and only came swimming up close to the bank when Clem stood on it with their evening meal ready for them in the blue plastic bucket they had come to know.

Laurie felt the cool river water round her like balm. She had told Joe she wanted the sea, but this silken water was a kind of cleansing, too . . . Scales and callouses; bruises and the grasp of hard, unloving hands—they all seemed to wash off in the river's quiet embrace. If I was a snake, she thought, I could slough my skin and come out all new and shiny. And each day she felt the sense of healing and newness grow within her.

Even Penny felt rested by the river. She floundered in it, rather like a fat and lazy seal, and Clem did not try to persuade her to do more than learn to keep afloat and turn on her back and kick out vaguely with her legs. But the children were learning fast. Jason could already dog-paddle himself across the backwater from one side to the other, and Midge wasn't far behind.

Laurie had been a bit pushed to find them all swim-suits. Midge quite happily wore nothing, and Laurie had managed to buy Jason a pair of trunks in the village shop. At the end of a week's work in the hop-garden and doing Stan's accounts as well, she found herself in possession of quite a bit of money. But to waste it on buying swim-suits for herself and Penny seemed absurd. So she turned to the friendly Dorrie for advice.

'Penny can have mine,' said Dorrie, grinning. 'She's about my size—in front!' She went and rummaged in her battered old suitcase and brought out a crumpled black swim-suit of gigantic proportions. 'Always took a dip in the old Mudway when it got hot,' she said. 'In the old days, we used to have quite a party, Sundays, down by the bridge. But I'm getting too old for it now.' And she chuckled hugely, waving the swim-suit like a banner. 'But

152

as for you . . .' she considered Laurie with an appraising stare—'I'll have to ask around.'

She waddled off, and returned after about ten minutes, triumphantly waving another one-piece swim-suit of a shiny, garish blue. 'All they could offer!' she apologised, grinning. 'At least it's your size. It won't fall off!'

Laurie was thankful it wasn't a bikini. Her bruises still showed too much for public display. She didn't want Clem's far-seeing gaze to cloud with pity when he saw her.

But now she swam quietly and confidently about beside the children, and let the water ease her aching ribs while she lay floating on its surface, gazing into the clear September skies above her head until her bruised mind began to feel healed of hurt as well. And Clem, bronzed and powerful but always gentle, swam round them like a watchful shepherd, encouraging every stroke.

Afterwards they would all sit round Clem's stove drinking hot tea, before they walked home again in the gathering dusk. It was an enchanted time.

He always seemed able to set this space aside for the swimming session, though he had a number of sick creatures to attend to each day, and more were always being brought in. But, one evening, Laurie found him bending over another swan and shaking his head sadly to himself as he examined it. He looked up as Laurie came near and said, 'I can't save this one—it's too far gone.'

'What is it? Lead-poisoning?'

'Yes. It's too weak even to lift its head.' He laid the snowy bird with its long, drooping neck on to the straw in the pen he had built for his sickest patients in his scullery. The swan lay there, limp and helpless, and under the gentle pressure of Clem's stroking fingers it closed its eyes and did not open them again.

'The poor thing!' murmured Laurie, with tears in her eyes. 'It's so beautiful. Can nothing be done?'

'No.' Clem's voice was sad but quite definite. 'It's too late. Even if I could get the pellets out, it wouldn't survive the shock. The best I can do for it now is let it die in peace.'

153

He got up and led Laurie away out into the sunshine, where the children were already swimming round Penny, who lay placidly on the surface, more like a basking seal than ever.

'Don't grieve over it,' he said softly. 'Some we save . . . some we lose.' He waved an expressive hand at his little flock of convalescents on the water. 'At least *they'll* be all right—for a time!'

* * *

On the last evening, they invited Clem to come back with them for supper round their camp-fire. He hesitated a moment and then said, 'Yes—I'd love to. But I must stay and see to the invalids first. I'll follow you on.'

Penny stood up and took Midge firmly by the hand. 'We'll go and start the fire,' she said, with an imperious glance at Jason. 'Laurie can walk down with you.'

Laurie was not sure that she approved of Penny's tact— or that she wanted to be left alone with Clem at all. But it seemed ungracious to walk off, and he had been very good to them all. And anyway, she did want to be with him, really—this was all stupid panic. She watched the three of them set off along the river path, and turned back to help Clem with his sick birds. He put down food and water for the ones who could manage on their own, and dressed a knife-wound in a swan's white breast and one shattered wing that needed more antibiotics to stave off infection. He left some chopped-up food for the badger cub, and some more for the injured fox who kept leaping up and down in his cage like a welcoming little dog. And then he straightened up and looked round at his patients with moderate satisfaction.

'They'll do,' he said. 'I'll have another look at them when I come back.'

He washed his hands in the sink, and followed Laurie out into the westering sun. They had been swimming earlier today, as it was Saturday and there was no picking left to do. Some of the casual workers had gone home already, but there were still a few families left in the old hoppers' huts—including Dorrie and her numerous relations—and there was going to be a grand farewell party that night in the scuffed, empty field. Laurie had finished her last attack on Stan's accounts the night before, and he had given her an extra bonus and a box of apples to take home for Jane at The Hide. He seemed very pleased with Laurie, and told her she'd be welcome to come again when the next year's fruit-picking started.

But now the stripped hop-gardens and orchards lay silent—there were only the late apples left to pick, and they could be done by Stan's own men. The hop-poles lay in neat stacks on the ground beside the piles of bushel baskets and empty bins, and everywhere seemed strangely quiet.

Laurie and Clem walked side by side in the slanting sunlight and watched the shadows grow long on the river meadows.

They did not talk much. Clem was always inclined to peaceful silence rather than too many words—and Laurie was grateful for it. But at last they paused, by mutual consent, to look at the reflections on the river and the two white swans that still preferred to stay near Clem, drifting gently on its gleaming sunset surface.

Clem was very tempted then. He turned to her swiftly and suddenly, with something blazing in his eyes that he could not say, and put his arms round her. But at once he felt her stiffen slightly within the circle of his arms, and he said to himself despairingly: You fool! Too soon . . . too soon. So he slackened his embrace and smiled at her and murmured by way of apology, 'It's a magic time, sunset. Even the swans feel it.' And he bent his head and kissed her, very gently and quietly, on her anxious, upturned face.

Laurie watched the blaze die in his eyes and the familiar, undemanding calmness return in its place. She knew she had hurt him, but she could say nothing to reassure him. Not yet. Her reaction had been instinctive and terrifying. She was not ready for it. Something so strong and overpowering was too much to cope with— too much to bear, just yet.

155

So she nodded quietly, trying to match his calmness, and turned to look at the graceful swans on the river.

As they watched, the two swans suddenly took off in a long, slow glide, trailing their feet in the water until the power of their wings took over. They flew off down river in a wide, thrumming arc—their wings glinting in the setting sun—and when they were almost out of sight and the sound of their throbbing flight was almost gone, they turned in the blue air and flew back upstream, landing in a shower of glittering spray almost at Clem and Laurie's feet. They seemed to look at Clem, as if satisfied that he was still there, and then sailed placidly into the shallows and stayed there, floating like white ghosts in the gathering shadows under the great grey arms of the tangled willows.

'Freedom,' said Clem softly, 'isn't only taking off. It's knowing where you want to land . . . and when it's time to come home.'

He did not look at Laurie. He did not say any more. But there was a whole world of future promise in his voice.

'Yes,' murmured Laurie, with her eyes on the swans. 'I know.'

* * *

The singing went on very late that night. Everyone was packing up and leaving in the morning. Even the gipsies in their smart trailers joined in the final party—though Dorrie said to keep a sharp eye on your money with 'them thieving rascals' about.

Clem joined in the singing with his deep, musical baritone, and Jason sat beside him and piped up in a clear treble whenever he knew the song. They sang all the old favourites—'Daisy, Daisy' and 'Roll me Over' and 'Knees up Mother Brown'—and 'Yellow Submarine', which Jason knew, and some pop songs that Penny knew but Laurie didn't—and some more scurrilous ones that Dorrie roared out with the men while the others looked on and laughed.

And there was dancing, too. When they got tired of singing, someone turned on a transistor and the young

156

ones rocked and wriggled and stamped and clapped in the flickering firelight. And, when they got tired of that, someone strummed a guitar and someone brought out an old squeeze-box and someone else produced a mouth-organ, and the familiar tunes and the singing began all over again.

At one point, Spider the tallyman—who never took no for an answer—caught Laurie round the waist and whirled her into the dance. She had no time to refuse, and anyway it was the last night, so she let herself be pulled and twirled, breathless and laughing, through the fire-lit throng of dancers.

Clem, watching her, surprised himself with a sharp, unmistakable stab of pure jealousy, and after a moment got to his feet and pushed his way into the crowd of wrigglers and rockers till he came face to face with Spider.

'My turn, I think,' he said, smiling, and neatly twisted Laurie away from her partner's arms and into his own. She did not protest, and Spider could only glower and watch them whirl away in and out of the shadows.

They did not speak, and Clem knew he must keep things cheerful. What he did not know was how right it felt to Laurie to be in his arms. But she did not tell him. So he merely twirled and spun a bit harder, till she was dizzy with laughter and Kentish cider, and then led her back to the leaping flames of their own camp-fire. There they sat peacefully, side by side, listening to the singing, and were strangely content to say no word.

Little Midge fell asleep against Laurie's arm, and she was carried inside the hut and laid on one of the bunks, but Jason stayed wide awake and excited till the end. But at last the singing died down and the fires burnt low, and people began to drift off—some to the huts to sleep it off, and some to the green orchards and empty hop-gardens for other games.

Laurie had been watching the circle of faces round her fire in a kind of dream. Clem's, brown and serene, his eyes crinkling with laughter as he sang with the others. Penny's, cheerful and glowing with simple enjoyment—like a child's. And Jason, his eyes fixed on Clem, trying to follow his every word. And Dorrie—huge, kind-hearted Dorrie—full of fat chuckles, shaking with laughter, roaring out her outrageous songs to the receiving night. The firelight, springing and dying, flickering on all their faces, turning them into brightly etched characters on a darkened stage.

Yes, she thought, it was like a dramatic scene—Dante's Inferno, perhaps—only they were happy, and they weren't devils or even the damned! They were just ordinary, friendly people having a bit of fun.

She realised suddenly that she hadn't sat around like this, part of a cheery uproarious group enjoying themselves, for years and years—if ever. In her prison of anxiety and fear and violence, she had been totally cut off from all this good-natured, undemanding companionship. She had almost begun to believe that life was all grind and terror and no one was to be trusted. It was good to be back among the human race.

Clem had got to his feet and stood looking down at her, smiling. 'Welcome back!' he said softly, and Laurie found that she was not astonished that he understood her thoughts.

Jason was looking at his hero in the firelight. 'Will we ever . . . can we come to see you again?'

'Of course,' said Clem, and rested a calm, reassuring hand on his head. 'Any time.' He was not looking at Laurie, his attention seeming wholly on the anxious small boy beside him.

'When?' asked Jason, his young voice sharp with anxiety.

'In the spring, I expect,' Clem answered for Laurie—sensing her hesitation.

'Will you still be here?'

'Sure. I'm always here.' He sounded rock-like and utterly dependable, and watched the anxiety begin to dissolve in the boy's too-serious eyes.

'And . . . will you let me help with the swans again?'

'Why not?' Clem smiled his slow, comforting smile. 'You're a great little assistant! I can always do with another pair of hands—provided they're kind, that is.'

Jason looked down at his own hands in wonder, and then at Clem's strong brown ones. 'Kind?' he murmured, as if it was a new word he had only just discovered. 'Kind,' repeated Clem gently, crinkling up his eyes again. 'That's the secret, Jay. Kind.'

His eyes strayed now to Laurie's face, and his gaze became deep and sure. 'And letting them go when they're ready . . . ,' he said softly, 'and being there when they come back. That's all it takes.'

His smile rested on Laurie quietly. He did not seem to expect any reply. But her own smile flooded out to match his with sudden radiance.

Then he turned back to Jason and laid his hand once more on the boy's fair head before he left. 'Don't worry, Jay,' he said gently, 'I'll be there.' And he strode away into the darkness without looking back.

But Laurie, staring after him, felt a brightness gone from the air, and a warmth and security lost. She knew she must stand alone—and there was a whole new life to build, and all kinds of problems to face. She could do it, she knew—if she kept her head and stayed strong. Only, it wasn't going to be easy. But Clem had said, *'I'll be there,'* and she suddenly understood that he meant exactly what he said. He would be there—with her. His calm, enduring presence would go with her wherever she went. Comforted, she looked up at the sharp stars, and took Jason by the hand. She would sleep now—in peace.

## PART III

# FREE FLIGHT

B ack in London, Laurie resolutely turned her mind to her immediate problems and tried not to keep seeing the golden September sunlight on the river instead of the grey London streets and thrusting roof-tops. She left Penny and the children at Jane's hostel — firmly refusing to let them go with her when she went back to the shabby little house to fetch some clothes.

The weather had changed, and a thin drizzle drifted out of a leaden sky, smearing the pavements with greasy moisture. People turned up coat collars and looked as glum as the day, and Laurie walked head down in the rain, hurrying to get the most dreaded task of all out of the way.

She hated the cramped, squalid little house and all its grim memories—hated and feared it. Even putting the key in the lock was an effort of will, and her heart lurched in remembered terror as she stepped inside the door. The rooms had a musty, unlived-in atmosphere and smelt of damp and decay. She did not go into the kitchen—she could not face it yet—but went straight upstairs to the bedroom to collect some clothes. There were two old suit-cases at the back of the cupboard, and she dragged these out and took one into the children's room. She crammed it with all the clothes she could find and with their shoes as well—though she had a feeling that their feet had grown during those two weeks of freedom in the hop-gardens. Then she returned, unwillingly, to the dark bed-room she had shared with Jeff, and hastily flung her own clothes into the other case. She did not look at the bed. Already her flesh was beginning to crawl, and she could not bear to remember the many ghastly experiences she had suffered there—the times Jeff had fallen on her, drunk and savage, and forced her, without love or pity, in a kind of unseeing rage . . . the times she had submitted, despairing and silent, knowing he would only be more violent if she tried to protest.

She shuddered, and kept her eyes away from that corner of the room—sweeping the last few bits and pieces off the dressing-table into the suitcase and snapping down the lid.

She carried the cases down the stairs and stood for a moment irresolute in the hall. Should she just walk out and leave it, or should she set to work and clean it first? But the thought of going into that kitchen made her sweat and tremble all over again. No, she could not do it. Jeff would have to cope with it himself—when he came out.

She had just decided to leave, when there came a short, sharp knock on the door. Laurie froze where she stood—paralysed. Could it be Jeff? Had he got out of prison—or had they let him go early?

The knock came again, insistently. Laurie took a deep breath and went to the door.

Joe stood outside on the step, looking anxious, and his old green van was parked by the kerb. Beside him was an unsmiling woman with a clipboard in her hand.

'Thought you could do with a lift,' said Joe cheerfully. 'And this, er . . . this lady is from the housing. Met her on the step.'

'Oh.' Laurie hesitated, and then said quickly, 'I'll get the cases.' She left the woman standing on the steps till she returned carrying the cases in either hand. Then she set the cases down on the top step and slammed the door firmly behind her. 'Well?' she said, sounding a little belligerent because she was still frightened.

'I . . . the authorities sent me round,' explained the woman, confused by Laurie's uncompromising stare, 'to ask if you had really considered their proposal.'

'What proposal?'

'Why—to come back to live here with your children.'

Laurie's stare grew colder. 'And leave them open to further attacks by my husband?'

The woman blinked. 'Surely he wouldn't . . . ?'

'Oh yes he would.' Laurie's face was bleak. 'He'd wait outside and accost the children. He'd get drunk and beat on the door, demanding to be let in. He'd climb in through the windows. I'd never have a moment's peace.' She looked at the woman, almost with contempt. 'You want to subject us to that?'

'I . . . we could take out another injunction, if he got violent.'

'*If?*' Laurie's voice snapped with anger. 'It'd be a bit late then, wouldn't it?' She turned away. 'No thanks. I'd rather not take the risk.'

'But . . . you do realise that by refusing to live here you make yourself ineligible for other housing.' She consulted the lists on her clipboard, as if asking them for help in the face of Laurie's continued icy stare. 'I mean—it is a roof over your head.'

'No!' said Laurie. 'I'd rather sleep out. It'd be safer in the streets.'

The woman looked shocked.

'In any case,' Laurie pointed out, 'this is a council house—let in his name, not mine. And since I have left him, he has more right to it than I have.'

'That's just the point,' explained the woman. 'It has been the marital home. If you and the children are already living in it—and have nowhere else to go—and you've got a separation order or a divorce pending, he can't come back.'

Laurie's gaze became incredulous. 'And can you imagine how he would feel about that? He'd have a real grudge against me then. He'd be more vindictive than ever.'

The woman looked into Laurie's face and saw that she had lost the argument. She put away her pen with a snap of her handbag. 'Very well,' she said. 'I'll report back what you say. But I'm afraid the Department will not feel that they are obliged to help you further.'

I'll bet they won't! Laurie thought. But she did not say it. In fact there was no need, for Joe spoke up suddenly. 'You needn't bother. Not at the moment, anyways. She's got herself fixed up till the spring.'

165

The woman suddenly smiled and looked human. 'I'm glad to hear it.' She turned to go back down the steps, but then added as an afterthought, 'I don't make the rules, you know. In any case, we'd better keep your name on our lists. Things may look different in the spring.'

'I hope so,' said Laurie fervently.

Joe seized her cases and pushed her unceremoniously down the steps to his waiting van. 'Get in!' he growled. 'Can't stop all day!' He slammed the doors and shot away into the traffic.

'Phew!' he said, after a bit of tricky bus-dodging. 'Those housing berks give me the creeps!'

'Me too!' agreed Laurie, and found that her teeth were chattering. 'How did you know . . . ?' she began.

'Jane told me, didn't she? Can't have you lugging suitcases all over London. Besides . . .' he cocked a wary eye in her direction, not missing the signs of tension—'I thought that place might give you the shakes.'

'Yes,' admitted Laurie, with a pale grin. 'It did!'

Joe dropped her off at The Hide and refused to come in. But he arranged to take her and Penny with the children to the coach station in two days' time. In the meantime, Laurie had to see the solicitor, Madeleine Williamson— and she also had to make up her mind if she was going to visit Jeff or not.

Jane, when consulted, would not commit herself, though she clearly thought it might be too much for Laurie. She only said, 'I should ask Madeleine what she advises—and get her to come with you.'

That seemed a good idea. The prison authorities, when the situation was explained to them, agreed to let Laurie see Jeff, and also agreed to let the solicitor be present. Laurie put on her tidiest clothes and brushed her cropped hair till it was smooth. She was very nervous.

Prison life did not agree with Jeff. To begin with, there was exercise, which he disliked, and 'slopping out' which he disliked even more. And then there were the inmates. Word had somehow got around in the way that prison grapevines mysteriously work that Jeff was a wife-beater and possibly (probably, they said) a child-beater, too.

They didn't like that kind. Burglars and petty thieves, yes. Even muggers and knifers they might tolerate—provided it wasn't old ladies. But Jeff's kind of violence they did not care for—and they let it show. The matiness of prison was not for him. He was mostly met by a stony silence at meal times or in the 'recreation' room. And in the workshops, where a couple of exasperated warders tried to teach them some useful skills, he was even subject to a few unpleasant practical jokes. Benches slid from under him; hammers missed nails and caught his unwary hands; piles of neatly stacked timber fell down all round him. And once a group of men doused him upside down in the lavatory pan in the wash-room. No, he did not enjoy prison one bit—and, to make matters worse, there was no comforting drink to blot out the humiliations of the day.

The prison chaplain came round once or twice, and so did an earnest prison visitor who lectured him about the demon drink. But Jeff was not impressed. He felt sure he should not be here in this place. It was all a mistake. He hadn't meant to let fly at that policeman in the hospital corridor—and he hadn't meant to hit Laurie so hard, either. She never used to make a fuss about it, and he couldn't understand why she had got so stroppy and independent now. In any case, it was a man's right to do what he liked with his own—and when he got out of here he'd soon show her who was boss. It was her fault, after all, that he was shut up in this place. She had no business to make such a fuss—gulling the hospital into believing all sorts of things about him, and taking the kids away too. He'd see about that, as well—*when he got out*.

So he was brought out of his cell, angry and resentful, by a laconic warder who said simply, 'On your feet, Collins. Visitor.'

He went where he was told in a black mood, expecting to be lectured by yet another do-gooder who did not understand his urgent, desperate need for a drink and some good company 'outside'. But, instead, he found himself sitting on a chair, with a window in front of him and Laurie's face on the other side.

But it was a different Laurie. Her hair was cut short, making her look older and somehow tougher. And her face was stern and set into lines of firm decision—a look he did not know, and one which scared him rather.

'How are you, Jeff?' she said.

'How do you think? Shut up in here!' He glowered at her, not sure what this visit meant.

'It's not for long,' she said, almost kindly.

'Long enough,' he grumbled. 'In this bloody place! I suppose you're crowing.'

'No,' said Laurie gravely. 'No, I'm not crowing, Jeff.'

'What did you come for then? Don't tell me you're having a change of heart?'

She sat regarding him with an assessing, puzzled expression. Is this the man I married? she seemed to be saying to herself. This bitter, resentful wreck? And is it my fault he has come to this?

'No.' She spoke slowly, carefully. 'I simply wanted to see how you were.'

'Oh *thanks*. Since you put me here in the first place. A nice, condescending visit. That makes it all right, I suppose?'

She seemed to sigh. 'I didn't put you here, Jeff. You put yourself here. Just as you drove me away—and your children.' She was looking at him intently now, willing him to see the truth. Only then could he begin to pull himself together and shed the perpetual chip on his shoulder.

'You bloody self-righteous cow!' he shouted suddenly, and banged his fist against the window. 'I'll get you when I come out!'

The warder in the corner got up off his stool and came over. 'None of that,' he said, 'or the visit's over.'

Jeff subsided.

On the other side of the screen, Madeleine Williamson also came forward and laid a hand on Laurie's arm. She did not say anything, but Laurie looked up at her and smiled. It was all right. She was not frightened—or intimidated by his threats.

And oddly enough it was true. From the distance of

that glass panel dividing them, she saw not the monster she had feared but a bewildered, shrunken man whose whole jaunty world of make-believe had crashed about his ears. And—just as she had predicted to Jane—she found that she was sorry for him—not angry any more. 'I came to say goodbye, Jeff,' she told him in an even voice. 'I'm going away.'

'Goodbye?' he snarled, outrage mounting again. 'You're not going anywhere, see? You're my wife—and they're my kids.'

'Not any more,' she answered, gently enough. 'Don't you understand? It's over. The divorce is going through. And if you want to see the children, I'm afraid you'll have to wait till they're older. They're much too frightened of you now.' She saw him blink at those words. Maybe that, at least, would make him pause for thought.

'Frightened of me? Rubbish!' he growled. 'You've put them up to it.'

Laurie did not answer that directly. She merely said in a mild tone, 'You don't really want them, Jeff—you never did—any more than you want me. We're only an encumbrance. Now you can go off anywhere you like and start again.' She watched that idea settle into his mind. She fancied there was a flash of unexpected hope in the angry eyes opposite. Jeff had caught a glimpse of a new, free life, with money to burn and girls to conquer.

But he still didn't like the idea of his wife and kids being on the loose. They were his—and they ought to stay where they belonged. He could always make money somehow—and find girls on the side if he wanted. Like Brenda, the barmaid—she was willing, wasn't she? But his wife and kids—a man needed them at home to give him stability, and status. He could always have some fun, one way and another, if there was someone to come home to afterwards—though, of course, a snivelling, incompetent slag like Laurie wasn't much use. Only, this new, crisp Laurie with the boyish hairstyle and steady, unruffled voice was something different. He rather liked a strong woman. They kept your life in order for you, which made things a lot easier.

'You can't just go like that,' he protested, trying to sound pathetic. 'I need you.'

Laurie got up from her chair. This was the Jeff she could not stand. She could bear him violent or resentful, but Jeff trying on his maudlin act she could not take.

'I'm sorry,' she said. 'It won't wash, Jeff. You can get in touch through my solicitor. Goodbye.'

Jeff could not believe it. She was really walking out on him. He let out a stream of furious obscenities. The warder took him by the arm and hustled him away, none too gently.

Madeleine Williamson steered Laurie out of the room and down the corridor. A prison officer let them out. The gates clanged behind them.

'Come on,' said Madeleine, holding on to her arm. 'What you need is a drink.'

She hailed a taxi and took Laurie as far away from the prison as she could get, stopping at a friendly bar near her own modest office.

'Here,' she said, putting a brandy in front of Laurie. 'Get that down you. I told you it would do no good.'

'I know,' Laurie sighed. 'But I had to try.' She took a gulp of her drink and waited for the world to settle round her before she asked anxiously, 'About access . . . ?'

Madeleine shook her head. 'He won't get it. Not with that injunction still standing—and the magistrate's ruling about no molesting for a year.'

'That's only a year . . .'

'We can get it renewed.'

'Are you sure?'

'Yes. Remember, we also have Jason's statement. And Midge's reaction. The evidence is quite clear.'

Laurie shut her eyes. 'It's my only worry. The rest I can cope with. But the children . . .'

'I know.' Madeleine's voice was firm and kind. 'Leave it to me. Go away and make a fresh start. I'll see to all the chores.'

Laurie took a deep breath and gave her a shaky smile. 'Well, I'm glad that's over!' she said.

\* \* \*

The parting with Jane was unexpectedly emotional. Laurie felt that a lifeline of sanity and rock-like support was being severed.

But Jane said steadily and kindly, 'We'll keep in touch, Laurie. And you know you can always come back here if you're stuck.' Then she handed Laurie an envelope, saying, 'This is the rest of your emergency grant from social security. I've got the maximum out of them! And I've told them you will contact their Penzance office for your normal maintenance payments as soon as you arrive.'

Laurie looked at Jane and shook her head wordlessly. Then she flung her arms round her neck and hugged her. 'I don't know what I'd have done without you!' she said in a voice like a gasp.

'Go on!' Jane's own voice was warm with affection. 'Have a good winter—and give my love to the sea.'

'How can we give your love to a lot of water?' asked Jason practically.

Jane looked down at him, smiling. 'You can get an old bottle and put a message in it,' she said. 'Write: "Jane loves you" on it, and throw it in. Maybe it'll land up in the Thames estuary and come all the way to London. You never know!'

'All right,' agreed Jason, his eyes alight with resolve. 'I will.'

'On the other hand,' said Jane solemnly, 'it might just get washed back on shore at your feet. Then you can open the bottle again and read the message. It'll still be true.'

Laurie looked at Jane over Jason's head and smiled. That was their farewell.

Joe packed them all in his van and delivered them to Victoria Coach Station. Their cases were put in the luggage boot of the coach and they climbed on board. Laurie went last and—as with Jane—she put her arms round Joe's neck and said, 'Thanks for everything.'

Joe gave her a cheerful squeeze back and said to them all at large, 'Be happy, kids,' then turned away rather swiftly to go back to his little green van.

The coach doors closed with a hiss, the engine started

into life, and they eased their way out into the London traffic. We're away! thought Laurie. A new life is beginning! The wings in her head almost got out. She thought they might break free altogether when she got to the sea.

Behind her, she heard Penny say to Jason, who was beside her, 'I feel quite excited. From now on, life's going to be really good!'

I hope so, thought Laurie. Oh God, I hope so. With Penny's baby to come, and the children's security to build—I hope I can cope with it all.

The coach made a left turn and started to run along the Embankment, so that the silver Thames accompanied them close by.

'Mum?' Jason's voice came close as he leant towards her, 'Could we put a message in a bottle for Clem as well?'

She turned her head, startled, and smiled at him. 'I should think so, Jay. Why not?'

'Would it get there?'

She answered almost in a voice of dream. 'It might. The Medway is tidal. All rivers run to the sea.'

* * *

In Penzance, they all bundled out with their luggage and took a trundling country bus into the deep Cornish lanes. They were set down at a crossroads beside an ancient Celtic cross, with the terse words, 'Tregarrow is that way,' from the bus driver. 'That way' seemed to point down the narrowest of the lanes before them, and they set out hopefully, carrying their cases between them. They had not been walking for very long when a farm truck drew up beside them.

'Where you making for?' asked the driver, pushing his cap back from a seamed brown face.

'Tregarrow,' said Laurie. 'Mr Veryan's place.'

'Luke Veryan?' The weathered face broke into a smile. 'Passing that way meself. Hop in.'

They piled in with their luggage, and the truck went lurching on down the steep lane, with the tall banks rising ever higher on either side. Around one of the sharpest bends there was a gap in the broad stone 'hedge' and they caught a glimpse of very blue sea between two sloping headlands.

The farmer pointed with a blunt finger. 'That's Tregarrow Head. Luke's place is up the valley a bit.'

'Near the sea?' Jason's voice was hopeful.

The farmer turned his head and grinned. 'Not far. Nowhere's far from the sea down here.' He negotiated another sharp bend and added cheerfully, 'But the cove's easy to reach. Not like some . . .' He lifted a bushy eyebrow in Laurie's direction. 'You like cliff-walking?'

Laurie smiled. 'Yes. But I'm not here on holiday. I'm here to work.'

The farmer's brown face registered approval. 'Glad to here it. Luke could do with a hand. Since his wife died, he's managed alone. But it's not been easy.'

He drew up at the side of a grassy cart-track and pointed to a cluster of roofs and barns. 'That's it, down there. Happen you'll be in the cottage?'

Laurie nodded. 'Yes, I think so.'

'Well, that'll be farther down towards the cove. But you'll find Luke in the milking-parlour about now, I should guess.'

'He's got cows as well?'

'Only a few. He supplies one or two hotels and guest-houses round about, and sends a churn or two to the depot—like I do.' He grinned at Laurie again, and went round to help the others out. He lifted Midge down and smiled at her tired, grubby face. 'Going to make sand-castles, are you, little 'un?'

Midge didn't answer, but Jason said stoutly, 'We can swim!'

The farmer laughed. 'Can you now? Well, just you be careful, my handsome. Keep near the shore. These seas can be very rough—and very cold!'

He handed them their cases and climbed back into his truck. 'Button, that's me,' he said.

'Button?' Laurie was mystified.

'My name. George Button. Bit of a joke round here, 'cos I'm six-foot-four!' He laughed, and let in the gear.

173

'Some button!' he added, still grinning. 'But at least I can see over my own hedges! Anything I can do, just let me know.' And he shot off round the next bend in the lane.

The little party stood looking after him, feeling suddenly very alone in the empty lane. Then they picked up their luggage and trudged down the track until they came to a farm gate and a cattle-grid across the track. Beyond the gate they could see a muddy yard and a jumble of buildings, mostly of crumbling stone and flint-grey slate. A small farmhouse stood at one corner of the yard, and a clatter of churns and milking-pails came from the open doors of the nearest barn adjoining it.

Laurie left the others standing in the yard and approached the long, low barn which was, she supposed, the milking-parlour. Six red-brown Jersey cows stood patiently in their stalls, and a tall, thin old man in a stained brown overall was pouring milk from a pail into a big metal churn. He looked up when he saw Laurie in the doorway and a faint spark of acknowledgement crossed his bleak grey face, but he did not stop what he was doing till the pail was empty.

'Can I help?' asked Laurie, seeing the other full pails waiting to be poured.

'Why not?' said Luke Veryan in an abrupt, clipped voice. 'Save time, t'would.'

She came inside and carefully poured the frothy milk into the waiting churn. He did not speak again till the last pail was emptied. Then he straightened his back and looked at Laurie with a shade more warmth.

'You're Laurie Collins, I take it?' he said, and peered at the rest of her little party standing uncertainly in the yard. 'Not much of a welcome is it?' He smiled a craggy smile, and led the way out of the barn. 'Take you down to the cottage in a minute,' he said, eyeing Penny and the children speculatively. 'Getting late. Show you round tomorrow.' He seemed to hesitate, scratching his head in perplexity. 'Got to get the cows out first,' he muttered.

Jason came forward, knowing his mother needed support. 'I can help,' he volunteered. 'Where do they have to go?'

Luke Veryan looked the boy up and down. Then he nodded briefly. 'Mostly they knows the way. Just keep behind 'em, and walk on.'

He went back into the milking-shed and let his cows out into the yard. Automatically, the leader made for the open gate into the field beyond—and slowly, ponderously, the others followed. Midge was a little scared of the cows and clung to Penny's hand. But Jason walked confidently behind them and only stepped out of line when one of the cows tried to go the other way.

'No!' he said softly, waving his arms. 'Not that way, silly! Come up, you old lazy-bones, come up! This way.' Laurie, watching him, thought he might have been herding cattle all his life.

Farmer Veryan walked behind Jason, saying nothing. When the cows were all in the field, he turned to shut the gate and found the boy before him, pushing it shut. 'Good!' he said, nodding. 'You'll do!' And the thin smile creaked out again as he saw Jason flush with pleasure.

'Give me a couple of they,' he said, picking up two of their cases in large, competent hands. 'Follow I down,' and he led the way past the farmhouse and down a stony track along the side of the hill. They walked on for about five minutes in silence, and then the track widened and they came to a small, square cottage set with its back to the hillside. Below them lay a sloping cliff covered in late gorse and bracken, and beneath its curving slope, stretching out to a darkening horizon, lay the sea.

'Oh!' said a chorus of enthralled voices. 'The sea!'

Luke Veryan grunted noncommittally. The sea was not new to him, but he loved it too—in his way—with all its moods, threatening or beguiling. And he was always glad when the visitors to his cottage uttered that initial 'Oh' of delight.

'Tregarrow is under the hill,' he said, 'farther up from the cove.' He jerked a thumb towards the narrow head of the valley where the two arms of the cliff met. 'Shop down there,' he added. 'But I stocked up for you, temporary-like.'

He took an old-fashioned key out of his overall pocket

and unlocked the sturdy cottage door, ushering them in with a wave of his hand.

Inside, there was one square room, whitewashed and clean, with a sofa and two small armchairs at one end, round an open fireplace. At the other end there was a small, square dining-table and four straight-backed chairs. Beyond this simple living-room was a small kitchen with a new-looking electric cooker and a fridge and some neat cupboards set under white Formica working-tops.

Luke Veryan was surveying this well-equipped little unit with a sardonic eye. 'Summer visitors,' he explained to Laurie, 'they likes everything quick and shiny. Me, I prefers an Aga—slow or no.'

Penny nodded. 'Cooks better, too.' She was rewarded by a surprised glance and a slightly less creaky smile.

'Let you loose on it then, girl, shall I?' he said, and then added on a note of caution, 'One of these days.'

Penny just looked at him and grinned.

But Laurie had already gone upstairs to have a look at the bedrooms. There were two—one with twin beds and one with two bunk beds and a single divan. Both of them had small, square windows looking out across the sloping hillside to the sea. It was wonderfully quiet, and there were no tensions anywhere.

'Leave it to you, then,' she heard Luke Veryan say to Penny, and she hurried down the stairs to say to his retreating back:

'What time time shall I start in the morning?'

The thin, spare figure turned back to look at her. In the half-light, his eyes—brown like his son Joe's, but bleaker and less warm—seemed to sum her up with asperity. 'No work tomorrow. Settling-in day. Come up after breakfast and I'll show you round.'

'All right,' agreed Laurie, and took a shy step towards him. 'And . . . Mr Veryan . . . thanks!'

He nodded at her abruptly and stumped away up the hillside to his farm. They sorted out their meagre possessions, and Penny firmly chose to share the children's bedroom. 'Give you a bit of peace,' she said, grinning. 'Besides, I like being with the kids.'

176

Laurie was looking out of the window at the slowly darkening sea. 'Is it too late to go down to the cove?' she wondered.

'Not if we hurry. Won't be dark for another hour.' Penny was almost as eager as Jason and Midge to get down to the shore.

'Better buy a torch tomorrow,' murmured Laurie, still staring out at the sloping cliff path downwards.

They wasted no more time, but each took a child by the hand in case the path grew steep. Between gorse and bracken, tall Cornish heath and myrtle, the narrow track wound downwards. Only once did it come near the edge of the cliff, and they looked over at a dizzying drop and a jumble of jagged rocks below, with a deep-green sea-swell swirling round them and sending up a thin spume of spray.

The path went on down. Presently it spread out into a little oasis of springy turf starred with pale autumn squills and bright clumps of late thrift growing among the rocks. Below this clearing the sand began, in a steep, creamy dune, and below that lay the cove—small and perfect, set in a curve of white-gold sea-shell sand and guarded by two arms of curious gold-brown rocky cliff, shimmering in the last rays of the sun like tawny lions. The sea itself was green—green and calm and quiet. It lapped gently against the gleaming sand in a lacy frill of foam. Only near the strange Aztec-carving shapes of the golden rocks did it fret enough to throw dazzling cascades of sea-spray into the air.

'Oh!' cried the children, and threw off their shoes and went running towards the sea.

Laurie ran after then across the firm, white sand, and Penny followed them, ruefully admitting to herself that she had to move more slowly these days.

'It's cold!' danced Jason, wriggling his toes in the translucent water.

'Ooh, it is!' echoed Midge, prancing about at the edge.

Even Laurie waded in, and stood there surrounded by swirls of jade and emerald—ice-cold and clean and pure. She stood gazing out to sea, westwards, where the sun was setting in streaks of flamingo fire. The sea looked immensely wide, immensely far—darkening with the shadows of evening towards an indigo horizon.

Pure, she thought. Implacable and strong. Nothing can spoil it. Those clear glass-green deeps are beyond the taint of our grasping fingers—beyond the slow stain of the world. Tomorrow, she thought wistfully, . . . tomorrow I'll swim in it. There'll be time tomorrow. And then I might begin to feel clean and whole again.

Aloud, she said gently to the enchanted faces beside her, 'Tomorrow we'll swim. It's getting late now. It'll still be here tomorrow.'

They looked at her trustfully, and then back to the sea. 'All right,' they agreed, but there was a note of loss in their rapt young voices.

'Come on,' Penny sounded as sturdy and practical as ever. 'We've got to cook the supper in our new house! Let's get back before we fall over the cliff in the dark!'

They turned to leave the sea behind them, but Jason lingered, looking longingly at the lift and fall of the sea-swell farther out. 'Mum?' he said, sudden urgency in his voice. 'Could I earn some money?'

Laurie looked at him in surprise. 'I should think so, Jay—if you helped Mr Veryan. Or if you helped me, maybe I could pay you. Why?' She saw the anxiety in his eyes, and added, 'Is there something you want to buy?'

He hesitated, scuffing his bare feet in the sand. 'Only . . . two bottles of pop.'

Penny laughed. 'That won't cost much! Even I could buy you those!'

'No,' said Jason, sounding obstinate and confused both at once. '*I've* got to buy them—myself.' He looked beseechingly at his mother, willing her to understand. 'And two corks . . .'

'Oh,' said Laurie, smiling. 'Of course! To send a message in to Jane.'

'And to Clem,' Jason insisted. 'Clem must have one as well.'

Laurie nodded quietly, and took his cold hands in hers.

'Tomorrow,' she agreed. 'We'll do all the things we promised. Now it's time to go in.'

Together they climbed the pale dune glimmering in the dusk and made their way back up the cliff path to the cottage on the hill.

* * *

In the morning, Jason went up to help Luke Veryan with the cows before anyone else was up. He came back to breakfast glowing with sea air and happy achievement. 'He's waiting for you to come up,' he reported. 'And the farm is smashing!'

Laurie found Luke Veryan in the yard, hosing out the milking-parlour. There were a lot of things she wanted to ask, and she hoped he wouldn't be too busy to answer.

'Show you the glasshouses first,' he said, leading the way to a long row of greenhouses behind the cluster of barns. 'Winter lettuce,' he explained, pointing to rows of seed-boxes. 'And various. Late chrysanths and pot plants for the Christmas market.'

'Oh!' breathed Laurie, enchanted by the long rows of flowers and their sharp, aromatic scent. 'Lovely!'

Luke Veryan glanced at her and grinned. 'Like flowers, meself. Pretty faces and don't hurt no one.'

Laurie grinned back and bent to bury her face in a snowy tangle of petals. Patiently, Luke Veryan took her through all the greenhouses, explaining about the winter market and the picking and packing. Then he took her out to his orderly market garden with its neat rows of vegetables and a glorious riot of late dahlias grown for cut flowers along one end of the field.

There was an old, bent man hoeing patiently between the rows. 'That's Bob,' said Luke, jerking a thumb in his direction. 'Comes up from the village most days—when his lumbago lets him!'

Laurie smiled in sympathy. 'I suppose stooping doesn't help?'

'You're right. Gets him cruel—specially in wet weather. He'll be glad of an extra pair of hands.'

Laurie agreed, and stood looking round her in the mild

179

sunshine. Everywhere there were flowers waiting to be picked and bunched—late asters and outdoor chrysanthemums, and several gleaming rows of gladioli besides the blaze of dahlias, their vivid colours aflare in the morning sun.

'Where are the daffodil fields?' she asked, gazing round at the close-packed space.

Luke Veryan's difficult smile broke out. 'You come through them, girl—on the way up from the cottage.'

'Did I?'

'All them green spaces between here and the sea— they're full of daffs come spring. And there's more fields of 'em over there.' He seemed to be enjoying a private joke. 'You was walking on 'em, girl,' he said, chuckling. 'Thousands of bulbs—under your feet!'

Laurie looked down at her own feet in their mud-caked wellingtons and laughed. Thousands of bulbs, she thought. All that green and gold life under my feet, waiting for winter to be done and spring to come.

'Do you get any frosts?'

'Not here.' He shook his head. 'Mild, it is. Though I do remember snow, once or twice. But it never lasts down here.' He stood staring out at his own fields in a dreaming way. 'Now then,' he said, being brisk with himself as much as Laurie. 'Seen all you can. Business next.'

He took her into the farmhouse and along a stone-tiled passage to a small room used as an office. He showed her his order books and his accounts, his milk returns and his packaging schedule, together with a whole lot of unspecified orders and bills on loose sheets of paper which he had not been able to file under any kind of order. 'Chaos!' he admitted, waving a hand at them. 'Never catch up.' Then he pointed a stubby finger at another book, full of names. 'Take on pickers and packers come February,' he explained. 'Only trouble is, we has to pack Sundays. To deliver to the Monday markets. Flowers isn't fresh enough, else. Or veges. D'you mind?'

Laurie smiled. 'No. All days are much the same to me. Except . . .' and here she asked the first of her important

180

questions. 'Jason, my boy, ought to go to school. Is there one within reach at all?'

Luke nodded. 'Right here in Tregarrow.' He straightened up and looked out of his window at the sloping hillside. 'You been down to the village yet?'

'No.' She shook her head. 'Only to the sea.'

He grunted, not displeased with her answer. 'More important to you than the shops?'

'Much more!' she agreed, smiling.

'Mind, there's only one shop, anyways!' He grinned. 'One pub, one church, one school.' His voice was dry. 'We're the biggest village hereabouts, see? So we've kept our school. Kids come from miles around.' He paused, considering. 'I dessay it's not too full, though. Better ask Mrs Weelkes—head-teacher. Nice enough and not too bossy.'

'And then,' Laurie pursued her next anxiety, 'there's Penny. Joe told you about Penny?'

He nodded noncommittally.

'Well, she ought to see the local doctor, shouldn't she? And get fixed up with a hospital bed. I suppose that'd be in Penzance?'

'Ar, it would.' He sounded a bit abrupt, and Laurie felt obliged to add, with a hint of mischief, 'I mean—I wouldn't want the baby to arrive on your doorstep! I'm no midwife.'

'Neither am I!' growled Luke, but there was an unmistakable twinkle deep down. 'Dr Trevelyan,' he said then. 'Surgery in the village, three days a week. And there's Agnes Penwillis—she really *is* a midwife!'

Laurie nodded in relief.

But Luke was looking down at his books and frowning, already back to business and the endless difficulties of running a smallholding almost single-handed. 'Think you can manage these plaguey books?'

'Yes, I think so—after a bit of running in.'

His creaky smile twitched at the ends of his mouth. 'Don't look much like a car to me.'

Laurie laughed. But I feel a bit like one, she thought.

A bashed-up heap, running on a new engine. Got to go slow at first—not sure what I can or can't do.

Luke was saying something about wages and quoting a figure that made Laurie's eyes open wide.

'All that—as well as the cottage?' She felt almost outraged on his behalf. 'You'll never make a profit that way!'

Luke's sudden laughter was more like a bark. 'Are you refusing?'

She looked at him severely. 'No. I'm not that daft! But I think it should include a bit of help from the others. Penny can do packing—providing it's not too much stooping. And Jay loves helping with the cows.'

'So I've noticed!'

But Laurie had just thought of something and didn't quite know how to put it. At last she decided to tell Luke about Jane and the message in the bottle. She thought he might understand, since his own son, Joe, was so involved with all Jane's work. '. . . so you see, I'd be obliged if you'd knock a bit off my wage—just a little— and give it to Jason. He'd feel so much better if he thought he'd earned it.'

Luke stared at her thoughtfully. 'How much?'

'Oh . . . say 50p? He's not been used to spending much.'

Luke considered. 'Make it a pound,' he said. 'And see he puts half in the post office. Good for 'im. Used to do it with Joe.' He seemed almost to glare at Laurie. 'And I won't knock it off yourn, neither.'

'Oh, but . . .'

'No,' he said firmly. And then, qualifying it, 'But I'll make him work for it, mind!'

Laurie grinned. 'You know,' she said conversationally, 'I told your Joe he was one of the kindest men I'd ever met. He must take after you.'

Luke made a growling noise in his throat and turned away to rummage needlessly on his littered desk. 'Well,' he said after a moment, 'all settled then? Take today for your own affairs. Get settled. Start tomorrow.'

Laurie agreed thankfully, and started to go out of the dusty little office. It suddenly occurred to her that Luke lived alone now, since his wife had died, and was probably far too busy to clean his house or to do much in the way of cooking. A hunk of bread and cheese now and then was probably all he bothered with . . . And Penny loved cooking . . . She even quite liked cleaning, so she said—but that could come a bit later. Probably enough had been said today. Luke was clearly a fiercely independent, proud old man, and a ready-made family trying to take over his life was certainly more than he'd bargained for!

'Break us in gently,' said Luke, following her out into the yard. It was not clear which of them he was referring to, but Laurie was somehow not surprised at his swift assessment of her thoughts. There were no flies on old Luke.

She just smiled at him and nodded briskly. 'Be up tomorrow, then,' she said.

\* \* \*

Dr Trevelyan was a bluff, grizzled man who seemed to Laurie more like a vet than a doctor. He looked at her from under bushy eyebrows and said, 'What can I do for you?'

Laurie explained about Penny, about coming down to Luke Veryan's cottage for the winter—and said as little as possible about herself and the children. But seeing a dark spark of sympathy flash far down in his eyes, she added bluntly, 'I expect you're used to incest?'

'I am. It's very common. Much more common than people believe—especially in country districts.'

Laurie nodded. 'Well—I only told you all this because Penny's very young, and I don't want her bullied or harassed. She's had enough of that in her young life.'

He agreed. 'People are still not all that kind to unmarried mothers—whatever the circumstances!' Then he looked at her more keenly. 'How do you come into it?'

Laurie sighed. 'I met her at . . . at a hostel for battered wives. She's a kind girl, and she was very good to me and to my children when we . . . when we first came there.'

183

He was still looking at her. 'And she intends to keep the baby?'

'That's what she says . . . though I suppose she might change her mind at the last moment.' She looked doubtful. 'But in any case,' she spoke as if continuing an argument, 'one extra child won't make all that difference.'

'You intend to give her a home—permanently?'

Laurie shrugged. 'Why not? I've got nothing to lose—and everything to gain. She's wonderful with my kids. But as to permanent . . . Nothing's all that permanent, is it? I haven't even got a permanent home of my own, yet.'

'She might go off when she gets older and wants some freedom.'

'She might.' She glanced at the doctor, almost defiantly. 'I wouldn't blame her—would you? She's only a kid herself, after all.'

The doctor grunted. 'Leaving you literally holding the baby?'

She laughed. Then she grew grave again. 'There's only one thing I want to ask—since I don't think it's occurred to Penny, and I don't want it to.'

'Yes?'

'Is there any . . . ? How much likelihood is there of the baby being . . . handicapped or deformed?'

Dr Trevelyan's eyes seemed to go darker. 'Very little. As you probably know, inbreeding is only dangerous because any inherent fault is apt to be doubled. If there is none to start with—that you know of—it should be all right.' He looked again at Laurie rather sorrowfully, and added, 'Of course, there's always a possibility—but I'd say it was remote.'

'Good.' Laurie got to her feet. 'Well, now I'll leave you to see her. But, please, if there's anything you think I should do for her, let me know.'

Dr Trevelyan smiled and nodded. But he too got up and laid a detaining hand on her arm. 'What about you?'

'What about me?'

'You haven't said a word about yourself. But you must understand, I'm in touch with Luke Veryan—and he's in touch with his son, Joe.'

'Oh!'

'Yes, oh!' He twinkled. 'No more headaches?'

She hesitated. 'A few.'

'Blinding?'

'Sometinies . . .' She hastened to amend it. 'But they're getting better.'

'And what about those ribs?'

Her eyes opened wide. 'You know too much!'

'My business to!' he retorted.

She grinned at him apologetically. 'They only hurt when I run up hill!'

He patted her arm. 'Just take it easy—and if you have any problems, come back to see me.'

'I will.' But she did not really mean it. Her job depended on good health.

'Children all right?'

'Yes . . .' she spoke slowly. 'I think so. The little one—Midge—is still a bit scared of strangers—particularly men.'

'Don't blame her.'

'But Jason's come through it very well—only he's a bit too good and too anxious.'

He nodded. 'Let him run wild by the sea. Not too tight a rein. . . . It'll get easier.'

Laurie's smile was sad, but a lot more confident. 'Yes. I'm sure it will.' As she turned to go, Dr Trevelyan said suddenly, 'Are you sure you don't want me to contact the adoption people? Sixteen is very young to cope with a baby.'

Laurie looked at him levelly. 'I know. You can ask her. But I think she needs to feel wanted by someone. Since her father disowned the child and her mother threw her out—she said, "I've got to have someone to love, haven't I?" '

The doctor's face changed. 'Haven't we all?' he said.

\* \* \*

She left Penny at the doctor's surgery and went on up the village street to look for the school, with Jason and Midge running ahead. The road was steep and narrow, with the small flinty cottages crowding together with their backs to the rock-strewn hillside. Some of them were

185

white-washed and clearly done-up to look more pictur-
esque for the tourists, but most of them remained what
they had always been—plain, grey-stone, work-a-day
dwellings without any frills or any pretentions. A few
houses stood farther up the valley, perched above the
main village on stony outcrops of rock, and one or two
were lower down towards the sea, with the cliffs rising
behind them. All of them looked sturdy and strong, but
not in the least inviting.

The little school was at the far end of the village, higher
up, with its playground bordering the wild heathery hillside and its wide windows looking out over the sloping
valley to the sea. There were quite a lot of children in the
concrete playground, all rushing about and shouting, and
a squarish, pleasant-looking woman with grey-flecked
hair was standing watching them from the doorway. She
seemed unperturbed by the noise, and made no attempt
to interfere with the children's activities until a group of
boys began fighting about something. Then she strode
over to the struggling heap of bodies and hauled the two
ringleaders out by the scruff of their necks. 'None of that!'
Laurie heard her say. 'If you can't find anything more
useful to do than fighting, go and sweep the playground.
Go on. Both of you. Find a broom. Now.'

The boys went. The rest of the children gave them a
cursory glance and went on playing. Laurie thought, It's
small, and not too tough—not nearly as tough as Jason's
London school. But she won't stand any nonsense. I think
Jay will be all right here. But aloud she said to Jason, who
was also staring at the shouting children in the playground, 'What do you think, Jay? You don't *have* to go to
school for a while, unless you want to.'

'Don't I?'

'No. The doctor said you could run wild by the sea!'

He turned his head to look at her and grinned. But his
eyes strayed back to the leaping, running children. 'I
could do that weekends,' he said slowly.

Laurie's eyes were on his expressive face. She knew
then that Jason was lonely—that he needed the routine
and easy companionship of school. It would reassure him

that life was getting back to normal. Satisfied, she opened the gate and went towards the woman standing on the steps. But Midge clutched her hand very tight and shrank from the running feet and the shouting. Yes, with Midge it would be more difficult.

Emma Weelkes knew who Laurie was. The village grapevine had already spread the news of Luke Veryan's winter tenants. Tregarrow was used to hordes of summer visitors descending on its narrow streets and quiet beaches, but winter visitors were rare—and Luke Veryan was a respected member of their community. He'd had a bad time since his wife was ill, and the farm had been difficult to maintain. He could do with some help. Tregarrow people were not unkindly. They were cautious, and slow to accept newcomers, but basically they were warmhearted enough—and staunch allies in trouble. Living close to the sea as they did—with many of their menfolk still working as fishermen out in the fierce grip of the Atlantic—they were used to trouble. Disasters brought out the best in them. And over the years they had come to recognise the look of dazed bewilderment that people got when fate had dealt them too many blows. Laurie had that look—you couldn't mistake it. And already the word was out that she could probably do with a helping hand. About the girl, Penny, they were not so sure. Pregnant? At that age? You could guess what sort of girl *she* was— and what kind of a life she'd been living. And who was she, anyway? The young woman's kid sister? She was obviously too old to be her daughter. But since Laurie had brought her down with her, she must be responsible for her in some way. And since Laurie had clearly come through a rough time herself already, they supposed they'd better not say too much about the girl—looked like she'd got enough on her plate already, without them adding to it.

So the village gossip went. Most of it was harmless and reasonably charitable—though there were one or two beady stares that summed up Penny without much sympathy.

Emma Weelkes, though she heard most of what went

on in her village, did not gossip. She knew all the mothers and children, and listened to all their problems, but she kept her own counsel. And she formed her own opinions, regardless of the general mood of the village.

Now, she welcomed Laurie with a smile and said, 'You must be Mrs Collins. Would you like to come in and have a look round?'

'If you're not too busy . . .' began Laurie, shyly.

'No, it's all right. It's still break-time, and Jean can keep an eye on them.'

She led them into a big sunny schoolroom, decorated with bright-coloured children's paintings and wall-charts. 'We do most of our work in here,' she explained. 'The numbers are too small for separate classes—though we take small groups for special subjects in a couple of the smaller rooms.' She took them into each room, and beyond them to a well-equipped kindergarten full of brilliantly painted toys and small tables and chairs, with glass doors open to the side of the playground.

'How old is your little girl?' asked Emma Weelkes.

'Four—she'll be five at Christmas.' But Laurie was very conscious of Midge's hand clutching hers ever more tightly. 'Only, I think . . . we may have to wait a while before she's ready for school.' She hoped desperately that Emma would understand the urgent warning in her voice, and not press the matter.

But the head-teacher was no fool. She turned to Midge and said, 'Would you like to see our pet rabbit? He's called Maurice, and the children look after him themselves.' Talking easily all the time, she led them out through the glass doors to a couple of cages built close to the wall, with small wired-in runs on the grassy edge of the playground. Maurice was a large lop-eared buck with golden-brown fur and a bold look in his eye.

'Mrs Taggy lives in the next cage,' explained Emma gravely. 'But she's going to have babies any day now, so she likes to be left in peace. I daresay when you next come there'll be a whole lot of baby rabbits to see, too.'

Jason was enchanted. 'Can I stroke him?'

'I should think so. He's very tame. If you could find

any dandelion leaves left, he loves those.' She showed Jason how to reach inside the cage. 'Don't let him out, though—he might escape.' She straightened up and pointed out to the open hillside. 'We've got a goat, too. She's out there, munching heather. Melanie, she's called, and she's got a kid that the children call "Buck's Fizz".'

Midge was watching Jason with the rabbit, fascinated. 'Can I feed him too?' she asked, and suddenly let go of Laurie's hand.

'Of course. If you hold that saucer steady, I'll put a little of his bran mash into it.'

After a few minutes, Emma and Laurie moved quietly away and left the children by the rabbit-hutches.

'Would you have room for Jason?' asked Laurie, when they were sitting in Emma's small office.

Emma Weelkes smiled. 'I don't see why not. We're not overcrowded.'

'He's missed a few weeks . . .' She paused, and then added, 'And life has been a bit . . . difficult for him. But he's a good boy, and he's bright.'

The head-teacher nodded. 'I'm sure he'll fit in.'

Laurie was thinking of that scene in the playground. They didn't look anything like so tough and unruly as London kids, but yet . . . Violence was still too close to Jason's life, and she had to make sure.

'You needn't worry,' said Emma gently. 'I can see he needs a peaceful, trouble-free existence—just as much as our Maurice!'

Laurie laughed. Her eyes met Emma's, filled with relief at being understood so swiftly.

'And as for your little girl . . .'

'Midge?'

'Yes, Midge. I suggest you bring her each time you come to fetch Jason. Let her go to see the animals . . . She has to pass the kindergarten to get to them. I think she'll soon want to stop and play with the others.' She smiled tranquilly at Laurie. 'Let it come from her.'

Laura nodded. 'You're very understanding.'

Emma Weelkes said serenely, 'We're used to almost every problem here. Even in a small backwater like this, human beings get into the same sort of difficulties! The children usually solve them on their own—given time.'

At this point Jason appeared in the doorway, with Midge by the hand. 'She wanted to know where you were,' he said apologetically.

'That's all right.' Emma smiled at him. 'We were just talking about you. Would you like to come to school here?'

'Yes, please,' said Jason.

Midge said nothing. But her eyes strayed to the window which looked out at the playground. The children were filing in now for lessons. And a small group of very young ones were gathered round a laughing girl who was teaching them how to skip, turning the coloured wooden handles of the skipping-rope for each eager child in turn.

'Tomorrow, then?' said Emma Weelkes to Jason, getting to her feet to indicate that the interview was over.

'Magic!' said Jason.

\* \* \*

Penny met them outside the village shop, looking a bit pink but still smiling. Her flaming red hair seemed to light up the street like a banner—and Laurie fancied from the toss of her head in greeting that she was a little at bay.

'Come on,' Laurie glanced at her flushed face. 'We're going down to the cove for a breath of air.'

'But . . . the shopping?'

'It'll keep.' Laurie's voice was firm. 'We've all had enough ordeals for one morning. Let's go and look at the sea.'

The sea was waiting for them—pearl and silver this morning, with a hint of mist on the horizon. A few gulls were sunning themselves on the new-washed sand, and took off with a lazy drift of wing as the children came running down to the shore.

Laurie watched the children laughing and chasing sea-gulls for a few minutes, and then turned abruptly to Penny. 'What did the doctor say?'

'Oh, he thinks everything is OK. But he's fixing a scan for me at the hospital.'

190

Laurie nodded, still not convinced by Penny's airy manner. 'Wasn't he nice to you?'

'Oh yes, he was,' she replied at once. 'Very.' She flicked a glance in Laurie's direction. 'But then you'd been talking to him!'

Laurie grinned. 'What about the district nurse?'

Panny's grin almost matched Laurie's. 'She's coming up to see me at the house. And she'll fix the trip to the hospital in Penzance. There's a local ambulance bus, or something.'

'That's good.' So the nurse hadn't upset her. Then who had? It must have been someone in the shop or in the street.

'Penny,' she said suddenly, 'do you want to wear a wedding-ring? Would it make things easier?'

Penny tossed her red-gold mane. 'No thanks. Who would I say I was married to? My father?'

Laurie sighed.

'Besides, I don't *need* a man to protect me. I can manage on me own! Men are very good at getting you *into* trouble and very bad at getting you out of it!' Her indignant glance flashed at Laurie. 'I'm surprised at you—you of all people!'

Laurie laid a protesting hand on her arm and laughed. 'It was only a suggestion.'

Penny's indignation dissolved like the morning mist. 'I know—to save me trouble.' Her eyes softened as she looked at Laurie. 'But I don't need it. I'm OK.'

Laurie gave her a swift hug. 'Of course you are. I'm going to leave you here with the kids while I get the shopping. Then I'll bring our swim-suits down. We probably won't get many more warm days.'

She went back up to the village street, pondering what she should do about Penny. If they were going to stay here for six months, she couldn't let unfriendly gossip go on upsetting her.

As she went up the step to the little general store, the door opened and a woman came out, carrying a bag full of shopping. Behind her, another woman who was leaning on the counter said, 'No better than she should be, I shouldn't wonder—and at her age, too!'

I suppose I must keep silent, thought Laurie. No one ever talks about what's happened to Penny—not in English everyday life; not in a small country village. You can't. Though it must have happened here sometimes, too, I suppose. But a sudden hot anger surged up inside her. After all, she thought, I'm not the victim this time—it's Penny. And I don't have to keep silent—I can fight for her.

So she marched into the shop and plonked some money down on the counter with a sharp click. 'No one is any better than they should be,' she snapped. 'Especially a victim of rape. Or would you prefer the term "child-abuse"? '

There was a horrified silence in the shop. The woman on the step who had just been going, turned back in appalled protest. 'We didn't mean . . .'

'Oh, I know . . .' said Laurie, pushing the hair out of her eyes in her familiar gesture of stress. 'It's not something one talks about to strangers, is it? But that child has suffered enough, believe me. And since I've taken her under my wing, I've got to protect her as best I can.' She looked at the three women appealingly. 'She needs all the help she can get—especially when the baby comes. It's no joke being a mother at sixteen!'

The women suddenly thawed and began to cluck in sympathy. 'The poor girl!' said the one by the door.

'We'll do what we can,' said the one by the counter.

'This is a good sort of place to come to,' said the postmistress, smiling at them over her counter. 'We look after people in Tregarrow.'

Laurie smiled back—an enormous wash of relief flooding over her. She had been afraid of what might happen to Penny in this small place—more afraid than she cared to admit. But now it looked as if these women at least would be on her side. 'That's good to hear,' she said, and the sudden radiance in her face made the other women blink. 'Now I'd better buy some food. We can't let her starve, can we?'

After that, since she had subtly drawn them into the conspiracy, they couldn't do enough for her. They pointed out the cheapest brands of food and advised her where to go to find mushrooms in the morning fields, and when the fishermen came in with their catch and had fresh fish to sell. And, finally, Annie Merrow—the postmistress— handed Laurie a small tin of Ovaltine, saying, 'Here. Have this on me. Good for expectant mothers!'

Laurie looked at the wispy grey hair and alert dark eyes of the woman before her, and detected unexpected warmth behind the scraped, unsmiling face. 'Thanks,' she said. 'You're very kind.'

She left the shop with a smile all round and a laden carrier-bag in her hand, and began to climb the winding hill path to the cottage. Behind her, the three women began another round of gossip, clucking and tutting together. But it was an altogether different kind of discussion. Laurie had won Penny's first battle for her.

* * *

The sea, she thought—the cool, clean sea. It will wash it all away. In fact, it was more than cool. The deep Atlantic swell swept in and out of the little cove at every tide and gave the swirling shallows little chance to warm up over the pale, smooth sand. It was cold—breathtakingly cold and clear—and as green as glass, as pure as translucent crystal, as buoyant as strong arms holding you in their lilting embrace.

They all swam—though Laurie kept them near to the shore and privately blessed Clem for his foresight and his patience in teaching the children to be safe in the water. Clem, she thought, floating on her back and looking at the sky . . . Clem and his swans and the gently flowing river. But here it is all deep-sea swell and white spray springing against the tawny flanks of the rocks. And small shells and curling amber ribbons of weed, diamond-clear on the bleached sea floor—perfect and untouched.

But this is only today, she thought. Now. An interlude. Tomorrow I've got to work, and I've got to keep my family together and heal their hurts—not only mine—and make

193

them feel safe and secure. I've got to fight my way through and order my own life. I must not think of Clem.

It still hurt her to swim—a deep ache began behind her ribs, and her back was still a little stiff and painful when she kicked out with her legs. But the bruises on her body were healing. The ones in her mind would take longer, she knew.

'Come on, she said, pushing the children forward in a shower of spray and laughter. 'You'll get cold. Time to come out.'

Golden October, she thought, looking up at the sun. Aren't we lucky? They tell me the weather can get very rough down here in the winter, but it's wonderfully calm now—like a dream of gold. The bracken on the hillside had turned golden in the mild autumn air, and the few stunted hazel bushes had gold discs for leaves. The gorse flamed yellow on the clifftops, and the strange orange-tawny rocks glowed golden in the sun. Even the sea had a golden swathe laid across the silver, and gold coins sparked on the swell like the flickering fire of the hazel leaves.

It's so beautiful, thought Laurie, so calm and quiet, drowsing in the October sunshine. It almost makes me want to cry.

'We're lighting a fire!' called Jason, rushing past her with an armful of driftwood. 'Penny's got some matches.'

'Coming,' said Laurie, and stooped to pick up a silvery spar of sea-washed wood lying on the sand.

* * *

The next day, Laurie took Jason to school and then went on to her first day's work, leaving Midge with Penny. But, mindful of Emma Weelkes' suggestion, she arranged that the two of them should go down to fetch Jason home—by way of the rabbit-hutches. Jason protested that he could perfectly well come home on his own, but Laurie said firmly, 'Not till you're used to the cliff path, Jay. Then you can.' And by then, maybe, little Midge would be staying for the mornings, too—if only her built-in terror

194

of being separated from Laurie—her only safe haven—would recede from her mind.

The first morning's work was a bit bewildering. But Laurie began to make sense of Luke's books, and also went into the packing-sheds and the greenhouses to help with the daily deliveries of vegetables and flowers. She found old Bob stooping over the rows of late chrysanthemums and dahlias, and stayed to help him tie them to their stakes so that their heavy heads did not snap off. Old Bob looked up with a toothless grin and said mildly, 'Mornin', Missus. Weather's still holdin'.'

At lunch-time when Laurie was wondering if she ought to go and make Luke a cup of tea, she heard purposeful clatterings going on in his kitchen and went to investigate. Penny was already there, encased in a large apron and clearly in charge, while Midge and Jason were putting knives and forks round the table.

'Jay!' said Laurie, hugging him through Midge's instant, clinging embrace. 'How was your first morning?'

'Smashing!' said Jason, whose vocabulary seemed to be limited to his own brand of superlatives at present. 'How was yours?'

Laurie laughed. 'Good enough—if not exactly smashing!'

'I should hope not!' said Penny, busily stirring something on the Aga hotplate.

Laurie looked at her exquiringly. 'Does Luke Veryan know you're here?'

Penny nodded. 'Told 'im, didn't I? Daft to cook Jay's dinner at the cottage and leave you and Uncle Luke to go hungry.'

Laurie's eyes opened wide. 'Oh, so it's Uncle Luke now, is it?'

Penny's grin was wide and infectious. 'Easier for the kids,' she said briskly. 'Midge couldn't get her tongue round all that.' She tossed her red mane and gave the stew one more stir. 'Besides,' she added, head on one side in consideration as she tasted her cooking, 'I think he rather likes it. Gotta have some kinda family, hasn't he—with Joe so far away an' all?' She lifted the pot of stew off the stove and carried it over to the table.

'Jay,' she commanded, 'go and find Uncle Luke. And that old man, Bob, could do with something hot—out there in the fields all day.'

So a routine was established. Luke Veryan never said he approved or disapproved, but he came in to Penny's meals, and so did old Bob, and both of them looked the better for it. Also, Luke's house mysteriously began to take on a more lived-in look. The rooms got cleaned and dusted, the windows got rid of their film of salt sea-spray and sand, and the patch of earth round the kitchen door suddenly sprouted winter violet plants and tubs of geraniums.

Jason always brought the cows in before breakfast and let them out again into their pasture before he went to school, and usually ran all the way back in the afternoon to help again before it got dark. And even Midge had learnt how to collect the eggs and how to help old Bob pack the cut flowers for market.

Laurie had little time to herself, but she took to wandering down to the cove very early in the morning. It was peaceful then—cool and quiet. The creamy sands were new-washed by the tide—smooth and unmarked, save by the thin feet of the gulls who strolled unconcernedly along the edge of the water. There were cormorants out on the rocks, their long, elegant necks silhouetted against the morning light, and a small, perky shag kept diving and coming up in the clear green water close to the cliffs. And the sea—the sea was all round her: pouring in from the deep Atlantic, breaking with a sighing rush on the shore and receding in a shower of pebbles and shells.

In the early morning light, the small cove looked very clean and bright—the rocks scoured by the sea, the sloping beach swept bare, the fine shells of the tide lines rinsed and jewel-bright, and the deep water of the little bay clear and unsullied. And above it all, a pure unclouded sky.

Pure, sighed Laurie. And empty. No one here but me. Only the sea-birds and the endlessly moving glossy backs of the Atlantic rollers. With a sense of strange release and freedom, she slid out of her clothes and into the water, scarcely breaking the opal surface.

She could feel the scales falling (even more than in the old, slow Medway), the fierce armour laid aside, and her mind reaching out, unguarded, unafraid. She lay on her back and looked at the sky—remote and limitless—and watched the dazzling wings of a seagull turn in the air, lifting and falling and hanging almost motionless on the small offshore breeze. So effortlesss and calm—but not so powerful or full of magic as the flight of a swan.

She did not stay long. One brisk swim across to the rocks and back was all the time she could spare—and a small, quiet moment when she turned over and gazed down through shadow and sunlight to the pale sea floor below. Then it was running across the sand to get warm, climbing the high dune and the cliff path to the cottage to get the breakfast with Penny, seeing Jason off to school along the easier path to the village, giving Midge an extra hug to make up for leaving her with Penny, and going on up the hill to Luke Veryan's farm and the day's work.

She was busy all day long—and sometimes the work was fairly back-breaking, especially when she stooped over the crates of vegetables or went out to help old Bob with the picking or the hoeing. But she did not mind. She was somehow glad to be endlessly busy. And putting Luke Veryan's accounts in order gave her an unexpected satisfaction. She even went to consult Farmer George Button about market prices and opportunities, and found that Luke's turnover could be improved in various useful ways.

The only thing that troubled her was her eyesight, as she seemed to have recurrent attacks of double vision, so that Luke's columns of figures suddenly multiplied alarmingly. But she decided that this would disappear in time and was just a hangover from the concussion and the hairline fracture. She didn't think it was worth consulting Dr. Trevelyan about it.

Penny, though, was a different matter. She went with her to the hospital—begging time off to do so—and was relieved to learn that the scan was satisfactory and the doctors considered everything to be in order. The baby, they told Penny, was due about the last week in December. It might be a Christmas baby, or of course it might be a bit early—first babies often were.

It had occurred to Laurie that Penny had made no provision for the child as yet—no baby-clothes, no cot, not even a packet of nappies, and certainly no pleasant-looking garment for Penny herself to wear in the last few weeks. She was still struggling into the same old shirt and the same pair of dungarees several sizes too large.

'Come on,' she said, when they came out of the hospital with Midge between them, 'we're going shopping.'

'What with?' asked Penny, tossing her bright hair in the sun.

'Your maternity grant,' said Laurie, grinning. 'And my wages.'

'But you can't . . .'

'Oh yes, I can.' She was still smiling. 'It's my baby, too. I'm going to be sort of an aunt.'

'What's an narnt?' asked Midge.

Penny looked down at her and laughed. 'Someone who wastes her money on other people,' she said.

But they were all happy that day, and they came home on the rattling country bus laden with parcels and full of cheerful chatter. They decided Penzance was rather beautiful along the waterfront, with St Michael's Mount floating like a mirage in the bay—and Newlyn with its fishing fleet and steep coast road was even better.

When they got back, Jason was home before them and had dutifully put the kettle on.

'We brung you a present,' stated Midge, and held out a crumpled-looking flat parcel.

Inside was a new pencil case for school, and a thin little paperback about the Cornish coast and its wildlife, with a picture of a seal on the front.

Jason was delighted. 'There's seals in the cove sometimes,' he said. 'Mrs Weelkes told me.'

Midge held up her own small present. 'I've got a sea-lion, 'stead of the lion I lost.'

Laurie almost shuddered, remembering the part Midge's yellow lion had played in the last awful scene with Jeff. But she was relieved to see that the little girl didn't seem at all disturbed by the memory of that battered woolly toy.

'And there's things for the baby,' Midge was saying happily. 'Lots of them!'

Not enough, really, thought Laurie, a little anxiously. And how are we going to afford all the other things we'll need? We'll have to have a carry-cot or something on wheels, if Penny's to be able to go out at all while I'm at work.

'I've got a new dress!' said Penny, holding it up to show then. 'Shall I put it on?'

Seeing the brightness in her face, and the children's eager response, Laurie privately put her worries aside and set about cooking the sausages for tea.

'Mum,' said Jason, leaning over her arm by the cooker, 'Mrs Taggy's had seven babies. But she sat on one.'

'Oh dear.' Laurie was busy turning the sausages under the grill. 'Were the others all right?'

'Yes. They're a bit skinny though, at first. Will Penny have seven, do you think?'

'Good grief, no!' Penny exploded with laughter. 'Only one, Jay, I promise you!' And she twirled round the kitchen in her new bright-green dress and added, giggling helplessly, 'One's quite enough!'

\* \* \*

At the end of the week, Jason got paid too. His eyes went round with wonder at the sight of the money.

'We'll go down to the post office,' decreed Laurie, 'and take you out a savings book right away. Mr Veryan says you're to put 50p away every week!'

'And then I can buy my bottles,' agreed Jason happily.

Laurie was not working that Saturday morning, so they all went down to the village post office together. After Jason had become the proud possessor of a savings book, they bought some Cornish pasties and a bag of sticky

199

buns from the baker, and two bottles of pop to go with them, and went down to the cove to have a picnic.

The weather had changed in the night, and a heavy white mist had rolled in from the sea, blanketing the headlands and safe harbours with a deathly pall of invisibility. The deep voice of the foghorn on the clifftop had called its warning all night long to the ships and little boats out on the dark ocean, and the fishermen from the next cove round the point with its tiny slipway had been unable to return from their night's fishing.

But now, as Laurie and the children settled damply on the beach, a small offshore wind got up. The mists suddenly rolled back, leaving a drenched and glistening world behind, and the sun broke through, lighting the trails and wisps with silver as they drifted and dissolved on the sea's face. And then, out of the silvery swirls, came the fishing-boats—a long, sturdy line of them—making steadily for home after the night's toil.

'Oh!' breathed Jason. 'Don't they look super coming in!'

'I bet they're glad to be home,' said Penny, and crinkled up her eyes against the sun.

They watched the steady line of boats cross the bay until they went behind the headland to their own safe haven and the throb of their engines faded on the morning breeze. Then Jason said, in a voice of dream, 'Now I can launch my bottles.'

He took a pencil and a scrap of paper out of his pocket—Jason was the kind of boy who always had useful things in his pockets—folded the paper neatly in half and tore it in two. On one half he wrote, very carefully and neatly. "*I love you, Jane*" and sat looking at it with his head on one side. 'Is that right?'

'Yes,' agreed Laurie, smiling.

He looked at her seriously. 'She said, "Jane loves you". And even if it came back it would be true. But I thought . . . this was truer.'

'Why?' demanded Midge.

Jason did not look exasperated. He was patient with Midge. 'Look,' he said, pointing to his lettering. "I love you, Jane" means she loves the sea—OK?'

'OK,' repeated Midge, like a small parrot.

'And it means we love Jane—OK?'

'OK.'

'But if it comes back, and we read it again, it means Jane loves us. See?'

'Oh,' said Midge doubtfully. And then, as an afterthought, 'Can I write on it, too?'

He hesitated. It was his special magic, after all—his private ritual. He didn't want it spoilt. But he was generous, too. 'You can put a cross on it,' he said, and handed her the pencil. 'That means the same.'

'Does it?' Midge had reached the age of endless questions. But she solemnly put a cross on the paper and watched, fascinated, while he rolled it up tight and shoved it into the bottle through the narrow top. Inside it unrolled a bit and spread out, but, however hard she peered through the glass, the message was hidden.

Jason had remembered about the corks, too. The original metal caps wouldn't go on again so he'd begged two corks from the sweet-shop, and even brought a penknife to cut them down. Now he skilfully corked the first bottle and turned to consider the one to Clem.

'Can I put the same?' he wondered, and looked at Laurie with his wide, too-adult gaze.

'Why not?' said Penny, lazily pouring sand through her fingers.

'But is it *true*?' he asked, pencil poised.

'Yes,' said Laurie quietly—and felt strange echoes and certainties stir in her mind, like rings in a pool. 'It is true.'

Jason was still looking at her with deep enquiry. Now, he nodded once and then bent his head over the paper. *"I love you, Clem"* he wrote. And Midge carefully put her mark there, too.

They all went down to the water's edge to see them go.

'Not near the rocks,' said Penny, sensibly. 'They might get smashed—the waves are too big there. Try wading out a bit over the sand.'

Jason was already in his swimming trunks and went confidently into the water—not even gasping at the cold. He waded out until the water was up to his waist.

'Now!' called Laurie. 'No farther, or you won't be able to throw them.'

He turned to look at them then—the three people that he loved standing on the shore—and felt a strangeness about the moment, as if he was casting a spell of deeper magic than he knew.

Then he looked out to sea, where the long swells were beginning, and lifted his arm and threw. He threw Jane's first, and watched it bob and turn and ride the water and then drift out on the next withdrawal as a spent wave receded. A bigger swell was coming in now, and the careening bottle was suddenly swamped in a great sweep of jade-green water. When it had passed, the bottle had gone.

There it goes, he thought. I wonder where it will get to. Then he took a deep breath and threw Clem's bottle as far as he could reach. Like the first, it bobbed and lifted, sailing the first waves bravely, heading away from him. But then another big swell poured in, unbroken, and swept on over the shelving sands of the little cove in a smooth green curve of power. And when he looked, the second bottle was gone, too—taken by the sea.

He stood there a long time, gazing out across the lift and fall of the waves, trying to catch a glimpse of the bottles as they sailed towards the far horizon. But they were gone, and all he could see was the dazzle of the sun on the water, the rising swell of the next oncoming wave, and an occasional wheeling sea-bird in the blue air above.

Presently he felt a wet hand slide firmly into his, and turned to find Laurie beside him, her jeans rolled up to her knees and her hair haloed with salt sea-spray.

'They're safe now,' she said gently. 'The sea will look after them. Come and get warm. Penny's lit a fire.'

Together they waded back to the shore. Jason did not speak. A great welling sadness seemed to have got inside him, and he did not understand it. The world was too big, the great Atlantic ocean was too mighty and turbulent—and his friends were too far away to reach. And somehow, all this beauty round him—the sea and sky, and life itself—was full of a terrible sadness. There were no words for it, but it was there—deep inside him, like an ache, deeper than tears.

But Laurie understood him. She gave his hand an extra comforting squeeze, and led him silently back to the driftwood fire and Penny's warm and welcoming smile. 'We're toasting buns,' she said. 'Don't they smell good?'

\* \* \*

In November, the first of the winter gales came tearing across the sea. The trees bent almost double, and the leaves were torn off them in a horizontal stream of sodden gold. The seas grew mountainous out in the bay, and crashed against the tawny rocks in great white towers of spray. The long Atlantic rollers raced into the cove and pushed the tide-lines farther up the beach, hurling themselves in solid ice-green chunks on to the shivering sands.

Laurie was fascinated—almost terrified—by their power, and forbade the children to go anywhere near the water. Even so, they all watched the great waves smashing themselves against the drenched cliff-face, and listened awestruck to the roar of the surf and the shouting, raging wind,

The fishing fleet from the next cove stayed inside its safe little harbour wall, and the fishermen sat about under the shelter of the fish-packing shed, mending their nets and gossiping about other storms and other wild nights at sea when they got caught out and couldn't get home. Even now there were one or two foolhardy ones who had ignored the shipping-forecast and gone out for the night's fishing—and they hadn't come back yet.

There was a sense of watchfulness and waiting anxiety about little Tregarrow. The villagers knew about the winter gales, and the toll they sometimes exacted. Old Bob, who had been a fisherman all his life until his rheumatics got too bad, shook his head over his battered chrysanthemums and said to Laurie, 'Bad, she is. I never likes 'er blowing in sou'west—takes 'em too near the rocks.'

'Aren't most of the fishermen ashore?' asked Laurie, pulling her hood down against the streaming rain.

'Ay, *they* is!' He grunted. 'But there's allus strange craft don't know their way around these waters. They'm the ones as causes the trouble.'

Sure enough, late that evening the maroon went off for the lifeboat down at Newlyn or Mousehole, and a small knot of people—old retired fishermen and a few anxious women—gathered on Tregarrow Head to peer out to sea.

Luke Veryan and George Button passed Laurie, running, with a coil of rope and a lifebuoy in their hands and a scatter of village boys after them.

'Ship on the rocks,' panted Luke. 'May be able to get some of 'em off . . .', and went on running. And now, various other men from the village were following him down to the edge of the cove.

Laurie, after a glance at the darkening sky, lit Luke's storm-lantern, which always stood ready in the porch of the farmhouse, and followed them down. Penny and the children were safe in the cottage, she reflected, and there might be something she could do.

There were people on the clifftop, but there was also a string of small lights bobbing about among the rocks at the far end of the bay. Laurie took the familiar path down and went on round the edge of the cliffs towards the shadowy figures on the shore. There were occasional shouts and sudden flashes of light from the edge of the sea, but the howling wind and the crashing surf drowned what was said and the driving rain and gathering darkness made it impossible to see what was happening.

At the cliff's end, where the jumble of rocks began, Laurie stumbled into another small knot of people—and among them saw the grim face of Agnes Penwillis, the district nurse.

'What can I do?' asked Laurie, trying to make herself heard above the gale.

'Nothing much any of us can do,' sid the nurse, shaking her head. 'Ship's broken her back on the rocks. Lifeboat's coming. We may get some of 'em off this way. They've got a line to her.' She looked at Laurie and added kindly, 'The lads are bringing down a couple of stretchers. There may be injuries. But blankets and a flask of tea—they might come in useful.'

Behind Laurie came Penny's cheerful voice in the dark, 'I've brought those—and a ground sheet to keep them dry.'

'Penny!' Laurie sounded almost angry. 'You shouldn't be out in this. You might slip on the rocks or something.'

'Safe as a house,' said Penny, grinning. 'And nearly as big!' Then, seeing Laurie's anxious face in the glimmer of the storm-lantern, she added, 'Old Bob's staying with Midge at the cottage. Says he's too stiff to be any use. But Jay's coming down with the boys and the stretchers.'

There was a sudden flurry of movement and a chorus of shouts from the rocks, and then a flare lit up the scene for a blinding moment. In its glare, Laurie saw the bows of a ship jammed hard against the rocks at the far corner of the spit of land enclosing the cove, and a line stretched taut from its shattered superstructure to some point closer in on the rocks. And a man was dangling from the line, trying awkwardly to help himself hand-over hand as the men on shore pulled him in.

'One!' muttered Agnes Penwillis, and got ready to receive her first casualty. 'How many more, I wonder?' Then she tugged at the next man's sleeve, and a concerted shout went up to the men on the ropes. 'Over here!'

Silently, efficiently, the drenched villagers passed the injured man from one to the other until he was handed gently down to the nurse waiting on the shore. 'What's the damage?' she asked, lowering him gently on to the sand.

'Broken ankle, I think,' he said, speaking good but halting English. 'Spar fell on it . . . It's nothing much—there's others worse . . . She hit head-on . . . We couldn't save her.' He sounded much more upset about his ship than his ankle.

'Stretcher party's here,' said a dark shape in oilskins at her elbow. 'Ambulance coming to the top.'

'Better splint it first,' said Agnes. 'Save jarring it. Try to hold still.' And she set about her work with swift decision. 'Here,' she snapped at Laurie, 'you look sensible. Hold this!'

When she had finished, Penny leant forward and

draped a blanket round the man's shoulders, and the stretcher-bearers carried him off up the winding path to the clifftop.

Two more men were winched off uninjured and passed on down to the waiting rescuers on the beach. These were given blankets and cups of tea to warm them up. Laurie discovered that several of the women had come equipped with these immediate comforts. They were used to such emergencies.

Then came one who was more seriously injured, wrapped in oilskins and tied to the lifeline from the beach, where he dangled helplessly like a broken doll. Agnes did what she could for him, shaking her head a little, and sent him on to the waiting ambulance as fast as possible. Laurie seemed to have become her assistant, and handed bandages and scissors and swabs when required.

By this time the lifeboat had arrived and stood off the rocks, unable to come too close for fear of also being smashed to pieces. The seas were breaking over their bows in massive fury as it was, and they were tossed about in the mountainous waves like a cork. And soon, overhead, was the thrum of a helicopter from Culdrose — though the blinding rain and thick darkness of the storm made it impossible to see much down below.

The rescue went on nearly all night, and between the three parties on beach, sea and sky, they got every man off, except one who was lost overboard at the first impact and couldn't be found in the pounding dark.

Towards dawn, the wind dropped a little and the lashing rain eased off — but the seas went on hurling themselves at the rocks in unrelenting anger. The weary party of rescuers looked out at the wrecked ship one last time before turning their backs on the sea and beginning the long walk home, drenched and tired.

But Penny and Jason had already thought of this and had gone back to Luke's big farmhouse kitchen and laid on a huge pot of soup, and two boiling kettles hissed on the Aga, waiting to make hot tea for everyone. Jason, full of useful importance, stopped everyone as they came up the path and invited them into Luke's kitchen — having

206

first run all the way back down to the rocks to ask the old farmer's permission.

'Why not?' growled Luke. 'Do *something* useful!' He was already wet and cold, and a bit sad to find that he was getting too old to be much help in an emergency—though he had been able to direct the rigging of the line, and he and George Button had hauled on the rope with the best of them.

Laurie walked back up the cliff path with Agnes Penwillis and called in at the cottage on the way, to reassure Midge and Old Bob that everyone was safe. But when she looked in through the door, she found the old man fast asleep in the chair by the fire, with little Midge curled up on his lap like a kitten, also fast asleep.

Smiling, Laurie tiptoed out again and left them undisturbed, following the sturdy figure of the nurse to Luke Veryan's kitchen door, where warmth and light and hot drinks awaited everyone.

It was an exhausted party, but a cheerful one. They had done their best. Between them, twenty-one lives had been snatched from the sea. Even the captain was safe, though he had refused to leave his crippled vessel until the last of his men had been taken off. Now he stood with the remnants of his crew by Luke's stove, warming his hands on a mug of soup, and trying in halting English to express his thanks. It turned out they were a Dutch trawler fishing out in the Atlantic off Ireland, blown off course by the storm. In a very short time, all the crew members had been offered beds for the night (or the morning) by their rescuers—even Luke Veryan had volunteered, and the Dutch captain had agreed to stay with him. (Laurie thought there was a certain reluctance on the part of both crew and captain to be too far from their ship and its battered contents on the rocks. They had obviously heard the old tales of Cornish wreckers and their swift, illegal salvage from the sea).

Penny went off to see if there was a bed fit to sleep in for the captain, and Laurie went round again with the saucepan of soup, while Jason and Agnes Penwillis went on pouring out cups of tea.

No one wanted to linger. They were all tired and long-ing for sleep, though the warmth of Luke's kitchen was very welcome. But as soon as the soup and tea were demolished, they drifted off to their own homes, calling a cheerful goodnight or good morning to Luke as they went, and taking their shipwrecked guests with them. All at once the big farmhouse kitchen was empty—save for Luke and the weary sea-captain, and Penny and Laurie washing cups in the sink while Jason went round the room collecting more.

'Leave all that,' commanded Luke. 'It'll keep till morn-ing. Get the boy home to bed. It's late,' He paused, straightening his back a little painfully, and added, 'You'm did a good job there, the three on you,' and smiled a creaky tired smile as he sent them home. From Luke Veryan that was high praise.

So Penny and Laurie, with Jason between them, went stumbling back down the path to their own cottage door.

'Don't wake them!' breathed Laurie, and they all slipped past old Bob and little Midge, still sleeping peace-fully in the chair, and crept up the creaking stairs to fall into bed and exhausted sleep almost in one breath.

We're safe, thought Laurie, before sleep engulfed her completely. Everyone's safe. The storm is over. We can sleep in peace.

Outside, the wind was dying but the sea still roared, and a few seagulls cried, wheeling above the waves. But inside it was warm and quiet, and soon even Laurie slept.

\* \* \*

Laurie thought that it was from that night—the night of the shipwreck—that the villagers of Tregarrow began to accept her and the family. Even Penny noticed the differ-ence, and met friendly faces in the village when she went shopping or took Midge to meet Jason from school. And Midge herself met a small boy called Billy Tremain at the kindergarten, who called out to her every time she came by, 'You comin', then? You comin' soon?' And one day Midge suddenly answered, 'Yes!'

Penny held her breath. But Midge made no further

comment. She marched on to see Maurice the rabbit and Mrs Taggy and her six fluffy babies, and then waited for Jason by the gate as usual. But the next morning she announced quite calmly, 'I'm goin' to school today.'

Penny looked at her sternly. 'They may not let you stay—not without asking.'

'We'll ask,' stated Midge. And ask she did, as soon as she got to the door.

Jean, the kindergarten supervisor, had already been briefed by Emma Weelkes about Midge, so she merely smiled and said cheerfully, 'Of course you can stay. Where shall we put you, now?'

'Next to Billy,' said Midge, and promptly walked over to where her dark haired admirer was waiting for her— his grey eyes fixed on her honey-gold curls in fascinated wonder.

'Hallo,' he said, suddenly shy. 'You come, then.'

'Course,' agreed Midge. 'I said so, didn' I?' And she sat down beside him companionably on the floor.

Above her head, Jean and Penny looked at one another and smiled.

'I'll come back at twelve,' said Penny, and went very quietly out of the door before Midge could see her go. But she needn't have worried. Midge and Billy were entirely absorbed—dark head and fair bent close together, building a leaning tower of Pisa out of bricks.

When Penny reported this small triumph at lunch-time, Laurie picked Midge up and whirled her round with a whoop of delight. 'Aren't you clever! Staying at school all by yourself!'

'I wasn't by mineself,' pointed out Midge logically. 'I was with Billy.'

Both pairs of eyes above her head danced a secret dance of amusement—but nothing was said. Only Jason added approvingly, 'You can go to school with me now—like a *proper* sister.'

There was no answer to that, except Midge's indignant retort, 'I *am* a proper sister!'

Neither of the children understood quite what the others were laughing at, but they joined in just the same.

* * *

That weekend there was a village jumble sale in the Methodist Hall, in aid of the Lifeboat Fund, and Penny—tipped off by Annie Merrow at the post office—insisted on making them all go to have a look because there might be a pram for sale. The hall was crowded with women and children, but when they managed to push their way through, there was indeed a pram for sale—a carry-cot on wheels that had seen better days but was still quite serviceable. Penny bought it for £2, and considered herself very lucky. She also bought a vivid knitted blanket in patchwork colours and a set of bright plastic beads to hang across the pram. Laurie bought the children some quite good winter jerseys and an extra pair of jeans for Jason, who seemed to be growing out of everything. She also bought Penny a frilly nightie for going to hospital, but she put that away in her bag rather quickly and said nothing about it, in case Penny got cross and said it was extravagant. Jason, on the other hand, had no qualms about spending his 50p on a small compass set in serpentine stone—a left-over tourist souvenir—and a red rubber ball for Midge.

Laurie had a moment of private rebellion in her mind about always having to buy second-hand clothes for the children and always having to worry about money. It would be wonderful, she thought wistfully, to earn enough to keep them all—Penny and the baby included—in real comfort. Not to have to depend on hand-outs from social security, and a precarious maintenance order—and not to have to work quite so hard and so long, or to get so cold and wet and stiff as she did sometimes on Luke Veryan's farm.

But then she gave herself a shake and admitted that she was a lot better off down here in Tregarrow than she had any right to expect. She loved their trim little cottage, and she loved the cove and the sea. The children were both happy at the village school, and the shadows were beginning to leave Midge at last. And young Penny seemed well content with the way they were living, and remained well and unfailingly cheerful.

What am I worrying about? she thought. Everything's all right. We don't need anything more.

She had been standing beside one of the stalls, staring unseeingly at the pots of honey and home-made jam placed in neat rows along it. But now her eyes suddenly played their alarming tricks again, and she found herself looking unsteadily at double rows of jam-jars, and double-edged trestle tables. She swayed a little, feeling strangely dizzy and off-balance, and put a swift hand up to her head.

'What's the matter?' said Penny's voice close to her. 'Anything wrong?'

'No,' Laurie spoke vaguely. 'Hot in here . . . Get some air . . .', and she lurched away through the crowd and fought her way to the door. There was a wooden bench outside and she sank down on to it, struggling to get the world back into focus. I mustn't pass out here, she thought. I *mustn't*! What will people think? . . . What will Luke Veryan think? . . . It's more than my job's worth . . . I must pull myself together.

Almost at once, Penny and the children came out after her, looking a bit anxious. 'You all right?' asked Jason.

Laurie sat up straight and summoned a smile. 'Of course I am. You go on ahead with Penny and get the tea. I'll . . . I think I'll have a bit of a walk—clear my head.'

They looked at her gravely for a moment, and Midge's eyes began to go dark with shadowy memories. But Penny seized her by the hand and said cheerfully, 'Come on. You can help me push the new pram'—and she set off up the hill towards the cottage without looking back.

But Jason lingered a moment, and then said like an adult, 'Don't go too far if you're tired.'

Laurie reached out a rather groping hand and touched one of the two Jasons in front of her. 'All right, Jay . . . I won't be long.'

She waited till they had gone, watching their blurred images retreat up the hill path, and then got to her feet and made her way slowly down the narrow street towards the cove. The sea, she thought—the sea will put me right.

She reached the pale dunes at the head of the cove and began to climb down towards the beach, her feet sinking into the soft sand at every step. She had just reached the level, firmer sand of the little bay when a group of seagulls who had been scavenging on the high-tide line saw her coming and flew up almost into her face with a clatter of wings and a chorus of noisy shrieks. The air seemed all at once to be full of noise and flapping wings. And suddenly there were other wings back in her head, beating frantically to get out, and she fell forward under their onslaught into a small, quiet heap on the damp sand.

She came round, groggily, to feel a wet tongue licking her face and to hear a man's voice saying, 'No, Corny. Leave her to me.'

At first she thought it was Clem's voice—it sounded so calm and competent, and so full of underlying strength. But it couldn't be Clem, she remembered sadly—Clem was far away. A sudden childish longing seized her for the warmth and reassurance of Clem's unquestioning kindness. She wanted to lie back and give up and leave it all to him—to stop trying to fight her way through alone . . . Oh, just to have someone strong to turn to—someone wise and kind who would know all the answers! Not to have to take all these decisions on her own, or to have to keep on working and worrying all day long in order to make ends meet and keep her young family safe. Oh, just to lean on Clem and let him look after them all, like his swans . . . And never have to lie awake in the night, too scared of the future to sleep.

But she was ashamed of this sudden collapse of her will, really. She knew she had to be independent. She had to stop being afraid, and learn to cope with life without running away. She had to turn into someone strong enough to stand alone—to order her own life and that of her children—and Penny's—without relying on *anyone*. Only then could she ever go back to Clem and say: I'm a whole person now. I can manage on my own. But I'd rather be near you—like your swans who got well and stayed close by you on the river. Only then would the wings in her head finally quieten and leave her in peace.

'Come on,' said the same kindly voice. 'Are you with us? Open your eyes and see.'

Laurie did as she was told.

Beside her was the square, weather-worn face of Dr Trevelyan, and beyond him a beautiful creamy retriever was sitting on the sand, looking at her with its head on one side in interested enquiry.

Laurie blinked, feeling confused and somehow guilty, and tried to struggle into an upright position. 'I can't keep doing this!' she muttered crossly, pushing the hair out of her eyes.'

The doctor sat down comfortably on the sand beside her. 'Have you done it before?' he asked in a casual voice.

'Yes. But I thought I was over it.'

He was looking at her shrewdly. 'Headache?'

She shook her head faintly, and then realised it was a mistake and put up her hands to steady it. 'Not exactly. More like . . .'

'Yes?'

'Wings . . .' she murmured, her eyes on the seagulls wheeling and turning above the sea.

The doctor looked startled. 'Wings?'

'Trying to get out,' explained Laurie. And then, more confidently, 'They will one day.'

He grunted. 'Wings in the head? Don't think I've ever prescribed for them. Anything else?'

Laurie hesitated—half-reassured by the flick of mischief behind the dry voice. 'No-o. Except that I see double sometimes still.'

'Double wings, eh?' He grinned encouragingly at her faint smile. 'Often?'

'N-no. Just occasionally.'

'Like just now?'

'Yes.' She felt, guiltily, that she was taking up his time with trivialities, and said suddenly, 'This is absurd. You're off duty.'

He was still half-smiling. 'A doctor is never off duty! Besides, Corny found you. He'd be most indignant if I just walked off and left you in a heap on the sand!'

Laurie laughed.

'That's better.' He watched the colour coming slowly back into her face.

She took a deep breath of clear sea air. Clear, she thought desperately. I must get things clear! But aloud she said with sudden shyness, 'I don't want to take up your time.'

Trevelyan's laughter startled the seagulls. 'You must be unique. Everyone wants to take up my time!' Then he reached into the small haversack beside him on the sand and took out a thermos, and briskly poured her out a cup of tea. 'Saturday', he remarked, 'is my walking day. Corny waits all week for this moment. And so do I.' He leant back on one arm and looked round him at the quiet cove and the gleaming, empty sands with calm satisfaction. 'Cures everything—better than I can,' he murmured. Then he looked at her sternly with his shrewd, assessing stare, and wagged a reproving finger at her. 'Now, listen to me, young woman. Can't have you fainting in coils all over the place. Clutters up the beach! Come up and see me at the surgery—*tomorrow!*'

'Tomorrow's Sunday. And I'm packing for Mr Veryan.'

He glared. 'Well, Monday then. After work.'

She sighed. 'All right. But it's not necessary.'

'That's for me to say. We may need to get another X-ray.'

Panic overcame her. 'I *can't*. I can't spare the time.' She looked suddenly desperate and frightened. 'I can't afford to be ill.'

'Nonsense!' Trevelyan spoke brusquely. 'Luke Veryan's not going to throw you out just because you take half a day off to go down to the hospital.'

She was still looking distraught. 'You don't understand. There's Penny, too. I'll probably have to take some time off when her baby comes. She won't be able to manage at first. She's only a kid herself. What will he think, poor man? That he's taken on a houseful of helpless cripples?'

Trevelyan snorted. 'He'll think he's taken on a brave, hardworking young woman, I shouldn't wonder.' He got to his feet and gave her a kindly pat. 'Shall I see you home?'

214

'No,' said Laurie, smiling at his kindness. 'You go on with your walk. I'll be all right now.'

'Sit there until you feel stronger,' he commanded. 'And then go home and have a rest. See you on Monday. No skiving, mind!' And he whistled to Corny, who was digging a hole in the sand, and stumped off towards the rocks and the high cliff path round the edge of the bay.

Laurie closed her eyes for a moment against the dazzle of the sun which had suddenly broken through the low-hanging sea-mist above the headland.

Peace, she thought . . . quietness and peace. There's nothing to be afraid of. When she opened her eyes again, Jason was coming down the dunes towards her.

'Thought you'd be here,' he said. 'Tea's ready. Penny sent me to fetch you.' And, like a true protective male, he put his arm through Laurie's and led her home.

\* \* \*

Dr Trevelyan was as good as his word and insisted on Laurie getting another X-ray. So she went down to Penzance on the country bus, guiltily missing half a day's work and leaving Penny behind with the children. Penny had wanted to come with her, but Laurie had been adamant. She was getting too near her time for long and tedious journeys, and the bus was very bumpy, jolting up and down all those hills and country lanes.

The weather had suddenly changed too, from being mild and drizzly to another spate of furious gales and torrential rain. Old Bob and Luke could do nothing out of doors but could only potter endlessly in the glass-houses, so Laurie did not feel quite so bad about missing work. There wasn't a lot to do anyway. Everything was awash, and the farm was a sea of mud.

The rain poured down on the sodden countryside, and all the little streams turned into raging torrents, sweeping across roads, carrying away young trees and even breaking down walls and small stone bridges. The bus churned on through clouds of spray and mud unitl it came round the coast road in sight of Newlyn and Penzance, and a cold grey-black sea beaten flat by the rain stretched before it.

Laurie had to wait a long time for her X-ray, and then a long time more before they decided the pictures were satisfactory and she could go home.

Once more the bus set off in driving rain and early darkness, trundling up and down hill in the teeth of the gale. Laurie could see nothing out of the windows, and the driver could see little beyond the swish of the windscreen wipers and the curtain of rain like a silver wall against the lights. But inside it was warm and light, like a bubble of comfort and safety in the midst of the storm, and the few passengers felt lulled by the throbbing engine, secure in their cocoon of rattling glass.

But all at once there were lights and waving arms on the road ahead of them, and the dim figures of men in oilskins with torches and storm-lanterns in their hands. 'Bridge down!' came the shout from one of them. 'Four feet of water on the road.'

'Better turn back for St Buryan,' called another.

The bus driver got out and consulted with the men in the road. Then he climbed in again, already drenched by the rain, and called out to the passengers, 'We're returning to St Buryan. Can't get through this way. Anyone want to get out and walk?'

There was a general laugh at this. But one worried woman said anxiously, 'I suppose we can telephone from St Buryan?'

'Sure,' agreed the driver. 'Though I doubt if anyone'll get through with a car to pick you up on this road.'

'Will you be trying the top road instead?' asked another traveller.

The bus driver looked doubtful. 'I dunno. Have to phone the depot first and ask for instructions. And get a road report if I can.' He looked at them all apologetically. 'Sorry, folks. At least I can get you back to somewhere warm and dry.'

'The pub, you mean?' said someone hopefully, and there was another laugh.

The bus turned in the road, guided by the men with

lanterns, and set off back towards the little town it had left twenty minutes before. Laurie wondered anxiously if she would be able to get home at all that night, and whether Luke Veryan would take a message down to Penny at the cottage. If the bus couldn't get through that bit of flooded road, nor could Luke's van. Maybe, though, if the bus went along the top road it could cut back on to the Tregarrow road later on—or maybe she could walk from some point or other.

The bus pulled up in the main square and the driver and all his passengers crowded into the nearest pub, where the driver made for the telephone while everyone else bought drinks. The bar was full of people sheltering from the storm, and the talk was all of trees down here and roads blocked there, rivers overflowing their banks, and village streets becoming torrents of mud.

Laurie did not buy a drink. She listened to the talk around her, and waited for the bus driver to get off the telephone. She wanted to ring Luke Veryan. Finally, the driver returned and said to the assembled passengers, 'Can't go farther tonight. Very sorry. They say even the top road is bad, and there's more trees coming down. I've got to return to Penzance. I'm afraid you'll either have to stay here for the night or come back with me to the bus station. Or try to make your own arrangements to get home from here.' He looked troubled by this, and added again, 'I'm sorry.'

Laurie went through the back of the bar to the telephone, not waiting to hear what the other passengers said. The phone rang a long time in Luke Veryan's house, and then a quavering, out-of-breath voice said, 'Hello? Veryan's Farm.'

'Who's that?' asked Laurie, surprised at the thin, old voice. 'This is Laurie Collins here.'

'Oh, Laurie!' The voice sounded relieved and upset both at once. 'It's Bob here. There's trouble here, missus.'

'What kind of trouble, Bob?'

'Your young Penny's started . . .'

'What? But she's not due yet.'

'I know. Slipped on Mr Luke's floor, 'er did.'

'Have you sent for Dr Trevelyan?'

'Missus, we'm tried. He's out on his rounds in his car, and he can't get back on account of the floods.'

'What about Nurse Penwillis?'

'She'm over to Poldurran, delivering another baby. We've tried to get a message through to the Shipwright's Arms and they've promised to tell her, if they can find her. But she'd have to walk over by the cliff path. No one can get here by road.'

Laurie seemed to go cold with fear. 'I'm stuck too, Bob. The bus had to turn round and go back to St Buryan. What are we going to do?'

Old Bob on the other end of the line seemed to sigh. 'Mr Luke's gone down to look after her and the kids.' The shaken, reedy voice hesitated. 'He's used to birth, missus. Delivered a-many calves in his time, has Mr Luke. I dessay he'll know what to do.'

Laurie tried to picture Penny struggling to produce her baby with only the inexpert guidance of an old country farmer to help her. I must get through somehow, she thought. I simply *must*.

Aloud she said, 'What's the weather like there now, Bob?'

There was a pause while the old man seemed to listen. 'Sheeting down still, missus—and a force nine gale blowing onshore. I stayed on here for Mr Luke—he said to man the telephone—but I tell 'ee, I'm not much good with phones—they fair moithers me.'

'You stay there, Bob. At least it's warm and dry. No sense trying to get back down to Tregarrow in this. But if you can get to the cottage a bit later, tell Mr Luke I'll get there somehow, and be sure to give Penny my love and tell her I'm coming.'

'I'll do that, missus. But you mind how you go! Them roads is dangerous. It was even on the radio!'

Laurie rang off, determined now to ask for help in the bar. Surely someone would have a Land Rover or a truck that would be able to get through the floods to somewhere close to Tregarrow.

She went back and spoke urgently to the landlord. He

listened intently, head cocked inquiringly towards her against the noise of the bar. Then he nodded briefly at her and rapped hard on his counter with a beer mug.

'Young lady here', he said, 'wants a volunteer to get her as near Tregarrow as maybe. There's a baby on the way, doctor and nurse both out and can't get back, and she's got to get home to help her sister through. Anyone feeling like braving the weather?'

There was silence all round the room for a moment, and then someone said, 'Where is it, exactly? You'll never get through to Tregarrow.'

'Luke Veryan's,' said Laurie. 'But I can walk, if anyone could get near the cliff path.'

'Dangerous in this wind,' said someone else doubtfully.

But a square, burly figure got up from a stool by the fire and said, 'I've got a Land Rover here. See what I can do.'

Laurie went across to him, her face alight with a mixture of hope and urgency. 'Are you sure you want to risk it?'

The man looked at her out of shrewd brown eyes. 'Why not? Can't say how far we'll get. But if there's a baby coming, I reckon we'd best have a try.'

They went out into the rain and wind together. At the last moment, the landlord thrust a torch into Laurie's hand, and also handed the Land Rover owner a quarter-bottle of whisky from his off-licence shelf, saying, 'You might need it', and then called over his shoulder, 'Good luck, Tom!' which was repeated as a chorus by the rest of the customers in the bar.

The night seemed more black and tempestuous than ever, and the stocky man beside Laurie took her arm firmly and led her out into the teeth of the gale where his Land Rover was parked in the main square. He helped her in, and climbed in himself, cursing amiably at the cascade of water that went down his neck as he opened the driver's door.

'We'd best try the top road and cut back,' he shouted at her over the sound of the engine and the roar of the wind outside.

Laurie simply nodded, clutching her hands together

and willing herself to keep still and not start shouting 'For God's sake hurry up!'

The Land Rover swung out on to the wet ribbon of road and churned steadily on into the night. Her companion did not speak much but kept his eyes on the road ahead, watching for patches of water or fallen trees.

'Whereabouts do you live yourself?' asked Laurie, suddenly aware that he was probably going miles out of his way for her sake.

He glanced round at her and grinned. 'Tremayne's Farm. I'm Tom Tremayne.' The Land Rover gave a sudden jolt over a stone, and his eyes went back to the road. 'This side of Poldurran. But I'll work my way backwards—if the floods'll let me.'

There was a lot of water on the road—sometimes quite deep—but the Land Rover ploughed steadily through it. Once they had to swing over and brush close into the hedge to avoid a fallen branch in the road, and once they nearly went into a pile of stones from a broken wall.

'You work for Luke Veryan?' he asked presently. 'Seem to remember George Button saying . . .'

'Oh, you know Farmer Button?'

He laughed. 'Everyone knows George. Tallest man in Cornwall, he says!'

All at once he caught sight of a signpost on his left, and swung round into a side-road. 'This should take us back,' he said. 'Doesn't drop too low, neither. Might get us through.'

The Land Rover lurched and bucketed along the lane, through pools of standing water, pot-holes and slicks of mud. At one point they came to a heap of rubble in the road from a fallen wall and a swirling mass of water round it. The way through seemed impassable. But Tom Tremayne simply turned his vehicle into an open gateway and drove, jolting and sliding, across the top end of a field and came out the far side into a farm track that led him back on to the road again.

'Good thing I knows these parts!' he grinned, and held the wheel steady while they lurched through another water splash and out on to firm road again beyond.

They had to make another detour round a fallen tree—once more skidding through a quagmire of a field—but at length they came to yet another crossroads and a signpost which said 'Tregarrow' on one arm and 'Poldurran' on the other.

'This is the one that's flooded,' said Tom. 'Don't think we'll get much farther. It drops down too low.' He glanced at Laurie again, doubtfully. 'Think you could walk from here?'

'I'm sure I could.' She sounded entirely confident. 'If you tell me the way.'

He nodded but did not stop driving. 'We'll go on as far as we can. But if I go right down, I may not be able to turn.'

They swerved again to avoid a broken wall and a fallen gatepost, and then the Land Rover suddenly slid to a halt. Ahead of them was a steep drop in the road and a gleaming expanse of black floodwater—and two red paraffin lamps set across the road as a warning.

'No getting past that!' said Tom, shaking his head. 'We'll have to leave it and walk.'

Laurie looked at him. 'I'll have to. You can turn here and go back.'

He grinned again, but made no comment. He simply got out and went round to help her down. 'Got the torch? Come on, then,' he said, shouting against the wind again. 'I'll see you across the cliff path—tricky in this weather.'

He took no notice of Laurie's half-hearted protest but simply took her firmly by the arm again and leant forward into the driving wind and rain.

They walked for a long time in silence, listening to the roar of the wind and the surf crashing far below them on the rocks of Tregarrow Head. There were few lights to be seen, except an occasional wink from the lighthouse on the point and a subdued glimmer from one or two isolated farms tucked into the fold of the hills. But at last they saw in front of them a couple of lighted windows in a cluster of long, dark buildings on their right, and below it a smaller light in a smaller, squarer building that was unmistakably Luke Veryan's cottage.

221

'There you are!' said Tom. 'You'll be all right now.'

'Oh, but . . .' Laurie spoke swiftly. '*Please* just come in a minute—there might be a message you could take or something—and you could at least have some hot tea!'

He stood there for a moment, considering, while the rain streamed down round him. 'All right,' he said, seeming to shrug off the storm and the delay with complete serenity. They squelched on down the cliff path together and came up to the cottage, pushing their way inside and shutting the door on the raging wind and rain.

Laurie left Tom Tremayne where he was and went running upstairs, calling over her shoulder, 'Take off your wet things. I'll be down in a moment.'

She rushed into the bedroom and found Penny lying stretched out on the bed, clutching at the headrail with desperate hands. Luke Veryan was in his shirtsleeves, bending over her and saying, 'Take it easy, girl, take it easy. Don't be in too much of a hurry.'

He looked up as Laurie came in, and his face broke into a wide grin of relief. 'Glad you got here,' he said.

Laurie leant over Penny and laid a cold, wet hand against her flushed face. 'I'm here now,' she said. 'Don't worry. Everything's going to be all right.' She didn't know how it was going to be all right. But it would be. After all, she'd had two children of her own—and a miscarriage, too, she thought grimly. She ought to know what to do. And there was Luke, too. He was experienced, and no fool.

Looking round at his tired, grey face, she said gently, 'Go down and talk to Tom Tremayne—and get yourself a cup of tea. He's been a tower of strength—and he may be able to get a message through to Poldurran for Agnes Penwillis.'

Luke nodded, and gave Penny a reassuring smile before he left the room. 'Back in a minute, girl,' he said. 'But you're in good hands now.'

Penny groaned and clenched her hands on the bedrail, and arched her back against the pain. 'Waters broke . . . a while back,' she panted. 'Probably . . . won't be long . . . now . . . Oh Christ!' She gritted her teeth and groaned again, and then fell back exhausted as the pain left her. 'You're all wet,' she said to Laurie, between gasps. 'Better take off . . . get a chill . . .'

Laurie had forgotten. But now she stripped off her wet coat, sodden jeans and pulpy shoes, and padded around barefoot to find a dry skirt and jumper to put on before the next pain attacked Penny. And she was by her side, holding on to her hands, when the next more violent one came.

Until now, she had had no time to ask if the children were all right, but then, just as she was beginning to wonder about it, Jason came into the room, carrying a cup of tea for Laurie. 'Uncle Luke said you'd need it,' he said gravely. 'Are you very wet?'

'Not now,' smiled Laurie. 'Where's Midge?'

'She's asleep. We put her in your room. But I stayed up. I thought I might be useful.'

'You are!' agreed Laurie.

'Would Penny like some tea?'

'No!' ground out Penny between her teeth. 'No time for tea! Oh . . . bloody hell!' And then, between tears and laughter, she added, 'Go away, Jay—I'm going to swear even louder!'

Jason smiled at her, not seeming in the least disturbed by the violence of imminent birth, and tiptoed away downstairs.

Laurie was trying desperately to remember all the different stages of birth, and all the things she ought to do. She wished Penny wasn't quite so young. Would it be harder for her? Would there be complications? She wished Agnes Penwillis was here, with her sturdy good sense — or Dr Trevelyan. What would she do if things went wrong? And why was childbirth so damned agonising?

At this point in her thoughts, the pains got worse and Penny needed more help. And then Luke Veryan came back, carrying a jug of hot water and some clean sheets and towels.

'Tom Tremayne's going,' he reported. 'He'll do his best to get through to Agnes.'

'Oh!' yelled Penny. 'Oh God, let it hurry up and come!'

'Relax,' begged Laurie, holding on to her hand. 'Try to relax . . . and breathe . . . breathe deeply. Try, Penny—it may help.'

She tried to remember what she had done herself. But after all, she had been in hospital, and they had given her pethidine, hadn't they? And gas and air for the pains when they got bad. Whereas Penny—young, vulnerable Penny, not much more than a child herself and not knowing in the least what to expect—had nothing to help her, and no doctor or nurse within miles on this stormy night.

Grimly, her eyes met Luke's over the writhing figure on the bed.

'Easy . . .' murmured Luke, 'easy does it, girl. It'll come soon.'

Together he and Laurie worked over Penny, doing what they could to help her and keep her calm. They lost count of time and forgot to note the spaces between the contractions—and even seemed able to shut their ears to Penny's groans and curses, though Laurie was riven by her suffering and possessed by a kind of driving anger at the whole messy business and the injustice of it all. But they all felt the inexorable rhythm of birth building up in each new contraction, gaining momentum and rising to its climax. And suddenly there was a final, desperate heave and a short, hoarse scream from Penny—and a small red creature lay squirming on the sheet between her legs, and a thin, fierce little cry of protest pierced the air.

Laurie remembered how to tie the cord before she snipped it. And it was Luke's old, steady hands that held the new-born infant while she washed it clean and wrapped it in a blanket.

'What is it?' murmured Penny, limp with exhaustion. *'Is it all right?'*

Then Laurie knew that Penny had understood all along what the hazards might be, and had been as filled with anxiety about the outcome as Laurie herself. 'It's a girl,' she said, smiling. 'And she's perfect. Look!'

She was just putting the baby in Penny's arms, and Luke was just bending over and saying gruffly, 'Well done, girl!' when there was a commotion downstairs at the front door, steps came running up the stairs, and Agnes Penwillis burst in, dripping rain from every angle — even from her battered medical bag.

'Sorry!' she gasped, out-of-breath and anxious. 'Walked over by the cliff path. Weather's terrible.' Her eyes went to the bed, and her face broke into a cheerful grin. 'But I see you've managed very well without me!'

'Look!' said Penny, holding the baby up for her to see. 'Isn't she lovely?' And then her face contorted as another wave of pain brought on a new contraction to carry away the afterbirth.

Quickly, Laurie took the baby from her, and Agnes Penwillis went into action with the calm deliberation of long practice. Laurie smiled at Luke, who was beginning to look very tired by now, and said softly, 'Thank you — we couldn't have done it without you.'

He grunted noncommittally and gave a small, dismissive shrug to his shoulders. 'Not all that different from calving,' he said, with a glimmer of mischief, 'except that cows is bigger!' Then he added, soberly, 'And more difficult to handle. Yon little lass was splendid!'

From Luke this was high praise, and Laurie glanced across at Penny to see if she had heard. But her eyes were shut, and her face was suddenly pale and drained with exhaustion under its golden sprinkling of freckles, and the vivid red hair lay limp and sweat-darkened on the pillow. She looked terribly young and quenched, lying there — a child in the grip of an experience too big to bear — and Laurie's own heart seemed to lurch with pity for her. Too young for all this, and a new young life to care for now, and years of responsibility and emotional ties and struggles ahead.

Sighing, Laurie turned away and spoke gently to Luke. 'Come downstairs and have a rest by the fire. I expect Jay's kept it up. And I'll make some more tea for everyone.'

'The kettle's boiling,' said Jason's voice from the doorway. 'I heard the new baby cry. Can I see it?'

Laurie nodded, and drew him close to look at the tiny creature in her arms. Already the angry redness of birth — the outrage of being forced into the outside world — was receding from the child's face, leaving it pale and petal-soft, and the small eyelashes lay in minute crescents on the curving cheeks. 'Here she is,' Laurie spoke softly. 'See how perfect her fingers are.'

Jason reached out a shy, awe-struck hand and touched the baby's damp, downy head. 'So little!' he whispered. And then, drawing himself up straight, he added, 'I'll get the tea. Penny still needs you.'

So Laurie found the new baby's first clothes, and the pink frilly nightie she had bought for Penny, and brought them over to Agnes Penwillis, with some more clean sheets and towels. 'Here,' she said, smiling at Penny's tired young face, 'let's make you both beautiful.'

When Jason returned with Luke Veryan and a tray of tea, Penny was sitting up in bed in her new frills, her glorious hair tamed and brushed, and her eyes alight with tender triumph. And the new baby was lying peacefully against her arm, neatly wrapped in her new white shawl.

'What are you going to call her?' asked Jason, offering Penny a mug of tea first, as befitted the heroine of the occasion.

'I dunno.' Penny looked down at the tiny, perfect oval of her daughter's face with an expression of rueful tenderness. 'Should be a mixture of early-bird and storms-and-tempest . . . But I'll think of something.'

'Christmas Rose,' said Luke Veryan suddenly.

They looked at him in amazement. But he went on quite calmly, 'They comes up sudden-like—in early winter. They doesn't mind rain and wind—very sturdy, they be . . . and all white and pure-like.'

There was an astonished silence in the room for a moment. They had none of them expected such a poetic speech from an old Cornish farmer—though they knew he loved the flowers he grew.

But Penny looked across at him and smiled with sudden radiance. 'Right then,' she said. 'Christmas Rose it is! But I 'spect we'll all call her Rose.'

'Rose?' echoed Jason, trying it out.

'Rose!' repeated everyone else, and lifted their mugs of tea in salute.

But little Rose just slept.

* * *

The next morning Dr Trevelyan stumped in, having also had to walk back over the cliffs, leaving his car behind. But he reported that the floods were going down and the roads would be passable soon. An ambulance would be coming to take Penny and the baby to hospital. But here he met a sudden, stubborn resistance from Penny. She didn't want to go to the hospital now. It was all over. Everything was all right. The baby was fine. What did she have to go all that way for?

In vain Dr Trevelyan talked about safeguards and possible complications—the baby's welfare, especially as it was probably a couple of weeks premature, and Penny's own future health.

He met with a flat refusal. Penny's usually cheerful face went suddenly white and pinched, and she looked piteously from Laurie to the doctor and said in a tight, unrecognisable voice, 'No. I don't want to. I'm all right as I am. I mean, *we're* all right as we are.'

Laurie turned to Dr Trevelyan and said, 'Have you made all the examination you need to? Perhaps I could talk to her? I think Jay's got the kettle on again.'

Trevelyan was a wise and experienced man. He nodded briefly and went off downstairs to have a chat with Jason.

Laurie sat down beside Penny and laid a hand on her arm. 'It's all right. Don't look so upset. No one's going to send you anywhere if you don't want to go.'

'Aren't they? Can't they make me?'

'No. Of course they can't.' She paused, watching the desperate pallor recede in Penny's face. She still looked like a creature at bay. 'What frightens you about hospital?' she asked gently.

Penny drew a quivering breath, and held little Rose tighter in her arms. 'They might try to take her away from me.'

Laurie was shocked. 'They wouldn't do that!'

'They might. The social worker might come. She was on at me again last time she came—about adoption.' She

227

shot a fierce, defiant glance at Laurie. 'And I'm not letting them take her. She's *mine!*'

Laurie nodded. 'Of course she is. No one's going to take her from you.' She hesitated, and then went on carefully, 'But they are probably thinking of you, too, you know—just as much as the baby.'

Penny looked astonished. 'Me? How d'you mean?'

'Well, they probably think you're awfully young to tie yourself down to bringing up a child at this stage of your life. They think you might want to go off and do something else—take some exams, get some training . . . and meet other people—perhaps even find a nice boyfriend, or get married—instead of staying at home minding the baby!'

Penny snorted. 'Why don't they ask me what I'd like?' She looked at Laurie with sudden anxiety. 'You . . . you did say . . .'

'Of *course* I did. I'll be there. There'll be nothing to stop you doing the things you want, I promise you.'

'I want to look after Rose,' she said obstinately. 'And Jay and Midge. That's what I'm good at.'

Laurie smiled her reassurance. 'I know. But maybe they don't. They probably think all teenagers are scatty good-time girls with no sense of responsibility!'

Penny began to smile. 'Little do they know.'

'But as for Rose . . .' Once again Laurie hesitated, but, before she could go on, Penny cut in—her face still full of anxiety.

'You don't think . . . Would she . . . have a better chance with . . . with someone else?' There was anguish and doubt in the young voice.

Laurie sighed. 'She might be better off—financially. But I don't think that's as important as what you can give her.'

Penny's still-childlike face was pitifully torn. 'I . . . I do want what's best for her.'

Laurie was looking at her with compassion. 'I know you do.'

'Do *you* think I'm right to keep her?'

A lot hung on Laurie's answer, she knew. But looking

into Penny's face she could not ignore the passionate protective love she saw there as the girl stared down at her sleeping baby.

'Yes,' she said slowly. 'I do. It's just that you're awfully young.'

Something flashed in Penny's face then. Not too young to be raped by my own father, it said. Not too young to have a baby. Doesn't that make me old enough to look after it and give it a decent life of its own—with nothing ever happening to it like what happened to me?

'You never told me,' said Laurie suddenly. 'Did you have any brothers and sisters in your family?'

'Oh yes.' Penny's eyes were bleak. 'Two young brothers, and a baby girl. I used to look after them mostly— especially the baby. My mum was usually out . . .' She glanced at Laurie, still with the same bleak, hard gaze. 'My Dad wasn't after *them*. Not yet, he wasn't. But . . . after I left, I did wonder about Evie—my little sister.' She drew in a sharp breath. 'I did tell him, though.'

'Tell him what?'

'What he did to me was criminal, wasn't it? I told him I'd tell the police about it when I left. So if he laid a finger on Evie, they'd know—and they'd send him to prison.' Her voice suddenly shook then. 'But the thing is—how would they know? I wouldn't be there to tell them.'

Laurie's hand still lay on Penny's arm. Now she gave it a comforting squeeze. 'The threat was probably enough— especially as your mother knew, too.'

'She wouldn't believe me.'

'No. Not openly. But I bet she did inside. And she'd be on the watch from then on, wouldn't she?'

'I hope so,' She let out a shaky sigh, and then added in a shamed, pitiful whisper, 'It seemed awful—to threaten him, I mean. Because I did . . . I did sort of love him, in a way . . . and that made it worse!'

Laurie nodded. She could find no way to answer that. But after a small silence she said tentatively, 'So—if we've dealt with what's worrying you about it—do you still not want to go to hospital?'

Penny looked away from Laurie. 'No.'

229

'Why not?' Laurie was nonplussed.

For a moment Penny did not answer—but then her face crumpled like a child's and she said in a strangled voice, 'I don't want . . . to go away from you.'

Laurie understood then that she was standing in for the mother who had rejected Penny when she most needed her, and she must not fail her now.

'Oh, my dear girl!' she said, and folded her in her arms, baby and all. 'Of course you needn't go away from me. We'll see this through together!' And she rocked her to and fro, while Penny wept as she had not wept since she had left home.

When she was quiet, Laurie went downstairs to tell Dr Trevelyan, patiently drinking tea by the fire, that Penny would not be going to hospital. He grunted his disapproval and then smiled suddenly and said, 'I'm not really surprised!'

But he made Laurie promise to send for him if anything unexpected happened, and told her that Agnes Penwillis would call in regularly during the first few days. He also made Laurie agree to take Penny down to the hospital for a post-natal check-up in six weeks' time. Then, feeling that he could do no more, he called up the stairs, 'All right, young woman, you win! But mind you behave yourself. I'll be back in a day or two to make sure.'

Penny called back jubilantly, 'I'll be good as gold, I promise. And so will baby Rose.'

'You'd better be!' growled Trevelyan, and strode out of the door, smiling a little to himself when Penny couldn't see him.

Laurie watched him go, and turned back to go upstairs again to Penny, wondering a little desperately how she was going to get through the next few days, what with her job and Penny and the baby to look after, and her own two needing her as much as ever.

But Jason came out into the hall with Midge beside him, and a cup of tea in his hand. 'Me and Midge'll look after Penny for a bit,' he said, and started up the stairs. 'Your tea's on the table.'

Laurie looked after him affectionately. Jason was being

quite absurdly adult and dependable. He seemed to thrive on emergencies. She wondered, vaguely, how he came to be so good in a crisis—he couldn't have got it from Jeff.

'Uncle Luke says not to come in today,' he added, pausing on the landing. 'The storm blew out some of the glass in the greenhouses. He and Bob will be all day mending them. He told me to tell you, when I went up for the cows.'

Laurie breathed a sigh of relief. Then another thought struck her. 'What about school?'

'Oh, stuff school!' replied Jason staunchly. 'Babies are more important.'

*　*　*

The next fortnight was very hectic. The Christmas trade was building up, and cut flowers and pot-plants were at a premium. So were vegetables—particularly sprouts and celery—and Laurie found herself frantically picking and packing and helping Old Bob to lift celery at all hours of the day. Luke's loaded van went into Penzance every day—sometimes twice a day—to the local markets or to the London train, or to catch someone's big long-distance truck that was driving through the night to reach the early morning London markets. Laurie's hands got rough and sore and her back ached continually, and the constant wind and rain made her feel even more battered, but she went doggedly on.

She had expected—and even ordered—Penny and the children to stay at home but they took no notice. Penny simply pushed baby Rose up the hill in the pram and parked her in the warm greenhouses, and got on with helping the flower-packers on the spot. Jason and Midge had already learnt how to be useful, fetching boxes, holding string for tying bunches, finding rubber bands, and standing patiently in seas of cellophane and wrapping paper.

Luke did not thank them—did not even acknowledge their help—he was too rushed and busy himself. But he did occasionally stop and look into baby Rose's pram and nod his head and smile. She was a good baby and did not cry a lot except when she was hungry, and Penny—to Laurie's secret relief—took to breast-feeding quite naturally and without the slightest difficulty, and seemed very practical and determined about it.

On Christmas Eve, Luke took the last load in very early in the morning and told everyone to stop clearing up by mid-day. He returned at lunch-time and stumped into the kitchen, where Penny and the children were just dishing up a hot meal.

'Something in the van for you,' he said to Jason, with a faint twitch of a smile.

Jason stopped stirring the stew and put down his spoon. 'Come on, Midge,' he said, taking her hand. 'Let's go and see.'

When he opened the back door of the van, there inside was a large green Christmas tree—its tangy fragrance filling the closed-in air of the truck. Together, he and Midge hauled it out and stood looking at it with awe. It was too big for them to stand it upright, but it was a beautiful tree—shapely and bushy below, with a long slender spike for the star at the top.

They rushed into the kitchen, babbling excitedly. 'Mum—it's a Christmas tree. Where shall we put it?'

Laurie looked from the children to Penny, and messages seemed to be passed and understood. 'It depends,' she said gravely, 'on Mr Veryan.'

'On me?' said Luke, surprised. And then he added gruffly, 'Tree's yourn. Do what you like wi' it.'

'No.' Laurie still sounded grave. 'You don't understand. We want you and Bob to be with us—either at the cottage or here, we don't mind which. But we're going to cook you Christmas dinner somewhere!'

Old Bob was standing beside his chair, waiting for the stew to be ladled out, and in the meantime giving Rose a surreptitious nod and wink and an occasional chirrup, for he adored the new baby. 'What?' he said surprised. 'You wants I?'

Penny nodded. 'Course. All together. It's Christmas.' She looked across at Luke, and then back to Rose who was vaguely waving a fist. 'Christmas Rose's first Christmas! Can't miss it, can you?'

The two men looked positively embarrassed. But at length Luke said—as gruffly as ever—'Come down to you, then. Easier for Penny than lugging Rose up here.'

Laurie smiled. 'That's settled then.' She began ladling out the stew.

*　*　*

When they went outside to collect the tree, they found a box of decorations and some Christmas lights standing beside it.

'Sell 'em in the market,' growled Luke. 'Did a swop. Glad to get rid of 'em just before Christmas.'

The others gazed at him, speechless. Then Luke turned to Penny and added, "Spose she might notice 'em . . . being shiny-like?'

Penny grinned. 'You bet she will! She notices everything. Jay and Midge will fix it all, won't you, kids?'

'You bet!' echoed Jay, giving a small, private skip of delight.

'Me bet!' agreed Midge, also prancing, and wondered why everyone laughed.

They carried the tree home together, rejoicing all the way.

*　*　*

In the morning there were more surprises. First of all there was a small pile of presents on the doorstep which, when they opened them, turned out to be from the villagers of Tregarrow to the three children at Veryan's cottage. There was a small doll for Midge with a label attached saying, 'Love from Billy' which made her dance even more. There was a red racing-car for Jason from someone called 'Brandy-ball' who, Jason said, was a mate of his at school. There was a rattle with bells on for Rose from Agnes Penwillis, and a box of crackers from the shop.

'Honestly,' said Laurie, pushing the hair out of her eyes, 'aren't people marvellous!'

'Yes,' agreed Penny, opening another parcel, which contained a knitted blanket for the baby. 'Aren't they?'

She and Laurie had been cautious about presents. Both felt the necessity of saving up what they could for the future. But they had each managed something for everyone—and even Jason and Midge had gone out with their own pocket-money and bought a bar of soap and some cheap scent and a tiny woolly bonnet for Rose.

But that was not the end of the morning's surprises. When the Christmas dinner was nearly ready, they heard steps on the path, and not two but three shadows passed the kitchen window.

Puzzled, Laurie went to the door—and there, beside Luke and old Bob, stood Joe from London.

'Joe!' she exclaimed, and called over her shoulder, 'Penny, look who's here!'

Everyone rushed to the door, and laughing, Joe lifted Jason and Midge high in the air. 'Well then, kids, how's tricks?' he said to them. 'Life treating you OK?'

'OK!' repeated Midge, jumping up and down. 'OK, OK!'

'Got enough to spare for an extra one?' he asked, sniffing the air appreciatively.

'Of course!' said Penny, smiling all over her face. 'Come on, Joe . . . Come and meet Christmas Rose!'

They drew Luke and old Bob in after them and took them to admire the tree, which stood winking and shining in the corner of the living room. And Joe picked up little Rose and held her up to look at the lights and the shiny glass baubles hanging from the branches, and watched delighted while her eyes followed the bright things as they swung before her.

It soon transpired that Joe had come laden with presents, too. There was an armload of second-hand clothes for the children, sorted out by Jane from her many donations—and even a special bundle for baby Rose.

'How did Jane know?; asked Penny. 'I didn't tell her.'

'Ah!' Joe laid a finger against his nose. 'My spies told me.' He looked across at his father and winked. 'And then there's this for Jason, specially from Jane,' he added, and carefully handed over a strange round-looking package.

When Jason unwrapped it, there was a beautiful little bottle-garden gleaming up at him, with a wealth of tiny green plants and twining ivies inside.

'I gather,' said Joe solemnly, 'that you and Jane have something going about bottles.'

Jason looked at him wide-eyed and went pale with joy. 'She . . . she must've got it, then,' he muttered, and glanced up at Laurie questioningly.

'Obviously,' agreed Laurie, and did not dare meet Joe's bright, observant gaze.

Then there was a small music box for Midge that played 'Silent Night' when you wound the handle, and a woolly ball on a string to dangle from Rose's pram.

And last, Joe brought out another parcel for Jason, and said, 'This is from your friend Clem, and he says be careful—it's fragile.'

So Jason unwrapped it with fingers that trembled a little, and this time there was another small green bottle with a tiny ship inside, its snow-white sails spread wide.

'Oh!' breathed Jason, entranced. 'How did it get in there?' Then he looked at Laurie again, doubtfully but joyfully, and said, 'He must've got mine, too!'

But Laurie stood gazing at it and did not answer.

In the package there were also some tiny carved wooden animals—whittled by Clem in the quiet, dark hours at his cottage. There was a small model of an otter for Midge, and a fleet of little mallard ducks for Penny to float in Rose's bath. And last of all, Jason drew out one pure-white swan's feather with a label tied to it which said 'For Laurie' and nothing else at all.

Laurie took it in her hand and bent her head over it, ashamed of the quick tears that brimmed in her eyes. One more token of freedom, the feather said. . . . Are you flying yet?

Jason picked up his two bottles very carefully and put them side by side on the window-ledge, and stood for a moment quite still, admiring them. He thought of his two ordinary pop bottles bobbing about in the sea, and the messages they carried, and it seemed to him that there were still wonders and mysteries in the wide world, bigger than he could understand. 'Magic!' he breathed.

'Joe,' said Laurie at last, 'I think this is the happiest Christmas we've ever had. And it's all thanks to you!'

'Rubbish!' retorted Joe. 'Gotta come and see me old Dad, haven't I?' He grinned, wilfully misunderstanding her, and ruffled Jason's hair briefly in passing. Then he demanded loudly, 'Where's this Christmas dinner then? Can I help bring it in?'

While they were all laughingly occupied in bringing in dishes of sprouts and potatoes, and Laurie was getting the turkey (also cut-price through Luke) out of the oven, old Bob shyly approached Jason with his offering. 'This is for all on you,' he said, and laid the square package on Jason's knee. Inside was a black painted board with a whole series of beautifully tied sailors' knots in crisp white string. There were several precise rows of them, intricate and delicate, and all neatly labelled. 'See . . . ,' he said stooping beside the boy and pointing to them one by one with a gnarled finger. 'Tied 'em meself. Used to be famous for 'em once—they'm got a set o' they in the museum.' He looked hopefully at Jason's interested face. 'I could teach you how to tie 'em, if you'd like?'

'Could you?' Jason touched the knots one by one with a tentative finger. 'That'd be brill.' He gave old Bob an admiring smile. 'You're a wizard at knots!'

Old Bob was enormously pleased.

And then the turkey came in, and the Christmas party began.

After the festivities were over, Joe and Laurie decided to walk down to the beach, leaving the two older men dozing by the fire and Penny occupied with the baby. Jason and Midge demanded to come too, and after a moment's hesitation Laurie agreed, provided they went off on their own along the sand for a bit. She wanted to talk to Joe.

'Well,' Joe was watching the children run on ahead, 'you seem to be making a go of it here.'

236

Laurie nodded. 'Up to a point. I don't know how satisfied your father is.'

'Oh, he's as pleased as Punch with the whole set-up,' stated Joe.

'Is he?' She smiled a little. Then she grew serious. 'Joe— I sent a message through to Jane. Did she get it?'

'Yes.' Joe looked at her severely. 'She did. Though I reckon you're daft to bother!'

Laurie's face tautened a little with resolve. 'Maybe, Joe. But it's Christmas . . . and Jeff's in prison. I . . . I just wanted to know if anyone was doing anything for him. Or visiting him. What about his barmaid friend?'

Joe snorted. 'Huh! She ditched him soon as she found out what he was nicked for—and I don't blame her!' He glanced at her again, a little grimly. 'Anyways, Jane says your solicitor—Madeleine—made enquiries. A social worker tried to visit him, but he refused to see her. He got beaten up inside by some of his mates, and started a fight, which lost him his remission. But he's over that. He'll have a probation officer to keep an eye on him when he comes out, whether he likes it or not.'

'What about his drinking? Will anyone help him over that?'

Joe sighed. 'They can't,' he said flatly, 'unless he asks them to. He's got to admit he's got a problem first.' He shook his head. 'Can't say how he'll be. He's been forcibly kept off it for four months. But whether he'll stay off is anyone's guess.' He looked at her again, quite sternly this time. 'In any case, Laurie, he's a man—not a flippin' child. He's gotta learn to deal with his own life *himself*. You've got enough children here to cope with, haven't you?'

Laurie nodded silently.

Seeing her expression, he laid a kindly hand on her arm. 'Mind if I talk to you like a Dutch uncle?'

Laurie turned to him affectionately. 'Try me!'

'Well—as I see it, kid—you've made a new life for yourself here. You look a different person from the wreck I first saw! Years and years younger, you look! And you've made a good job of Penny, too. She's as happy as Larry

237

with you and the kids and the new baby. You don't intend
to go back on it all, do you?'

Laurie stared at Joe. 'No. Of course not. I couldn't—
not now. But . . .'

'But that doesn't stop you having a few twinges of
guilt?' Joe's tone was flat and sardonic. 'Well, *don't*, kid!
You've made your choice. You don't owe that bastard
anything—not after what he did to you, and to the kids.'
His voice changed a little and he added, with his eyes on
the distant figures of Jason and Midge running about at
the water's edge, 'How are they, now, anyways?'

Laurie's eyes also followed the two dancing children,
and she sighed. 'They're fine, really. Only, Jay's still a bit
too good.'

Joe looked startled. '*Too* good?'

'Yes. Too serious—like an adult, sometimes. He was
wonderful when Penny's baby came. But I . . . I just wish
sometimes he'd be a bit naughty—or mischievous, like a
normal, carefree boy!'

Joe laughed. 'You wait! You'll be wishing the opposite
soon!' But his gaze still rested thoughtfully on the children. 'How about the little 'un?'

'Midge? Oh, she's come on a lot. She goes to the kindergarten now. And she's quite taken to your father and old
Bob—though she's still a bit scared of strangers, particularly men.'

Joe nodded. 'See what I mean? The damage isn't over
yet.'

'I know,' agreed Laurie. And for me, most of all. I weep
at a swan's feather, but I still don't dare trust human
relationships enough to do anything about it. Even Clem's
gentlest message simply terrifies me. Aloud she said
slowly, 'There's one thing that troubles me, Joe.' She
hesitated, unsure how to go on.

'Well?' Joe had been looking at the sea, but now he
turned back to her, his bright, intelligent eyes fixed on
her face.

'It's about your father . . .' she began again. 'He's been
very good to us—and I think he's got quite fond of us all

in his way—specially Penny and the baby. After all, he helped bring Rose into the world!'

Joe grinned. 'So I heard!' But his gaze still rested on her, alert and waiting. So?'

'So . . . will he . . . ? I mean, he's got used to Penny cooking for him—him and old Bob—and his house being cleaned occasionally and so on. What will he do when we go in the spring?'

'More important, what will *you* do when you go in the spring?' retorted Joe.

Laurie closed her eyes for a moment and drew a long, steadying breath. 'I don't know yet, Joe. I . . . I can't plan very far ahead at present. But I'll think of something.'

Not even to Joe—shrewd and experienced Joe—could she admit to the long wakeful hours of the night when sleep eluded her and worries about the future crowded in. 'But I've been thinking,' she went on, a little shyly. 'I like this kind of out-door work.'

'Even in winter, when it's hard?'

'Yes. Even then. It's sort of . . . satisfying. And I'm not too bad at keeping other people's books in order! So maybe I'd better aim at those kinds of jobs—on farms and such. And perhaps later on I could do a course in . . . in book-keeping and management or something.'

Joe nodded again. 'Sounds sensible. I'll think about it.'

'And what about your Dad?'

He smiled then, and patted her arm. 'Leave things be. He's enjoying himself. He hasn't been so well looked after in years!'

'Yes, but . . .'

'He'll be OK,' insisted Joe. 'Things is easier in the summer, anyways. And he rents out the cottage, so he can afford more labour if he wants it. You don't have to worry about him as well as everything else.'

But I do, thought Laurie—a small rueful smile touching her as she considered it. She had grown mysteriously fond of the gruff old farmer, and she did not like the prospect of him being lonely and uncared-for again when they had gone.

'Come on!' Joe gave her arm a friendly shake. 'It's

239

Christmas Day. Can't have you getting broody. Let's go and look at the sea.'

Laughing, he ran off in a scatter of sand to where the two children were dodging the incoming waves at the edge of the shore. And, laughing a little too at his wild dash across the sand, Laurie followed him. The sea, she thought, gazing out at it with a sudden sense of release and well-being—the sea resolves everything. It cuts us all down to size. We are alive, and the sun is shining on the water. Nothing else matters.

And, laughing still, she began to run with Joe and the children in the sun.

* * *

Jeff was released from prison at the end of January, on a cold, blustery day when the streets were wet with rain.

His first action was to get a drink. Someone from the prisoner's aid society had given him a little money 'to start him off' and the address of a day-centre for ex-prisoners where he could get a hot meal before he went home.

He didn't want a hot meal. He wanted a drink. Hunching his shoulders against the rain, and trying to disguise his short prison haircut, he dodged into the nearest bar. It was featureless and anonymous—no one knew him and no one cared. With a sigh of relief, he put down his parcel of 'personal effects' and got himself a drink. After two whiskies, he felt better. After three, he looked at his dwindling money and decided to go home.

He let himself into a cold, empty house. There was a pile of bills on the floor, and a layer of grey dust over everything. The place smelt musty and unlived in. He wandered disconsolately from room to room, occasionally kicking things out of his way to relieve his feelings. Upstairs, he discovered that Laurie's things were gone. So were the children's. There was nothing in the place that belonged to them any more. Everything there was his—such as it was.

But he didn't like it—empty and echoing, and somehow reproaching him with its silence. Cursing, he kicked another chair out of the way and went out again, slamming the door.

He tried the local which he used to frequent, but no one seemed to want to know him—and Brenda the barmaid eyed him coldly and refused to serve him. She left it to the landlord, who gave him one whisky, grudgingly, and said, 'Better go elsewhere, Mr Collins. They know too much about you here.'

And when Jeff began an indignant protest, Brenda tossed her head and added loudly, 'No wife-beaters in my bar,' and banged all the beer mugs down on the counter with a resounding clatter. The other occupants of the bar fell suddenly silent and eyed him uneasily. One or two of them took their drinks rather ostentatiously away from his company and went over to their cronies on the other side of the room.

But there was no fight left in Jeff—not at present. This cold silence unnerved him. Quickly, he swallowed his drink and left the bar behind him. He could not even slam the door, as it was a swing one and only came back at him when he shoved it too hard.

He tried another pub down the road, where nobody knew him. But it was not the same without his mates and the old cheerful camaradie he used to know. He drank alone, a solitary, morose figure, and wove his way home along the darkened streets after closing time in a haze of lonely self-pity.

The next morning, he went down to the social security office and signed on—and asked for special supplementary benefit to help him on his way. They told him he could not have it. There was a maintenance order for his wife and children, and that had to be paid first. It would be deducted from his money accordingly, as ordered by the court. Was he staying on in his council house? If so, they would give him a rent allowance. There were arrears to pay, they understood. But it must be used on rent, so they would pay it for him.

Jeff was appalled. All these encumbrances round his neck, and not allowed to touch his own money!. He asked them politely if they could give him his wife's address.

241

He said he had lost touch with them while he was, er. . . away. He wanted to help them, and he had some extra belongings of theirs to deliver.

But the authorities said blandly that they did not know his wife's address.

Defeated, Jeff went back to the house, wondering what to do next. On the way, he bought a bottle of whisky to cheer himself up. It made a large hole in his dole money but, still, he reckoned he needed it.

The next day he began to scan the job adverts—knowing he'd got to set his sights low, now that he'd got a prison record, however short. There wasn't much to choose from in his line, anyway. He wondered about a shop assistant in a computer and video shop? Or a garage attendant? Or an attendant in an amusement arcade?

He hated the empty house without Laurie and the brats. They'd been an infernal nuisance when they were there—always whining and always under his feet—but now that he was left on his own he missed them. It occurred to him, too, that he *had* been a bit rough with Laurie. He wouldn't do it again, if only she'd come back. He'd show her he'd changed. She wouldn't have to be afraid of him any more.

But then a sudden vision of her face in that smashed-up kitchen came to him—Laurie, his wife, pale and blood-stained, the eyes dilated with shock, deep in their heavily shadowed sockets, staring at him—not in fear but in total disbelief that he could be so senselessly violent. And he shivered.

No good, he said. No good brooding. She's gone—and the children with her. Good riddance, really. That unnerving silence of hers, and that God-awful reproachful look. Now I can start again, without encumbrances.

He was just turning to the sink counter to pour himself a drink, when he caught sight of his own face in the mirror. Something about it startled him, and he went closer to have a look.

Is that me? he thought, appalled. That sagging, unshaven wreck with the hot, angry eyes? *Me?* Smart young Jeff Collins, up-and-coming salesman, with a sharp suit and a flashy car, a briefcase full of orders, and a pretty wife at home? *A pretty wife at home?* Once again the image of Laurie's face came to him—pale and defeated—and incredulous. Yes, she might well look incredulous. He was incredulous himself. How had he come to this?

For a long, frightening moment he went on looking in the mirror at himself, seeing himself clearly for the first time in many months. In prison he had been too angry to see himself or anything else—and, anyway, there hadn't been a mirror on any wall. But now there was, in Laurie's kitchen, and—he was suddenly appalled to admit—there were still spots of dried blood on it. Laurie's blood. *Mirror, mirror on the wall, who is the lousiest of them all?*

He took stock then. He saw a picture of the whole sorry story of his own disintegration, the despair and the drink, the drink and the despair, the increasing seediness and the jobs that never materialised, his failing marriage and his awful, senseless hitting out against fate. Against Laurie and her accusing eyes; against the kids who tied him down. No, it wasn't against Laurie. It was against fate. Yes, fate. That was why he was so angry. Why should it happen to him?

But then, all at once, in this moment of painful clarity, he knew it wasn't fate. It wasn't Laurie or the kids who had brought him to this. It was himself. He—Jeff Collins—had done this to himself. He had picked up the extra glass of whisky—gone out with his pals once too often—slept around too many times—neglected his wife and kids—got himself into debt—drunk a bit more to forget—and hit out, hit out, blindly, savagely hit out at the senseless, uncaring world that rejected him. No. At Laurie. He had hit out at Laurie. He had blamed it all on his young wife. And it wasn't her fault at all.

Jeff took a deep, shaken breath of terror when he reached this point in his thoughts. He did not like what he saw—not one bit. He stared into the mirror again—at that grey, unrecognisable face—and addressed it bleakly. 'You are a bastard, Jeff Collins. Do you know that?'

The face seemed to mock him in the mirror. 'Bastard?'

it sneered. 'You know best. And what are you going to do about it?'

Jeff did the only thing he could. He smashed his fist into the glass and broke the mirror. The grey, mocking image disintegrated into a thousand fragments. It wasn't there any more. Jeff Collins, failed bastard, was wiped out. The moment of truth was shattered into jagged shards of glass on the kitchen floor.

'I need another drink,' said Jeff, and poured himself out a large one. He noticed that he had cut his hand, but he couldn't be bothered with it. He gulped down his drink in desperate haste and went out of the house as if devils were after him. Too early for the pub. Or was it? The one on the corner might be open. He could sit there till he calmed down. Then he would think what to do next. He would be sure to think of something.

After a while, and several drinks which he could ill afford, he did think of something. In fact, he had an idea. He went down to the social services building again, and asked this time to see one of the social workers. He did not specifically ask for the one who had been dealing with Laurie's case. Just someone he could talk to . . .

The girl in the outer office was impressed. He seemed so nicely spoken and so reasonable—very civil and humble, really. She felt sure he was sincere and meant well. She went to fetch a counsellor to talk to him.

Jeff stated his case. It was a spurious one, but he was always a persuasive talker and his story seemed to hold water. Before long, the woman opposite him had a picture of a conscientious, penitent husband, out of work and anxious to keep his young family together, who had once—just *once*—lost his temper, and never ceased to regret it. His wife was young and inexperienced—she didn't understand the pressures he was under. He wanted to make amends. He wanted to see his wife, just to say he was sorry. He desperately wanted to persuade her to come back. He missed his children. That was understandable, wasn't it? And, after all, a boy particularly needed his father. A reconciliation would be so much better all round, wouldn't it? Could she help?

The counseller considered. She did not know Laurie's case history and she did not know the background to Jeff's final burst of violence. But she thought she knew a penitent man when she saw one—and, after all, family life was what her work was all about, wasn't it? A reconciliation would be splendid, if she could arrange it. She left Jeff sitting there while she went away to find out a few more details. Maybe if she simply passed on the situation to the other DSS department where Laurie was registered now, they could take the next step? Then she at least would not be to blame if it went wrong—and it might, it just might, go right.

She returned, having discovered what she needed from the Giro payment records. She still had not tried to look up Laurie's case history—those papers were somewhere else and it would take too long. Besides, that was the province of the other office now. All she could do was set the wheels in motion.

'Well, Mr Collins,' she said brightly, 'I'm very sympathetic to your story, of course. But I'm afraid I can't give you your wife's address—it's against the rules. In any case, her income support payments are being handled by another office now, not in this area at all.'

Jeff looked disappointed.

'Were you thinking of contributing further maintenance? If so, of course we would get in touch with them.'

Jeff's disappointment grew. 'Er . . . not at the moment, I'm afraid.' He tried to look disarmingly frank. 'I'm out of work, you see.'

The counsellor nodded. 'Quite so. Then I'm afraid I can't help you.' She saw his face take on the familiar despairing acceptance of the ex-prisoner who found the whole world against him and added quite kindly, 'But if you were to write to us formally requesting a meeting with your wife, I would see that your letter reached the right department.'

Stymied, thought Jeff. Now what? He looked across the desk at the neutral grey face of the woman counsellor, and his glance fell on the papers in front of her. One of them seemed to be a notice of payment with figures on

245

it—and an address at the top from another office. If only he could just get a glimpse of that address.

'Where should I send the letter to?' he asked humbly.

'Why, to me at this office. But of course, to effect any meeting with your wife you would have to be willing to travel.'

'Travel?' An eager light came into his eye. 'Where to?'

But the counsellor was not to be drawn. Jeff saw his mistake and added carefully, 'If it was . . . a long distance, would I be able to get a travel allowance?'

The counsellor thought she understood his dilemma. 'Yes. That could be arranged, I think.'

'Is there a form I could fill in?'

There was indeed such a form, and the kindly woman counsellor went off to get it. Jeff leant forward and swiftly read the address on that top page on her desk. It was from the DSS office in Penzance.

Penzance?

The counsellor returned with a form. 'You can return it with your letter,' she said, smiling at his relief.

Jeff accepted it gratefully and thanked her for her time and patience. He escaped then as quickly as he could and went off to the nearest pub to think things out. Penzance? What the devil was Laurie doing in Penzance?

If he went down there and tried the other DSS people, maybe they'd tell him something. Or maybe he could catch another glimpse of an address. It was worth a try.

But in the meantime he needed several drinks to boost his confidence. Quite an ordeal it had been, talking to that woman. He also badly needed some more money if he was to get to Penzance and have any left for a drink. (A pity about that travel allowance!) After some thought, he went into a pawnbroker's he knew and flogged his watch, the gold signet-ring Laurie had given him and his leather briefcase which he always carried about with him, still pretending to himself that he was a salesman with a job to do. He minded about the briefcase most. Somehow he lost status without it. He felt less cocky, less sure of himself than ever. He was not quite sure who he was. Still, a drink would help.

By the time he made his way home, life looked a lot rosier but had shifted rather out of focus. He wove along the street and stopped outside his own front door to get his breath. He still didn't much like going inside to that empty, accusing silence. But he had to go in because that nosey old biddy Mrs Banks from next door was leaning on the fence looking at him. She was always standing about gossiping and watching what went on—and he was always trying to dodge her. He had even stopped Laurie talking to her because she never would mind her own business.

'Gone for good then, has she?' said Mrs Banks loudly, standing with arms folded and looking him up and down with contempt.

'Who?' said Jeff, taken unawares.

'Your wife. Took her bags and went off with a fella in a van.'

'What van?' snapped Jeff, whose head was spinning. 'What fella?'

'New boyfriend, I shouldn't wonder.' The voice was edged with malice and put Jeff's teeth on edge.

A couple of the neighbourhood kids were playing outside on the pavement and listening to this exchange with unconcealed glee. One of them started hopping up and down and chanting, 'Laurie went off in a lorry. Laurie went off in a . . .'

'What lorry?' Jeff shouted, and found himself shaking the boy's arm.

'Joe's,' said the boy, wrenching his arm free and grinning malevolently at Jeff.

'Joe who?'

The boy shrugged. 'Said it on the van, see? *Joe's.*'

'Veges,' added the other grinning urchin helpfully.

Jeff's head was whirling worse than ever, but he had just enough sense left to realise that this might be important. 'Veges?' he repeated, bewildered.

'Kite Street,' said the first boy, who never missed a trick.

'Market,' added his mate, still grinning, but keeping a wary eye on Jeff's outstretched hand.

'How do you know?' asked Jeff, not sure about anything—least of all their veracity.

'Said-it-on-the-van-see?' they chanted, hopping up and
down some more.

'Are you sure?' Jeff clutched at their arms, just as he
was clutching desperately at clarity.

'Said-it-on-the-van-see?' began the boys again, jeering
outrageously. But then, seeing Jeff advancing on him for
another shaking, the first boy added swiftly, 'Seen it up
there, didn't I?'

'Green, it was,' added his friend, also dodging smartly.

Jeff supposed that was as much as he could hope to get
out of them, and turned away to go inside. He would
have to think about it first—have another whisky to clarify
his mind—go down to this market, wherever it was,
tomorrow. Yes, tomorrow would do.

'Hey, mister,' called out the first boy, watching Jeff
fumble with his key, 'is Jason coming back, then?'

'I don't know,' muttered Jeff. 'I hope so.'

I hope so. He went inside and shut the door.

\* \* \*

He found Kite Street Market without much difficulty. It
was in a seedy part of town some way from his own road,
tucked into the centre of a maze of grubby little side-
streets. It looked prosperous and busy enough, though,
and was full of stalls and people. But there was no sign
of Joe.

It was just as well, because by this time Jeff had built
up a totally false picture of a leering rival carrying off his
wife in a green van, and was ready to do battle at the
slightest provocation.

The stallholders all knew Joe—and all liked him a lot.
He was cheery and kind, he didn't undercut on his prices,
and one way and another he did a lot of good around the
place without saying much about it. But they knew. So
when a stranger came asking questions, they didn't say
much. Joe, they said, wasn't there Thursdays. Went down
to Kent to collect his veges, didn't he? He'd be there

tomorrow, though, when the stuff came through from Penzance.

'*Penzance?*' said Jeff, staring at them wildly.

'His Dad,' explained someone. 'Gotta small-holding somewheres. Sends stuff up regular.'

'*Where?*; asked Jeff. '*Where from?*'

But they didn't know—or wouldn't say. A shrug. Somewhere in Cornwall. Silence.

'Lovely daffs, 'e sends,' added one woman suddenly, remembering the early golden buds that lit up the market on grey, wet mornings.

'What's his name?' asked Jeff.

They looked blank. Joe's? Joe was Joe. His father's? They didn't know.

Cursing inwardly, Jeff pushed his way through the market stalls to the corner pub and got himself a drink. Just one to give him time to think. Or it might be two.

After several drinks and not much thought, he suddenly had an idea. He enquired where he could book a market stall, and was directed to a shabby little office above a warehouse in the corner. Once there, he was a bit intimidated by the large, unfriendly man behind the desk, who looked like an ex-prize-fighter. But he asked politely about a stall. He had been recommended to try by someone called Joe, er . . .

'Joe Veryan?' growled the man, looking even more belligerent. 'What's he to you?'

But Jeff had got what he came for. He demurred a bit about the letting price, made an excuse to escape from that suspicious stare, and left in a hurry.

Veryan. Penzance. And Laurie had gone off in Joe's van. There must be some connection—and if there was, he'd find it. He'd go to Penzance tomorrow. Right now he needed another quiet drink—away from this unnerving place where they didn't like questions about Joe.

My God, when he did catch up with Joe, whoever he was, he'd teach him to go off with his wife—sending him off on a wild-goose chase like this. He'd teach him a thing or two.

\* \* \*

249

In Penzance it was wet and blowy, with a fine sea-mist spread over the bay like a pall. Jeff had hitched most of the way in a series of lorries, for he was rapidly running out of money—again. But he was tired and cold, so he thought he deserved a drink. In any case, the DSS office was closed till tomorrow. He'd have to find somewhere to sleep. Maybe someone in the pub would help.

Various people suggested various bed-and-breakfast places, but Jeff thought of his dwindling money supply, so in the end he slept rough in a small shelter on the sea-front, with a newspaper and the rest of his bottle of whisky to keep out the cold. In the morning he was hungry, so he spent some money on breakfast in a steamy seamen's café near the fish market, and shaved off his dark stubble with his pocket razor in the men's washroom. Even then it was too early for the social security office to be open, and the pubs weren't open either. So he sat in the warmth of the café as long as he could and then walked along the sea-front, his shoulders hunched against the grey wet drizzle.

By the time the office was open, he had decided he wanted a drink first—preferably two, for he needed some Dutch courage. So he rolled up at the office a little later, feeling a little more forceful.

The girl in the outer office knew nothing of Laurie's history, nor did she seem to care. She listened to his polite enquiries indifferently, and then told him she could not disclose any information about Mrs Laura Collins—if they had any.

Defeated yet again, Jeff went into the first pub he found open and tried to think what to do next. After several boosts to his flagging confidence, he got to his feet and enquired for the main post office. There, he took out the phone books and looked for the name Veryan. There were several—some in Penzance, some outside. Should he try ringing them all and asking for Laura Collins? But if she was in hiding, as seemed probable, they might not tell him—and it might alert her to run away still farther. No. Find the right one and go and see her. Talk to her. Persuade her. He was good at persuading. Always had been.

He took out the Yellow Pages and looked up Farmers. There were three Veryans—all in places he had never heard of. He would have to try them all.

He took a bus to the first one. They had never heard of Laura Collins, and eyed him with deep suspicion. At the second they were equally blank, and set the collie dogs in the yard to see him off. He grabbed a bit more Dutch courage in the village pub, where people seemed even more suspicious, and got the next bus back to Penzance.

That only left this place Tregarrow. But it was getting dark now. he would have to go there tomorrow. In the meantime, the Penzance pubs were warm and anonymous. No one looked at you at all, if you kept quiet. He kept quiet, and drank till his money was in danger of running out. He spoke sternly and rather drunkenly to himself about saving some for tomorrow, and wandered out into the damp, cold night. Then, once again, he slept in a shelter, wrapped in old newspapers and a comforting haze of whisky, and mercifully unnoticed by the patrolling police.

In the morning, he counted the rest of his money and took a bus to Tregarrow, promising himself a drink when he got there. But he felt bad without one—thin and empty and not very sure of himself.

At Tregarrow post office, it just happened that Annie Merrow was out at the back checking stock, and her niece, Donna, was serving in the shop. She did not have Annie's built-in wariness of strangers, or her professional reticence about post office matters. Nor her awareness of Laurie's situation. She simply saw a reasonably well-dressed, soft-spoken man who was enquiring politely about his friend Mrs Collins who he believed was staying nearby. Oh yes, she said, at Luke Veryan's on Tregarrow Farm. Cliff Cottage, she thought Mr Veryan called it.

Jeff gave her a dazzling smile and asked her to point out the way. He also asked, still politely, if there was a pub in the village where he might get a sandwich and a pint?

Several drinks later, and with a curious angry tension

251

rather like fright building up inside him, Jeff set off to look for Veryan's farm. As he climbed the hill, he came in sight of the little village school and a straggle of children just coming out to go home. A thought struck him, and he looked at them more closely. Were Jason and Midge among them?

Yes, there they were—hand-in-hand, turning aside from the road to the winding cliff path.

'Hey!' he called, lurching into a run. 'Jason! Midge! It's your Dad!'

The two small figures stiffened—the two faces turned to him in frozen horror. Then, without a second's hesitation, they began to run.

'Wait!' called Jeff despairingly. 'I only want to talk to you! Wait a minute!'

But they didn't wait. They went on running, streaking away up the narrow, rock-strewn path till they were out of sight. Jason had two thoughts in his mind as he ran. I must get Midge home to the cottage—to Penny, where she'll be safe. They can lock themselves in. And then I must go and warn Mum—I must get to the field before he does. Desperately he went on running, with Midge's tense, frightened little hand in his.

Jeff, meanwhile, had given up chasing them. His wind wasn't very good nowadays anyway and, what with several drinks on an empty stomach, he found the cliff path weaving about in a most unsafe manner. Better keep to the road, he told himself. They said the farm was up here somewhere. Better see Laurie first. The children could wait.

But he was angry—furious that his own kids had run away from him like that. What did they think he was—some kind of ogre? He only wanted to talk to them—like he did to Laurie—just talk, reasonably, and sort things out. But they wouldn't even listen. They ran away, looking terrified, as if the devil himself was after them. What had Laurie been saying to them to make them behave like that? It wasn't fair of her to make them afraid of him—and by God he'd tell her so when he saw her.

He had a small drop of that whisky left in the bottle,

and now he stopped and took another swig. It was the last of it. God knows where I'll get any more, he thought, but Christ I need it now.

* * *

Laurie was picking daffodils. Things had been slack on the farm for a bit after Christmas. The winter had stayed mild and very wet, and the fields of beet and swedes for the cattle were like seas of mud. Even the sprouts and broccoli were drenched and sodden. But the daffodils were early. Old Bob, casting an experienced eye over the rows of thin, green spears coming up, reckoned they'd be ready for picking before Mothers' Day. Soon as the buds showed green, he told her, they'd be picking like mad. Meantime, his rheumatism was bad, and there was plenty to do in the greenhouses—enough for both of them—and the boss would know when the daffs were ready and he had to lay on extra pickers.

So when Luke Veryan came in one morning and said, 'They're ready. Better get out there now,' she knew what was happening.

It was fairly back-breaking work, but for some reason Laurie loved it. She liked the feel of the sturdy stalks in her fingers and the fat, green buds trying so passionately to burst into golden flower.

During the morning, a lorry-load of pickers came in from St Buryan and moved slowly down the green daffodil fields. Laurie got used to seeing them out of the corner of her eye, so she did not look up at once when someone came and stood near her.

'Hullo, Laurie,' said a voice close above her head.

Laurie froze. Her hands, clutching the bunches of daffodils, went stiff with terror. She looked up in dazed disbelief into the taut face of Jeff smiling dangerously down at her.

A number of thoughts passed swiftly through Laurie's head as she knelt there among the daffodils. But uppermost was the quick realisation: He's drunk and angry. I must not take him near the cottage—Penny and the baby are there, and the children will be on their way back from school soon. *I must lead Jeff away from there—and I must face up to him and make him see reason somehow.*

She got to her feet slowly and laid down her bunches of daffodils. So far she had not said a word, but her scalp was prickling with danger and there was a hard knot of fear in her stomach.

'Surprised to see me?' asked Jeff, his voice like the flick of a whip.

'Not very,' said Laurie truthfully. 'I thought you'd get around to it.' She glanced down the field to where old Bob was directing the pickers, and added in as calm a tone as she could muster, 'Wait there, will you? I must tell Bob I'm going.'

'Going where?' The question hung in the air like a threat.

'I suppose you want to talk?' Laurie spoke reasonably. 'We'd better walk along the cliff. It's more private.' She left him standing there and went quickly over to Bob, who was knee-deep in bunches of daffodils which he was carefully packing into boxes.

'Bob . . . I've got to knock off early. Someone wants to see me.'

Bob looked up at her shrewdly. 'OK, missus.' Then he added, with more concern in his voice, 'You all right, then? You looks very pale.'

Laurie tried to smile. 'Yes, Bob. But if . . . if the children come looking for me . . . tell them to go home and wait.'

Bob nodded, still looking at her oddly, and then went back to his packing. Laurie walked back along the daffodil rows to where Jeff was standing, impatience clear in every line of his body. 'All right,' she said evenly. 'Shall we go?'

Jeff was a bit nonplussed by this cool, efficient Laurie— he did not quite know how to handle the situation, and his frustration was growing.

'Well?' Laurie stopped walking when they were out of sight of the farm and as far away from the cottage as she could manage. 'What do you want?'

Jeff was amazed. '*What do I want?* I want you back where you belong—and the kids, too.'

'Why?' The question was flat and uncompromising.

'Why? Because you're my wife, and they're my kids—that's why.'

Laurie sighed. 'No, Jeff. Not any more. I explained all that before.'

'Explained, my arse!' shouted Jeff rudely. 'You're mine, I tell you, and you're coming back with me—*now*!' And he leant forward and seized her by the arm.

'Let go of me!' Laurie spoke quite softly, but there was somehow menace in her voice.

Jeff stepped back a little and raised a hand—in an almost automatic gesture of defiance—to hit her across the face. But he paused, staring down at her—for Laurie did not flinch this time. She stood her ground and said firmly, 'Don't be idiotic. If you hit me, you'll only land in prison again. There's an injunction out against you molesting me—remember? Why don't you calm down and be reasonable?'

'*Reasonable*!' Laurie's calm seemed to madden him still further. 'How can you expect me to be reasonable when my wife and kids have walked out, my house is filthy and cold, and there's nothing to eat!'

Laurie actually laughed. 'Ah! Now we're getting to it. You need a housekeeper, Jeff, not a wife. Only, of course, you couldn't knock *her* about. Or, alternatively, you could learn to cook.'

Jeff swore and lunged at her with flailing fists. One caught her a swinging blow to the side of the head, and Laurie stepped back a little, blinking at the pain which suddenly shot through her already damaged skull.

My own fault, she thought. I shouldn't bait him. I must try to reason with him—and she put out her hands to fend him off, while she tried to summon enough courage to talk some sense into him.

But before she could say anything more, several things happened at once. Jeff lunged again, and she found herself wrestling wildly with him. Midge came running along the cliff path, calling 'Mummy!' in a scared voice, and, just as Jeff turned his head to look at the child, Jason came racing past her and launched himself straight at his father like a small tornado.

'Stop it!'; he shouted. 'Stop hitting her! Go away!' and he pounded Jeff with his small fists in a blaze of protective anger.

'Jay!' called Laurie sharply.

But it was too late. Jeff let out a savage oath and felled Jason to the ground. Midge screamed, long and high, and backed away towards the edge of the cliff.

'No, Midge!' Laurie's voice rose desperately. '*Stay where you are!*'

But the child was beside herself with fear. As Jeff moved towards her, she screamed again and took another step backwards. Her foot slid on rock and slippery turf, and she flung her hands up wildly, trying to keep her balance, and disappeared over the edge of the cliff in a slither of stones and a wail of terror.

For a second, Laurie stood transfixed. Then she flung herself down on the edge and peered over—almost afraid to look. And there was Midge, crouched in a terrified heap on a ledge of rock, her skirts caught in a small gorse bush leaning out from the cliff-face. She seemed unhurt, though almost beyond the limits of fear.

Jason was picking himself up by this time, bruised and shaken but not badly hurt. Laurie glanced round at him and said, 'Run, Jay! Run and get help!' and was relieved to see him take a deep, gulping breath of resolve and obey her. At least he would be out of trouble.

But now Jeff was moving nearer—a strange, mad glitter in his eye—and Laurie knew she had to reach him somehow.

'Jeff!' she said holding back the rising hysteria within her. 'Think what you're doing! It's your daughter down there. It's your *daughter*. Do you want to kill her?'

Jeff stopped, weaving on his feet a little as the combination of drink and anger and unexpected emotion surged round inside him. 'Midge?' he said uncertainly. 'Midge?' And then he too looked over the edge. 'My God!' He sounded suddenly stone-cold sober. 'We must get her back!' And he began to move forward again, as if he intended to climb down after her.

But Midge saw him and screamed again—crouching

256

closer to the rock and clutching the rough stem of the gorse bush in her small, cold hands.

'No!' Laurie saw the danger. 'Not you, Jeff. She's terrified of you.'

She didn't have time to notice the sudden flick of bitter awareness in Jeff's face—the realisation that his own small daughter was so frightened of him that she'd rather risk death on the cliff-face than have him come near her.

'I'll go down,' Laurie went on, persuasively. 'In any case, I'm lighter, and you can hold on to me and haul us up.'

She didn't wait for his reply but began cautiously lowering herself over the edge, a little to the right of Midge in case she sent down a cascade of stones on top of her. The rocks were shaly and slippery, but there were still tufts of heather and thrift growing in the crevices which gave some sort of foothold. Slowly, inch by inch, she got nearer, trying not to look down at the dizzying drop to the tangle of sharp rocks below and the pounding seas beyond. At length her foot touched the ledge where Midge lay crouched. But here Laurie paused, uncertain what to do next. If she tried to hold on to the same gorse bush, her added weight might pull it from the rock—just as it might cause the little ledge of rock itself to crumble away.

So she edged her way down a little lower than Midge and anchored her feet against a jutting piece of rock. Only then did she reach up and fold her arms round the terrified child above her.

'It's all right,' she murmured, holding her. 'It's all right. . . . You're safe now. . . . We'll soon have you back on top.'

But Midge was past reason. She clung tightly to the gorse bush, rigid with shock, and could not move.

Gently, Laurie went on talking to her until she saw some of the tension beginning to leave the child's frozen body. If I could get her to stand, she thought, with me holding her from behind, maybe Jeff could reach her.

Jeff, meanwhile, had taken off his jacket and was lying full length on the clifftop, with the coat dangling over the edge. It was just not long enough to reach Midge. He took off his tie and tied it firmly to the end of one sleeve. Then he dangled it down again. This time, Laurie could just reach it, by stretching up dangerously high.

'Tie it to Midge somehow,' he called, 'and I'll try to pull her up . . . if you steady her from behind.'

Laurie did as she was told. But Midge took a lot of coaxing to move at all—especially when she saw Jeff looking down at her.

'Try, darling,' begged Laurie. 'Try! Daddy's trying to help you. . . . Please try to climb up . . . That's it . . . Now the other foot . . . I'm right behind you.'

Carefully, with infinite and awful slowness, Laurie coaxed and cajoled the terrified little girl forward, inch by painful inch, up the treacherous cliff-face. And slowly Jeff pulled her up and held her steady as each small foot fumbled for a new hold and each frantic small hand scrabbled for another grip.

At last, Midge's head came up level with the overhang, and swiftly Jeff reached down and hauled her to safety over the edge.

But as he did so, the shaly overhang began to crumble under him in an ominous rumble of stones. 'Get away, Midge! *Quick!*' he shouted, and shoved the child backwards with a convulsive heave before he began to topple in horrible slow motion over the edge of the cliff.

Laurie was stranded beneath him, neither safely supported on Midge's ledge by the gorse bush nor within reach of the top. She crouched there in horror as a shower of loose rock and sandy pebbles began to pour down towards her—and with them, helplessly caught in the torrent of stone, came Jeff.

'Look out!'; he screamed, as the rocks bounced down towards her.

Laurie shot out a hand to him as he spun past, and he reached out desperately and grasped it by the wrist. The shock of his weight pulled at the shoulder socket with such violence that Laurie cried out. It's gone out, she thought. I wonder if it'll hold? And when a heavy piece of rock bounced off the cliff-face and struck her on the same outstretched arm, she scarcely felt the added pain. She had shut her eyes at the initial jolt, but now she opened them again and found herself looking down directly into Jeff's face. He was dangling in space, his legs reaching out wildly and finding nothing, while the cascade of rocks went on falling round him—his grip on her wrist the only hold he had against certain death.

'Hold on!' she called faintly, sick with pain and unable to help him or herself further.

And Jeff held on. But the weight of his body was more than Laurie could withstand, and she felt herself beginning to move very slightly downwards. Soon it would be a slide and then an unpreventable rush—and they would both be gone.

'Hold on!' she repeated, trying to keep her mind clear. And she looked down again, straight into Jeff's pale, terrified eyes.

But they weren't terrified any more. Somehow, as Laurie gazed down, they seemed to clear and grow deep with awareness—the whole, inexorable pattern laid out before him in split-second clarity. What he had once been, what he might have been—the hopes and ambitions that had mocked him and broken him with their false promises. What his young wife had been when he first knew her. What she might be now, given half a chance. And his children, too, caught up in the same bitter tide of destruction that now threatened to engulf them all.

Maybe his failing strength just suddenly gave out. Maybe his fingers just lost their grip and could not hold on any longer. Maybe his whole, disintegrating, drink-sodden body just gave up in despair. No one would ever know the truth. But to Laurie, seeing the expression in those eyes, it was perfectly clear. Jeff had seen the stark choices of the future—and he could not bear it.

His mouth seemed to be framing the word 'Sorry', and she caught a faint whisper of it above the crash of the waves below. Then his fingers, grasping her wrist in their desperate, convulsive grip, slipped and failed, and let go.

'Jeff!' screamed Laurie. 'Jeff! No!'

But it was useless to call. For a second he still seemed to hang in space, his eyes still looking up at her with their strange awareness. And then he was gone, hurtling down and down, turning over and over, wreathed in a cascade of stones, till his body hit the rocks below and spread out into a sprawl of limbs that lay utterly still.

Laurie could not see him. Mercifully, the cliff-face bulged out a little before that final, sickening drop. She could only see the far edge of the rocks, and the white spray springing up over them, ceaselessly washing them clean.

She clung there, helpless and weeping, with her useless right arm still swinging before her and her other hand gripping the only solid piece of rock she could find.

Jeff was gone. There was no way she could have saved him. No way she could have stopped that terrible fall. But she wept painfully and with aching pity for the bright-haired young man with the engaging smile she had once loved so much when she was young.

They found her still clinging there—and still weeping helplessly—when the rescuers came running with ropes and clamps and stretchers, and Jason racing at their head.

*    *    *

Midge was unhurt except for a few bruises, though badly frightened; and Jason only had one sizeable bump on the side of his head. But Laurie was not so lucky. Her arm was broken in two places where the rock had fallen on it, and she had to have it set and the dislocated shoulder pushed back into place. She didn't remember much about it, since she was already half-fainting with pain and shock before the rescuers reached her. And she never saw the second stretcher party bring Jeff's body up from the rocks. But sometime later she found herself lying in a neat hospital bed in a small side-ward, with her plastered arm and strapped shoulder held securely in a sling and propped up on an extra pillow, and a friendly young nurse smiling at her from the open doorway into the general ward.

'The children?' she asked anxiously, failing to add anything else.

'They're fine,', said the nurse. 'They brought them in for a check-up—just to be on the safe side.'

'They?' She sounded puzzled.

'They'll be in to see you, as soon as the doctor's been round. They wouldn't go home without!'

'Can't I go home with them?' Laurie tried to sit up straight. 'This isn't serious.'

The young nurse looked at her warily. 'That's for the doctor to say.' And then, in a changed voice, she added, 'Oh. Here he is now.'

The house doctor came over and sat down beside Laurie. He took her wrist in his hand and felt the uneven, too-rapid pulse. 'How are you feeling?'

'I'm fine,' Laurie lied. In truth she was aching all over, and she was beginning to shake with reaction. But at least, she thought, I'm alive—while Jeff . . . 'Can I go home?' she begged, shuddering.

'Not tonight.' He shook his head firmly. 'Not after *another* blow on the head.'

Laurie looked innocent. 'Did . . . something hit me on the head?'

The young doctor stared at her reflectively. 'Several things, I should think. And we have to be cautious with head injuries.'

'Do you?' Laurie's thoughts kept flying off like black crows—refusing to stay still, but full of half-remembered grief and terror.

'So I think we'll keep you in for the night. You've been through a very harrowing experience.' He smiled at her briefly. 'Besides,' he added, not missing the tremors that were beginning to shake her, 'you've probably got some delayed shock.' He rose and patted her kindly on her good arm. 'Take it easy. I'll see you in the morning.' And he strolled off to talk to another patient.

But as soon as he had gone there was a rush of feet down the corridor, and Midge rushed in, followed by Penny and Jason.

'All of you?' gasped Laurie, under the onslaught of Midge's embrace.

'Had to make sure you were all in one piece, didn't

we?' Penny sounded quite fierce. She grinned at Laurie, ignoring the startling pallor of her face and the heavy shadows under her eyes.

'I'm all right,' murmured Laurie, answering all their unspoken questions. She held out her good arm to Jason and drew him close to her. 'You fetched help so fast!'

'He ran all the way to the farm, and all the way back!' Penny told her. 'And he got George Button as well.'

'Was he there, too?'

'He came running. We all did!' Penny was smiling now. 'But Jay ran fastest!'

'Laurie gave him a silent hug.

'Now then,' ordered the young nurse, returning with a cup of tea. 'Time to go home.' She smiled at Midge, who was looking very doubtful about leaving, and added cheerfully, 'She's coming home tomorrow.'

For a moment Midge clung on tightly, but then Penny came forward and hugged Laurie too, a trifle convulsively, and said in an uneven voice, 'Come on, Midge. Your Mum's tired,' and took her by the hand.

Jason looked at his mother for a moment and then said, 'You OK?'

She nodded, all at once too full to speak, and he smiled at her with sudden radiance and followed the others out.

'Drink your tea,' said the nurse, pretending to sound severe. 'You've got one more visitor. But he can only stay five minutes!'

Luke Veryan looked quite grey with shock—and Laurie felt a lurch of guilt when she saw him. She hadn't meant him to be drawn into her affairs—especially not a catastrophe like this.

'Won't stay long,' he said gruffly. 'Came to say I'll keep an eye on young Penny and the children. Police want to see you. I said tomorrow—too tired tonight.'

Laurie nodded. 'I suppose . . . Jeff? No one's told me anything.'

'He was dead before we got to him.' His face was suddenly kind. 'Must've been instantaneous.' He put out a gnarled hand and gripped hers hard. 'Don't grieve, girl. Better this way, I dessay.'

262

Laurie did not answer. She was too occupied trying to swallow useless tears. I was afraid of him, she thought. And sometimes I hated him. But I never wished him dead.

'Won't talk now,' said Luke, comfortingly. 'Get some sleep, girl. Deal with things tomorrow.' He got up and patted her awkwardly.

Everyone seems to be patting me and trying to soothe me down, she thought, with a flick of desperate humour. But aloud she said gently, 'Thanks for coming . . . and . . . and for everything.'

Luke gave a kind of snort. 'Glad you're alive, girl!' he snapped, and stumped out of the room without looking back.

* * *

Laurie had a bad night. She woke several times shouting Jeff's name, caught in the nightmare of that suddenly failing grip on her wrist . . . the falling body . . . the shower of stones . . . the terrible drop below. 'No!' she shouted. 'No, Jeff! No!' and sometimes, desperately, 'Hold on! Hold on!'

She sweated and shook and wept in the darkened room, and then fell back into exhausted sleep again. After the third time the little night nurse had come in to quieten her, the night sister appeared with an injection. 'Get her another cup of tea, nurse,' she said, and then smiled at Laurie consolingly. 'It'll take effect soon.'

Laurie slept dreamlessly till the early activity in the main ward woke her.

* * *

Later on, a sympathetic policewoman came to see her and took down a careful statement. Laurie told her story as calmly as she could. She did not leave out the initial row with Jeff on the clifftop, because she realised Jason and Midge had seen it all, and Jay himself bore the marks of that first attack. But she went on to recount how Jeff had rescued little Midge, and had tried to save Laurie, too. In fact, *had* saved her by letting go her wrist. But here, at

last, her composure broke and she said in a choked voice,
'I tried . . . I tried to make him hold on. But I couldn't—
he was too heavy. I couldn't pull him up.'

'Don't distress yourself,' said the kindly policewoman.
'It's all right. I've got all the facts now.'

'I tried . . .' whispered Laurie. 'I tried . . .'

The young woman beside her looked thoughtfully
across at Laurie's injured arm and shoulder. 'I can see
you did,' she said softly, and got to her feet. 'Thank you
for being so frank, Mrs Collins. We'll be in touch if we
need to know anything more.' She hesitated a moment
and then added, 'I do hope you'll be feeling better soon.'
Then she went away and apologised to the sister in charge
for upsetting her patient.

Laurie was tired after her visit, and lay back with her
eyes closed. So she did not see someone come and stand
in the doorway of the little side-ward, looking in at her—
did not know anyone was there until a voice said,
'Laurie?'

It can't be, she thought. I'm dreaming, of course. It's
only because I'm so tired . . . and I need comfort so much.

'Laurie?' said the voice again.

Her eyes flew open—incredulous and glad. 'You? Is
it . . . really you?'

'It's me,' said Clem, smiling at her gravely. 'Can I come
in?'

Laurie's face suddenly crumpled, and she tried to hold
out her one good arm. 'Oh God . . . *Clem!*'

He was across the room with one stride and folding her
close so that she could lean against his shoulder like a
tired child, feeling his warmth and strength encompass
her in a cloak of well-being. And suddenly the awful
events of the day before caught up with her and she began
to weep desperately, and found that she could not stop.
'I tried . . .' she kept saying—as she had to the policewoman. 'I tried . . . but I couldn't hold him, Clem, he *let
go*. . . . He knew he was pulling me down too . . . He
just . . . *let go!*'

'Yes,' said Clem calmly. 'Of course he did.' And he
rocked her in his arms and waited for the storm of grief

to pass. If it occurred to him to have doubts about Jeff's intentions, he did not show it. It was clear to him that Laurie needed to believe it. She badly needed to believe there had still been some good in Jeff, if she was to come to terms with his death. And anyway, Clem too was apt to believe the best of people, given half a chance.

At length Laurie was quiet, though tremors still shook her. She took a deep shaken breath and sniffed—looking so like a tearful child that Clem could not help smiling at her. He reached for a handful of tissues that lay on her locker and gently mopped her face and brushed the hair out of her eyes with loving fingers.

'Come on,' he said, handing her a tissue. 'Blow!'

Laurie laughed and gulped—and did as she was told. Then she said, still amazed at his presence, 'I don't understand why you're here.'

Clem took her hand in his and held it firmly. 'It's simple, really. I was coming to see you anyway. I had business in Exeter and Truro. I thought you might be glad of a visit.'

Laurie was still gazing at him, almost with disbelief.

'And I had something to suggest to you about the spring,' he added quietly. 'But we can talk about that later.' He reached out his other hand and touched her face gently. 'It's all right. . . .' He spoke as if she was one of his injured swans, too filled with terror and shock to understand that it was safe. 'Everything will be all right. Give yourself time.'

Laurie closed her eyes and drew another perilous breath.

'I rang Luke Veryan last night,' Clem was saying. 'He told me what had happened.' His firm fingers gripped her hand tightly. 'So I arranged with him to come and fetch you home today.'

'Now?' A sudden, enormous wave of relief seemed to engulf her. Clem was here. He would see to everything. She needn't fight any more.

'As soon as they say you can go,' he told her, watching the tension and anxiety slowly recede from her face. 'Don't worry. I'll look after things.'

He got up quietly, and stooped to brush the hair out of her eyes again. He did not kiss her. It was not the time, he told himself. Not yet. Here was a shocked and injured creature—needing rest and comfort and a sense of safety, with no demands upon her. He knew what his role must be. But he was patient. And love could grow as surely and imperceptibly as a swan's new wing feathers.

'Rest a moment,' he murmured. 'I'll find out when you can leave.'

Laurie lay there in a dream, scarcely daring to believe it was true. The world seemed to turn under her hand and take on a new dimension. She was safe.

\* \* \*

Clem did not immediately take her home. He stopped at a quiet pub with a bright log fire in the hearth and ordered her coffee and a small brandy to drink with it, taking her over to a secluded seat in the corner.

Then he glanced at her pale, shadowed face and said gently, 'I'm not going to talk about the future. It's only the present we need to think about now.'

Laurie nodded.

'So . . . first, I must warn you that the press may bother you.'

She looked startled. 'Oh God. I hadn't thought of that.'

Clem's face was a little grim. 'No. Well, I had. And so had old Luke Veryan. He gave them the bare details, but he wouldn't let them talk to Penny or the children.'

'I should hope not!'

Clem grinned. 'Quite an old battle-axe, Luke is, when he tries! And so am I!'

Laurie managed a pale grin, too. 'I don't believe it!'

'Well, I routed 'em for you at the hospital. But I think you'd better see 'em and say something.'

'I don't know why they're so interested.'

'It was a pretty spectacular rescue, so I'm told.' He was squinting at her through a smile.

'I suppose it was.' She took time to consider. 'What should I say?'

'Oh—not a lot.' He also seemed to be considering. 'What did you tell the police?'

'The truth,' She spoke flatly. And then, amending it, 'I mean, I couldn't leave out the . . . the violence, because Jay and Midge had seen it. He knocked Jay down and bruised his face—and it showed. I . . . I didn't know what Jay might say.'

Clem nodded. 'Just as well. When he got to Luke, his first words were, "My Dad's trying to kill my Mum on the cliffs!" '

Laurie had tears in her eyes. 'He tried to fight him off, you know. He went for him like a little wildcat.' She shook off the tears. 'But I . . . I'd rather just say Midge went over the edge and Jeff got her back. . . . And then he slipped.'

Clem looked at her sternly. 'Yes. That will do for now. But it depends on what comes out at the inquest.'

Laurie seemed to go even paler. 'I suppose I'll have to attend?'

'I think so.' He was still looking at her, his eyes full of reassurance. 'But I'll be there. And so will Luke, I'm sure.'

Laurie closed her eyes for a moment. 'Clem, . . . do you think . . . after the history of violence and . . . and prison and the injunction and all that . . . anyone would suppose I'd *pushed* him?'

Clem laughed. 'With that arm injury? And where you were found—half-way down the cliff, clinging for dear life to a piece of rock? Don't be absurd.' He reached out and took her hand in his, holding it firmly. 'You needn't let that nightmare haunt you, on top of everything else!' Ha paused, as if considering what to say next. 'I'm only warning you of what you'll have to face in the next few days. It won't be easy. But I'm also telling you that I'll stay till everything is settled.' His smile rested on her again, calm and loving. 'I just thought we'd better talk here, rather than at home. We needn't disturb the children any further.'

Laurie shuddered. 'They were just getting to feel happy again—and secure. Even Midge. And now it will all have to be done over again.'

Clem kept her hand in his, and tightened his grip for added emphasis. 'No it won't. They're stronger than you think, those kids of yours. And I think Jeff's final action may have released you all from more than you know.'

Laurie looked at him gratefully. 'I think he knew that.' Then her gaze darkened and turned inwards, clouded with memory. 'I think he saw it all—the whole wretched mess. His eyes were somehow . . . filled with knowledge. He was like . . . like he might have been when he was older—and wiser. As if he understood himself as well as us. It was uncanny. He knew—and he *chose*.'

Clem did not contradict her. He waited a moment and then spoke quietly. 'Yes, and, that being the case, you mustn't undo his choice.'

'What?'

She stared at him, caught by his sudden intensity. And now he reached out his other hand and gently pushed the hair out of her eyes.

'You did your utmost,' he said, his voice as gentle as his hand. 'Your absolute utmost. Look at you! So no misplaced feelings of guilt, understand? You'll be defeating his purpose if you let it haunt you all your life.' He drew a long, steadying breath and added, trying to keep his voice as calm and steady as ever, 'You've got a lot of living to do yet—and a lot of happiness to look forward to, one way or another.' He smiled now directly into her eyes, making his meaning plain. Then he added softly, 'Give yourself a chance!'

It was a long speech for Clem, and Laurie was shaken. She saw something flash deep down in his grey, cloud-flecked eyes that almost made her heart stop. But it was gone almost at once, and only his calm, loving smile was left. 'I . . . I'll try,' she said, and bent her head to hide the betraying tears that threatened her again. Then she added, like an apologetic child, 'I'm sorry I'm so wet!'

Clem laughed. 'Enough lecturing. I'd better take you home.'

But there was something else bothering Laurie, and now she spoke of it shyly. 'Clem—what about your swans? How can you leave them? Won't they mind?'

He smiled at her anxious expression. 'I have an assistant now. The Wildlife Rescue Service gave me one, to help with the increasing work. And anyway, I was on official business down here.'

'Were you?' She was looking at him in a puzzled way. 'I never asked you—what do you do for money? How do you finance the Sanctuary?'

His eyes were still crinkled with laughter. 'You don't know much about me really, do you?'

No, thought Laurie painfully—only that I feel I've known you all my life, and there is nothing about you that is strange to me. She looked up and found the same thought clear in his eyes. But he did not speak of it—not then.

Instead, he went cheerfully on. 'Well, I earn a sort of living as a lecturer. Mostly at evening institutes, so I can be free for the birds during the day—with an occasional book about wildlife or conservation to add to the funds.' His eyes were sparking with mischief. 'I get a grant from the wildlife people, but I rely on donations as well.' He was smiling now, talking easily and happily about his work. 'And then, as you know, I'm also a vet—though I don't practise much now. But I do help out the farmers and the local vet sometimes in emergencies, so I earn a bit extra that way.' His smile seemed to grow as he went on. 'And now that Alec's there, they're talking of setting up another sanctuary or two in other places. It happens when they get hold of someone useful—we're always trying to expand.'

Laurie was looking at him strangely. 'So—what were you doing down here?'

His smile remained entirely open and innocent, but she knew he was not in the least guileless and it made her wonder a little. 'I was delivering a pair of swans to a man with a private lake.' Sudden warmth came into his eyes. 'They were mended, and the water was unpolluted, so I knew they'd be safe and probably live happily ever after.' For a moment the new, unexplained warmth in his glance rested on her. 'They mate for life, you know—swans.' Then he continued more briskly, 'He was very pleased

269

with them. So, after that, I went on to arrange a couple of lectures in Exeter and Truro—just in case.'

'Just in case of what?'

The mischief was back in his voice. 'In case you were glad to see me.'

Laurie was still staring at him, but at the dancing light in his eyes she suddenly began to laugh.

'That's better,' approved Clem. 'Satisfied?'

'Not entirely,' admitted Laurie. 'I think you're up to something. And I still don't understand how you knew I needed you *just now*.'

The smile died in Clem's face. He looked at her with sudden piercing gravity. 'Nor do I,' he said softly. 'But thank God I did.'

* * *

Jane, when she heard the news, went storming down to the social services office to lodge a fierce complaint. 'Do you realise,' she raged, 'that it is due to your breach of confidence that a man is dead, and his wife and children were nearly killed as well? Added to which, that poor, wretched girl will be carrying a totally undeserved weight of guilt for the rest of her life.'

'But it wasn't her fault.'

'No. It was yours.'

The woman looked bewildered. 'But I didn't tell him anything.'

Jane stopped short. 'You must have let something slip.'

The counsellor shook her head. 'No. We are always most careful.' She looked at Jane earnestly. 'Believe me, we have strict instructions.'

'Are you sure you didn't leave any papers where he could see them? Did you leave the room for anything?'

There was a silence. The counsellor remembered Jeff— how humble he had seemed, how contrite. And how he had asked for that travel voucher. 'Yes,' she admitted slowly. 'I might have.'

Jane snorted. 'They're not to be trusted you know, these husbands.'

'But he sounded so sincere.'

270

'Oh, I'm sure,' said Jane. And I suppose he told you that his "lapse" was a one-off mistake and he was desperate to make amends?'

The colour was rising in the woman's face. 'Yes. He did.'

Jane swore mildly. 'How gullible can you get! D'you know how long Laura Collins was married to that man? Nine years—*nine*! And for eight of them he was continuously violent. She left home once before. She landed in hospital twice. She had a dreadful miscarriage caused by him throwing her downstairs. And the last time—when she came to me—she had a fractured skull, concussion, broken ribs, and such horrific bruising you could scarcely see her face. And you think you can let that . . . that mindless, uncontrolled animal near his wife and children!'

The woman counsellor shook her head in shock. 'I didn't know.'

'You should have found out!' snarled Jane. 'Didn't you even know there was an injunction out against him?'

'No.' She shook her head again. 'The papers were with another department.'

Jane laughed. 'British bureaucracy!' Then, unexpectedly, she calmed down. 'Listen, I know you did your best. And I can see that you didn't intentionally divulge any information. But these women—many of them—are in fear of their lives when they get to me. I promise them safety—at least while they stay at The Hide. I try to give them time to sort themselves out—*in safety*. And I've got to keep that promise.' She drew in a sharp breath. 'D'you know what the housing people suggested to Mrs Collins? "Go back and live in your husband's council house. We can get another injunction to keep him away." ' She laughed again. 'Did this injunction keep him away?'

The counsellor said slowly, 'I . . . we hoped to arrange a meeting. It would have been carefully monitored, of course.' She looked at Jane with despairing honesty. 'We always have to *try* for a reconciliation, you know.'

Jane nodded. 'I know. And sometimes it works. But in a long history of violence, it hardly ever does. The women always want to give them a second chance . . . and they always revert.' She looked back at the counsellor with equal honesty and despair. 'I've seen it too often. And they always try to follow their wives, no matter how careful we are.'

The counsellor sighed. 'I'm sorry this has happened.'

Unexpectedly, Jane smiled her curiously sweet smile. 'I can see it wasn't your fault. But if anything had happened to Laurie or her little girl . . .' She paused, and then added more gently: 'We're on the same side, you know—trying to repair the damage. But these husbands . . . they can be very persuasive.'

'I can see that.' The counsellor's voice was dry.

They looked at one another with understanding.

'Some of these young social workers,' said Jane, speaking with oblique bitterness, 'are altogether too idealistic. They don't live in the same world.' She glanced at the counsellor almost casually. 'Maybe you could tell them?'

'I daresay I could,' agreed the grey woman gravely.

Jane knew she had said enough. She had to protect her women. But she had to work with the social services people, too. It was important.

Once again her singularly sweet smile flashed out. 'Thanks,' she said, and went out of the office without another word.

* * *

Laurie had insisted on going up to the farm each day. She could keep an eye on the books for Luke Veryan and, though she could not help with the bunching and packing, she could at least pick daffodils with one hand. When both Luke and Penny protested, she said jerkily, 'Please. I'd rather be busy just now,' and Clem unexpectedly supported her and came with her into the fields to lend a hand.

'Two hands to your one,' he said, and smiled at her encouragingly over the green and golden sea of flowers.

He was unfailingly kind to the children, too, and spent a lot of time persuading little Midge to laugh again and run about in the early spring sunshine. And he fell for young Christmas Rose on the spot. She was an exceptionally pretty baby now—with the beginnings of soft, reddish curls like her mother's, and the bluest of wide, enquiring eyes.

'Penny,' he said approvingly, 'she's enchanting! You're a lucky girl.'

'Don't I know it,' agreed Penny, tossing her own bright-red head.

But then more serious things encroached. There had to be a post-mortem, and after it the police told Laurie as kindly as they could that it was death from multiple injuries and it would have been instantaneous. Laurie was white and quiet, but she thanked them politely for their consideration and did not falter. She did not falter either when the press came and got their promised interview and asked a lot of impertinent questions. But Clem got rid of them for her when they got too tiresome.

He went with her to the inquest, where she gave her evidence quietly and clearly—and emphasised with careful honesty Jeff's rescue of Midge and his final attempt to save Laurie herself.

'Are you saying, Mrs Collins,' asked the coroner gently, leaning forward a little to see her face, 'that at the last moment, when he was hanging on to your wrist, your husband *let go?*'

'Yes,' said Laurie, her head held high. 'I think he realised I was being pulled down after him. He did it to save me.'

There was a silence round her in the little courtroom. Then she spoke again, in a broken whisper, as if reliving that moment: 'He was too heavy for me. I couldn't hold him . . . And he knew it.'

The silence continued for a moment. If the coroner had any doubts about that final gesture of Jeff's, he did not say so. It did not seem to him relevant now. And clearly it mattered to this young woman to believe what she did.

'Thank you, Mrs Collins,' he said quietly. 'You have been very brave and helpful. I'm sorry to have distressed you.'

Clem came forward then and led her away. He took her out of the courtroom, out of the town altogether, and drove away up on to the moors beyond the busy main road, where there was nothing to see but moving cloud shadows on wide hillsides and splashes of sunshine on golden outcrops of rock—with the liquid sound of curlews on the wind.

Laurie drew in deep breaths of cold, clear air and stood gazing out at the line of hills and the dark sea beyond. And Clem—blessed, undemanding Clem—stood beside her and said nothing at all.

They walked a long time that day, side by side, and only returned to the cottage when it grew dark. And there were the children and Penny waiting for them in the firelight, and they drew the curtains against the night and sat round the table together to demolish the meal Penny had got ready for them. Even Laurie ate something that evening, for the long walk in the spicy moorland air had made her hungry.

Clem watched her and said nothing. But seeing her there in the firelight with her children round her put a darkness into his eyes that he could not hide. Only Penny saw it. Laurie was too tired to notice, and for that he was thankful. But he kept very still in his chair.

* * *

The funeral was small and quiet, but even so one of Jeff's family came. Laurie hadn't known who to contact, so on Clem's advice she had put a notice in the papers, and Jeff's sister appeared at the crematorium. She was a big, awkward woman—older than Jeff and without his easy charm of manner. Laurie had met her once before—at their wedding. Now, she came forward rather shyly, her face a mixture of commiseration and embarrassment, and took Laurie's hand, saying simply, 'I'm sorry. You've had an awful time . . .'

Laurie smiled at her but did not reply. She found it hard to think of anything suitable to say. She just wished, desperately, that the thing would be over soon and she could get away.

'I'm Hilda,' said the woman, answering Laurie's smile with a tentative one of her own, 'in case you've forgotten.'

Her eyes are like Jeff's, thought Laurie, but her smile is kinder.

'I would've kept in touch . . . but Jeff wouldn't let me.'

Laurie looked surprised. 'Wouldn't he?'

Hilda shook her head sadly. 'He was his own worst enemy, you know,' she said, and turned away with sudden tears in her eyes.

After the bleak little service, when it was time to go, Laurie felt compelled to go up to her again. 'We aren't . . . having any other . . . gathering. But . . . if you'd like to come home and meet the children . . .'

Hilda's craggy face softened. 'Not this time. You've had enough of the Collins family. But some other time I'd like to.' She fumbled in her bag. 'I'll give you my address. If there's ever anything I can do . . .' She hesitated and then said abruptly, 'Father was the same, you know. Jeff saw it all. They do say the pattern gets repeated.'

Laurie nodded. But not with Jason, she thought, in sudden panic. Not my brave, gentle son, Jay—who tried to protect me . . . who loves his small sister, and Penny's baby and all defenceless creatures . . . who loves Clem, too, and reflects his kindness and compassion. Not Jay.

'Don't blame him too much,' Hilda was murmuring, stark appeal looking out of her eyes.

'I don't,' said Laurie. 'I blame myself.'

'Not that either.' Hilda's voice was insistent. 'Let him go in peace.' Then she patted Laurie's good arm and hurried away.

Laurie turned a little blindly and found herself looking down at a surprisingly beautiful heap of flowers lying at her feet.

'Old Bob put them together,' said Luke Veryan's gruff voice beside her. 'He said you'd think it was right.'

Laurie felt absurd tears prick her eyes. So much care and shy kindness lay in that simple statement. So Jeff was gone—and there was nothing left now but a few ashes and a bunch of bright spring flowers.

Clem's hand came out quietly and clasped hers in a strong, calm grip. And Luke Veryan came and stood sturdily flanking her other side. 'Car's waiting,' he growled. 'No more to do here. Best get home.'

* * *

Clem waited three more days before he went home. By that time, he decided, Laurie was over the worst and had no more ordeals to face. She had talked to her solicitor, Madeleine, on the phone, and arranged to go up to London later on to sort out her affairs. Jeff had not had much to leave—only the furniture in the house and a life insurance which would mostly be swallowed up in paying off his debts. But at least Laurie would be clear, with a little extra left at the end.

She also spoke briefly to Jane on the phone—who was firm and kind and told her to take a deep breath and get on with living.

After all these things were settled, Clem took her out on to the hills again and sat her down on a rock in the pale spring sunshine and prepared to talk.

'I miss the swans,' said Laurie suddenly. 'There's everything else down here—sea and hills and sky, and seabirds everywhere—but no swans.'

Clem smiled. It was the opening he was waiting for. He reached into his pocket and took something small and metal out of it and laid it in her hand.

'This is the key to my caravan,' he said. 'Do you remember it? Quite old, but watertight. There are four bunks— and room for a baby's cot. A little kitchen area, not smart but practical. Water and light laid on. You'd be all right for the summer.'

Laurie was gazing at him, speechless.

He laughed a little at her expression and laid a gentle arm round her shoulders and gave her a small, loving shake. 'Don't look so startled. It seems obvious to me. Or do you want to stay on at Luke Veryan's? I'm sure he'd let you.'

'No,' said Laurie swiftly. 'I couldn't after . . . not after all that's happened.'

'That's what I thought.'

'Though . . .' she sounded troubled again, 'it will be

276

hard to leave him—especially for Penny. She'll worry about him.'

'Will you?'

Laurie sighed. 'Yes. A little. But he's very independent. He'll manage. And he needs the cottage in the summer—it brings in a lot of income to tide him over the winter.' She looked at him doubtfully. 'I . . . I did talk to Joe about it when he was here.'

Clem nodded. 'As to the practical details . . .' He seemed determined to be brisk and businesslike, though Laurie's puzzled, half-incredulous stare unnerved him a little. 'There's quite a good little primary school in the village—rather like Tregarrow's, small and friendly. I think Jay and Midge would like it. And if you—or Penny, for that matter—wanted to go into Maidstone for evening classes or something, I'd be going in most nights, or there's a bus. And . . . well, I'd be on hand if you needed anything.'

'Clem—stop!' said Laurie, with tears standing in her eyes.

He paused, looking anywhere but at her. 'And as to jobs . . . I'm sure Stan would welcome you back—not to mention several of his farmer friends who are all hopeless book-keepers.'

'Stop it!' said Laurie again, and turned him round to face her. 'Oh, Clem!' She reached out and touched his face with a shaking hand. 'What am I to say to you? I'm not . . . I don't know if I . . .'

'It's all right,' he said quickly. 'No strings attached. Of *course*, no strings. I know you have a long way to go yet—but one day . . .'

'That's just it.' Laurie sounded upset and desperately honest at the same time. 'I don't know if I'll ever . . . if I'm capable of . . .'

He laughed suddenly, and without warning bent his head and kissed her. It had been meant to be a light kiss—easy and gentle—but it became something else entirely—long and strong and passionate—and Laurie felt her own unexpected longing rise within her into vivid response.

After a strange, pulsing moment out of time, Clem

withdrew and looked down at her, smiling. 'You were going to say you didn't know if you were capable of loving anyone, weren't you?'

She nodded, and the tears spilled out and fell in rainbow prisms against the sun.

'Well, you know now.'

Yes, she thought, panic-stricken. I know now—and I'm terrified. I know what passion can do to people. We can become wild and savage and ungovernable—like animals. No, not animals—not Clem's animals. They are gentler than we are. We can become mindless and ruthless and brutal. Not like ourselves any more. And I want to be *myself*, always. I want to *stay* myself—and not be taken over by a force I can't control.

'No,' said Clem gently, to all those thoughts, 'it needn't be like that, my dearest child. It could never be like that with us.'

'Couldn't it?' Laurie's gaze was piercing—seeking through layers and layers of human experience to the inner core of truth. 'Why not?'

Why not? She had seen it happen. She had seen how passion changed a man and turned him from a loving companion into a vicious stranger.

'Because'—Clem's voice was gentler and slower than ever—'we already care more about each other than ourselves.'

Laurie's expression changed. 'You do, Clem. You've already . . . already almost killed me with kindness.' Her tremulous smile was still laced with tears. 'But I . . . I seem to have done nothing so far but take . . .'

'That isn't true,' he said. 'You have given me more than you know.'

She sighed and took hold of his hand and bent her head to look at it. The fingers were long and brown, immensely sensitive at the tips—delicate and strong and somehow incorruptible. 'It isn't fair,' she whispered. 'As things are—it's not fair to you.'

'That's for me to decide,' said Clem, and his smile was loving again and full of quiet certainty. 'My swans have taught me not to expect too much too soon.'

278

Laurie looked at him despairingly. 'But it may take . . . forever.'

'Never mind.' He was still smiling a little. 'I can watch you learn to fly.'

She suddenly beat at his arm with her clenched fist, like a frightened child. 'Don't you see? I'm *using* you. I'm taking the easy way out. I've leant on you shamefully these last few days. I ought not to do this to you!'

'Yes, you ought.' He captured her beating hand. 'I *need* to be leaned on. I love you, dammit!'

Laurie laughed, and then, bewilderingly, began to weep. 'I'm s-sorry,' she gasped, trying in vain to stop the sudden onslaught of grief that assailed her. 'I'm not . . . not used to such generosity.' And when he folded her in his arms, she added in a helpless, tear-laden voice, 'What am I to do with you?'

'Just love me a little,' said Clem cheerfully, 'to be going on with.'

'I do . . .'

'And take me at my word. There's plenty of time.'

Laurie was silent. She did not know how to answer him.

'You don't have to decide anything now,' he told her, smoothing her tumbled hair into place. 'You have the key. You can come when you want. I must go back to my swans tomorrow—but you don't have to leave the cottage till April, do you?'

'No.'

'Then—I shall expect you when you're ready.'

'Oh, *Clem*! You haven't heard a word I said.'

'Yes, I have. You are as free to come and go as the wildest swan in the world! But I am also free to hope!' His eyes were suddenly deep and piercingly grave. 'And I hope that you *will* come soon—and be glad to come!'

'I hope so, too,' said Laurie, unable to look away from that searching gaze.

Clem folded her fingers over the key and kissed her again—this time very gently and softly.

Both of them knew that it was a promise given.

\* \* \*

279

After Clem left, the world seemed curiously empty and cold to Laurie. She did her best to fill her days with work—in so far as her one-armed state allowed—and spent rather more time than usual in the greenhouses or with Luke Veryan's books. She also spent more time with baby Rose, as Penny cheerfully took on most of the work outside in the daffodil fields. Laurie came out there too, though, and found a strange kind of healing in the clean, flower-scented winds of March and the great sweeps of burgeoning flower-heads all around her. It was mild weather, and old Bob said them plaguey daffs was coming on too soon—the shops liked them in tight green bud, not already open. They had a longer life as cut flowers if they were picked just right. There was something calming and satisfying about dealing with flowers, Laurie thought. She stood knee-deep in green stalks and stared out at the sloping hillside and white scudding cloud above it, and a deep indigo sea beyond.

She hadn't been near the cliffs since the day of Jeff's death—nor even down to the little cove where the sharp-edged rocks began. But she knew she must face it some time—some time when the kind green fields of daffodils had made her feel calm again. And after all, the sea itself was kind—implacable and kind. It came in over those rocks day after day, powerful and strong, unconcernedly washing the bright stones clean. There was no trace now of Jeff, or the tragedy that had befallen. The sea was used to tragedies, and it always washed them away in the end.

She also spent a lot of time trying to build up Midge's confidence again—and comforting Jason. For, to her surprise and dismay, the boy was heartbroken at Clem's departure. She hadn't realised—till then—how much the children, too, had come to rely on Clem's gentle warmth and kindness—particularly Jay. For him, as for Laurie, it seemed as if the sun had gone out.

For, yes, she had to admit it: she was desolate without him. And yet, she felt, she must learn to be strong again all by herself—not rely on Clem to fight her battles for her. Only that way could she be free in her own mind— free to choose. To spend her life with Clem, or to spend it alone? She did not know. But she felt, obscurely, that if she worked on in the sun and wind and rain close to the growing earth, somehow things would become clear to her. In the end, she would know what to do.

'Jay,' she said suddenly one day when he had come up to the daffodil fields after school to fetch her home to tea, 'do you miss Clem a lot?'

The boy looked at her levelly out of blue, honest eyes. 'Yes. Don't you?'

She nodded, hardly daring to admit how much, even to herself. 'Why, Jay?' All at once she was curious to know what he felt about it.

He paused to consider. 'Because . . . he's nice. No, because he cares what happens to us . . .' He looked at his mother again. 'And he's kind. . .' He frowned, and kicked at a stone on the path. 'No,' he said again. 'It isn't that . . . Because I love him.'

'So do we all,' said Penny's voice close behind him. 'Don't we, Laurie?' She was laughing, but her eyes were bright with challenge.

It occurred to Laurie then that Penny knew—even the children knew—how important Clem was to her, and they were all waiting for her decision—all longing for her to make up her mind and fill her life and theirs with the warmth and compassion of Clem's protection. And this knowledge only made her decision harder. It would be so easy to accept—so comforting and peaceful—so good for all of them. But was it *right*? Was it fair to Clem? Was she really worth it? Could she offer him the kind of totally committed love that he had every right to ask for—that he was prepared to offer her?

'Of course we do,' she said to Jay's anxious stare. 'But it isn't that easy.'

'Will we see him again soon, then?' asked Jay, persisting.

'See him soon, see him soon,' chanted Midge, and skipped up and down the daffodil rows, turning her face up to the last pinkish rays of the setting sun.

'Yes,' agreed Laurie, sighing. 'Soon.'

It was then that old Bob came running. His wispy hair

281

was on end, and his eyes were wide with fright. 'Come quick, missus! Come quick! It's the boss!'

Laurie put down her flowers and went running swiftly after him. Penny turned to Jason and said urgently, 'Take Midge and the baby up to the farm, Jay, and wait for us there.' Then she followed Laurie through the lanes of flowers to the end of the field where a small knot of people had gathered.

Luke Veryan lay on his face among a tangle of broken daffodils. His hands were clenched into claws of agony, grasping at the red stony earth.

Laurie bent over him and tried to turn him over. Someone helped her to lift him a little so that she could support his head. He was still breathing, but each breath was harsh and laboured and his face was grey with pain.

It's a heart attack, she thought. What ought I to do? 'Get Dr Trevelyan,' she said. 'Fast.' She loosened Luke's collar and tried to help him to breathe.

Presently some of the workers came with a wattle windbreak and laid him on it and carried him into the house.

The rest was stark nightmare. Dr Trevelyan was out and could not be found. Nurse Penwillis was over at a remote farm, but would come as soon as she could. The ambulance was on its way from Penzance, but would take at least half an hour. And meanwhile Luke Veryan's breathing got harsher and more desperate with every breath, and his face got greyer.

At last they heard the ambulance siren ringing as it came down the hill to the farm, and at the same time Dr Trevelyan's car arrived from the other direction.

Between them they got Luke fixed up with an injection and an oxygen mask, and lifted him into the ambulance. Laurie had thought he was unconscious by now, but he opened his eyes and looked at her as he was being carried out, and seemed to be trying to say something to her.

She came close and stooped over him, attempting to put reassurance into her voice as she said softly, 'You're in good hands now.'

He seemed to shake his head faintly, and his fingers

grasped at hers for a moment. He pushed the oxygen mask away and whispered, 'Good girl . . . thanks.'

The ambulance man clamped the mask back over his face then, anxious about his breathing. The doors were shut and he was driven away.

Joe, thought Laurie. Joe must be told. I must get through to him somehow. She managed to get through to Jane at the hostel and left an urgent message for Joe which Jane promised to deliver at once.

But by the time Jane reported back that Joe was on his way, the hospital had also rung Laurie to say that Luke Veryan had died in the ambulance before reaching them.

Laurie was stunned. There had been no warning of this. Luke had seemed as well and sturdy as usual, stumping about his fields, directing his pickers and looking after his cows. His cows! Had they been milked yet? Had Luke dealt with them before he went out into the fields? She did not know. She had better ask Bob . . . Or Jason—he would probably know. And what was going to happen tomorrow morning?

At this point in her anxious, shocked thoughts, old Bob himself came into the office where she was sitting and said, awkwardly twisting his old seaman's cap in his brown hands, 'I can see to the cows, missus—and get a boy up from the village to help. And your boy, Jason, will help too—till Mr Joe says what's to do.'

Laurie nodded and, seeing the old man's distress, leant forward and patted his arm kindly. 'Thanks, Bob. I know you're as upset as I am. We'll keep things going till Joe arrives. I should go home now and get some rest. We'll all be busy tomorrow.'

The old man gave a brief nod and turned to go. 'One of the best the boss was,' he muttered as he went out. 'They doesn't come like that no more.'

Laurie was left alone in the silent farmhouse. It felt very empty and cold, and she had a sudden desperate longing for Clem and his warmth and kindness. He would know what to do. But she was alone here, and she had to manage without him.

Sighing, she closed the farm books and went methodically round the house, tidying the rooms and closing doors and windows. It seemed strange and rather terrifying that she should have to cope with death and its endless difficulties and arrangements twice in a month. She began to wonder what on earth else could happen to her now—what other unlooked-for blows fate had in store for her.

When she had done all she could, she left some cold food on the table and a note for Joe and went sadly away down the path to the cottage. There would be plenty to do. Now she must comfort Penny and the children—particularly Penny. Time enough to grieve for Luke Veryan—that unbending, craggy man who had been so good to her—when all the work was done.

* * *

When Joe came he was crisp and efficient, and as bitterly upset underneath as the rest of them. But he got on with all the arrangements—dealt with the hospital and the undertakers, the solicitors and the farm—and came down to Laurie and Penny at the cottage for a hot meal and a bit of warmth and comfort.

The funeral was very unlike Jeff's bleak little ceremony at the crematorium. Luke was buried on the windy hillside, in sight of the sea, and his grave was heaped high with daffodils and jonquils and all the spring flowers he had loved. There was one small wreath specially made by Penny and the children—she had gone into a huddle with old Bob about it—and it contained a few fragile Christmas roses in its centre. She laid it down with the other wreaths and made no comment, but both Laurie and Joe understood.

The whole village was there. Luke had been widely known and respected for many long, hard years of farming, and they all wanted to say farewell to the tough old man. So Laurie and Penny laid on a spread at the farmhouse. 'He'd have wanted to do right by his mates,' said Joe. And everyone climbed the hill path from the little village church and its flowery churchyard full of the graves of dead sailors and farmers from Tregarrow's long history of hard toil and ceaseless struggle against the elements.

Farmer George Button was there—and so were Dr Trevelyan and Nurse Agnes Penwillis and Annie the postmistress. They all greeted Laurie with much kindness, and George Button went so far as to say gruffly, 'Bad time you've been havin'. Very sorry!'

Laurie had not been in the village since Jeff's death. She had left the shopping to Penny, making the excuse to herself that she couldn't carry anything with her right arm anyway. But in truth she had been afraid of the bright knowing glances and gossiping tongues of the villagers. It had been all over the local paper—her private life with Jeff, his prison sentence, the injunction, her flight to Cornwall and the final tragedy on the cliffs. She did not know how they would take all this melodrama—whether they would eye her suspiciously and with antagonism for having brought all this trouble to their quiet village. And now this as well—though it was not of her making this time. Or was it? Did Luke's collapse stem from his efforts over the cliff rescue? That frantic run from the house, carrying ropes and grappling irons? And the anxiety over her? And the fact that he had more work to do himself while she was laid up with a broken arm?

'Running out of tea,' said Joe in her ear. 'Better make another pot.' He looked at her shrewdly. 'No good brooding. Here, sit down and have a cuppa yourself. There's a drop of dregs left!' And he pushed her down on a chair at the long kitchen table.

'Joe,' she said sorrowfully, 'did I . . . add to it?'

'You did not,' he retorted. 'Massive heart attack. No previous trouble. Happens that way with men like my Dad. They told me at the hospital.' He was still looking at her. 'You did a lot for my Dad—made him very happy, you and Penny and the kids—especially baby Rose. He told me.' He gave her a cheerful push. 'Go on! You know he'd rather go out with a bang like this. Stands to reason!'

He stumped off, looking rather like his Dad, and went the rounds again with plates of sandwiches and beer for the men. Laurie made another pot of tea and carried it in to the crowded front sitting-room. The talk was quiet, but not subdued. The room was full of the warm sound of rich, deep Cornish voices—as rich and deep as the soil in those hidden valleys between the cliffs, the soil where the daffodils grew and which Luke Veryan's hands had been clutching as he lay dying among his flowers.

'Mum,' said Jason, close to her, 'I'm going to help Bob with the cows. And Joe says you're to drink this!' and he handed her a small tot of whisky in a glass.

Obediently, Laurie swallowed it, not aware of her own blazing pallor, and was surprised to find Agnes Penwillis at her side saying in her comfortable, forthright voice, 'Bear up, my dear. They'll soon be gone.'

Laurie smiled at her and protested, 'No. I don't want them to go. It's good to hear them talking about him.' She glanced round the room at the seamed brown faces, the square, determined jaws and the far-seeing blue sea-man's eyes of Luke Veryan's friends. 'They seem to have thought a lot of him.'

'Oh yes.' Agnes Penwillis nodded her wise grizzled head. 'Don't say much, Tregarrow people, but they have feelings—same as all of us!' She gave Laurie's good arm a comforting squeeze and went on to talk to someone else.

It seemed to go on a long time. But at last the final stragglers had departed, and Joe, Penny and Laurie were left to the clearing up. Midge had been running in and out of the crowded rooms without apparently feeling the solemnity of the occasion, and now she was occupied with the important task of rocking baby Rose in her pram.

'Keep her quiet a bit,' instructed Penny, 'till the washing up's done. I'll feed her in a minute.'

Rose seemed to think 'a minute' was not soon enough, but Midge managed to pacify her by bouncing the pram till the coloured balls strung round its hood danced and rattled and the baby laughed.

Joe helped them tidy everything away and then strolled down with them to the cottage. 'Want to talk to you,' he said. 'Are you too tired?'

'No.' Laurie took him in and sat him down by the empty grate.

'What we want is a fire,' said Penny. 'Won't be a jiffy. Thank God for firelighters.'

They laughed and watched her deftly get the new fire going. Laurie made yet another pot of tea. And finally they all sat down together to watch the flames leap up the chimney.

'My Dad,' said Joe, without preamble, 'knew what he was about. So I'd better tell you where we all stand.' He was not looking at anyone, but staring into the fire. 'The farm goes to me—debts and all. I can sell it, or try to run it, or put in a manager—though it would scarcely pay for that. But this cottage'—he looked round it, and then from Laurie to Penny with a curious half-smile on his face—'he left to baby Rose.'

'What?' Penny sat up straight in her chair, and baby Rose, who had fallen asleep in her arms, uttered a sleepy protest.

'Yep.' Joe nodded. 'Lock, stock and barrel. Baby Rose's.' He laughed at Penny's stunned expression. 'With me as trustee.'

Penny looked from him to Laurie in disbelief. 'But . . . what does that mean exactly?'

'It means you can live in it, or you can let it and bring in an income—but you can't sell it. Not till Rose is eighteen and can make the choice herself. It means you've got a roof over your head if you want it. Or you and Rose can have money to spend on her upbringing. Whatever you decide, at least she won't need to starve!'

Penny was still staring at him, open-mouthed. But now the tears rose in her eyes and spilled out on to her flushed cheeks in long, shiny trails. 'Uncle Luke!' she muttered fiercely. 'That wonderful, obstinate old man! I didn't want his money!'

'He didn't give it you!' retorted Joe. 'He gave it to Rose!' He was smiling at her now, with the same bluff, unexpressed kindness as his father's. 'After all,' he added, 'he did help to bring her into the world. I guess he felt kinda responsible!'

287

Then he looked at Laurie. Joe was shrewd enough to
see that this made life even more complicated for her.
'Now, about the farm,' he said briskly. 'I don't want to
run it myself—got my own patch in London. I like the
Smoke too much to leave it now. And I like helping out
with Jane's work at the refuge and all.' He sighed. 'I did
offer to come home, you know—at Christmas when I
came down. Thought he looked a bit stretched. But he
wouldn't hear of it.'

Laurie nodded.

'Well . . .' Joe was still looking at her in an enquiring,
tentative kind of way. 'I don't know how you feel about
it all. I reckon you could manage it yourself, if you wanted
to. You know the set-up, you've done the books and
you know the turnover. But you'd need another man—
younger and more active than old Bob (and I don't know
how long *he'll* want to keep going!). It'd be a long, hard
grind—more or less for ever. It's not a big enough holding
really to make a decent profit. But you could all live in
the farmhouse, and let the cottage.'

Laurie nodded again.

'Or . . .' Joe went on, now looking away again into the
fire, 'I could sell up. And in that case I'd have to ask you
to hang on with Bob and some help until things were
settled.'

'What do you want to do, Joe?'

He sighed. 'I don't know, girl. I think it depends on
you.' Once more his shrewd glance flicked towards her.
'And I don't want to saddle you with it . . . if you've got
other plans.'

Other plans, thought Laurie desperately. Clem. How
can I ever leave now? I can't leave Penny here on her
own.

'I . . . I'll have to think about it,' she said, and her
glance suddenly caught Penny's. 'We've . . . we've both
got things to decide.'

Joe nodded. 'I know you have. There's no hurry. I'm
gonna be down here for a bit anyway. But I wanted you
to know the worst.'

'And the best,' interrupted Penny, tossing her red head.

'Yes, well . . .' He looked directly at Laurie now, his eyes full of honest distress. "Tisn't much of a living, you know. Mostly hard grind and damn-all return. And as for you, Penny . . .' His gaze moved to the younger girl's face and back again. 'Not sure it's a good idea to bury yourself here for ever. Other things to do . . . and learn. Other people to meet!'

Penny was staring down at the baby's downy head and not looking at Joe at all. 'I want what's best for Rose,' she said slowly. 'And I'm not sure what that is—not yet!'

Joe got to his feet and touched the baby's head with one blunt finger. 'She's got the right idea. Sleep on it!' He grinned cheerfully at them both and went away without saying any more. If he grieved for Luke Veryan, he did not mention it. He kept that for the dark hill path and the quiet night where he walked alone.

* * *

Laurie spent the next few days in a state of tired confusion. Thoughts went round and round in her head— alternatives and proposals; suggestions and objections; endless questions and never any answers.

Could she manage the farm on her own? Would the children be happy there? Would it be right for Penny? Or could she leave Penny and Rose behind and go to the other side of England to be near Clem? Of course she couldn't. Penny depended on her. She wouldn't be able to bring up a baby all on her own—not at sixteen years old! How could she think of leaving her behind? But how could she take her away, now that she had got somewhere of her own to live in? And if she didn't, how could she reconcile staying on and trying to make a go of it at the farm with the increasing longing for Clem that was growing inside her?

It was all impossible, and she didn't know what to do. Also, the children missed Clem, and Jason kept asking her when they were going to see him. But, on the other hand, they were happy now at the little school in Tregarrow. Would it be fair to move them yet again?

Penny watched her trying to sort out her thoughts, and

forbore to say anything at first. Twice Laurie went off for a long walk by herself and returned tired and pale, but with no clear light of resolve in her eye.

But at last Penny could stand it no longer and said, late one evening after the children were asleep, 'Hadn't we better get things straight?'

Laurie sighed. 'Oh Penny—I wish I could!'

Penny thought for a moment. 'As I see it, you need Clem—and so do the kids.'

Laurie's face seemed to close like a shut flower. 'Yes, but . . . you and Rose need me here. And so does the farm.'

'Not important.' Penny shook her head. 'Not like Clem's important.'

'Don't be idiotic!' snapped Laurie. 'Of course you're important—both of you. Especially to me.'

Penny's tough young face softened a little. 'Well, that's nice to know. But it doesn't solve anything, does it?'

'Do you want to stay in the cottage?'

Penny looked round thoughtfully. 'I like it here . . . but it'd bring in good money, let.'

'What about the farm?'

'What about it?'

'Would you like living there?'

'It'd be OK.' She sounded strangely offhand, and Laurie was puzzled.

'Or you could come with us to Clem's caravan.'

'Or I could stay here on me own.'

Laurie looked at her in astonishment. 'Do you want to stay here on your own?'

Penny's face went pale. 'I didn't say that.'

Laurie felt like shaking her. But instead she said urgently, 'Penny—you've always told me the truth about things. I want the truth now—it's important. *Do you want to be on your own?*'

The girl stared at her defiantly for a moment, and then her face crumpled like a child's and she began to weep angry tears. 'Of *course* I don't. You're my family. How could I cope without you? But I . . . I thought . . .'

'You thought I'd want to run off to Clem and leave

you?' Her voice was gentle now. 'Then you've got another think coming!'

'But . . . do you really want to run the farm? It'll be bloody hard!'

'I know it will.' Laurie pushed the hair out of her eyes with a nervous hand. 'But you'll all help. I daresay we shall manage.'

Penny looked unconvinced. 'And what about Clem?'

Laurie tried to sound calm, and as if her own private dreams were not being destroyed with every word she said. 'He'd understand.'

'Jay wouldn't,' said Penny starkly.

Laurie closed her eyes in terror. Clem and Jay, she thought. They love each other already like father and son. What am I to do?

'Then . . . if we didn't stay here, would you come with us?'

'If you asked me,' said Penny, sounding suddenly stiff with pent-up emotion.

'Oh, for God's sake!' said Laurie, and suddenly held out her good arm to pull her close. 'Don't be such a goose!'

Penny took one half-disbelieving look and fell into her arms. 'I thought . . . I thought you didn't want me,' she sobbed.

Laurie sighed again, over the top of her head, but she did not say any more.

'You know what I think?' sniffed Penny, gulping back tears and trying to be reasonable. 'I think you should go and ask Clem.'

'*Ask Clem?*'

'Yes. Why not? He'd know what to do. He's got more sense than the lot of us.'

'But, Penny, . . . if I went all that way to see him, he'd think . . .'

'No, he wouldn't. He's fair, Clem is. He'd listen—and he'd know what's right. You go and ask him—you'll see!'

Laurie was silent, more shaken by this suggestion than she dared to admit. At last she said, 'Are you serious?'

291

'Yes. I am. Go while Joe's still here, and leave the kids with me. Joe'll look after us till you get back.'

Laurie was staring at her, almost as if she scarcely knew her. 'Penny? What's got into you?'

'Oh Christ!' said Penny, with sudden violence. 'I can't stand seeing you torn to pieces! And I don't go much for broken hearts, either. For God's sake, go and see Clem!'

So Laurie went.

# PART IV

# LANDFALL

It was April by now, and a scented spring evening with blackbirds singing in the orchards as she walked down through them towards the river. The old Medway looked calm and placid. Brown, sluggish water flowed under the stone bridge, and the willows leant down and looked at themselves, unbroken images on the glassy surface.

Laurie went on along the bank, following the curve of the river towards Clem's cottage, her feet slow with doubt. Ought she to have come—with nothing settled in her mind, nothing to offer him? Leaning on him again already for comfort and wise counsel! And how could he possibly answer her, feeling as he did? It simply wasn't fair to ask him.

As she came towards the next bend, two swans came out of the shadows under the trailing willow branches and began to sail towards her. She thought she recognised them—they were the same pair she had seen greet Clem on that very first occasion when he had come to sit beside her on the bank.

'Hello,' she said, pausing to look at them and holding out a tentative hand. 'Do you remember me?'

It seemed that they did, for they swam confidently towards her, and when they were within reach of the bank they stayed there peacefully treading water as if waiting for something. She remembered how Clem had stopped to talk to them and reached into his pocket for something to give them. She remembered the look on his face, too—smiling and affectionate—as the swans arched their long necks and reached over to accept his offering. 'In the end,' he had said, '*they eat out of my hand.*'

I've got the rest of my sandwiches, she thought. I

wonder if they'll accept them from me. Like Clem, she reached into her pocket and brought out a crumpled piece of bread and held it out to the swans. They looked at her questioningly for a moment, and then both beautiful slender necks bent towards her outstretched hand.

For some reason it seemed desperately important that they should accept her and be unafraid—as if she was just an extension of Clem and his loving care; just another safe and welcome image in their clear, wild eyes.

The swans ate all she had to offer, and when she held out her empty hand to them and murmured, 'It's all gone now,' they turned quietly away and sailed out again into the slow-moving current where the brown eddies swirled in the deep centre of the river.

Laurie watched them go. Then, sighing with pleasure at the quietness and peace of the spring evening, she walked on. There was no sign of Clem. She began to wonder if he might be out—or away. She had sent no message to him—nor even considered that he might be absent, or even there in his cottage with someone else. It suddenly seemed to her monstrously arrogant to come strolling in and expect him to be waiting for her—or even glad to see her.

She was so confused in mind—so troubled and lacking in confidence—that she almost turned tail and fled. But she remembered Penny's flushed and desperate face as she said, 'I can't stand seeing you torn to pieces!' And she remembered a bit more of that conversation, too. How Penny had demanded, accusingly, 'And what about Clem?' and her reply: 'He'd understand.' And Penny's swift retort: 'Jay wouldn't!' Yes, Jason. She must at least have the courage to talk to Clem, whatever transpired. She had promised Jay when she left, hardly able to meet those great anxious eyes fixed on her face. 'You will *tell* him I miss him?' 'Yes, Jason, I will.' I will, but I don't know what it'll do to Clem.

She came round the corner and found herself looking at Clem's old caravan standing on the little isthmus of reeds beside the backwater that led to his cottage. And she saw, with a painful lurch of the heart, that it had been

296

given a new coat of paint and was gleaming with polish and care—awaiting her arrival.

What was she to say to him?

Around her there was a sudden babble of voices from the mallards in the backwater, and several regal-looking swans swam up to have a look at her. But even at this noisy announcement of her arrival there was no sign of Clem—and nothing stirred in the cottage beyond.

Filled with new aching doubt and uncertainty, she went on across the dyke and along the mossy track to the back of the cottage, skirting the edge of Clem's dredged-out pond and its numerous, vociferous inhabitants. The back door stood open but, though dusk was falling, there was no yellow lamplight from within.

Maybe he was out tending some sick animal? Or collecting yet another stray creature in his animal rescue van? Or lecturing in Maidstone? But then he wouldn't leave his door wide open—would he?

Puzzled, she stepped over the threshold and stood looking into the kitchen. And then a soft exclamation of dismay escaped her. For there lay Clem, stretched out on the lumpy old sofa, a two-day growth of beard on his chin, his eyes shut, his face grey with exhaustion, and one stiff, plastered leg stuck out before him on a faded velvet cushion.

'Clem!' she said, going swiftly over to him. 'What have you done?'

He opened his eyes then—incredulously—and for a moment his piercing gaze looked straight into hers. 'You came!' he murmured—and then, unexpectedly, he began to laugh. 'Look at us!' he grinned, waving a hand at Laurie's plastered arm and his own propped-up leg. 'Between us, we'd just about make a whole person!' And then, as if he suddenly understood what he had said, the laughter died in his face and he looked at Laurie again with the same piercing gravity.

'Yes,' agreed Laurie softly, meeting that searching gaze with the utmost certainty. 'I think we would.' For, seeing him there, spread out and vulnerable and clearly in pain, she felt all her doubts and anxieties dissolve before his

297

need of her. This was where she ought to be—beside Clem. This coming together was entirely right, and nothing else had any significance.

'Be careful,' said Clem, smiling a little. 'I always knew you had too soft a heart! An injured animal always brings out your protective instincts!'

Laurie laughed. 'Who's talking?' But then she too grew grave, for already she knew she must not allow this new sense of enormous rightness to take hold. 'Clem . . .', she began—and reached blindly for his hand. 'I didn't . . . I haven't come . . . to stay.'

'I know,' he said calmly.

'How do you know?'

His smile was tender. 'My dearest girl—you didn't look like a radiant bride coming to meet her lover, standing there!'

His choice of words made her blink. 'How . . . how did I look?'

'Scared to death!' He reached out and touched her face with infinite gentleness. 'And worn with doubt. What's been happening to you?'

'What's been happening to you, more likely!' she countered. 'Tell me what you've done.'

He sighed and shifted his leg a little. 'It's only a simple fracture.'

'How did it happen?'

'I was out in the boat, trying to rescue a swan. It had got its feet entangled in some plastic netting. The poor creature was trapped and terrified—the more it struggled and flapped its wings, trying to break free, the tighter the tangle got. I was reaching down to cut it free with my knife, when one of its wings caught me off balance. They're very powerful, you know, swans' wings. Snapped my leg like a twig, and I fell overboard. Nearly drowned me, the poor demented creature!'

'Did you manage to save it?'

'Oh yes. I managed to cut the netting under water, before I went under again! And then I just held on to the boat and pushed myself ashore with my good leg.' He paused as if he had said enough.

298

'Well, go on,' said Laurie. 'How did you get home—with a broken leg?'

He grinned. 'Crawled—mostly. But that was ridiculously painful. So I managed to get hold of a branch of something to use as a crutch, and hopped the rest of the way. And then I passed out, I think.'

Laurie shivered. All that agony—and Clem probably in mortal danger, too—and she had not known. She glanced round the room anxiously. 'How did you get help then?'

'Telephone.' Clem waved a cheerful hand. 'Had it installed not long ago. The Wildlife Trust people insisted—for emergency calls, they said!' He laughed. And then, seeing Laurie's expression, he touched her face again gently and said, 'Don't look like that. It's all right now. All it has to do is mend—like your arm!'

Laurie shut her eyes. 'You might have died!' she whispered.

'Yes, but I didn't. I'm very much alive.' He was looking at her with the same watchful tenderness, and now he turned her towards him so that she faced him directly. 'Hadn't you better tell me what's on your mind?'

She hesitated. 'It . . . it may take rather a long time. Shall I make some coffee or something first?'

'No,' he said. 'You can tell me now. And I like tea, not coffee—*afterwards*!'

She looked into his face, and the same vivid awareness was in both pairs of eyes—the same longing . . . the same desire . . . and the same knowledge that a crisis of decision awaited them.

'Oh Clem!' she murmured. 'Try to understand . . .'

'I'm listening,' he said.

Then Laurie told him all that had happened, and all that Luke Veryan's death and his gift of the cottage to Rose implied.

Clem heard her out, patiently and quietly, without interruption. Only, when she described the frantic scene in the daffodil field, he reached out and took her hand in his and held it in a warm, steady clasp.

When she had finished, he sat looking at her intently for a moment, and then said, 'Laurie, before I . . . before

299

we decide what must be done, I just want to ask you one question.'

'Yes?' Laurie knew what the question would be—and half an hour ago she would not have known how to answer it. But now, astonishingly, she did—and everything seemed to fall into place in her mind as she faced the truth. She lifted her head bravely and met Clem's searching gaze with fearless certainty.

'Do you love me?'

'Yes.' Her voice was calm and clear. 'Of course I do.'

He nodded, as if he already knew the answer but only wanted to confirm it. 'Not afraid of it any more?'

'No.'

'Commitments? To love and to cherish . . . All that?'

'Yes, Clem.'

He smiled. 'You sound almost sure.'

She was still gazing at him, but there were tears in her eyes now. 'I am sure. I wasn't when I came. But . . . but as soon as I saw you, I knew.'

'Laurie!' he said reprovingly. 'I did warn you!'

Her smile matched his, and radiance spilled out with the tears. 'I can't help it!' Then she went on with desperate candour. 'But I can't leave Penny and Rose.'

'Of course you can't.'

'And . . . and there are the children . . .'

'Don't be absurd. They already seem like my own—especially Jason.'

'But . . .'

He stooped suddenly and stopped her with a kiss. It was a quiet movement—gentle and consoling—but there was a hint of hidden fires beneath it which she could not mistake. Clem—patient, loving Clem—was under stress as she was. Only, for some reason, he seemed to be smiling—even in the midst of kissing her, the corners of his mouth seemed to turn upwards into laughter.

'Stop fretting,' he said. 'We can work something out. As a matter of fact, I've been doing a bit of quiet spadework already.'

'What do you mean?'

'Do you remember that man I took the swans to?'

'Yes.'

'And the possibility of starting up other wildlife sanctuaries elsewhere?'

'Yes.'

'As I say, I've been working on it.' He was still smiling. 'I thought it was about time I took a hand in my own future for a change.'

She was looking at him expectantly. 'Well?'

'Have a look on my desk. There's a letter there somewhere from the Wildlife Trust.'

Bewildered, Laurie went over and searched on his desk and found the letter.

'Read it,' he commanded, and a fleck of irrepressible laughter laced his deep voice. 'And don't say I haven't made some attempt to prepare the ground!'

Laurie looked down at the letter, confused by his smiling look. 'Dear Clem,' it said:

You'll be pleased to hear that Lord St Curnow is very happy with his swans and has come up with a suggestion that ties in with what we were discussing the other day. He is willing to let his three lakes be used as a permanent safe haven for recovered swans—from any area. And he would also like to share the expense of setting up new sanctuaries elsewhere—initially in Devon and Cornwall, as they are within his area, but later on even farther afield if you can find suitable sites for them.

There is a lot of work to be done with oiled seabirds as well as the swans on the rivers and estuaries, and there are the usual casualties among the visiting migrants and geese. And I believe there are still a few remaining otters on the moorland streams. Plenty to do!

You say you are pleased with Alec. Could he be left in charge in the Medway sanctuary while you set up a couple of places elsewhere and find people to run them? I don't suppose it will be that easy—good wildlife handlers are hard to find—but, as I see it, the work needs to be spread around the whole of the country—given time and money! And this offer of financial support from Lord St C is probably too good to waste. It would mean a lot of travelling about, but I can't think of anyone else experienced enough to tackle it. Let me know what you think? I shall be at headquarters during April. Then I am off to Iceland.

Yours ever, John (Montrose).

Laurie read the letter through slowly. Then she looked at the date. It was written soon after Clem's return from Cornwall. He must have had it lying on his desk for at least three weeks.

'Clem—have you answered it?'

'No. I was waiting for you.'

'But I might not have come.'

'You'd have come,' he said tranquilly. 'You are much too kind and too honest to leave me in suspense for ever. Though of course I didn't know what you might say.'

'Nor did I . . . till now.'

He drew her close. 'You see? Nothing is insuperable. It'll take time to set up of course. I'll have to wander about a bit. But we've got time, haven't we? All the time in the world.'

She was looking at him curiously. 'You think very far ahead, don't you?'

'Very,' he said, smiling, and kissed her again.

She emerged rosy and laughing, but still serious underneath. 'What would you have done if . . . ?'

'If you'd turned me down?' He grew grave again, but there was still a hint of a smile lurking somewhere behind. It seemed irrepressible somehow. 'I'd have agreed anyway. It's my job, after all, and I think it's important. But I daresay I'd have found every excuse I could to come and make sure you were all right.'

She was silent, threatened by tears again. Such devotion still rather frightened her.

'After all,' he said reasonably, 'it needn't always be the female of the species who makes all the adjustments!'

She laughed, but it was rather a broken sound.

'You know something?' Clem's smile had grown very tender. 'You're scared of happiness.'

She nodded, unable to speak.

'Too much has happened to you,' he murmured, holding her cradled against his arm. 'But I'll make you believe in it, if it kills me!'

'That'd be a lot of help!' Her laughter was still more like a gasp, and he reached up an exploratory hand and found himself touching wet eyelashes.

'Hey!' he said. 'You should be rejoicing.'

'I am,' she answered, and helplessly allowed him to brush the tears out of her eyes.

'Sunshine and somersaults,' he said obscurely, with an astonishingly tender, reminiscent grin on his face. 'And that reminds me—we'd better do the rounds before it gets dark.'

Laurie was a bit alarmed. 'Can you? Are you safe?'

'Oh yes. I'm a dab-hand on crutches. Especially with you to guide me.' He reached out for the light metal crutches that lay beside him and heaved himself to his feet. For a moment he stood there, weaving slightly till he got his balance, and Laurie saw with a small lurch of shame how thin and tired he looked.

'You're thinner,' she said, standing beside him.

'Pining,' he agreed, with mischief in his glance. 'The only drawback with crutches is,' he complained, 'I can't kiss you without falling over.'

Laurie laughed. 'I can wait.'

'Ah!' said Clem darkly. 'But can I?'

Together they went into the glimmering spring evening. There was still a gleam of primrose light in the west, while above them a pale sky was deepening into sapphire night. One star winked through the tangled arms of the willows, and a small thin sliver of moon climbed like a bright sickle-blade behind the tall elms in the water-meadows. A late blackbird still sang of love and ecstasy on the topmost branch of Clem's favourite chestnut tree.

'He's got the right idea,' said Clem, looking up. 'Shouting it to the housetops!' And there was such a thrill of joy in his voice that Laurie was dazzled.

As they stood there side by side, gazing out towards the quiet river, there was a sudden thrum of wings across the water, and the two swans that Laurie had met earlier—Clem's special ones—came swinging down the river in a long, pulsing flight above their heads. And Laurie was reminded of Clem's voice long ago, when she first said goodbye to him among the silent hop-fields and empty orchards: *'Freedom isn't only taking off. It's knowing where you want to land . . . and when it's time to come home.'*

The great white birds swung on across the sky in perfect harmony, seeming to head straight for the pale golden light in the west.

'Where are they going?' wondered Laurie, feeling a strange sense of loss as the sound of their flight grew fainter on the wind.

Clem watched them with an experienced eye as they turned in the darkening sky and curved round in a wide arc, their wings still pulsing with that unearthly sound.

'They aren't going anywhere,' he said—and there was a world of love and reassurance in his voice. 'They're coming home.'